Dangerous
Grace

Dangerous Grace

A NOVEL OF THE PHILIPPINES

BY

Robert W. Whalen & Richard T. Goode

Based on an Idea by

Billy O. Wireman

Published & Distributed by:

856 Nicanor Reyes, Sr. St.
Tel. Nos. 741-49-16 • 741-49-20
1977 C.M. Recto Avenue
Tel. Nos. 741-49-56 • 741-49-57
Manila, Philippines

ISBN-971-23-1021-3

Printed by
REX PRINTING COMPANY, INC.
TYPOGRAPHY & CREATIVE LITHOGRAPHY
84 P. Florentino St., Quezon City
Tel. Nos. 712-41-08 * 712-41-01

DEDICATION

To Senator Jovito Reyes Salonga, Former President of the Philippine Senate, who embodies to an extraordinary degree the indomitable spirit of the Filipino people.

ACKNOWLEDGMENTS

We owe a sincere debt of gratitude to many people who made this book possible. We alone are responsible for the book's contents, and not all of our friends would agree with everything in it, but all made the book possible by their continuing support and encouragement. For that, we are thankful.

We wish to thank our friends in the Philippines, especially former Senate President Jovito Salonga, his staff, and son, Ricky Salonga, who taught us much about their wonderful country. Interviews with former Defense Secretary Fidel Ramos, now President of the Philippines, and Congressman Juan Ponce Enrile added important perspectives and insights to our understanding of the Philippines. We also want to recognize posthumously the valuable contributions of the late Philippine film producer and director, Lino Brocka.

We wish to especially thank Dr. Venice Mendiola, Chairman of the English Department of the Philippine Normal University and holder of the Alice Hollister Marquardt Professorial Chair, for his critical analysis and helpful suggestions which helped to ensure that the novel had an authentic Philippine flavor and character.

We wish to thank, too, our friends in the United States who provided both encouragement and financial support for the book, especially Ned Davis, Robert Gilley, Jerry Greenhoot, Sam and Carolyn McMahon, and Dan Taylor.

We wish to thank our friends at Queens College, especially John Slater and Lidia Figiel, who supervised much of the technical side of our work. Author Frye Gaillard reviewed the manuscripts and offered many helpful suggestions.

We wish to thank our publishers, Attorney Dominador D. Buhain and his staff at Rex Bookstore, Inc., for their encouragement and faith in our project.

Finally, we wish to thank the people of the Philippines for providing the courage, nobility, drama, and indomitable spirit which we have tried to reflect in our story.

AUTHORS' NOTE

This is a work of fiction. Though it reflects, we hope, some of the realities of life in the Philippines, it is entirely fiction. We have freely invented people and events as our story warranted.

We are not Filipinos. But over the years, we have come to respect, and indeed admire, the Filipino people. Their history, their struggles, their victories, have sparked our imagination. We hope that Filipinos will look on our errors with indulgence. We hope that non-Filipinos may learn something about the lives and challenges, hopes and dreams, of the Filipino people. We hope our tale can become a part, however small, of the much larger story of the Philippines.

Billy O. Wireman
Richard T. Goode
Robert W. Whalen

TABLE OF CONTENTS

PROLOGUE

A cry, smothered by the fetid night air. A second cry, a scream, a shriek.

Scuttling amid the mountains of garbage. Wet, sucking noises as dozens of feet wade through the darkness, over and through the smouldering human wastes, the debris and wreckage of the city.

The blackness, the very humidity of the tropic night stirring through the valleys of garbage, the thick, choking, foul odors parting turgidly as they struggle toward the scream.

A small woman, in rags, wags a finger toward the fattened garbage bags before her, the bags, filled with waste, darker even than the night. "What?" they whisper to her. "What is it?" But she only wails and wags her finger.

One of the bags has ruptured. From it protruded something slick, red and torn. One of them pokes it with a stick. Another tugs at the bag, revealing more of the thing, until it falls, stupidly, lazily, amid the rest of the garbage. "What is this?" they whisper, as more and more wraiths stir from the smoke, amidst the trash.

"Meat? An animal? Something butchered?"

A spinning blue light appears behind them. Two policemen, gagging, holding cloths to their mouths, struggle up the mountain of trash. They stare at what the people have found. Both become very ill.

This was the first discovery .

It was not the last.

The men around the table looked at the photographs and shook their heads. There were a dozen of them, all hard and muscular, with cropped hair, all were dressed in tiger-striped battle fatigues.

They were in a secured briefing room in what had once been the American Army-Navy club in Manila. The club was white stucco, long and broad, and one could almost hear the ghosts of Americans, in white tropical uniforms, sipping cool drinks in the Manila heat. Outside, before the club, Luneta Park, the old Spanish parade ground. Across the park, the venerable Manila Hotel, filled with its own ghosts of elegant imperialism. To the left of the club, the vast expanse of Manila Bay.

The men in the club, seated around the table, looked at the photographs and grimaced. A colonel, a very thin, taut man, spoke quietly, in clipped tones.

"There have now been seventeen killings. All the same. The victims were all," he paused here, awkwardly searching for the right word, "... were all badly abused. Most of the bones in the bodies were broken, but in a systematic way. All were..." he paused again, "flayed."

"As you all know," he continued, "at one time, the armed forces found it necessary to employ para-military measures. That was under the old leadership. That has ceased. But even then, we never did anything like this. This has not been done by our side."

"But we had uncontrollables in our ranks," an officer objected. "Could this be their work?"

"No. We have consulted with all our former operatives, even those now in hiding, even those who now become our enemies. It is not their work. Besides, all these people, at least the ones we could identify, were criminals, drug-runners. None had any political involvement."

"This is a criminal thing, then?" someone asked.

"That appears to be the case. Obviously some sort of take-over is happening. By someone, some group, that is remarkably brutal. The aim of all this is, of course, terror. Whoever is behind it is without doubt the most," the officer paused again, absent-mindedly stirred his papers, "I don't know, diabolical, evil, thing, person, we have ever had in this part of the world. Our investigations will continue."

But they did not. Orders came down to ignore the killings.

Not thirty minutes away, hidden in the labyrinthian alleys of Intramuros, the old Spanish town, in a well-guarded cellar, eight young men and women talked, too, about what had been found on "Smoky Mountain," the wasteland of northern Manila.

"I do not think it could be the military, or even their wild agents," one young woman said. "They say they have stopped salvaging. I think they have, maybe not. But this, this is worse than even them. There is a sadism here, a brutality I do not think even they are capable of."

"But if it is not the military, who is it?" a young man asked.

"This is something new," another young voice responded. "I am not a coward. I am a revolutionary and will face death, I hope, bravely. But this. This is evil. Of this I am afraid."

But the revolutionary leadership told them to stay away from this.

In his Senate office, Senator Raul Martinez Senior quietly lay *The Manila Times* on his desk, turned in his chair, and stared out his window, stared toward the palm trees and park outside the old Spanish walls of Intramuros. He felt suddenly very cold.

It had been a lifetime ago. He raised his hand to his cheek, and touched a long scar with his arthritic fingers. The first reports of these killings had stirred a vague memory, a memory like that of a nightmare which had been painfully forgotten but suddenly recalled. Terrorists, he had guessed like all the others. Right-wing terrorists. Left-wing terrorists. But the victims were not political. And the extraordinary brutality. The broken bones. The systematic mutilation. The flaying. The strange sign carved in the fore-head.

Senator Martinez had believed, or more hoped than believed, that this thing was gone, purged, destroyed. He had driven it out of his memory. This cunning. This cruelty. This evil. He knew it. And it knew him.

The ancient enemy had returned.

Luneta Park, in the heart of Manila, is the political and spiritual soul of the Philippines, and the place where all important national political events take place. Luneta is to the Philippines what the Washington Monument and Lincoln Memorial are to Washington, Red Square to Moscow, and Tiananmen Square is to Beijing.

There is a reviewing stand in Luneta Park, its back toward Manila Bay, its face toward the city. In front of the reviewing stand are life-size statues of the "carabao," the native work animal of the Philippines, and the "tamarau," another animal indigenous to the islands. Both are large, horned animals, like oxen or water buffalo.

The carabao is submissive. Its horns are turned downward, bowed to the yoke. This is the inscription below the carabao:

"Sturdy of patience, in the sun industrious,

bearing with us what burdens bow our breed.

Undaunted hail the common as illustrious,

even the sweat that gives the soil our seed."

The tamarau, by contrast, full of energy and anger, is poised to strike. Its nose is snarled and its head is straining to break loose and be free. This is the message below the tamarau:

"O symbol of a people's Dangerous Grace,

Power controlled the rage that startled

when a great cry rent the slumber of the race.

When will that horned fury stir again?"

Rising in the background behind these statues is a small cross on a long pole which reaches far into the sky above the park. The cross is the highest point in the park and can be seen from anywhere in the area.

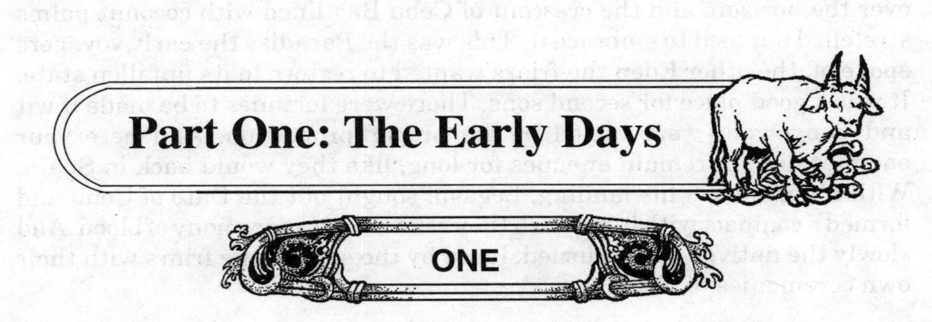

Part One: The Early Days

ONE

The trades were light and the sun threatened oppression as it climbed above the horizon beyond Cebu Bay. It was a steamy morning. From his tree hutch, Andres could see over the stockade that ran parallel to the beach and glimpse the mast of his ship, the San Pablo, silhouetted against the dull yellow disc. The bay at Cebu was a good anchorage, and the ship sat motionless on the glassy water. It had been riding at anchor for six months since the expedition under Commander Legaspi had reached the Islas del Poniente in April. The natives, like those at Ladrones back in January, had not been friendly at first, but one broadside from the San Pablo's guns had set them scrambling for the hills above the beach. They abandoned the settlement that had been there since Magellan first discovered this archipelago over forty years before. Within two months they had come out of the hills and embraced their new conquerors.

Andres and his companions took over the village and found plenty of food to fill their bellies and palm wine to fill their nights. Andres had become an expert on palm wine, with its pungent taste and syrupy texture that covered the tongue like honey. As Miguel said, it had a kick like a Cordoban mule. Andres shifted to one side on the straw mat, supported himself on his right elbow and inched his eyes open to let a bit more sun in. He knew the effects of palm wine had to be counteracted gradually.

He brought the ship mast into focus slowly and tried to ignore the pounding in his head. Back in Salamanca he had heard that people on this side of the world walked upside down. In school he had read about strange creatures whose heads were beneath their shoulders and others whose feet were so large they used them to shade the sun. After a night with palm wine, Andres had a good idea where these stories came from.

Things certainly were different on this side of the world. Even the sun rose differently. Not like it did over his parents' hacienda in Salamanca.

There the mountains kept the sun from view until it had already risen high in the sky and grown small. Here, huge in the morning mist, the sun peaked over the horizon, and the crescent of Cebu Bay lined with coconut palms stretched out as if to embrace it. This was the Paradise the early voyagers spoke of, the other Eden the friars wanted to restore to its unfallen state. It was a good place for second sons. There were fortunes to be made if wit and gunpowder were mixed in the proper proportion. And here your enemies did not remain enemies for long, like they would back in Spain. Within a month of his landing, Legaspi sought out the Dato of Cebu and formed a compact with him which they sealed with a ceremony of blood. And slowly the natives had returned, lured by the spell of the friars with their own ceremonies of blood.

Andres was impressed with the power the friars had over the people, with their magic rites, their words of worship. They seemed to put the natives into a trance with their hymns and incantations. Andres was a soldier and he respected power. Even if he could not understand it. Andres shifted his weight to his left hip, lowered himself to the mat and cupped his left hand behind his head to gaze on Itel. This was another power he could not fully understand. She was sleeping gently on her side with her back to him, legs curled up towards her chest. Her body was smooth and brown like the polished mahogany writing table in his father's study, the one that was shipped all the way from Seville. She was young, fifteen years of age or so. Only a few years younger than Andres. And she was the daughter of the Dato of Cebu. Her black hair fell loosely over her shoulder covering the side of her face. But Andres knew what was beneath it. A wide mouth with white teeth, a fine little nose, high cheekbones and almond eye slits such as he had never seen. Andres knew that eyes are the windows of the soul. But there was a mystery behind Itel's eyes, and those of her people. One that Andres might never understand.

Andres reached out and traced his finger up Itel's right arm which was draped over her hip. She shivered as he came to the curve of her arm and rolled toward him willingly, exposing her soft round breasts, the flatness of her tight stomach and the diadem of hair beneath her navel. Andres ran his hand across her front as if he were smoothing out a strip of leather until he found the mound between her legs. She shuddered again, as Andres eased his left arm beneath her neck and lifted her on top of him.

They made slow undulating love. One of the effects of palm wine, Andres discovered, was sexual stamina. Andres had never been with a woman before Itel, but he found it to be much like learning to sail. You had to get your sea legs first, then roll with the motions of the ship. Itel had a particularly interesting way of making love. Just as she was reaching the height of her pleasure she would squeal in little bursts of delight. The sounds seemed to start back in her throat and then escape through her nose with the shrillness of a badly played flute. Andres mentioned this to Miguel one night and he said that Andres should count himself among the fortunate, especially in this godforsaken land of savages. Miguel had a tendency to exaggerate and speak out of turn. But he was right about Itel. Andres always tried to time his moment of ecstasy with Itel's little noises.

This time they were arriving earlier than usual. And it seemed they were not coming from Itel but from outside, down below and far away. Itel's motions were becoming more rapid as she moved her body faster and faster. The squeals came faster and nearer too. "Itel, Itel.... Dantu, Dantu...Itel! Itel!" The words became louder and more desperate, until Andres began to recognize that it was Itel's name being called. Itel was in a trance, moving her body over his in a frenzy of pleasure. Suddenly the words penetrated and she became alert, motionless, and broke off. In an instant she was standing above Andres with a wild look in her eyes. Then she turned and bolted for the rope ladder that stretched to the beach below. She was down it, jumping half the distance to the sand, before Andres could stagger to the edge of the porch. She began to run before getting her legs fully under her and lurched forward, hands and knees on the sand. With a yell of frustration she lunged forward and was off down the beach to the south end of the bay. She had not bothered to put on her sarong.

Andres stepped into his breeches and stumbled to the ladder as he eyed Itel disappearing into the deep undergrowth just beyond the village. Andres made a note of where it was she entered the jungle. When he reached the beach he found footprints, two sets of them, and confidently followed them to the point where he saw Itel flash out of the sun and into the green shadows. From here, it would be more difficult to track Itel and whoever it was that called her away so frantically. The brush was thick and the air was heavy, suffocating for one not used to it. Andres was a good hiker in the hills beyond Salamanca. But there the air was light and the breeze invigorating. Here it was stagnant, oppressive. There had been a good rain over night, and the sod was soft under Andres' feet. If there were footprints, it was too dark to see them.

Andres plotted a course directly in front of him and stayed on a line as best he could, only yielding to the trees and underbrush that obstructed his way every ten paces or so. Soon he realized he was on a path recently made by a band of Aetas, the little people of the mountains who often came to the lowlands to hunt and dig wild roots. Andres stepped in one of the many holes left by the Aetas' digging and fell forward into the mud. As he raised himself up, he heard screaming in the distance ahead of him. He struck out in the direction of the sounds, knifing through the heavy vegetation like a schooner.

When he arrived at a small clearing in the woods, Andres saw what the excitement was about. Trapped in a pool of black mud was a carabao, one of the lumbering beasts of burden that populate the Islas del Poniente. The creature was stuck midway to its chest in the sucking mud. The more it struggled to extract itself, the deeper it dug itself in. Andres thought it a comic sight. And Itel was going about it all wrong. Her shouting and frantic gesturing were simply exciting the stupid animal. She should rather have tried to calm it. Later when the mud hardened in the hot sun, they could dig it out.

But Itel was shouting at the beast, cursing it, Andres thought. In her nakedness, she looked small and vulnerable as she stood over the half-submerged animal. The strength she had given him just an hour ago was not there now. Terror was on her face. Anun, her sister who had led her to the place, stood aside sobbing. The carabao bellowed and shifted its weight forward. Andres moved around the edge of the pool and saw that Itel was knee deep in the mud herself. And she was holding onto something, desperately. It was a hand! A small hand stretching out of the mud just above the wrist. Itel grunted and pulled backward with all her strength, falling flat on her back at the edge of the mud pool. She brought part way with her a small arm attached to the hand she had been clinging to so doggedly. A head appeared briefly above the muddy froth. It was Itel's little brother Dantu. Andres rushed forward and reached over Itel to grasp the boy's arm flailing in the air just as the carabao shifted again, this time on its side, rolling over the boy and driving him down into the mud.

Itel howled as the mud displaced by the carabao's movement flowed over her. Andres reached under her armpits from above her and pulled her out of the dank pool and onto the turf. There was not much time. He pushed his way into the mud, leaning over up to his shoulders and feeling everywhere for the boy beneath the mud. The frightened beast was churning up what solid ground there was on the bottom and making it more difficult for Andres to hold his footing. If he had to go in up to his waist, he would not have the leverage to pull the boy out.

To get deeper with his arms, Andres held a long breath and bent over, submerging his head. At first he thought he had found the boy's arm, but it was only the animal's tail. Then he felt the boy's upper arm and was able to get a good hold. But he would not budge. His lower body must be wedged under the animal's hip, Andres thought.

Andres stood erect, his chest and face dripping with the sticky mud, and motioned to Itel to coax the carabao forward and to the left, off of its right hip. It was the boy's only chance. Itel rushed to Anun and ripped off her sarong. She ran to the front of the carabao waving the bright cloth wildly. The carabao followed her frantic motions. Its eyes were rolled back in fear. Froth sprayed from its mouth and nostrils. In one lurch toward Itel the beast moved off its hip. Andres dove into the mud and found the arm as the carabao shifted its weight. The boy came lose. Andres straightened up and held him over his head in triumph. It was as if he were a midwife, aiding in a difficult birth.

Andres' feet gave way in the slick mud and he sat down hard at the edge of the pool laughing. Itel ran to him and threw her arms around his neck from behind, reaching for her brother's face. Andres threw back his head and laughed. When he turned to Itel he saw the terror was still on her face. The boy was not breathing. Quickly he wiped the mud from Dantu's face, his lips and nostrils. The mud was down his throat and in his nose blocking the air.

On the voyage from New Spain, Andres had seen a drowned man brought back from the dead when one of the sailors blew into the man's mouth and forced the water out of his lungs through his nose. Andres dug his fingers into Dantu's mouth to remove the mud and then blew hard. Once, then again, and a third time. The boy wheezed and choked, his air passages blocked. Then in a single convulsion he spewed out water and mud in a great torrent and gasped for air. He cried out and then fell to panting for breath. In a few seconds he drew easier breaths and his wails became sobs. Itel hugged his neck and cleaned his face with her tears. Andres fell back on the grass exhausted. He had saved the boy's life.

Anun had heard the men from the village just beyond the clearing and had brought them to the place just as Dantu was returning from the dead. Now they had attached a rope around the water buffalo's neck and were heaving him out of the mud. Andres hoisted Dantu onto his broad shoulders and with his arm around Itel they made their way back through the jungle to the edge of the settlement. Itel chattered the entire way. She was breathless in her excitement but Andres could not understand a single one of her words. Still he felt every bit like Adam with his Eve beside him as they broke out of the undergrowth into the sun and began the short walk toward the piked fences that formed the south barricade for the settlement.

It had been such an early morning adventure that few of his comrades were awake. Until now. Anun had preceded them with the story of the great exploit with the carabao. They saw him coming with his naked Eve, striding together down the beach. And they flooded out of the stockade to welcome him, with the irrepressible Miguel in the lead.

There were shouts of "Hero!" and "Andres, are you all right?" Then they stopped in their tracks. Miguel fell to his knees clutching his stomach as he doubled over with laughter. The others did the same. Miguel mustered enough strength to lift his arm and point. From a distance it had appeared that Andres was wearing his stockings and doublet. But now it was clear that he was only covered in mud. He had lost his breeches in the mud pool, and now he stood triumphantly before his fellows as naked as Itel. Adam and Eve indeed, he thought. Without a hesitation he grasped Dantu even tighter, pulled Itel closer to him and strode defiantly through the band of his comrades who were now thrashing on their backs in the sand, hopelessly out of control.

That night there was a special celebration in Hidalgo's canteen. Miguel made all the arrangements. There was rum, and palm wine, and a bottle of Canary that Miguel had stowed away through the entire Pacific voyage. This was an occasion worthy of "killing the canary," as Miguel put it. Most of Andres' squadron was there, hunched over their flagons of rum on wobbly stools around rough wooden tables. With them were the women of the canteen. The village women who did not go with Father Martin were left for Hidalgo to recruit. The soldiers needed women and Hidalgo supplied them. They kept the canteen clean and the men satisfied. The canteen of course gave Father Martin something to preach about on Sundays.

"You are a hero," Miguel slobbered between draughts of rum. "And he is the son of the Dato. You will be richly rewarded." Andres was less interested that Dantu was the son of the village chieftain than he was that the boy was Itel's brother. The Dato, after all, did not make little noises.

"Where is *ruidos bajos*?" Miguel wanted to know. This is what he called her — "little noises."

"I don't know. Off with her brother somewhere, I suppose. Making things ready for me when I return. I don't know." Andres was beginning to droop under the influence of the palm wine. The air in the canteen was heavy with the acrid smoke of the oil lamps and he was having difficulty keeping his eyes open. "I'll tell you one thing, though."

"What's that?" Miguel was pretending to be interested. His attention had wandered to a plump Bisayas girl of about sixteen whose companion, one Corporal Carlos Huenta, had just slumped forward and rolled onto the floor.

"I must learn her language," Andres went on. "Today. That boy might have died. If I had known what she was yelling I could have reacted faster. I will go to Father Martin tomorrow. He will teach me."

"That's fine. Then she can tell you how much she loves you." Miguel's voice was tinged with sarcasm. "And you'll understand what she says. I'm sure the Father knows all the right words."

"The least she can do is tell me when I don't have any clothes on." Then Andres remembered that Itel had been trying to tell him something all the way back to the settlement. "First thing tomorrow I pay a visit to Father

Martin." Andres sealed his contract with himself by taking a long pull at his flask. Miguel had already moved off to Corporal Huenta's vacant seat.

The doorway at that moment was filled with the considerable bulk of Humabon, the chief advisor to Dato Tupas and the medicine man to the village. He was dressed in what seemed to be war gear — an old breastplate, a feathered robe, and a helmet from the time of Magellan garnished with feathered plumes. He seemed a strange amalgamation of native and borrowed attire. Hidalgo had never seen anyone, or anything like it, and reached for his musket on the wall. Several other men in the canteen, always on the alert that the natives might sometime mount a resistance, slid their free hands silently over the hilts of the swords at their sides.

Humabon stretched out his arms over the assemblage in the canteen as if he were giving a blessing and everyone froze. The two men behind him were armed with spears, but he gestured to all who would see that his hands were empty. It was a sign that he came in peace. He grunted a command and the two men came forward and stood behind Andres who looked over to Miguel as if to ask, "What now?" The two men lifted Andres to his feet and began escorting him to the door.

"Do you have any idea what is happening?" Andres asked Miguel as he was whisked past his friend. "No, but I am right behind you." And indeed as Andres was ushered through the door with Humabon, the whole canteen emptied out onto the beach in close pursuit. Humabon led the way with his plumed helmet catching some of the moon's rays and reflecting them off into the darkness. Andres had not quite recovered the use of his legs and was practically being dragged across the top of the sand by Humabon's guards. Miguel and Hidalgo followed in their tracks, bearing torches. Even Corporal Huenta had stumbled awake and with the rest was making his way toward the center of the compound. There a circle of torches awaited them.

"It is Legaspi himself," breathed Miguel with reverence and a bit of astonishment. The great commander seldom appeared like this before his men. He made it a practice to remain aloof, both to the natives and to his men. It garnered respect. And on this side of the world, respect was the first step towards power. Miguel pointed toward the edge of the circle and it was indeed Miguel Lopez de Legaspi, grand commander of the third expedition from New Spain to the Islas del Poniente, or, as they were coming to be known, the Philippines. Every inch the conquistador, Legaspi stood there in his gilded breastplate and plumed helmet, with his snowy beard sticking out from beneath the chin strap like so much down forced from a metal pillow.

Beside him stood Tupas, the Dato of Cebu. Tupas was arrayed much like Humabon only his feathers were grander and his helmet, given him by Legaspi, was newer than Humabon's by forty years. Tupas' large hand rested on the shoulder of the boy Andres had saved that day. Andres could not see Itel. Evidently this was no place for women. But what kind of place was it?

Humabon led Andres to the center of the circle. The Spaniard's two supports left him there and he almost fell to his knees. Humabon's icy stare gave him nerve. Tupas advanced to the center and Humabon retired. A chant went up from the circle around them. In Tupas' hand was a knife, a *Sula Barong* they called it. The arched handle was of gold and carefully wrought with braided gold. The blade gleamed in the moonlight. Tupas extended his arm and held the blade horizontally. He then crooked his arm and brought the blade toward his chest. With a swift back-handed motion he opened a wound in his pectoral muscle from which the blood flowed freely. He then offered the barong to Andres whose knees threatened to buckle again. The chanting rose in intensity and put sinews back in his legs.

"It is the ceremony of blood covenant," he heard Miguel shout from behind him. "You are a fortunate man." Andres glanced over to his commander who signaled his approval with a nod as if to say "It's your turn. Show them what you are made of. You are a Spanish soldier. Make me proud."

Magellan himself forty years before made a blood compact with one of Tupas' predecessors. That time they sucked the blood from each other's chests. The ceremony had since become more civilized. As Andres drew the blade across his breast Humabon came forward with golden cups in which he caught the blood flowing from each man. Then with an elaborate gesture he crossed his arms, offering each man the other's blood. The circle fell silent. In the hushed moment, beneath the stars on the other side of the world, Andres drank another man's blood.

Tupas dropped his chalice in the sand at his feet and Andres followed suit. Then the chieftain put his arm around Andres and led him to the other side of the circle where Dantu stood. Tupas positioned Andres next to his son and smiled broadly. He then motioned beyond the circle which divided to let Itel enter. Tupas positioned her beside Andres. He then joined Legaspi and made a broad sweep with his hand as if to present his "family" to the Spanish commander. Itel reached out furtively and claimed Andres' left hand, entwining his large fingers with all of hers. Had he been made her brother? Or had Tupas given her to him as wife?

Now more than ever Andres wished to speak her language. Tomorrow he would see Father Martin, tonight there was Itel.

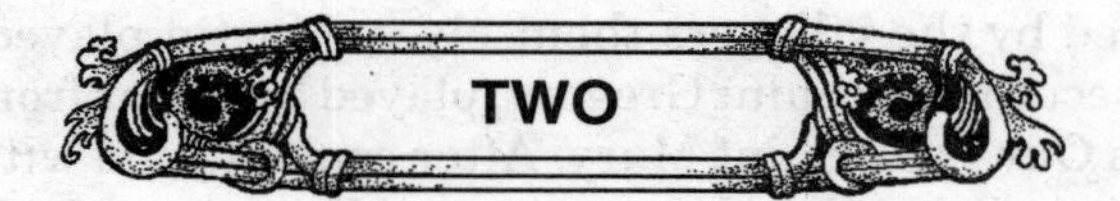

TWO

Father Martin's missionary church was not at the center of the settlement at Cebu as the churches for coastal settlements usually were. It was not yet even a church, but a chapel built next to a shrine on the site of a house where a small wooden image of the Christ Child had been found the day after the Legaspi expedition overran the village. A friar from the Magellan expedition forty years earlier had given the image to a native. It had become an object of veneration and worship and was preserved until it was found by one of Legaspi's soldiers on a routine sweep of the houses that were abandoned by the natives when the San Pablo offered its broadside.

Martin had moved the "Santo Niño" to the site where he had planned his church. But the little wooden image kept returning to the house where the natives had worshipped it. Back home in his native Castile, Martin was familiar with stories about saints' statues that found their way back to the site where a miracle occurred or where a saint appeared to a pious shepherd. The peasants said it was a sign that the Lord meant the saint to be worshipped there, and a shrine with a chapel was dutifully built on the spot.

So Martin had shifted his plans for the Church of the Holy Infant from the center of the triangular settlement to its present site. What better spot to build a church and perform the job he had come halfway around the world to do.

Martin Herrada grew up on a farm outside of Segovia where he and his three older brothers helped their father scratch out a living in the rocky soil beneath Mount Penalara. Martin made the church his destiny when he was thirteen. He was fond of telling people what prompted him to make this decision. The way he told it, the area around Segovia was plagued with locusts back in 1540 after two years of drought. The country folk tried everything they could think of to get relief. They prayed to the local saints and even to the Holy Mother to rid them of the pests that were destroying their crops. They made vows to Saint Gregory of Nazianzus who was held to be a special enemy of insects and vine worms. They held processions and novenas. They held public confessions of sinners. They even sent a representative to Navarre to bring back holy water from the shrine of St. Gregory to sprinkle on the fields. When all else failed, the townspeople of Segovia decided to put the locusts on trial.

The trial was arranged by the neighboring Augustinian monastery. The witnesses for the prosecution were the patron saints of the nearby villages, played by the villagers themselves. Martin played Saint Sebastian. The prosecutor was Saint Gregory, played by a friar from Segovia, and the judge was Our Lady Saint Mary. After consultation with her advisors — Saints Jerome, Sebastian, Lawrence, and Francis — the Blessed Virgin proclaimed that the locusts would be excommunicated if they did not leave the territory. The next year there were no locusts and Martin left the farm for the Dominican monastery at Toledo. There he studied hard and proved to be a brilliant scholar under the tutelage of Brother Jofre de Henares.

Jofre was one of the new breed of priests who had studied the teachings of Ignatius of Loyola and had joined the Society of Jesus. The Jesuits, as they came to be called, were militantly determined to re-educate the world in the wake of Luther's blasphemies. Theirs was a missionary zeal, and the object of their zealotry was no less than the salvation of humanity. The first thing Jofre did was convince Martin that his future involved more than the exorcism of grasshoppers.

What Jofre convinced Martin of was that the church had to convert the heathens of the East Indies. Did not one-third of the host of heaven follow Lucifer to the fiery pits of Hell? he would ask rhetorically as he slammed his hand down flat on a map of the Moluccas and the archipelago of the Islas del Poniente. Had not most of the souls of northern Europe followed Luther to the same destination? "These Philippines," he would say, "are named for our king, and King Philip does not wish to rule over a pagan nation. Here are the souls the church needs to replace those lost in the north." It was a compelling argument for one filled both with the spirit of the Lord and with adventure as Martin was.

Before he was twenty Martin had given testimony before the Inquisition in Madrid and even had a hand in several prosecutions. It was Jofre, after he had become Bishop of Seville, who hand-picked Martin to sail with Legaspi to the Isles of the West and bring the word of God to the natives. There were many lost souls to capture, and Martin Herrada was just the man to get the job done.

It was almost nine o'clock and Father Martin was readying the candles and the wine for the mass he delivered each morning at that time. Several villagers were already assembled in the small chapel Martin had hurriedly erected beside the shrine of the Santo Niño. A garden with flowered trellises connected the chapel with the small workshop where Martin and Brother Carlos, a stonemason, worked on the plans for the church. It was through this garden that "sister" Teresa scampered to announce the arrival of a visitor. "Who is it?" Martin inquired. "A soldier. He did not give his name." Teresa's Spanish was broken. Martin did not press the matter in Bisayas but hurried across the garden, stopping to cross himself before the Madonna in the niche on the far wall.

Entering the shop, he found Carlos at his bench carving figurines of the Apostles. Along the bench were scores of little figures, mainly crucifixes, which Carlos had carved from the island's soft wood and from the horns of animals. He gave them to the natives to inspire their devotions. Martin had tried to rid the natives' houses of their anitos, the images of their ancestors which they superstitiously worshipped. The crucifixes served as replacements. "Keep them coming," Martin joked, "we need all the working Christians we can create if we are to build our church." Andres was looking over Carlos' shoulder and turned at the sound of Martin's resonant voice.

"Ah, our hero of the mud." Martin seemed to be in a hurry. He gestured Andres to a table across the room before the open fire where Teresa was stirring a large cauldron of porridge. Sometimes Teresa put slivers of coconut and cinnamon in the porridge. It was a treat the natives had come to love. Martin knew it was easier to be faithful on a full stomach. "The spirit is willing," he often said, "if the porridge is hot."

Martin heaved himself onto the bench opposite Andres, fixed him sternly with his eyes, and asked brusquely, "What do you want?" The sound of Martin's voice startled Andres. It came up from the friar's chest which was as large as the bell he rang early each morning to summon the islanders to worship. Andres was unnerved by the directness of Martin's question. He had expected some idle chatter first. There was nothing but time on the island, and as a rule people did not get right down to business. Andres thought Martin should have asked him something about his heroics of the day before.

"Well, what is it? What do you want?" Andres decided it was best to give a direct answer and skip the explanations.

"I want to learn Bisaya." The bells for the mid-morning mass had begun to ring, and Martin motioned to Carlos to take over and conduct the ceremony. Through a window Andres could see the worshippers entering the chapel door from the street. They were mostly women. The women were the first to accept the new religion. The men came afterward, if at all. Andres turned back to Martin across the table from him. "You know the native language, Bisayas." He paused. "That's right," Martin said. "I have constructed an alphabet and developed a vocabulary. I have even preached to them in their own language."

Andres allowed a moment to indicate that he was duly impressed with this last piece of information. Martin clearly wished him to be so. "Will you teach it to me?" Martin did not answer immediately.

"Why do you want to learn to speak Bisayas? Have you got a woman? Is that why you are so anxious to learn their language?" Martin's tone was threatening. Andres backed away from the table to put more space between himself and the friar who seemed to be tuning up for a sermon.

"These people are godless heathens. It is my duty, your duty, to show them the right path. We were sent here to bring them God, not our filthy lusts and diseases. I have spent hours mastering their language so I could speak the word of God to them. And now you want to learn it so you can converse on matters of the devil. Our job is to educate these people, not to sleep with them."

"But I want to know what she is thinking, what is going on in her mind. It is true we sleep together, and we enjoy that. But there is more. I want to talk with her about other things, what she likes, what she fears, what she did during the day, the sky, the water, sunsets, and the lagoon on the other side of the island." Andres was earnest in his pleading, but he was not sure he was getting through. Martin was a hard man.

"I heard about last night. You know that I don't approve. The drinking of blood."

"What did you expect me to do? It wasn't my idea." Andres was irritated that Martin had changed the subject. "And anyway, how is it different from what you do?" Andres gestured toward the chapel where Carlos was intoning the mass. That, Andres thought, was probably not a good idea. After all, he was here to ask the man a favor. Martin ignored the impertinence. "How is your wound this morning?" It was going to be difficult to pin the friar down. He was fond of changing the subject.

Andres reached to his chest. It was a reflex action. "It's still sore. Itel put a poultice on it last night. I haven't looked at it since." Martin reached over and spread Andres' blouse open. "Let me see." His hands were large and rough. The hands of a farmer. He found a palm leaf stuck to Andres' chest. Brown ooze leaked from beneath it.

"Teresa, bring me some alcohol and bandages. Sergeant Andres is in need of repair."

As he cleaned the wound and applied the fresh bandages, Martin described the plans he had for the church. He had taken on the duties of architect and builder with relish. He had the men to do the job, he explained, because he had performed over seventy-five baptisms in just the last two months. And there were even more women, those who were not with Hidalgo, to work the fields beyond the stockade and serve his needs at the chapel. The church's larder was always well stocked. Anyone who worked for the Padre could be certain of a full belly.

"Now about the language lessons." Martin seemed to be musing out loud or just making conversation while he applied the fresh bandage to Andres' chest. "That will take some work. And what can you offer me in return?"

"What did you have in mind?" Andres was surprised by the sudden turn. Martin had given no indication that he had changed his mind and Andres wondered what had caused it. He did not think it had been anything he had said.

"You have strength in your arms and legs. When your wound heals perhaps you could help me with the building of the church." Martin had put the last touches on the bandage. Andres closed his tunic over it and pulled back from the Padre. "I'm a soldier, not a laborer," he said with a finality that he hoped would close the discussion. "Well, we'll have to think of something," Martin said as he returned to his place across the table. "I have it. The boy." Andres was a bit confused. "The boy? Who do you mean? Dantu? What about him?"

"I need your help with him. He is the son of the dato, and yet he is lost to me."

"What do you mean?"

"Your episode of the mud yesterday. Had you ever been on that path before?" Andres indicated he had not. "Are there any fields of rice or maize or other crops being cultivated in that direction from the settlement? We both know there are not. So what was Dantu doing with a carabao out there with no one but his younger sister?"

"I'm sure I don't know. I haven't given it much thought. I was rather busy at the time." Andres was not at all sure what it was that Martin was driving at.

"Surely you know that pagan rites and sacrifices and devil worship are practiced in the jungle beyond the village. Humabon leads these heathen rites with their ungodly dances and fornications. He is jealous of my... God's power. His magic is no longer the force it once was on this island. He is fighting for his life. And it is up to me to wipe out the gods of the forest. Dantu is the son of the dato. Our future will depend on his good will. The church needs him. I cannot lose him to Humabon and the forest. Will you help me?"

The bells signaling the end of the service punctuated the friar's speech and gave urgency to it. Andres listened with little interest to the story of Martin's battle with Humabon for the souls of the islanders. His attention wandered to a scene unfolding outside in front of the chapel. Through the window he could see the worshippers filing out to the street. A man was shouting at one of the women who had just emerged into the dusty morning sun. He struck her several times and then pulled her by the arm down to the ground.

Martin's voice brought Andres back. "Just be his friend," the friar said quietly as he turned toward the window and the commotion outside. "Bring him with you to our lessons. That might be a start."

A reasonable request, Andres thought, and one not too difficult to comply with. Andres could care less about Martin's mission to convert the natives, and it was little of his concern whether or not Dantu joined Martin's flock. It was the boy's sister that Andres was interested in, and Martin held the key to the language that would give him access to her thoughts. What had he to lose by befriending the boy?

Andres was about to accept the friar's proposition when the street-side door behind him burst open. The man Andres had seen through the window now stood in the doorway, his leg raised as if he were sighting across the toes of his left foot while he balanced adroitly on the other. In his raised right hand was a spear, its teardrop head of iron attached to a bamboo stock four feet in length.

Andres reacted instinctively. He leapt across the table towards Martin, pulling the table over with him to act as a shield. He knelt down and reached for his pistol. Martin stood up to face the intruder who with a wild shout heaved the spear at the friar who was now presenting a full target. Martin raised a tin dish that had fallen into his hand as the table tipped toward him and stretched it at arms' length toward the flying spear. The platter broke its force just enough as the spear point penetrated the soft metal and came to rest an inch from Martin's left ear. Martin threw spear and platter aside and Andres, pistol at the ready, stood up and took aim. The assailant shouted again and rushed Martin, fists flailing, while he cursed the friar in words Andres could not yet understand.

Andres cocked the hammer of his pistol but Martin waved him off. The intruder covered the distance from the door to Martin in an instant and began striking the friar's chest with his fists. The friar towered over him; only the upturned table stood between them. As the man struck repeatedly at Martin's chest, Martin grabbed his left hand in his own and began to squeeze. Andres could hear the bones crack as the man fell to one knee howling in agony. Martin's expression did not change. Andres imagined the knuckles popping out of their sockets and the sinews around the fingers snapping. Then he saw what was really happening. Martin had wedged his large fingers between the man's ring and little finger and was separating the little finger from the rest of the hand. The web of skin between the fingers was splitting open and blood ran down the man's arm and dripped from his elbow onto the floor.

The pain drained every ounce of the man's energy and he drooped sobbing to the floor on both knees, his right arm dangling free and his left extended like a broken wing with the little finger, red with blood, pointing helplessly to the floor like a divining rod that had just struck water. Martin stood over the hapless figure now kneeling before the table like an altar and placed his hand on his head as if in benediction. "Teresa," he shot over his shoulder, "we'll be needing some bandages."

Teresa came in. Brother Carlos was with her. Together they escorted the wounded man out of the room. "What was that all about?" Andres asked as he eased the hammer on his pistol out of the cocked position and holstered the weapon. Martin was righting the table and the bench on his side. Andres moved around the table to the other bench. "It seems he lost his wife... to the church. She has been attending services and helping out around here instead of working in the rice fields and keeping his house. Understandable he became angry. Now he will join us and he will no longer be angry with his wife."

"How do you know that?"

"Because he has suffered pain and the church will heal him. He will be grateful and he will respect my power. That is the way it works. When will you begin your lessons?"

"I am due to go on patrol tomorrow. I'll be gone about a week."

"Then it is agreed. We will start a week from today."

"Fine." Andres began moving toward the door which still stood wide open.

"And don't forget. Bring the boy." Andres closed the door behind him. The crowd that had gathered for chapel was now dispersed. The morning heat was setting in and most people were about the business of the day. Andres stood alone in the street. Yesterday he had saved a boy's life. Today he had almost shot a man. And it was early yet. He did not have to report for duty until tomorrow morning when the patrol was set to start out, so he decided to take the rest of the day off. By the time he got there, Hidalgo's canteen would be open, and Miguel would enjoy hearing how the Padre made converts to Christianity.

* * *

Patrols to the interior of the island were sent out every other week. Usually twelve men or so led by a sergeant like Andres. Their purpose was to check for any signs of Moro pirates and to secure the area. What this meant was they were to make their presence known to any natives in the hills. Spanish control of the island was not to be confined to the narrow strip of coastline occupied by the village. But the real reason for the patrols and why the men did not mind the steamy days of jungle march and the sleepless nights when everything on the ground around you was in motion, crawling, darting, slithering; the real reason was very simple. Gold. Since Magellan's time there had been reports of gold in Cebu. The villagers like Itel and her father Tupas and even the women of the mission, all wore gold earrings. The goblets used in the ceremony of blood were made of gold. The knife handles were gold. There had to be gold on the island. Their job was to find it.

Andres knew, all the men knew, that if their fortunes were to be made, if this island was to mean anything to the Spanish crown it would be because of the gold mines the natives were hiding from them. Cebu would never produce a commodity of any value for Spanish traders. The Spice Islands to the south were in Portuguese control and Mindanao where the cinnamon tree grows was under Moro control. Unfortunately, the cinnamon tree did not flourish in Cebu. So it had to be gold. If they were patient, they would find it.

But this patrol like the four before it that Andres had led uncovered nothing, nothing that Andres could report. On the second night out, Miguel shook Andres awake to report a flurry of movement on a trail beyond their camp. Andres, Miguel, and two other men followed the sound until they came upon a small band of the Aeta, the pygmy hill people. The band joined a larger group gathered around a smoldering fire in which wild roots and tubers were roasting. The band Andres and his men had followed were most likely a hunting party. One that had not been successful.

The little men squatted around the fire, and Andres could see better than he ever had before the designs on their chests, backs, and arms which they made with rows of cuts that left scars in ornamental patterns. Their hair was rough and matted and decorated with bamboo combs and feathers from the mountain cock. Some of them had filed their front teeth into sharp points. The fire flickered and cast eerie shadows on their faces. Andres imagined he was watching a congregation of imps or little devils like he had seen carved over the western doors of the church at Salamanca. These souls, he thought, were beyond the power of even Father Martin. There was no gold to be seen, so Andres and his men slid back into the darkness and returned to their woodland camp, leaving the strange men to their roasted tubers and hopes of a better hunt the next day.

On the way, Andres was attracted by a noise off the path, faint sounds of voices. It could be just more of the Aeta on their way to join the others. Andres motioned the men to go on and he ducked under the heavy leaf of a banana palm to investigate. The darkness enclosed behind him, shutting him off from his comrades. In a few seconds he was upon another clearing where he found several men in heated discussion. Andres could not understand what they were saying, but by their gestures they seemed not to be arguing but to be trading, striking a deal. Large bundles made of fish netting lay at the men's feet.

The four large men with their backs to him wore colorful silk robes with elaborate patterns that Andres could barely make out in the moonlight that filtered through the opening in the trees above them. The wedged-shaped swords and the oval helmets with the high ridge down the center like a lizard's spine left no doubt in Andres' mind. He had seen this equipment before. They were Moro pirates. He and his ancestors had been fighting the Moros in the Spanish peninsula for two centuries. And now half a world away they were fighting them again.

Andres crouched quietly and then eased himself down to his hands and knees. Careful not to rustle the undergrowth, he crept to his right so he could see who the other men were. The one who had been doing most of the talking was just turning and moving off into the dark foliage beyond the clearing. A smaller figure had preceded him into the dark. Andres recognized the one remaining figure. It was Humabon. "What is the dato's lieutenant doing out here in the middle of the night with Moro pirates," Andres wondered.

Andres was not prepared for what he saw next. As Humabon turned to go, the leaves parted on the far side of the clearing and into the light stepped Dantu. This was not the boy he saved from the mud pool. He had a robe thrown over his shoulders and wore a headdress of feathers. He had an air of confidence about him that belied his years.

One of the Malayans gestured for Dantu to come closer. He lowered his arm to reach Dantu's outstretched hand. Andres could not see what the Moro gave the boy, but Dantu seemed pleased. He took a step backward and nodded his thanks. Then he turned on his heels and followed Humabon into the darkness.

Andres held his position until the Moros picked up the bundles and left the clearing. After a few minutes, Andres crept backwards, staying low, until he reached the path he had left earlier. He reached his camp quickly, but he did not sleep that night.

It was Sunday when Andres' patrol returned to the settlement. First, Andres reported to Captain Martin de Goiti, Legaspi's field marshal. Then he went home where Itel was waiting. Dantu was with her. This was the first time that Andres had been gone for such a long time and Itel had wanted some company. So Dantu had stayed with her. Since there was only one room, Andres hoped that this was not going to be a permanent change of residence for the young boy. Itel made a great fuss over Andres, and so did Dantu who, shy as he was, tried to show his gratitude. Itel placed a garland of flowers over Andres' head and led him to the wooden block that served as a table on the far side of the mostly bare room. They sat on the broad palm leaves that served as mats. After a dinner of rice and fish and some coconut, Dantu presented Andres with a little wooden animal. It was a carabao. That night, Dantu slept curled up in the corner of the room. For the first time, Andres and Itel slept together but did not make love.

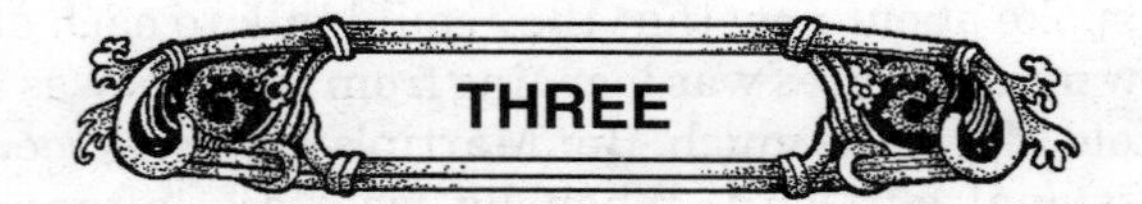

On Monday morning, Andres began his lessons with Father Martin. Martin was an energetic teacher and truly excited about the Bisayan language. "It has the best qualities of the finest languages in the world," he told Andres before they got started. "It has the mysteries and obscurities of the Hebrew; the precision of the Greek; the elegance of Latin; and the good breeding and courtesy of Spanish." Martin began with pronunciation of the three vowels and twelve consonants. By the end of the day he was drilling Andres in the pronunciation of common objects in the room around them: table, chair, dish, spear. The spear was still lodged in the platter which served as its base of support as it leaned in the corner of the workshop opposite the fireplace.

The first time he saw it, Andres had not inspected it very closely. It had been a weapon aimed at him and the padre. Now he could look more closely. The tip was of iron, forged in a way he had not seen before in the islands. The point was not fixed permanently but was attached to a short stub that fit into a hollow in the end of the stock. Together, these were attached by a rope to the stock which served as a hurling stick for the deadly projectile. Martin saw the direction of Andres' gaze. "It's a Moro hunting spear. A frightful instrument. But no match for our powder, eh?" The spear seemed rather peaceful as it leaned against the wall, its head dangling limply beside the bamboo pole. Perhaps Martin was keeping it as a reminder to stay on his guard, Andres thought. Religion could be a dangerous business on this side of the world.

Martin gave Andres the Bisayas word for "spear." "You just may have some need to use that word in the future." The lessons had started.

For the next weeks, Andres became a dutiful student. He reported to the chapel early before the morning mass, and Martin helped him build a vocabulary and guided him with pronunciation. After the mass, they would wander around the building site, and sometimes Andres would help the laborers carry the blocks of stone that brother Carlos had chiseled to a fine shape. The walls of the mission church were waist high and grew to their full height in the time it took Andres to begin speaking his new language with any confidence. Their conversation was mixed with simple sentences in Bisayas and more complex Spanish ones about the hunt for souls and gold on the island. Martin was interested in both.

He was also interested in Itel. At times he would ask Andres what he and Itel spoke about now that they could talk to each other. He wanted to know how much Andres was learning from Itel. Itel was a good teacher, and Andres told Martin as much. But Martin's inquiries seemed more than idle or professional curiosity. When he was free, after guard duty on the parapets of the stockade and after drilling his squadron in the dust behind the barracks, Andres would walk with Itel in the late afternoon. They would talk of sunsets and gulls on the wing, and the noise the surf makes slapping against the sand at low tide.

Learning the Bisayas language gave Andres a keen sense of the Bisayas people. They were after all people, with words for things, with ideas, with intelligence. They had words for love, and life and beauty, and war, and death. And God. Martin wanted to use their words to change their minds about things like God. It was part of his power. Andres wondered if his motive was any less innocent.

As the weeks passed, Andres was able to speak more fluently with Itel. Sometimes they held long conversations, late into the night, about the island, her father, what she thought about the new order of things. Andres discovered a thinking person. Itel had opinions and they were strong ones. But the more he learned about her, the less he really knew. Some nights, after they had talked, and made love, and then slept, Itel would go off in the night.

Andres did not know how long it had been going on. But ever since the night in the forest when he saw Dantu with the Moro pirates, he had not slept well. Perhaps it was also because he frequented Hidalgo's canteen less and consumed less palm wine now that he had someone to talk to late at night. And he also had those early morning obligations with Father Martin. Some nights when he awoke, she would not be there. The place on the mat next to him would be empty. One time, he was sure that it was her smell on the breeze she made as she moved toward the door that woke him. Or perhaps he was just dreaming. Some mornings when he woke early, she would be lying where she should be, breathing hard, her brown skin moistened with sweat. Andres imagined that she had run from somewhere to return to her place beside him before he awoke. But from where?

It was strange, Andres thought. Now that he could talk with Itel, there was a question he did not want to ask. It had not occurred to him yet that he might be losing her. But he was losing part of her, the part she was keeping secret from him. When he looked in her eyes, there was mystery. Part of her was closed off from him. He might have told Father Martin and asked his advice. But Martin was only his confessor. He was not his friend. And there are some things that you can only talk about with your friends.

"How is the boy, Dantu, these days?" Martin asked Andres in Bisayas. Andres was well aware that he had not yet brought the boy with him to one of his lessons.

"He lives in the sun," Andres replied, using a Bisayas idiom to mean that the boy thrived and was healthy. Then slipping back into Spanish, Andres was able to be more direct. "He fills his days like most of the boys with working in the rice fields. But he also spends time with his father on matters of business in the barangay."

Martin stretched his arms wide and heaved a great sigh as if he were releasing pressure that had been building up for weeks. "What would you say to moving the lesson outside tomorrow?"

Martin was changing the subject again. But Andres knew him well enough now. Sometimes he only seemed to be changing the subject.

"We could take a little trip up the coast in a boat. Go sailing. There are Bisayas expressions about sailing and the sea you need to know. Why not bring the boy along?" Andres was right. "It might be a nice break from his 'living in the sun'."

The next morning, Andres and Dantu arrived earlier than usual at the door of the mission workshop. Teresa was already up and bustling about. She let them in and went off to find Father Martin.

Andres had slept the night through and felt refreshed. Itel was beside him when he awoke; Dantu was also there, asleep in the corner. He did not know whether she had been there all night, but he suspected that the two of them had been somewhere together and had returned before dawn.

"Well, there you are," said Martin cheerfully in Bisayas as he entered the room. The greeting was directed more to Dantu than to Andres. "And you brought our friend with you, I see. Are you ready, my son?"

Dantu did not answer. He was already moving cautiously toward Brother Carlos's workbench. He was fascinated with the little crucifixes Carlos was carving.

"What are these?" he asked as he picked one up and rolled it over in his hands. Carlos inferred the question and answered in Spanish. "They are images of our Lord Jesus Christ."

Dantu looked toward Martin for an explanation. He repeated Carlos' words in Bisayas. "It is our Lord who died for our sins and is our salvation. He is the God to whom we pray for the safety of our souls."

Dantu nodded his understanding. "Anitos," he said, referring to the images of ancestors that he and his people continued to worship. He picked up one of Carlos's carving tools and began to whittle on the crucifix he held. Martin's reaction was swift and violent. He pulled the wooden figure from the startled boy's grip and hurled it across the room where it struck Teresa's pot with a sharp ping. "The little blasphemer," he shouted. His voice crackled with danger. "When will they learn?"

Dantu backed away from Martin toward Carlos's end of the bench. The milder monk picked up another crucifix and handed it to the boy in a gesture of reconciliation. Dantu took it gratefully, eyed Martin suspiciously and then crossed behind a table to arrive at Andres' side.

"We'd best get going," Martin said in a calmer tone, trying to put his outburst behind them. "Blasphemer or not, this young fellow has a day of adventure before him. And we don't want to keep him waiting."

Martin put one arm around Andres' shoulder and made a friendly effort to encircle Dantu with the other to escort them to the door. Dantu ducked under Martin's arm and walked boldly back to Carlos at his table. The boy reached into the pouch tied around his waist and pulled forth a small figure of a bird. It was made from a crocodile tooth and was colored blue.

Dantu placed it on the bench beside a crucifix in front of Brother Carlos. "Laon," he said proudly, and then he turned and ran to catch up with the two men.

The party of Martin, Andres and Dantu left the settlement by the north gate. Martin led the way along the beach where several native sailing vessels were perched uncomfortably on the sand. Fishermen already returned from their morning's work were busily making over the nets which were stretched along the beach between the boats. One boat remained in the water, bobbing with the slow undulations of the bay. A man squatted facing the boat, holding a rope attached to its stern.

The San Pablo sat quietly guarding the entrance to the bay. A few white caps appeared from the breakers along the jetty on the bay's southern edge in the distance. If they made a sound it did not carry to the shore where Andres stood with his face turned to the gentle westerly breeze and judged it a good day for sailing.

The man pulled the boat closer to the shore and tossed the rope in. He stood knee deep in the surf beside the skiff, holding it steady under his right arm so the three could climb aboard. Dantu pulled himself up to the chest, then scissored his legs over the side. He moved forward to the prow to balance the craft before the men entered.

"You know our captain for today, I presume," Martin said gesturing to the man holding the boat as he hoisted himself over the side. His coarse robes collected more water than other garments and made his entry a struggle.

"Yes, of course," Andres acknowledged as he vaulted gracefully into the boat. It was Cid-Hamel, a Muslim Malay from Borneo who had been taken to Spain by an earlier expedition, then sent to Mexico where he joined Legaspi's expedition as a translator. He had accompanied de Goiti on his discoveries of the nearby islands of Masbate, Ticao, and Burias. His knowledge of the central islands of the archipelago and his navigational skills had earned him the title "The Pilot" among Legaspi's troops.

Cid-Hamel gave the prau a shove, then leapt over the stern. As they skimmed over the green sheet of water, Cid-Hamel moved to the center of the craft, positioned the mast and raised the sail. The wind caught it and they shot forward. Then he took his place at the helm and they were under way. Dantu knelt at the prow and let his hand skim across the water.

In a few moments they reached the north end of the bay and broke out into the open sea. But never more than two hundred yards from the shore, just beyond the gentle breakers that washed onto a narrow strip of sand. Cebu itself was just a thin sliver of an island nestled between Bohol to the southeast and Negros to the west. The northern tip of Cebu, where they were heading, projected beyond the protection of the neighboring islands and became exposed to gale force winds at times. The palms along this coast, Andres noted, were bent backwards away from the sea like tall gaunt men hunched over a private game in the streets of Salamanca.

Andres marveled at the different hues of blue and green that presented themselves to him in the water and the sky, near and far. Martin gave him the words for the colors, and for the parts of the boat and the actions of sailing, and the compass directions. Cid-Hamel helped in the instruction. Dantu listened attentively and interrupted occasionally to offer a synonym. Dantu was even more attentive to the Spanish that Martin used to identify the Bisayas words. Perhaps Martin would teach the boy Spanish, and then they all could learn Arabic from Cid-Hamel.

As it neared noon, the sun began to blaze white hot. Martin dipped a piece of cloth in the water and draped it over his tonsured head. His nose was turning a bit red already and no doubt his bald pate was blistered by now. The padre then pulled open a pouch he had brought with him and began to distribute pieces of dried fish and some biscuits, first to Dantu, then to Andres and "The Pilot". Cid-Hamel started a flask of fresh water back the other way starting with Andres.

After the light lunch, Andres stretched out and leaned back against the side of the boat facing the open sea. He was struck by the beauty of the day, the pleasure he had found in Cebu, the newness of the world he was discovering every day, and the vastness of the sea that stretched out before him as far as he could see to the horizon. Beyond that horizon were continents that did not exist a hundred years ago. And beyond them was his peninsular homeland.

It seemed even farther away than it was. All Europe was aflame with new ideas. Powerful men sought riches and treasure to decorate their splendid courts. The church had gone on the offensive against heretics. Fierce faith battled with treachery and elegance mingled with horror as princes and priests struggled for men's souls and their minds. But in Cebu, Andres had found quiet dawns and gentle days. And Itel.

The thought of Itel confused him. There are things I do not yet understand, he thought. The world Andres had left and the world he had found were filled with contradictions. And some of the contradictions were here in this boat with him.

Andres was stirred out of his reverie by Cid-Hamel's shout. "A ship!" The Malayan was pointing to the northeast in the direction of Leyte. It was a Portuguese warship riding high and at full sail. It had just cleared the headlands of Leyte after negotiating the straits between Leyte and Samar to the east and Masbate to the west. It was most likely sailing for Panay to trade with the Moro pirates there. The Portuguese had aligned themselves with the Moros to resist Spanish expansion in the islands.

"Quick, into the water," Cid-Hamel instructed as he moved forward to take down the sail and mast.

The four slid gently over the sides into the water, holding on to the boat with one hand. Without a command from anyone they began paddling for shore with their feet and free arms. Given the wind and the currents in this region, Cid-Hamel knew that the Portuguese ship would come nearer before it moved off around the cape and down the west coast of Negros. If they remained in the open sea they would be spotted for sure. And even though the Portuguese probably would not be interested in them, would probably take them for a Bisayas fishing boat, Cid-Hamel did not want to take any chances. If they were caught, Martin and Andres would surely be killed.

When they reached the shore they found a small inlet with a good cover of trees where a clear stream tumbled down a hillside into the sea. Cid-Hamel tied the prau to one of the trees that jutted out from the bank and waded over to where the others were washing themselves in the cool fresh water.

Martin stood up to his knees in the rushing torrent. "Oh, this is cold," he shivered. "This water has never seen the sun, I believe. It has come from beneath the earth, through the dark forest, to this place where it joins the sea."

"It is not that cold," Cid-Hamel observed. "It is rather that you are so hot from the sun." "Perhaps," Martin agreed. "But it is cold to me." It was cold to Andres too, and he stepped out of the stream after washing the brine from his eyes and found a spot of sun on the bank to sit down in.

Cid-Hamel waded up stream to where Dantu was stalking a fish. "How many guns do you suppose she has?" he asked. Dantu returned a blank stare. "Let's go count them," Cid-Hamel offered. Dantu brightened. They walked up the bank toward a promontory that looked out over the sea toward the Portuguese ship. They had good cover and would not be seen as the ship passed by on its way south.

Martin was wringing the water out of his robes as he walked over to share Andres' sunlight. "They make quite a pair," he began. Andres did not respond. He figured Martin had something to say and was going to say it whether he joined in the conversation or not.

"Quite a pair of heathens," Martin continued. "The Mohammedan is a pagan, you cannot trust them. They have no honor. Think of how they slaughtered Roland at the pass in the Pyrenees. They are treacherous all and cannot be trusted."

Andres could not resist correcting Martin. "But Roland was betrayed by one of his own fellows, not a Muslim."

"But it was for Saracen gold. That is what betrayed Roland. Worldly riches. When Ganelon betrayed Roland, he was a Saracen at heart. The Mohammedans aspire only to worldly riches. They deny the savior. Their hearts are filled with hate, their eyes with deceit, and their mouths with blasphemies. For centuries they contaminated our homeland and now they threaten to spread their poison in this new world." Martin looked beyond Andres to Cid-Hamel and Dantu and to the Portuguese ship beyond. "There are our enemies all in a line," he said flatly. "Greed, heresy, and superstitious ignorance. We're here to convert the native pagans. The Muslims are our competition, and the Portuguese are trying to stop us for reasons of their own."

"And you want to change them all, make them believe like you do. Back home there has been great change. People believe one way, and then another. And then we fight wars with people to make them change. Is that religion?"

"Be careful, my boy. Do not question Mother Church. We all will change from this corrupt flesh to spirit in the end, if we believe, if we repent. Heaven is our reward. For the nonbelievers there is hell and torment. Eternal pain and agony."

Andres cocked his head in the direction where Dantu and the Muslim stood counting Portuguese cannons. "And what has a child to do with eternal pain and agony?" Andres asked.

"Everything, if he is not cleansed by baptism. I would rather he die right now and be assured of heaven than live to sin in ignorance. I would kill him right now if it would save his soul."

"So there was no point to my saving his life? I think your religion is strange, Padre."

"Not at all. You have saved him so I might save him. You kept him alive so I might give him a new life. You don't realize it yet, but we are working together."

"I think he likes the life he has now."

"How can he enjoy a life that does not have God in it? He worships animals and trees." Andres shifted uneasily on his hip and faced Martin. "But he does believe in them. Doesn't that count for something?"

"No. Not if heaven is his goal. He must accept Christ as his savior and take the sacraments daily, and give up his idol worship. Right now his god is a blue bird he calls Laon which represents all the spirits of his ancestors."

"I think I can understand that." Andres pondered for a moment. "The birds here are striking in their beauty. They soar toward heaven like spirits leaving the earth. One day last week, Itel and I saw a blue heron skim across a mirror-like lagoon and then rise heavenward leaving its reflection behind. It seemed to be going up and down at the same time."

"A beautiful sight I am sure. And all of God's creation."

"And this Laon. Isn't that what God is? All the spirits we become, including those of our ancestors?"

Martin placed a heavy hand on Andres' shoulder. "Be careful, my son, you are treading near to blasphemy. You want to go to heaven, don't you?"

"And what exactly is heaven, Padre?" Andres had a needle into Martin now and he wanted to twist it a bit.

"It is complete felicity and happiness. You are at peace and at one with God. It is what every soul desires and longs for."

"Are there wars in heaven?"

"There was one, once, when Lucifer was expelled. Why do you ask?"

"Do you think Legaspi will make it to heaven?" Martin leaned back, startled at the line of questioning. "I certainly think so. Why is his fate of concern to you?"

"Well, Legaspi is an adventurer and an explorer and a warrior. If heaven is to make him happy there will have to be lands to discover and battles to be fought. Otherwise, he will think himself in hell." Andres leaned back satisfied, sure he had made his point.

"You have a very materialistic concept of heaven, my son," said Martin. "If you wish truly to know the joys of the spirit you must meditate on the corruption of the flesh. I will teach you the spiritual exercises of St. Ignatius. You will feel the love and the power of God like you feel the passion of your heathen whore, only it will be divine love, not a worldly sin that depends on corrupt flesh to be felt."

"I trust we can put this off until another day," Andres said sarcastically. Martin stood up abruptly. "You must clear your mind of these thoughts, Andres. They are dangerous."

"I will do what I can, Father, but it was you who put them there. I swear I had none of these thoughts before today." As Andres got up, Cid-Hamel and Dantu were returning. The Malayan gathered up the leather water flasks and filled them in the stream. "We can go now," he said as he untied the boat and pushed it toward Martin and Andres. Dantu was already aboard. On the journey home, he sat at the stern with Cid-Hamel. They talked lively. Martin and Andres said not a word.

That night, Andres suffered from a sunburn. He was warm to the touch, but no matter how gentle Itel was during their lovemaking he groaned with pain. Itel could only laugh. The next morning she pealed off the dead skin from his forehead and the back of his neck. And Andres learned a new word in Bisayas, the word for "stupid."

FOUR

Andres had no idea why he was summoned to meet with General Legaspi at his headquarters. Goiti had simply sent word that he was to be there at ten o'clock.

Andres peeled some dead skin off the back of his hand as he waited to be called into the general's presence. Mendoza, Legaspi's aide, appeared at the door and beckoned. Mendoza was a small man in stature and in spirit, the kind of man who borrows his importance from the men he serves and then trades it as if it were his own.

Inside, Andres found Legaspi and several others leaning over a map of the islands spread out over a large table. "Sergeant Urdaneta," Legaspi greeted Andres in a way that acknowledged his presence and pulled him further into the room to the edge of the table. "Are you familiar with these islands?" The general made a sweep with his hand over the region north of Cebu which included Leyte and Samar to the east, Masbate to the north, and Panay to the west.

"Yes, sir. The Islas de Los Pintados." Andres had heard that the Bisayas on these islands were distinguished by their habit of tattooing their bodies with ornamental designs so they came to be called the Islands of the Painted. It was in this very area that Andres had seen the Portuguese ship just the day before.

Legaspi straightened up and faced Andres. "Yes, islands of painted savages. And a nest of pirates. Goiti here has been interrogating prisoners he took the other day, from a Moro prau. It seems our Bisayas friends have a profitable trade going on with the Moros." Andres already suspected this after what he had seen that night in the forest.

"And through them with Borneo and points west," Goiti added. "The Portuguese are not ignorant of this. We have to move quickly or our enterprise will be lost."

Legaspi continued. "The traffic our scouts have observed indicate Panay or Mindoro as the location of the pirate's base of operations. The Moros threaten the safe passage of our ships and if they join with the

Portuguese...." Legaspi's voice trailed off into silent meditation. The conclusion was obvious. His orders, from the King of Spain, were to explore and secure the islands of the Philippines as a source of treasure for the Spanish crown. The Portuguese had always been rivals in the area and an alliance with the Moros would spell disaster for Legaspi's mission.

"Our choice is simple," Goiti interrupted. "We destroy the Moros." He brought his hand down hard on the island of Panay. "Or we do business with them, get them to join us against the Portuguese."

"It sounds simple," Andres offered. He felt a need to show an interest, to join the conversation. After all, they were telling him all this for some reason.

"And that is where you come in," Legaspi said. He put his arm around Andres' shoulder and turned him toward the map. "I want you, with ten men and a company of our Bisayas friends, to sail up the coast of Panay here and search for the Moro camp. Probe inland for a few miles every now and again. If you don't find anything, go on to Mindoro. We have to know what we're up against."

Legaspi turned Andres toward him and put both hands on his shoulders. "We're counting on you. You speak the language pretty well, or so the padre tells me. And The Pilot here will be with you, to navigate and to translate." Cid-Hamel had been standing at the edge of the room. He stepped out of the dark and stood next to the table across from Andres. "If you make friendly contact with the Moro, Cid-Hamel can translate for you. If not, you'll need his sword."

"Choose your ten men and inform them immediately, Sergeant." Goiti's voice was all business. "You leave day after tomorrow, at dawn. You will be using Bisayas fishing boats so you won't attract Portuguese attention. Tupas has already selected the Bisayas who will go with you. He assures me they are all good warriors."

Andres looked across at Cid-Hamel who shrugged and returned a friendly grin as if to say "We're in this together." Andres began to wonder how much the language lessons and going sailing in native boats were part of somebody's master plan. Was Itel part of it too? Andres thought of the puppet shows he had seen at festival time in Salamanca. A wooden world of make believe.

A deception. He felt someone's hand inside him now, making his arms and legs move with a force that was not his own.

"That is all, Sergeant." Goiti's voice cut off Andres' thoughts with the crispness of a military salute. Andres turned and crossed the room to the door. As he was leaving, Father Martin breezed past him with a "Good morning" in Bisayas. Martin laughed as the door shut behind him. It pleased him to let Andres know that he was aware of what his language lessons had earned.

Martin strode across the room and reached for Legaspi's hand and shook it boldly. "Well, is the mission under way?" He leaned on the table with the knuckles of both hands and surveyed the area like a would-be conqueror. Legaspi motioned to Goiti that he wished to be alone with the priest and to Cid-Hamel he said, "You have much to prepare. You may go. Good luck."

The formalities concluded, Legaspi unbuckled his breastplate and slid it off his shoulder onto the floor beside a long-armed oak chair. He turned on his spindly legs and slumped into the chair with a sigh that revealed the fatigue of a fifty-seven year old man. Leaning back, he dangled one leg over the richly carved arm of the chair. "This will be a hard business, Father Martin."

"But well worth it, commander." Martin circled the table like a panther inspecting his most recent kill. He stopped near the islands that were the objective of Andres' mission. "There are many souls to be saved here."

"And cinnamon. That is my business."

"And gold."

"Be careful, Padre. That is my business, too."

"Perhaps. Philip needs money to fight his wars in Europe. But the church is at war, too. I agree with you that Cebu is not the source of the gold we find the natives wearing. It must be here." He waved his hand over the islands north of Cebu. "There are souls and gold to be mined here."

Legaspi heaved himself out of the chair with some difficulty and joined Martin at the map. "We have to secure those islands. The Moros patrol the waters to the north and west and the Portuguese seem to have a free reign with the Moros' blessing. Our only way home is westward around the cape of Africa which means navigating Portuguese waters. It is hard enough to escape the Portuguese ships on the route home. But first we have to run the gauntlet here in our own islands."

"When do you expect Salcedo to arrive?" Salcedo was Legaspi's grandson. He was due to depart from Acapulco in August and with the easterly trade winds south of the equator he was expected at Cebu within a few weeks, barring some mishap on the outward voyage. Usually the journey west was swift and without incident due to the favorable winds and currents. Ironically, it was these same currents and winds which blew steadily from the east that made the return voyage to Mexico impossible.

"Soon. Before we move against the Moros I will need him and the men he brings. A hundred men left for home last month on the San Sebastian with Montoya. I am rather shorthanded right now. We will need the Bisayas too. We will see what they are worth if the little expedition we put together this morning succeeds."

"And if it fails?"

"We'll send another. Perhaps you would like to go along next time. Do a little mining of souls firsthand."

"That won't be necessary. I am perfectly content to let you conquer their bodies first. That's how you help me do my job."

"Which is?"

"To tend to their souls."

"And what exactly do you do with their souls after I have conquered their bodies?"

"I give them hope."

"And that is how you help me do my job."

"How do you mean?"

"The kind of hope you give them helps me keep control over them. A man who worries about his sins does not worry so much about the boot on his neck or the emptiness in his belly."

"So you think a moral people are more easily defeated?"

"Don't look so smug, Padre. A defeated people are also more religious. We help each other, you and I. Between us we conquer them completely. We were destined to work together, Father Martin."

"It is comforting, then, is it not?"

"What is?"

"To know you are part of God's plan."

That night, Andres slept fitfully. His mind was racing with the events of that morning, his assignment, and the things he had seen in the last few weeks. He had seen Dantu and his sister in the jungle on a path that led nowhere, and he had saved his life.

He had seen the boy and Humabon in the middle of the night talking with Moro pirates. He had seen a Portuguese warship close to their settlement and possibly bound for Panay.

In all of this he had just been an observer. Now after this morning Legaspi had given him the chance to be an active participant in the events that would shape the conquest of these islands for Spain.

He was scared. Not just for his life only. But for Itel and the boy. And for what might happen to his relationship with them.

Itel stirred and moved towards him as if to test the soundness of his sleep. He lay motionless and breathed evenly. Satisfied that he was asleep, Itel stood up, wrapped herself in her flowered sarong and crept silently to the door. She was gone in less time than it took for Andres to sit up and stare into the blackness Itel was now moving through.

There was no moon out and it was difficult for Andres to keep sight of Itel as he followed her through the narrow streets of the village to the south gate. Once into the woods beyond the village he could no longer see her at all. He only sensed her somewhere in the heavy darkness in front of him.

He moved through the woods more swiftly than he ever had before. Recklessly. Dodging the branches and the overhanging vines as best he could. Some clung to his shirt and ripped it, scratching his arms and face. He tripped on a root and fell forward. The dank smell of the sod filled his nostrils.

He began to feel the darkness around him. There was a mystery in it he could not understand. Andres had no fear when it came to fighting a battle out in the open, where there was a plan and where you could see your enemy. He relished a good clean kill. He had experienced such battle in Mexico before he signed on with Legaspi.

But the forest was something different. Here you could not see your enemy. And there was no battle plan. Only keep going. Towards what he did not know. But Itel would be there, and that was enough.

He paused to catch his breath, filling his lungs with the water-heavy air. It choked him and he imagined this must be what it is like to drown. Standing motionless he could hear his heart beat and feel the pulse in his neck. It was quiet and he could hear the forest's life around him, crawling, slithering, constantly moving.

Then the silence was broken with voices, four or five of them, chatting calmly, just a few paces away from Andres to his right. He crouched down instinctively. The voices caught up with him and then moved on ahead in the direction he was going. Andres remained motionless. A lizard startled by the activity on the adjacent path scurried across his foot.

The voices receded into the distance before him. He decided to follow them. They guided him to a clearing where they flowed like a river into a hubbub of chanting voices that drowned them out.

Andres found himself at the edge of a large area that had been cleared out of the jungle. Torches illuminated a circular stone pavement which filled the center of the clearing. Men and women, and children too, swayed to the rhythm of their chant while they wandered aimlessly around the edge of the clearing. They bent at the waist and moved their heads from side to side. Drums and timbrels picked up the rhythm of the chant and intensified it. Some were still arriving from out of the darkness, drawn into the ceremonial area by the hypnotic rhythms. Gradually, they began to organize themselves into a circle at the edge of the pavement.

They moved faster and faster to the beat of the drums. The chanting reached a deafening pitch. Andres could not see very well past the swaying bodies, but he could barely make out a raised bench or altar at the upper end of the paved arena. On it was perched a large bird, like a macaw, painted blue.

The drums and the chanting stopped abruptly. The swaying worshippers stood still. Into the center of the circle marched Itel. She wore a robe of blue feathers. On her forehead was a garland of flowers. She was beautiful, Andres thought. She lifted the bird figure and held it over her head while she walked around the interior of the circle formed by the assembled worshippers. A new chant arose, guttural, spasmodic.

In the middle of the pavement were four drains radiating out from a hole in the center. Itel stood over the hole, reached up and opened the bird's chest. Out flew a blue heron. It disappeared quickly into the dark sky. Itel then opened the bird's beak, tipped the figure forward, and rice spilled out into the hole beneath her feet.

The chanting reached a climax and then stopped. Itel moved back to the altar where she returned the bird to its original position. Andres then recognized the towering figure of Humabon. He too was dressed in ceremonial robes. In his hands he carried a sword like no other Andres had ever seen. It had a thick, curved blade that ended in a wedge shape. It was of highly polished metal. The handle was of bronze and gold.

The worshippers began to chant, "Laon, Laon, Laon." The circle parted to reveal a carabao ambling into the arena. Riding on the animal was Dantu who guided it to the center of the pavement where Humabon waited. Dantu slid off the beast and joined Itel. The chant now lowered in tone to almost a whisper. The dumb animal stood patiently not knowing what was about to happen.

The light from the torches bounced off of the broad blade of the sword as Humabon raised it over the carabao's head. The beast stood patiently, dumbly. The chanting stopped and Humabon brought the blade down powerfully, opening a wedge-shaped gash a foot deep in the animal's neck. The beast's head tipped forward like a horned candle snuffer. The animal collapsed forward onto its knees. Humabon swung again, this time completely severing the head from the shoulders. The head tipped sideways coming to rest on one of the horns. The body, lifeless, discharged its bowels in a hapless gesture of revenge and slumped to the pavement.

Blood streamed from the open wounds and flowed down the drain into the hole where Itel had poured the rice. The chanting grew louder and louder and then stopped when Humabon raised his sword over his head. Itel was by his side holding the figure of the bird over her head. When they brought their arms down, the chanting stopped. For a moment everything was still. Then, as silently and cautiously as they had come, the worshippers turned and walked to the outer edge of the clearing where they disappeared into the darkness.

Andres knew for certain now that the forest held many secrets. This was one he had to keep.

Andres was waiting for Itel and Dantu when they returned to the hut just before dawn. He sat with legs crossed in the fashion he had learned from Itel, with his knees flat against the mat in the center of the room. His back was straight; his jaw fixed.

Itel registered only mild surprise when she entered and found him calmly waiting for her. She had known for some time that he would eventually discover her. What she did not know was how she would respond when he asked her where she had been.

"There is no need to lie," Andres said flatly. "I followed you tonight. I saw what you did. It was frightening. What was that all about?"

Itel sat down opposite Andres. "It is the season of harvest. We must give back to the earth what we take from it or next year our harvest will not be good. Each year Laon dies for the earth. And then he comes back again. It is the way of the earth. It is the belief of our people."

Andres eyed Dantu who sat quietly and sullen in the corner. He acted embarrassed, like a puppy that had just fouled a rug.

"You killed that poor animal. And you worship a bird. God is God and he is not a bird or a water buffalo. This is what I have been taught. I am no theologian. I do not understand everything. I am not a priest. But I think I understand this."

"Itel is," said Dantu from his dark corner. "Itel is a priest." Andres had seen that. Itel in her robes, holding the blue bird over her head and offering the rice. She was at the center of the ceremony, a Bisayas priestess. "You understand nothing," Itel said. "I belong to Laon. His spirit possesses me."

"And what about me," Andres complained. He was getting jealous. "There was another ceremony the other night when your father gave you to me."

Itel ignored this last remark and lifted herself up in a fluid motion from her cross-legged position, letting her sarong fall to the floor at her feet. She seemed to rise in full nakedness from the flowery cloth. She stood boldly before Andres as if to say, "You have this, what more do you want?" She glanced over her shoulder at Dantu who continued to squat in the corner. Then she glided to her mat and slid to her knees, then forward onto her pallet, her back to Andres. She spoke softly, with determination. She wanted him to know.

"My father Tupas has great power. In this world, for this time. He rules the barangay, tells the people where to plant, what food they can have. He is now. Laon is then. He is all our pasts . . . our ancestors, those who have come before. But he is not just then, they are not just then. He is now, too. We are all connected with each other, as on a string stretched out on the ground. Then and now and what will be. If you pick up the string and let it fall into your hand, all the parts touch each other. Then long ago and the soon to be touch each other. The past is everywhere in your hand, all along the string. That is the way our ancestors are in us now and we will be in our children. And Laon is the string. And the harvest is his sign. And that is what you do not understand. In the harvest season I am Laon's," she said with a finality meant to close the discussion.

"I'll be leaving tomorrow for quite some time," Andres said quietly to her back. "I've been chosen to head an expedition..." He stopped short. He was not sure how much he should tell Itel and Dantu. ". . . to look for cinnamon plants on some of the neighboring islands. It could be dangerous. We will have to look out for the Portuguese. And the Moros. I don't know how long I'll be gone. But it could be for weeks."

Dantu crawled out of his corner toward Andres. Andres sensed a camaraderie with the boy. Perhaps the boy felt his pain, his confusion at this moment. Dantu put something in Andres' hand, then threw his arms around the Spaniard's neck. Then he returned to his corner.

Andres opened his hand and adjusted the object he held to catch the moonlight. It was the crucifix Brother Carlos had given Dantu weeks ago.

FIVE

Andres did not leave the next morning as expected. A violent storm raged for three days. Sheets of water blew onto the coast of Cebu and winds howled across the bay like an angry argument. The streets of the settlement were flooded. From the mountains, swollen streams flooded the rice fields and then flowed through the village to the bay. Most of the houses in the settlement were raised on stilts. Some lost their moorings and crashed to the ground. Others lost their roofs to the gales.

On the fourth morning the winds died and the rain ceased. The sun rose bright and dangerous. "Like a woman's smile," Miguel observed.

Goiti stood with Cid-Hamel giving him last minute instructions. The rest of the company was busily checking provisions and loading the six small crafts that bobbed up and down in the gentle surf.

The storm had taken its toll on the beach. Great clumps of seaweed clung to small mounds of sand and stretched their tentacles down to the receding waves. The sand itself had been turned a dark brown by the silt dredged up from the bay and deposited on the shore which was strewn haphazardly with palm leaves and coconuts that balanced awkwardly on the uneven sand.

"At least we won't have to clean all this up," said Miguel with a laugh as he hoisted his gear into a native skiff that waited for him in the knee-deep water.

"In a few days you might wish you were back here picking up coconuts," Andres shot back over his shoulder as he moved to the prow of the boat he and Miguel were to share with four Bisayas warriors.

Cid-Hamel and a company of two of Andres' men and three Bisayas had already begun to pull out into the bay. The other boats followed swiftly. Andres and Miguel quickly joined them. In no time the little armada had cleared the north edge of the bay. Andres could still see Dantu and Itel waving goodbye to him from the shore. He turned and looked toward the open sea. For the first time Andres was worried about his future, because he had something, someone, to come back to.

The weather held and they made good time around the north point of Cebu. They spent the night on the western side of the island. The next day they made land-fall on the north coast of Negros where they collected fresh water and fruit and camped for the night. A northerly wind prevented their sailing the next day. By the fourth day they were exploring the east coast of Panay.

So far it had been an easy journey. The men actually seemed to be enjoying it. Except for the patrols in the forest of Cebu the men had been confined to the settlement for over six months since their arrival from New Spain. Some of the men fished as they sailed around the shore of Cebu. The second night on Negros they had sat around a campfire and told stories of home. Miguel led them in song. For the men this was an adventure, a chance to explore. It was also dangerous. Andres knew that.

Miguel was enjoying himself. But then he always did. "Why so melancholy, amigo? " he would ask Andres, and slap him on the back with the kind of slap that says not so much "How do you feel" but "I'm feeling great. "

Andres would remind Miguel that they were on a mission. "Of course we are," he would agree. "A dangerous mission, " Andres insisted. Miguel would register his impatience with a laugh . " I don't understand you, Andres. This is what we came halfway around the world for, a chance to find something, make our mark in the world, take possession of untold riches. I won't get rich sitting in Hidalgo's canteen back in Cebu. "

Andres wanted to say, "And you won't get killed there either, " but he resisted. In fact one could get killed at Hidalgo's. "It's that woman. She made you soft," Miguel went on. "Back in Mexico when we did battle with the Toltecs you had fire in your eye and your pistol in your hand. Now, I look around this island and see my future, wealth, and fame, and you see nothing but Portuguese ships, Moro pirates, and shades of death."

"Look over there and you'll see them for yourself, " Cid-Hamel said as he placed a hand on each of their shoulders and forced them to a squatting position behind thick foliage at the edge of the beach. "Look there," he whispered. Beyond the reef that encircled Panay was a Portuguese war ship at full sail, running before a northerly wind, patrolling the coast. The word was passed swiftly and quietly to the men who were strung out along the beach readying their equipment for the continuation of their journey.

"It is best we pull our boats under cover and remain here," Cid-Hamel advised.

"Right," Andres agreed. "Then we can set out up the coast under the cover of darkness." "That is not a good idea," Cid-Hamel shot back. "The shoals and reefs along this coast are difficult to navigate in the daylight. At night we would certainly lose a ship, and some men."

"Then what do you suggest?" Andres asked.

"It is better we stay the night here. In the morning the Portuguese ship will be at the southern end of the island and we can continue unseen."

Andres gave the order and the men pulled the boats ashore and covered them with broad leaves and the undergrowth that was plentiful along the shorelines of the islands. Then they made a temporary field camp. There was no fire and only jerky and fruit for dinner. Cid-Hamel posted guards around the perimeter. Andres removed his corselet and stretched out his cape on the damp ground. He leaned his head against his pack which served as a pillow and stared up at the sky with its unfamiliar stars. He soon fell asleep, but not for long.

Andres was awakened when he felt the cold steel of a Moro knife blade against his throat. He opened his eyes. Where there had been stars there was now a large mustachioed face grinning down at him. The man had his knee in Andres' crotch and pulled him up with his free hand with which he had gathered up a handful of Andres' shirt.

One of Andres' men put up a struggle. The man holding Andres barked out a command and a Moro ran Andres' man through with a spear while the Moro holding him from the rear sliced through his throat. Blood gushed from both wounds. The throat-cutter cast the dead Spaniard aside like a bag of rice. "Don't resist. Go calmly," Andres shouted. "Stay alive." As he was saying this, he glanced around quickly, searching out the darkness for signs of what had happened. Several Bisayas lay dead where they slept. The rest had fled. There were not enough Moros to restrain them all. They concentrated on the Spaniards.

Cid-Hamel was nowhere in sight.

"That bastard!" Andres thought as his captor pulled his arms behind him and bound them fast with rope. The rest of his men were being similarly tied. "This I would trade for Hidalgo's canteen," grinned Miguel as they were escorted roughly away from the camp to Moro praus which were waiting for them at the shore. Andres bristled with rage. He had lost a man. The mission was in jeopardy. He had been betrayed. Martin was right. This was a godless race. And one of them in particular belonged in hell.

Several of the Moro craft were small skiffs called vintas with room enough for four or five men. They were swift outriggers with curved prows, like ax blades, and bamboo poles extending on each side for balance. They were the craft of choice for raiding parties. Andres and his men were thrown aboard a larger boat, one big enough for twenty men. Its deck was level and even. A small flat top cabin occupied the center of the deck. Two wooden beams with decorative carvings soared forward beyond the bow providing ballast for the heavier stern. In the moonlight, Andres could see that the railings around the boat were similarly carved like fine furniture.

"Is everyone all right?" Andres was hunched in the corner of the boat toward the stern. The cold spray lashed his face as he searched the figures beside him. "Where's Hernandez?"

"He didn't make it." Miguel's voice was uncertain. "He's back there with Valasquez, with his throat cut. He never got his pistol out of its holster."

"We'll all have our throats cut soon." It was Lopez, the youngest member of Andres' band. He had joined Legaspi's expedition out of desperation. His father had lost all his money in Cadiz and his creditors were hounding him. Old Lopez had borrowed enough money against the family estate to outfit his son in the hopes he might restore the family's fortune. "These murderers have no respect for human life," Lopez complained. "We are all as good as dead."

"What do you think our chances are?" Miguel's tone was earnest.

"I'm not sure," Andres answered. "They could have killed us all back on Panay. They didn't so they must have something in mind for us."

"That's what worries me," Miguel said, eyeing the long beheading sword that swung from the side of a Moro standing spread-legged before him to keep his balance.

The wind had come up and the boat was pitched about by the black and swelling sea. Water cascaded over the sides and ran over the deck. The bow surged high into the air, then crashed down against the swells. The wind howled angrily. No one could hear the commands barked by the Moro captain. But the sailors calmly went about their work of securing the cargo aboard and battening down anything that might move with the pitching and rolling of the boat.

One Moro at the bow was struggling to tie down a cannon that had shifted from its moorings. He had lashed it to the railing with a rope. But as the bow surged upward the rope snapped and the cannon rolled down the deck, crashing into the side of the boat and bouncing dangerously backward as the bow came down, finally lodging itself sideways between the cabin and the lee side of the boat where Andres and his men were huddled in the stern. With the next surge skyward, it came loose and careened down the deck.

"Look out!" Andres shouted, but his words were lost in the storm. The cannon bounced wildly toward them. It landed squarely on Lopez' right leg, crushing it like a splinter. Andres imagined the sound of the bone cracking, and he could not hear Lopez' agonizing scream. The storm howled for him.

The boat lurched to the right, carried by a swell, and the cannon shifted its course in midair to crash into the side of the boat across from Andres. The wood gave way to the heavy metal and the cannon teetered for an instance and then was swept overboard leaving a gash in its wake. Water flooded in each time the bow surged heavenward.

In an instant Andres and his men were lifted from their places and dragged forward. "We're all dead now," Lopez cried. His fear had taken over from the pain. "They're going to throw us overboard." The Moro captain was shouting something to his men who were pulling the Spaniards up the deck. They dropped them like bales of hay on either side of the bow. They were being used as ballast, to keep the bow down and prevent the stern from riding so low. Andres was relieved. "We're safe as long as we're good for something," he thought.

The men braced themselves as best as they could to hold their positions at the forward end of the boat which continued to pitch. With their hands tied behind them they pressed themselves against the sides of the boat with their legs. Andres could reach the upper end of the cabin with his right leg and used this to secure his place. Lopez was not so fortunate. He could not put any pressure on his leg. Once when the boat was lifted high on a swell, Lopez was thrown free and he rolled helplessly toward the stern. Andres feared he might be swept overboard out the hole made by the cannon. But he came to rest next to a barrel of cinnamon that had preceded him down the deck.

The storm subsided as quickly as it had come up. The sea was calmer now. The Moro craft was damaged but still seaworthy. It rode evenly in the water. Andres surveyed the horizon. He could see only three of the smaller boats that had been part of the raiding party. The storm had blown the others far off course, except for one which followed at a great distance.

Water continued to rush in at the boat's stern. The pilot at the rudder who had displayed such skill and courage to bring them through the storm was calling out to the Moro captain. Several of the Moros were collecting the cargo that had been strewn about the deck. Some items they retained, others they threw into the water. "They seem to be trying to lighten their load," Andres confided in Miguel who was huddled beside him. "We're shipping water."

One Moro was standing over Lopez eyeing him and the barrel of cinnamon. Water rushed in and swirled around the barrel. Lopez was unconscious from the pain. His pants' leg was torn and a piece of bone protruded from below his knee cap. His ankle was smashed and his foot was swollen and turning green. The Moro paused as if weighing the relative value of the injured man and the barrel of spice. His decision being made, he moved with singular speed and purpose. In a continuous motion, he swept Lopez from the deck and hoisted him over his head like a sack of flour. He turned around to face Andres and his men who looked on in helpless terror. Lopez snapped to consciousness as he found himself stretched out horizontally in the wind above the deck. His right leg dangled limply, hanging on a few threads of cloth and skin. His eyes were wide with surprise, his mouth open but no sound came out. The Moro let out a scream, turned, and heaved Lopez into the water.

The night and the storm behind them, the Moros sailed before an easterly wind making good time. The day went by slowly. Andres could not wipe Lopez' dazed and frightened expression from his mind. Is this why he had sailed halfway round the world, to see his men slaughtered before him and cast overboard like so much useless cargo. Was this his destiny? To lose his men one by one and then be killed himself?

Andres tried to determine the direction the boat was taking. He suspected they were heading toward Mindoro. Legaspi had told him to explore this island for Moro strongholds. Well, Legaspi was right. But this is not what Andres had in mind when he imagined how he would investigate the island.

By dusk they found themselves at the headwaters of a river that flowed into the sea from the western shore of Mindoro. The Moro pilot steered his craft expertly past the breakers into the channel of the river. Within two bends of the river they had left the sea and the sun behind them. Darkness and the sticky heat of the jungle settled over them as they made their way up river for what Andres judged to be three miles.

The jungle noises were familiar. The squawking macaw and the chattering monkeys. It was so different from the open sea where the wind droned in the cup of your ear making an empty forlorn sound and timbers creaked and cargo shifted over the groaning planks of the deck. Here the wind was still. Only an occasional breeze relieved the oppression of the heavy air. The sounds of the night came from the jungle.

Before him on the north bank of the river Andres could see lights. This must be the Pirate stronghold, he thought. As they neared the lights, Andres could distinguish several rows of houses, many of them two stories high. In a few moments they pulled alongside a sturdy dock that extended like a wooden tongue into the river. The Moro sailors quickly lashed ropes to the pilings and pulled the boat firmly to the dock's side. Andres' legs were stiff and cramped and he could hardly stand as he was pulled up and shoved off the boat onto the dock. Miguel and the others came after him.

"I think we found what we were looking for," Miguel cracked as he was pulled alongside Andres. Together they were escorted into the bustling pirate town along timber gangways that served as narrow streets raised above the wet riverbank. All along the wooden streets were shops filled with food, spices, silks, and merchandise. Many of the things Andres had never seen before. Bundles of peppers, garlic, and cinnamon hung from bamboo awnings. Pots boiled with rice dishes. The smells were strange, unfamiliar, and exotic. The place was alive with people, selling, trading, buying, making deals. There were women, too, selling themselves. And being sold.

Andres and his men were shoved along the street. The people paid little attention to them, only grunting in disgust now and then as they were jostled out of the way by the group pushing its way along. They reached higher ground by a series of stairways which led to a level area surrounded by houses more elegant than those in the market below. One house in the center of the semicircular arena was most impressive and, Andres concluded, must have belonged to the leader.

A few more moments being pushed and dragged along through the undergrowth behind these buildings and they reached a hole in the ground carved out of the side of a small mound. Andres was the first to be pulled toward the hole. His captor stood him there for a second and then shoved him in. With his hands tied behind him, he could not break his fall. Andres measured his fall to be about four feet. He landed with a grunt on his left shoulder and rolled over to protect his head from hitting the dank hard floor of the cell. Miguel came toppling down after him. "What the hell," he shouted as he hit beside Andres. The others fell on top of the two of them. They could see nothing in the darkness.

"What is this place?" Miguel asked. Andres had brought his arms beneath his legs to his front and was busily chewing at the ropes to free his hands. He was crawling away from the direction of Miguel's voice to explore the dimensions of the cave.

"The last place you will ever see alive." The voice was a strange one, not one of Andres' men. It came from the far side of the room.

"Who is that?" Miguel asked in astonishment. "You speak Spanish?"

"I am Fillipe Ortega," the voice answered flatly. "A member of Montoya's crew on the San Sebastian. And who are you?"

"Fillipe, it's me, Andres Urdaneta. And this is Miguel. How did you get here?"

"That is a long story. Obviously, you did not come to rescue me. If you did, you are not doing a very good job." Andres didn't understand Fillipe's tone. He seemed to be making light of the situation. They were in deep trouble and he was making jokes. Like Miguel sometimes did. Maybe being in this dark cave for a long time had unsettled his mind. Or perhaps that is the way he faced danger.

"No, we were captured by the Moros on Panay. They brought us here. We don't know why, or what they intend to do with us. I thought you were sailing back to New Spain with Montoya. How did you end up here? And where exactly is here, and what is this place we are in?"

"I will answer the first question first. By the time I have finished, your eyes will have adjusted to the dark and you will be able to see for yourselves the tomb we are in." Ortega paused for a moment and pulled his crossed legs up under him and leaned forward on his knees. He spoke in even, measured rhythms, like a professor at the university who has an important message to convey.

"As you know, we set sail from Cebu two months ago to find a route back to New Spain going east. We found it! North of the equator the winds blow steadily from the west, not against us as they do below the equator. Montoya plotted a course that will take him to the California coast. From there he can follow the coast south to Acapulco. He's halfway there by now!"

Ortega paused to let this information sink in. Andres recognized its significance. They could now ship whatever they took from the islands directly back to New Spain and from there to the Spanish peninsula without having to run the gauntlet of Portuguese ships in the Indian Ocean and around the Cape of Africa. Ortega returned to his story.

"As we sailed north we put into a few islands where we heard of rich lands to the east, in China. There are treasures to be had there. With the little silver we had among the crew we could buy enough silk to make all our fortunes in New Spain. We urged the captain to make sail for China. He refused. His loyalty, he said, was to Legaspi and to the King. His mission was to find a return route. Well, my mission, and that of several others, was to get rich. So we mutinied. My companions were killed in the attempt and I was thrown in the brig for killing a man. I don't know what Montoya's plans were for me. But if I survived the journey, I would not survive our arrival. When we put into an island for fresh water I bribed a seaman and made my escape. I used what silver I had left to buy my way back south on a Chinese junk. They put in at a place they called Maynila on the big island north of here to trade their goods of silk and precious gems. The Moros in Maynila have a profitable trade going, Andres. The city is on a bay that is completely protected and excellent for shipping. I would have stayed but my Chinese traders offered to take me back to China with them. On the way we were attacked by pirates. I threw in with them. I even helped them take control of the junk by killing its captain. I arrived in Mindoro a month ago and began doing odd jobs in the market you saw on your way up here. I got a little drunk and offended one of their women. They gave me a few lashes and threw me in here. That was twenty days ago."

"I'm not so interested in how you came to be put in here. The question is how are we going to get out," Miguel shouted.

"You're not going to get out. Take a look around you. This is the last place you'll see alive." Andres and Miguel looked around and could just make out the particulars of the room. It was about ten feet across, a dank, dirty floor and walls of wet rock. Roots hung like tentacles from the ceiling ten feet overhead. "This is your grave. The bastards want you to see what your tomb looks like before you're dead." Andres stood up and brushed the roots aside as he looked toward the hatch above the far wall where they had been thrown into the cell.

"Be careful with those," Ortega warned. "You might be having that for supper one of these days."

"What do they feed you?" Miguel asked.

"A portion of rice. Once a day. It's spicy and makes you thirsty. But they don't give you any water. The bastards. They play with you. But I fooled them. Here, feel this." He took Andres by the arm and led him to the back wall. He took his hand and pressed it against the moist rock. "The water seeps in here. It tastes like mud, but you can get enough of it to keep you alive. They're not going to win. I'm going to beat those bastards." His voice trailed off as he backed away from Andres into the darkness of the cell.

Ortega continued to talk quietly in the distance. Andres could hear him but could not make out what he was saying. He could just make out his figure hunched over in the far corner. Andres crawled toward his voice. Ortega sensed his presence in the dark.

"Meet my friends, Andres. Here is Wednesday. And this is Saturday. And the Chinaman is yesterday." As he talked Ortega was arranging three figures, leaning them against the wall. Andres moved closer. He was not aware that anyone else was in the cell with them. He had not heard any sound from this part of the room since he was thrown in. Then he saw why. They were corpses. Headless torsos.

"You see what I mean about the way they play with your mind. They want you to see what you'll look like when you're dead. These fellows were all here when I got here. No, Wednesday there came later. But he went earlier. He was a thief, too. See, his hand was cut off. Must have been his second offense. That's when they cut off your head. Me, I don't know what they'll cut off."

Andres felt his gorge rising in his throat. The stench of rotting flesh was powerful. The smell of death. Andres gagged. "Come away from here." He pulled at Ortega's arm. Ortega pushed him aside and pulled free. "Go back to your men," he hissed. "I prefer the company of my friends here."

Andres slid away toward the opposite side of the cell where Miguel and the other men were huddled. Ortega was lost, Andres thought. He already considered himself dead. "That won't happen to me," Andres tried to convince himself.

"I'm dead," Ortega shouted from the darkness. "You are dead. We are all dead." The last word echoed against the rock and then silence fell like a pall over them. The smell of death entered Andres' nostrils again. A low sobbing began to build from across the room. Then out of the darkness broke a wild, demonic laughter, inhuman, uncontrolled, liberating, that Andres heard from behind his eyes and felt in the depths of his soul.

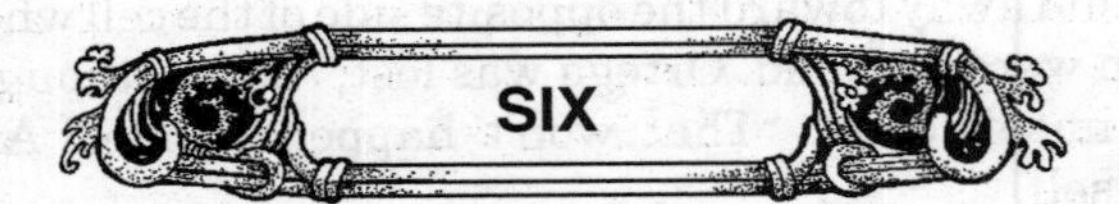

SIX

Andres did not know what to expect when the cell door opened and a short rope ladder was dropped into the room. It was a dark night and no light was let in. An armed guard climbed down the ladder frontwards, awkwardly swinging his sword before him to clear a way. In the dark a prisoner might have jumped him if he had not taken this precaution. Andres moved his men back to the opposite wall.

The guard let his eyes adjust and then he stepped forward and grabbed Ortega by the sleeve and pulled him to the ladder. He pushed Ortega up where he was gathered in above by a second guard. Then he came toward the other men. He eyed them up and down as if to indicate he was making a selection. If it was a random choice, Andres thought, which one of them would be taken? And where was he taking them? And why?

The guard reached out with his left arm and gathered in a fistful of Andres' shirt below his neck. With a quick tug he started Andres off towards the ladder. In a moment Andres was above ground, breathing in the heavy river air. He filled his lungs with it as the Moro pushed him down a path toward the complex of buildings he had seen the day before. Ortega was in front already halfway down the path being pulled along by a rope tied around his neck.

They entered a circle of torches gathered around the plaza at the center of the official-looking buildings. A boisterous crowd was gathered, pushing and shoving to gain a view. Andres was conducted to the center of the arena and stationed beside Ortega who already stood before a raised throne. On the throne sat an impressive man, clothed in yellow and red silk. He wore a jeweled turban and pantaloons that billowed in the evening breeze. He had a handsome face, Andres judged, with olive skin and a close cropped beard that came to a sharp point beneath his chin. His eyes were dark and serious like black pearls. He wore a circular gold earring in his left ear. On the right there was none because his ear lobe was gone. Pulled off in a fight, Andres supposed. The only blemish in the man's otherwise perfect features was a scar that began above his left eye and ran across his cheekbone until it disappeared in the hair above his lip. He twirled his mustache with delicate fingers that were covered with rings set with precious stones. Andres judged the man to be no more than forty years of age. A man of experience and courage, wisdom and craft. A leader of desperate men.

"It's the great man himself," Ortega whispered to Andres. "It's Saluddin. The Emir. The Raja hereabouts."

Saluddin heard himself being introduced and broke his silence. "And what has brought you to face our justice?" he asked Ortega in Spanish. "You are a rapist, I am told."

"I was drunk, sir. It was not my fault."

"Was it the woman's fault then? Did she intoxicate you?" Ortega had no answer. Saluddin turned to Andres. "And you. What brings you before our justice?"

"I am sure I do not know, your majesty." Andres was not sure whether he was being facetious or trying to compliment his accuser to gain a favorable judgment. "My men and I were captured and brought here against our will from Panay. Several of my companions were killed by your men. One was thrown overboard. If anyone should be brought before your justice, it would be your captain who killed my men."

Saluddin let out a roar and repeated much of what Andres said in Arabic to the gathered crowd. They hooted and cheered. Saluddin raised his hand and the throng fell silent. The captain Andres had referred to appeared on the raised platform that supported the throne. Saluddin reached into a box beside him and pulled forth a handful of gems and necklaces. He held them aloft and then gave them to the captain. The crowd cheered. Saluddin fixed his gaze on Andres. His eyes sparkled with menace.

"You are a thief," he hissed through clenched teeth. Andres cupped his hand over his right wrist, remembering what Ortega had said about thieves. "You are the worst kind of thief. One who does not admit it. You don't even know that you are one."

"I know what you are," Andres shot back. "You are the thief. These waters are not safe from the likes of you. You raid the settlements among these islands. Ships are not safe from you. You . . . ."

". . . are a thief, a pirate. I know," Saluddin interrupted. "And I admit it. Your crime is that you do not admit it."

"Who is it that we steal from? These islands are ours. We discovered them and claimed them for King Philip. The Portuguese have laid claim to them but the Pope has decreed that all lands 180 degrees west of the Azores meridian are Spanish possessions."

"The Pope decreed! A small, uninteresting man in Rome. What does he know about these islands? When has he sailed a ship in a typhoon or charted a course through these island reefs, or handled a cannon in the field? Who is he to say whose lands these are? Do you suppose there was no one in these islands when you 'discovered' them as you put it? No, my friend, you come here like I do, as a thief. Whatever you take from these islands you steal."

"It's not the same thing. We trade with people, give them something in return." Andres stopped short. A figure behind Saluddin in the crowd caught his eye. A torch lit up a face that was familiar to him. It was Cid-Hamel. Here. Among the Moro. His own race. "The traitor," thought Andres. "I wonder what Saluddin's justice would have in store for him?" Saluddin noticed Andres' fixed stare beyond him and turned to see what he was looking at. Andres watched him turn, then directed his eye back to where Cid-Hamel had stood. He was gone. Saluddin turned back to Andres.

"You trade. We watch you. And when you finish your deal, we decide which has gotten the better of it, which has what we want the most. And we take it. You might think of yourselves as our agents. You are our middlemen."

"And what do we get from you? A burning village. A cut throat."

"A lesson in business, my friend. Like us you trade to enrich yourselves. And what is it you give to the people you take from?"

"We bring our laws, our government, our church." Andres was growing more confident. He was certain he had taken the high moral ground.

"Your church!" Saluddin bellowed. "Your church! You take the riches of these islands and in return you offer a religion that preaches poverty. What is your name, lad?"

"Andres. Andres Urdaneta."

"Well, Andres Urdaneta, I have a question for you. Have you ever been to Jerusalem?"

"No."

"I have. It is a holy city of Islam, or didn't you know that. In the south wall of the old city there is a gate, a narrow gate, through which the caravans enter the city for the markets. The gate is called the Needle's Eye. Because it is so narrow, the heavily laden camels of the richest merchants cannot pass through it. That is why your Bible says 'Sooner a rich man will get into heaven than a camel will pass through the needle's eye.' You want to go to your heaven, I am sure. And yet you come halfway around the world to load down your camel with riches. I believe you are a confused young man, Andres."

"And you are still a pirate and a thief and a murderer."

"Think of me as someone whose purpose it is to lighten your burden. I'm trying to help you get into heaven, Andres."

"And I would help you to hell if I could."

"You would kill me if you had the chance. That's good, Andres. You have begun to learn something about yourself. Let me tell you a story. There once was a young man in Persia, the son of the Sultan's magician. When he came of age, his father gave him three gifts. A mechanical horse that could fly him anywhere in the world. An amulet that let him speak with the birds. And a ring that allowed him to become invisible. He tried the horse once and it frightened him. He spoke with the birds occasionally but there was little he felt he had to learn from them. The ring was his most prized gift. With it he became invisible and crept into the Sultan's harem and slept with his wives whenever he wished, and stole jewels to please himself, and spied on his father to learn his secrets. Now what do you suppose is the moral of this story? What would you do if you had the power of this ring?"

Andres did not respond.

"You want to say that it demonstrates that there is a little evil in everyone. That given the chance, everyone will pursue their desires and commit criminal acts if they know they won't be caught. Is that what you want to say?"

"Yes. I suppose so."

"Well, you would be wrong. What the story says is that the boy was stupid. He should have killed the Sultan when he had the chance. Then he could have had all the women he wanted. You see, Andres, he set his sights too low. He had a few pieces of fruit when he could have had the whole banquet. Power, my boy, that's what he should have gone after. Everything else follows. When you and the other Spanish have driven us from these islands, when you have the power, then you can trade freely here. Until that time, we will prey on you like crows."

Andres looked over at Ortega who had stood silently during this discussion. "If it's a fight you want, we will be happy to oblige you. If not us, then those who will follow us. Never fear, Saluddin, there are Spanish hearts that will stand you a good fight when the time comes." The blood was pumping through the veins in Andres' neck. His face flushed crimson.

"So you relish a fight, do you, Andres Urdaneta? I can see it in your eyes and in your face. Tell me, lad, have you ever faced death? I don't mean someone else's in battle, but your own. Have you ever thought about it, imagined it?"

Andres fell silent. He had seen death, certainly. On the battlefield. In Mexico. He had been in dangerous situations, taken risks. He had cheated death several times. But he had never faced it in the way Saluddin was asking about and Saluddin knew it.

As he thought how he would respond to Saluddin's challenge, Andres heard the hiss of the blade just before he felt the breeze made by the tip which passed by his left ear. The sound of skin being sliced and bones crunching followed immediately. Ortega's attempt to scream was drowned in a gurgle of blood that gushed from his mouth as the blade severed his head from his shoulders. His head popped off like a grape pinched from the vine, the eyes wide open and startled. It seemed to suspend in air for an instant as it looked back at the torso it once rested upon. The headless body stiffened, convulsed, then crumbled to the earth like a deflated bladder. The head rolled to a stop some four feet away and stared up at Andres who was paralyzed with terror waiting to hear that hiss again. Andres wondered if Ortega could see him. Did the head live on briefly while there was still blood to feed it? What was Ortega seeing in his face now? Fear? Pity?

"That is death, Andres Urdaneta." Saluddin's voice was firm and paradoxically reassuring, like a father's. "Yours will come soon enough. Take him away." Saluddin barked the orders with a finality that chilled Andres to the bone.

A guard dragged Andres, weak limbed, out of the ceremonial arena and through the throng who jeered at him as he went past. For a moment, Andres thought he saw Cid-Hamel again. Their eyes met for an instant. Cid-Hamel avoided his gaze and disappeared into the crowd. Quickly, Andres was escorted back to the earthen mound that was their cell. He now saw that it was just behind one of the official-looking buildings. It was dug into the side of a hill against which the semicircular row of houses was built.

Andres braced himself as the guard threw him into the black pit. When he hit the hard damp floor, he rolled forward to lighten the impact on his legs. He lay motionless for a second. Then a weight fell on his back. It was Ortega's headless body. Andres screamed with surprise and horror. The thought sickened him and he kicked the torso away from him and scuttled like an animal across the floor until he bumped up against Miguel's legs.

"What's going on?" Miguel asked fearfully.

Andres was breathless. "Give me a minute, Miguel. Did you see what came in after me? It's Ortega. Or what's left of him. Give me a hand." They returned to where Ortega's corpse lay in a growing pool of blood. Together they dragged it over to where Ortega had lined up the other corpses. "He wanted to stay with his friends," Miguel cracked, "now he's got his wish. How did it happen?"

"I was standing there calmly talking with the headman, Saluddin, when he gave a sign and they cut off Ortega's head. One minute he's standing next to me. The next he's looking up at me from the ground with screaming eyes. It was horrible, Miguel."

"You need some water. Come over here and see what we've done." Miguel guided him to the far side of the room where the other men were sitting in a circle. They had pulled a stone loose from the back wall and a little stream of muddy water was running into a trench they had dug out of the floor. Miguel dipped a piece of cloth torn from a pants leg into the dank liquid. "Here, squeeze this out into your mouth. This acts as a strainer so it's not so bad."

Andres was thirstier than he thought and dipped the cloth a second time. He ran what he had seen through his mind again. It did not change. He thought of Itel and he did not want to die. He thought of Cid-Hamel and he wanted to kill. He thought it strange that hate should be such a stronger passion than love.

For the next few days the Spaniards busied themselves with finding new sources of water. Andres encouraged them to see how Ortega's fate resulted from his crime. They, on the other hand, had done nothing to deserve death. He cautiously failed to tell them that Saluddin called him, called them all, thieves. He wanted to keep their spirits up. Still, he could not forget what Saluddin had said. Especially about death, and how he would have to face it. "I prefer to face life," he thought to himself. "I wish I had said that to him when I had the chance."

"I am not afraid to die," Miguel said with an air of bravado. "God gave us life, and we owe Him our death. It will come when He wills it. Do not resist, it would be sacrilegious."

"But surely God would want us to resist dying at the hands of that butcher out there, Miguel. Our mission is blessed by the church, and our cause is God's cause."

"That is why it will be sweet to die. In God's cause. We will find our place in heaven."

"I never figured you for a martyr, Miguel. I think I have more to do for God than to die for him. I'm not sure what it is, but I'm not ready to quit right now."

"I know I will face death bravely, Andres. It is important for me to do so. My death is my own. It is everything to me. My death is nothing to Saluddin, unless I scream, and cry, and plead for my life. That is what he wants. If I do that, I give my death to him, and I have nothing. A brave death is all I have now. Saluddin has made me see that. Ortega was right. This is our tomb. And we are already dead."

"I wish I had your courage, Miguel. But I will try to die a brave death. I don't want Saluddin to have the satisfaction a cowardly death would give him."

It was difficult to calculate the passage of time in the cell where no light penetrated. They were not certain that five days had passed since Ortega's death when Andres climbed atop Miguel's shoulders and using his belt buckle began chipping away at the dirt that framed the door to their cell. Miguel was weak and could not sustain the effort for more than a few minutes at a time. It took two days for Andres to break through. He opened up a thin sliver which let in a faint smell of fresh air. It was night. Andres strained to see down the pathway to the plaza below. He could see the torches burning and the crowd was gathered like they were that night a week ago, buzzing with excitement.

The guards must have approached from the other direction. They caught Andres by surprise when they jerked the door open. He fell backwards off of Miguel's shoulders onto the floor of the cell. The rope ladder was lowered and a sword-swinging guard entered their tomb. Miguel ran over to Andres and cleared him out of the guard's way, dragging him back to the far wall. The other men were grouped together like cattle waiting for one to be cut out of the herd. The guard went over and put a rope around Luis de Lope's neck and pulled him toward the ladder. He was weak with fear and hunger and offered little resistance as the guard threw the other end of the rope up and out of the cell door. Luis tugged at the rope as he was pulled up kicking and squirming.

"You bastards!" Andres shouted, running at the rope ladder as it was hoisted up after the guard. The six men sat in silence for the next hour, squatting, backs against the damp walls. Their thoughts were private and full of dread. Suddenly, the hatch-like door opened. A limp form tumbled to the dirt with a dull thud. It was Luis. And his head was gone!

After two days, Andres managed to dislodge a stone below the door and dig out a foothold where he could stand to monitor the activities in the Pirate village. He could see the crowds gather every two days. And he could watch the guards come up the path to collect one of his men. Each time the same routine was repeated. The door would open and a guard would climb down and select one of Andres' men. An hour later the headless corpse would be dropped back into the cell. It was maddening. Andres watched his band being murdered one by one. Miguel and Andres stood to one side while the other men huddled nervously. Each time the odds of survival for them grew less. When the guard came, they knew that one was to die. One man's death meant the others lived. For a day or two.

When there were five men left, Miguel challenged Andres. "What did you say to the man, what did you do, that makes him torture us in this way? Is death so random as this?"

"He is exercising his power," Andres decided. "It is his choice which of us dies and when. That is what power is."

After eight days, there were only three of them left. Andres, Miguel, and Roberto Urquel, the youngest member of the company after Lopez. The corpses were strewn about the floor. The smell of rotting flesh filled the air around them. Their cell was indeed a tomb.

For Urquel, there was now no doubt. He knew he was the next one to die. For two days he said nothing. Occasionally, Andres would hear a whimper through the darkness where Urquel sat with his knees drawn up to his chest. He stared blankly in front at nothing. His eyes were sunk deep in their sockets and his face appeared a skull. He had urinated down his leg. The smell of death was all around him. To Andres he was already dead.

When the hatch opened and the rope fell into the cell, Urquel did not wait for the guard to enter. He stood up mechanically and walked stiffly toward the ladder. "In the name of God, Andres," he whispered. "In the name of God," Andres answered. Urquel struggled up the ladder and disappeared into the night above. Andres found his foothold and pulled himself up to his viewing slit. He saw Urquel descending the path to the circle of light below. An hour later he came back the way the others had.

All the next day, Miguel kept his spirits up, talking about how he would die a brave death. In the afternoon, Andres was at his slit. "Look here," he cried excitedly. "I can't believe what I'm seeing." "What is it?" Miguel demanded.

Andres jumped down. His legs were weak and he crumbled to the floor. "What is it, Andres?"

"It's Dantu. He's here. With Humabon. We've got to get word to them. He can get us out of here."

"How does he know that madman?" Miguel wondered. "What is he doing here?" Miguel didn't know why he was asking these questions. He wasn't really interested in the answers.

"What difference does it make? Now there is hope for us."

"I don't want hope, Andres. I was just getting ready to die. Hope is not something I need now."

"Maybe he found out that I was here, and that's why he came. He's here to save us, Miguel." Andres shook Miguel by the shoulders. He had to convince him that they now had a chance. Miguel was screaming, "I want to die, I want to die." Andres hushed him.

"Shhh. There is someone at the door." Andres mounted his foot hole to get nearer the hatch. A voice from the other side whispered in Spanish, "Andres ... someone ... is anyone there?"

Andres answered back. "Yes, we're here. It's me, Andres."

"Dantu is bartering for you right now. Saluddin is a hard man to please. But we'll get you out somehow."

"And Miguel. He's with me. He's still alive."

"And Miguel." The voice was reassuring. It was confident. Andres dropped to the floor. "Miguel, everything is going to be all right. We're getting out of here." That night they slept like they were going to live forever.

The next day at dusk the voice returned, this time in Bisayas. "Andres. Dantu has not succeeded. Saluddin will not release you. If Dantu pushes him any harder he might be in danger himself. Be prepared to act fast. And be brave."

"Who are you?" Andres asked, but the voice was gone.

An hour later the hatch opened and the ladder fell into the cell. The guard climbed down this time with his back to the room. "What's going on, Andres? Are we getting out of here?" The guard turned to face him. It was Cid-Hamel. Andres' mouth dropped open with surprise. Cid-Hamel spoke to him in Bisayas. "We need time, Andres. Miguel will give it to us." Cid-Hamel reached for Miguel who recoiled as terror spread across his face.

"What is this, Andres?"

"Be brave, Miguel." Andres' voice was flat, final.

"Be brave? You said we were going to be free." He was clutching the front of Andres' shirt with all the strength that remained in him. "Don't let him take me, Andres, don't let him take me." Miguel finally recognized Cid-Hamel and realized what was happening. He pushed Cid-Hamel away and bolted for the ladder screaming, "They're trying to escape! This man is a spy. Don't let them get away."

Cid-Hamel fell on him from behind and brought his sword hilt down hard on the back of Miguel's head. Miguel slumped unconscious in his arms.

He fixed a rope to his neck and threw the other end out of the hole. Slowly Miguel's body disappeared into the night.

Andres fell back against the wall and slid down to a squatting position. He was drained of strength, physical and emotional. In what seemed like only a few moments the hatch opened and Miguel's corpse crashed onto the floor. Andres heard a groan from above and another body fell through the opening. It was a Moro guard. "Hurry up," Cid-Hamel urged him. "Take his clothes." Andres went over to the body and pulled it off of Miguel. He rolled it over and saw where the throat had been cut. Blood flowed down the sides of the neck and a low gurgling sound came from the wound. He wasn't dead! He was trying to talk and all that came out was a hollow growl and bubbles of blood.

Cid-Hamel leaned into the opening. He saw Andres kneeling over the body. "Finish him off," he ordered, and he threw a knife into the room. Andres picked it up. It was heavy in his hand. He mustered what strength he had, and held the knife over the man's throat. The injured man looked up. There was anger in his eyes, not fear, not pity, no plea for mercy. "This man is facing death now," thought Andres. "And I have the power. He is prepared. I will give him a clean death." And with that he drove the blade through the man's throat severing the aorta. He choked once on his own blood which rose in a fountain up to Andres' chest. His eyes rolled backwards and he was gone.

Andres quickly removed his clothes, put them on, and dressed the guard in his own. He then knelt down and cut off the guard's head, sawing through the flesh, and the sinews, and the bone. It was a clumsy job. When the head finally came loose, he tossed it up to Cid-Hamel who stuffed it in a basket he was carrying. "That will give them something to think about," Andres growled as he climbed up the ladder.

He looked back into the hole. His own grave, Ortega had said. He had risen out of his grave like Lazarus. But it remained a tomb for his men. Andres crossed himself and kicked the door closed. Then he and Cid-Hamel made their way down the stairs to the market and the docks where a boat waited to take them down the river and to the open sea. Andres had cheated death once again. But he had also looked it in the face. He now knew what it was like to die. He had been dead.

The next time, which would be the last time, he knew he would be able to die a clean death, his own death.

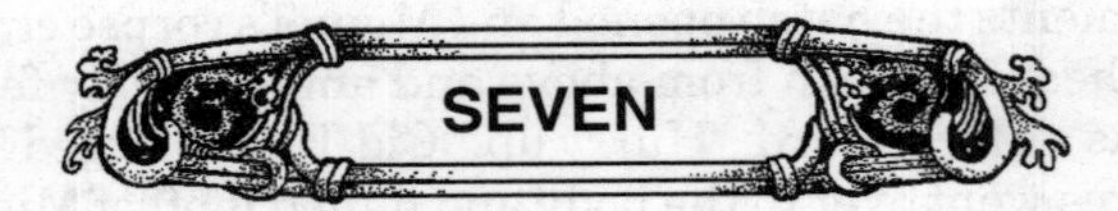

Andres jolted awake. He was lying flat on his back and the sun beat through his eyelids with such fierceness that he was afraid to open them. It had been so long since he had seen the light. He was still groggy from a deep sleep and his mind whirled as he tried to piece things together. So much had happened. Dantu and Itel, and the mysterious meeting with the pirates in the jungle. And Father Martin and Itel and God and sacrifices. And Saluddin. The images flashed behind his eyelids and made them quiver. It was the faces of his men that he could not forget, their heads stuck on pikes that lined the gangway he scrambled down with Cid-Hamel to the river and his freedom. They watched him go and he dared not look back.

He leaned forward supporting himself on his elbows and slit his eyes open slowly. A boat rocked gently in the water before him and the hunched-over figure of Cid-Hamel was silhouetted a few paces away.

"Where are we?" Andres' lips cracked when he spoke. His voice was hollow and grating.

"So, you're awake. Good. Here, you'll need some water."

It was the first fresh water Andres had in two weeks. It was delicious and he was grateful. "Thank you," he said softly. Andres needed to express his gratitude more forcefully. But that would come later. He hadn't yet decided if he would tell Cid-Hamel what he had thought about him. He was feeling a bit guilty. Andres drank carefully from the flagon Cid-Hamel had offered him. "Where are we?" he inquired again.

"We're safe, Sergeant. We are at the headwaters of the river, downstream from the Moro camp. I thought you should rest and regain some of your strength before we set out for Panay."

"Panay?"

"That's right. Legaspi has moved his forces to Panay. We can join them there." Andres stood up. His legs were wobbly at first, then he collected himself and strode off across the sand to the boat with the singularity of purpose of a man on a mission. "Let's get going," he barked.

"Are you sure?"

"I've never been so sure of anything in my life." He began shoving the boat into the surf. Cid-Hamel collected his equipment and the water and hurried after him.

"And we're not sailing to Panay. We're going north."

"North?"

"There is a city, Manila they call it, on a large bay overlooking the entrance to all of these islands. The people there trade directly with China. If we can take that town, we will have the Orient at our doorstep. China will come to us with her silks and embroideries and her spices. We can control the Philippines from there."

"But what about the Moro pirates in Mindoro? Legaspi is after them."

"They can wait. Nobody wants Saluddin more than I do. He owes me a death. But right now Legaspi can't be wasting his time and soldiers on a few pirates. The door to China is ours to open. And Manila is the key. I need to convince Legaspi of that fact. And to do that, I need to see for myself. So we sail north."

Cid-Hamel finished trimming the sail and settled down at the rudder of the Moro prau. Andres leaned against the mast facing him. For more than an hour they did not speak. The sun climbed hot overhead. A few clouds hugged the horizon. Andres broke the silence. The horrors of the last two weeks kept crowding into his mind. He needed a diversion.

"That night, Cid-Hamel, when we were taken in Panay. Tell me what happened."

Cid-Hamel recounted the following story. He had been on guard at the perimeter of the camp when a noise pulled him off into the jungle. When he returned to his post, the attack had already begun, so he watched from a safe distance. It appeared that the Moros were only interested in taking prisoners if no one resisted. Then he followed the Moro boats and was caught in the same storm. The next morning he found Lopez' body, or what was left of it, floating in the water. It had been badly mangled by sharks attracted by the blood from his wounded leg.

When they reached the Moro pirate camp, he had mingled with the crowd until he had assured himself that Andres was still alive and he had found where he and his men were being kept. Then he returned to Cebu to tell Legaspi what had happened. There he learned that the Portuguese ship they had seen from the coast of Panay had circled around Negros and Cebu and blocked the harbor at Cebu. For five days the ship had laid at anchor and threatened Legaspi's ability to go and come as he pleased. Then the Portuguese ship moved on. Legaspi decided that he was too vulnerable at

Cebu and gave orders to relocate his forces to Panay. There wasn't time to mount a rescue mission so Cid-Hamel had gone to Dantu who quickly determined that he would try to buy Andres' freedom. So he and Dantu and Humabon sailed to Mindoro.

"What happened to that plan?" Andres interrupted.

"Saluddin was too difficult. He wanted too much in return."

Andres grimaced. He wasn't too sure what was too much when it was his life and that of his men that lay in the balance. Cid-Hamel noticed the Spaniard's displeasure. "He asked for Itel," he said flatly, to answer the question he saw on Andres' face.

Andres did not respond. No response was necessary. Still, he wondered if given a chance, would Itel have let herself be bargained for. Would she have given herself for him? Would he have wanted her to?

"So we had to come up with another way," Cid-Hamel continued.

"Wasn't there some way you could have saved Miguel too?"

Cid-Hamel shifted to the lee side of the rudder and turned the boat into the wind. The sail swung sharply over Andres' head on the spar. "There was only one set of Moro clothes," he answered. His tone was as mechanical as his sailing maneuvers. "Besides, we needed a diversion. Miguel's death kept Saluddin busy. Dantu was there; he saw it. That way Saluddin wouldn't think Dantu had anything to do with your escape."

"Where is Dantu now?"

"Probably on his way back to Cebu."

"Not Panay?" Cid-Hamel did not answer. He didn't have to. Why should Dantu join Legaspi on Panay. His home was in Cebu, with Itel. Andres wondered if that would ever be his home again, or if he would ever see Itel again.

It was dusk when they reached Luban island where they made camp. The next day they sailed into Manila bay. The sun was setting behind them. Before them was a broad expanse of protected water. Many ships could lie at anchor here, Andres thought, and trade their goods from east and west. As they neared the shore, Andres could see the white sands of a beach beyond the Chinese junks that nestled together just off shore. Beyond the beach rose the walls of the fortified town. The walls were made of the trunks of palms. At regular intervals there were embrasures with mounted lantakas, Moro cannons. To the north of the citadel, a river flowed into the bay. Cid-Hamel directed their craft into the river and found a mooring where it would be out of sight to anyone on the walls of the city.

"You stay here," he ordered. "I'll get a closer look."

Andres slept. When he woke Cid-Hamel was at the rudder guiding the boat out into the current of the river. "What did you find?" Andres asked, rubbing the sleep from his eyes.

"It is as you said. A prosperous town. There are many rich merchants. Chinese. Moro. They have many weapons. But they are not pirates. The Raja is Soliman. He would rather make a business deal than fight. Your soldiers should have no trouble taking the town."

Andres leaned back satisfied. With control of this site, the trade with China, and the northern route across the Pacific, their fortunes would be made. Now he had to get back to Panay and convince Legaspi to attack Manila. Hopefully, his plans to invade Mindoro were not too far along. The voyage south to Panay took two days. Their little boat was pushed briskly along before a steady wind. The wind that always blew from the north and made it difficult for ships to exit the archipelago in that direction. Sometimes, ships were forced all the way south to the Moluccas by the northerly gales. "All the more reason for a secure harbor at the northern extremity of the islands," thought Andres.

It was the afternoon of the second day when Panay became visible on the horizon. "Salcedo has arrived," Cid-Hamel informed Andres. "Have you ever seen him?"

"No. But I have heard about him. Quite the soldier, isn't he?"

"It was his arrival that drove off the Portuguese ship that was blocking the harbor at Cebu." Andres remembered that Legaspi was expecting his grandson just as he was leaving on his expedition to Panay. "He came ashore with a squadron of men, all fancy dressed with plumes on their helmets, like a flock of birds. You would think he was laying claim to Mecca the way he strutted ashore."

"I had heard that he was flamboyant."

"And the speech he made." Cid-Hamel stood up at the tiller and swung his right arm around in a wide arc. "My friends," he mimicked Salcedo in bombastic tones, "patriots and loyal subjects of King Philip, emperor of the East and West Indies, I bring you greetings. Ours is a noble mission, sanctioned by God and the high host of heaven, blah, blah, blah." Here Cid-Hamel fell back to his seat beside the rudder, laughing, his full lips stretched back to expose his dark gums and his large white teeth. One gold tooth caught the evening sun and blinked at Andres.

Andres had never seen Cid-Hamel so animated, so full of fun. He had a healthy disregard for pomposity, a man of action, not of show. Perhaps Salcedo was also a man of action. Andres would find out about that later.

Right now, it was Cid-Hamel who interested him. He had saved his life and he owed him something for that. He owed him loyalty and respect and his life if it came to that. But it had not occurred to him that he owed him his friendship. And now, seeing him prancing about the stern of a small boat off the coast of Panay in the sunset making fun of a young Spanish officer, the grandson of the General, he was actually beginning to like the man.

Just after twilight, Cid-Hamel brought their little skiff aground on the shore just below Legaspi's camp. Andres could see the torch light of the encampment in the distance beyond the palms that lined the beach. As he waded ashore on wobbly legs he realized that he was still weak from his ordeal. Four days on the open sea in a small boat also made it difficult to stand straight on solid ground.

Andres identified himself to a sentry who challenged them and they were taken immediately to Legaspi's tent where a council of war was in session. Legaspi and several men encircled a table with a map of the islands spread out on it. Andres recognized de Goiti. A handsome young man, no more than twenty years of age, stood next to Legaspi. Andres judged that this must be Salcedo. Opposite de Goiti, Father Martin leaned over the table resting his weight on his huge hands.

"Ah, welcome Sergeant Urdaneta. We celebrate your safe return," said Legaspi as he raised a glass and gestured to the others to follow suit. "Now what can you tell us about Mindoro?"

Obviously, Legaspi was not in the mood for pleasantries and idle talk, thought Andres. He was all business. Good. That would make it easier for him to sell what he had come to say.

"Well, there are pirates there," Andres began. "And danger. But you know that." Legaspi nodded. Andres sensed that he was getting impatient already. "Their camp is here." Andres pointed to a spot on the map of Mindoro where he suspected Saluddin's fort was located. "About three miles up this river, on the north bank."

Salcedo moved around beside Andres to get a better look. "Cid-Hamel told us as much. But you have been inside the camp for two weeks. Did you observe anything that we can use to our advantage. Where are the gun placements? How many men are on guard duty? Where are they stationed?" Salcedo was itching for a fight.

"I was in a cell underground for most of the time. All I saw was my men being murdered brutally. I do know that the leader is a madman. He has no respect for life and will fight to the death against us."

"That is of course what we want," laughed de Goiti, "for him to fight to his death."

"But our men will have a hard time of it," said Andres. "The fort is unapproachable except by the river. We cannot surprise them. On the first level, there is nothing but a marketplace with innocent people. The fortification is higher up, against the side of a hill, with thick jungle all around. They will pick us off like flies."

"I believe I am beginning to smell a coward," said de Goiti and he brought his thumb and forefinger to his nose in a gesture of contempt for what Andres was saying.

"Yes, shouldn't you of all people want to get revenge on the man who slaughtered your friends?" asked Salcedo. "There is a question of honor here." Andres weighed the word honor for a moment before he continued. Honor indeed. He wondered what good Salcedo's honor would have done him in that tomb with no water or light for fifteen days, with corpses rotting all around him, and death staring him in the face.

"We don't have to charge him," de Goiti suggested. "We can blockade him. In the river. Or safer still, at the head of the river."

Legaspi was growing more impatient. He wanted a decision, a plan of action. "We have got to do something," he said. "Our orders brought from Spain by Salcedo are that we take possession of all of the islands, and secure them, in the name of King Philip."

"Then take possession of this!" Andres brought his hand down hard on the island of Luzon at the point of Manila Bay.

"And what is that?" asked Legaspi.

"The key to carrying out King Philip's orders, General. There is a large protected bay here for many trading ships. There is already a Moro settlement where the Chinese bring their silks and spices."

"The Chinese?" Father Martin seemed interested.

"Yes. Cid-Hamel and I went there after our escape from Mindoro. It is a lightly fortified citadel. We can take it easily."

"And why should we want to?" Salcedo moved around Martin, back to his view of Saluddin's camp on Mindoro. Legaspi leaned forward and stood over Luzon.

"Because this location can become the center of trade for this entire region. Think of it. We won't have to go looking for spices and silks and all the things they want back in Spain. They will come to us from here." He pointed to the China coast. "There is already trade going on, from here to here. All we have to do is take over Manila and our fortunes are made." Andres paused for a moment to see if he was getting his message through. He caught Legaspi's eye and continued.

"You have been in these islands for almost a year, General. You know that they do not support agriculture. Anyway, we will not inspire the youth of Spain to sail around the world to push a plow. The Moluccas have all the spices and they are controlled by the Portuguese. We haven't found any gold yet, or just enough to cover one of Cid-Hamel's teeth." At this Cid-Hamel stretched a broad grin for all to see his tooth. "So what we need to do is take control of the trade in the area. Can't you see it? Ship after ship laden with beautiful silk, porcelain jars, ivory combs, cinnamon, nutmeg, jade, and tea. All of the goods will pass through a central port, here at Manila, and we will take our profit."

"It doesn't sound like an occupation for a soldier," Salcedo groused.

"You will always find wars to fight, Salcedo," Legaspi said.

"And there will still be pirates to chase," Andres added. "When we have taken Manila, we will lure Saluddin out and meet him on our own ground." This seemed to please Salcedo, but de Goiti was still not convinced.

"Why should we listen to this sergeant? This sergeant who lost his men on his first command?" Andres bristled. He did not need to be reminded. The thought of his men had not left him in the four days since his escape. His anger at de Goiti weakened him. His knees buckled and he slumped back into a chair.

"Because I know something else, de Goiti. I know the route back to New Spain across the Pacific." This got everyone's attention. Andres continued. "The route lies north of the equator, not south as our ships have attempted before." Andres stood up and drew an arc on the map from the Philippines across the Pacific to the North American coast. "The winds are westerly here and the currents favorable. A ship carrying goods can cross to California and then follow the coast down to Acapulco. It can return bringing silver to purchase more goods using the southern route which we know."

De Goiti brought his hand up under his chin. He recognized the significance of Andres' proposal. "And how do you know this?" he asked.

"Montoya. He was forced north and discovered the favorable winds. He's probably in Acapulco by now. Ortega, one of his crew, told me. We found him in Saluddin's prison. He was the first to die." Andres' voice lowered to a hush. The argument was exhausting him. He sat down again and continued in a softer, more explanatory tone.

"Manila is already to the north. If we start out from there, we won't have to face the northerly winds that make it hard to navigate in the islands, that force us south. From Manila it will be easy to find our way east back to New Spain. And there is China to the west."

The mention of China brought Martin into the conversation again. "Yes, China. There are many souls to be saved there. Our missionaries can follow the trade routes to the mainland." His voice trailed off in private thought.

“What is this island here?” asked Salcedo, pointing to Luban to the west of Manila Bay. He was already setting his sights on Manila and was beginning to form a battle plan.

“There is a Moro fort there, heavily armed, guarding the entrance to the bay,” Andres advised.

“That will be my objective,” Salcedo announced.

Legaspi leaned forward and pointed to the south point of the bay. “De Goiti, you will land here with a company of forty men and a force of Bisayas. Work your way up the shore on foot and attack the fort from below. I will take the flagship into the bay and shell the fort from the front. Then when we have softened them up, with Salcedo protecting our rear, we will send crafts ashore and storm the battlements. It is a good plan.”

”And God be with us,” said Father Martin. They bowed their heads over the map, and prayed.

It was a good morning for battle. A good day for dying. Legaspi had timed the journey from Panay so he would enter the Bay of Manila just before dawn. It had taken three days to gather provisions and prepare the small armada of Bisayas praus and two Spanish galleons. And now, two days after they set sail, they were poised for battle.

"I smell victory in the air," Legaspi announced as he strode the quarter deck of the San Paulo. Andres and Martin were at his side. "So that is our target?" He looked across the bow at the fortifications ringing the far side of the bay. "It is time. Give the signal." At this command a flag was hoisted up the mast, and the skiffs with de Goiti's troops peeled off to the south, heading for a patch of sand that jutted out into the bay just below the fortifications of the city.

"De Goiti's men should meet no resistance? Is that right?" The question was thrown at Andres like a dagger.

"Yes sir. I mean, no sir. We saw very few soldiers the other night. There is not much of a guard. This is a trading settlement, not a military camp." Andres was becoming uneasy. This was, after all, his idea. There would be plenty of people ready to take credit for this enterprise if all went well. Legaspi for one. And Salcedo for another. And then there was Martin who would invoke God's providence and claim credit for the church. But if anything went wrong, it would all be on his head. No matter, he thought. He could just retire from Legaspi's service and live with Itel and Dantu on Cebu. If Legaspi let him live.

"Is Salcedo well-positioned?" Legaspi walked crisply to the stern of the ship to see for himself. Salcedo's task was to guard Legaspi's rear at the entrance of the Bay should Saluddin make an appearance. Salcedo was itching for a fight with the pirate and prayed that he would be foolish enough to try his luck against a swift Spanish ship with full cannon. When Legaspi had finished with the meager resistance on the shore, Salcedo imagined, he could turn and they would have Saluddin between them.

Legaspi acted like a man sure of himself and his plan. This was the leader Andres always imagined him to be. Now he could see him in action. Legaspi barked out his final orders. "In another hundred yards bring her into the wind. Starboard cannons prepare to fire."

As the ship came about Andres could barely make out the silhouettes of de Goiti's boats reaching the shore. The sun was peeking over the city behind the high bamboo wall that fronted the bay. Soon it would be in their eyes. But it was no matter. The target was large and they planned to fire indiscriminately. Legaspi had instructed the gunners to demolish the wall so de Goiti's men could take the city. He did not want the city itself to be hit. It was a good plan, he said over and over.

When de Goiti reached the shore, he found himself confronted with the greatest enemy of a heavily armored conquistador. Mud. It was a marshy headland that de Goiti and his men had been directed to and they were knee-deep in mud, unable to move.

"Remove anything that weighs you down," de Goiti ordered. The men quickly complied, tossing helmets and breast plates aside where they disappeared in the sticky muck with little gurgling sounds.

The next sound they heard was the whizzing of arrows. Hundreds of them. From the bushes beyond. From the trees. De Goiti's men scrambled for cover, but there was none. The sound of the arrows was deafening, and the small dull thud of the arrowhead meeting flesh, followed by the cries of pain and fear, the splash of bodies falling into the mud. The sounds of panic drowned out the first report of Legaspi's guns trained on the city. De Goiti tried to take it all in, but all he saw was confusion, flight, and death. The face of one of his men flashed before him, the eyes staring wide, blood dripping from the nostrils, an arrow through his neck. "My God, we're doomed," he cried. "How did they know?" he yelled at no one in particular. He expected no answer, and feared he would not be alive to hear one if it was offered.

At that moment a hand from below, somewhere down there in the mud, pulled him earthward. It was the leader of the Bisayas warriors who accompanied him. The Bisayas pulled de Goiti forward to the base of a fallen tree where they found cover from the onslaught of arrows. De Goiti looked out to the bay, searching for Legaspi's ship in the growing light of dawn. And that is when he saw the wall of flame encircling the Admiral's ship.

They had come from nowhere it seemed. Fifteen or twenty small skiffs, tied together and set in the path of Legaspi's flagship. They must have been doused with oil or painted with pitch before they were set afire because they burned with furious intensity.

"Bring her about." Legaspi's command filled his men with energy and urgency. He was the calm center of frenzied activity as the men ran to their positions to execute his order. There was not much time. If the ship pushed forward into the row of burning boats, they would be pulled toward the ship, ultimately circling it. Already the water was aflame with burning oil on three sides.

"Can we sink them?" Father Martin asked.

"We can try," Legaspi shouted. "Train your guns on those skiffs," he ordered, "and fire at will." What seemed like a good idea was not. The boats exploded on impact and sent fireballs high into the air. Some landed on the deck of the San Paulo. A powder keg next to Father Martin ignited and blew up, sending Martin reeling backwards and smashing him against the mast. He crumpled to the deck unconscious.

"Quick. Put out those fires." Legaspi's voice was still without panic. "If the magazine catches, there'll be an explosion none of us will forget. Hurry men, or we'll be shark bait." This last remark put speed into the legs of the men who scurried about the ship dousing fires.

From his location further out in the bay, Salcedo saw the ring of fire and the flaming balls shooting skyward and then falling on the San Paulo. Salcedo decided to come to his grandfather's aid. He ordered his sails to the full and set course for the middle of the bay. This is what Saluddin had been waiting for. Suddenly he appeared across Salcedo's wake in the perfect position for a broadside. A single volley brought down Salcedo's mast and he was dead in the water. Saluddin could pick him to pieces.

Legaspi leaned over the rail of the San Paulo inspecting the damage to the hull of his ship. "We must break free of these fire ships, Andres. No matter what direction we move, we will drag them with us like deadly sea weed."

"I will do what I can," Andres promised as he grabbed a knife from the belt of a passing sailor, threw off his armor and mounted the railing to dive into the fiery water. Legaspi watched him arch gracefully and disappear into the smoke below. Beyond he saw Saluddin's ship pressing the attack on Salcedo. "God's speed, Andres." There was now a tremor in Legaspi's voice. "Free us, for there is work to be done."

First there was the smoke and then there was the cold water covered with fire. But even before that, Andres saw from the corner of his eye another figure leave the railing and dive with him. He must have had the same idea, Andres thought. To cut the ropes binding the burning skiffs. That would end the immediate danger of the vessels crashing against the hull and setting the entire ship ablaze, and it would free the San Paulo to maneuver itself into position whether to attack Saluddin or to continue the assault on Manila.

It was cold under the water. And Dark. The silence was a welcome change from the cannons, and screams, and shouts of the ship deck. Cold and silent and calm. Like death Andres thought. He swam as long as he could under water toward the ring of boats. As he neared the surface he could see the flames and the bottoms of the boats and he imagined that he could smell the oil that was spread across the surface of the water. His lungs were bursting. He had to come up for air. But he had to find a clear space, one that was not on fire.

Finally he could wait no longer and he broke the surface gasping for air. It was hot and oily and it burned his lungs. Andres was lucky. He had come up where there was very little fire on the water. And there was a clear path to the boats just twenty yards in front of him. He swam quickly, diving under every now and then to avoid the scattered flames.

When he reached the ring of boats he decided to attack the problem from below the water. The fire close in to the boats was still raging. He could swim under each boat, reach up and cut the ropes that bound it to the next one. It would take some time to separate enough of them to insure the San Paulo a safe passage, so he went to work.

After cutting the first boat loose, Andres pulled himself under it to begin on the next. This one was burned out, only a charred hulk remained, but it was still floating. As he sawed on the ropes he felt a tug from beyond the next boat, as if someone were working on that one. Maybe it was my fellow diver, Andres thought. But why was he here. He should be working further along the line.

With that thought he pulled himself up chest high onto the boat to see who was on the other side. What he discovered was that the job had been completed. The boats, many of them still afire, now floated freely and aimlessly on the water. Legaspi had already turned the San Paulo and was sailing to rescue Salcedo from Saluddin's attack. Andres lifted himself into the boat and slumped down breathlessly into its charred bottom. A head appeared over the rim. It was Cid-Hamel.

"I should have known. So my old friend. You work quickly." Cid-Hamel pulled himself over the edge of the boat and fell inside. He was clearly exhausted.

"I had a little help," he said, as he rose to his knees, leaned over the side and pulled a small brown figure into the boat. It was Dantu.

"What in God's name is he doing here," Andres demanded. "Where did he come from?"

Dantu's hair was singed, and his eyebrows were gone. Andres wondered what he looked like, and he glanced at his forearms to discover that most of the hair had been burned off. He ran his fingers through the mat of dark hair that still remained and sighed. "Well, what have you got to say?"

"We don't really have time for explanations right now," Cid-Hamel protested. "But if you must know, Dantu learned of this little expedition when Legaspi sent to Cebu for warriors and he demanded to come along."

"Somebody else found out about it, too. Somebody not so helpful. This is a trap we sailed into, that's pretty clear. Someone sold us out. We've got a traitor among us, Cid-Hamel."

"I suppose you're right. They do appear to have been ready for you."

"I despise treachery. Men must have trust, otherwise it is the jungle." Andres looked again at Dantu. He recalled when he saw him in the jungle with Humabon and the pirates. And again with Humabon and Itel in that bloody ritual. Cid-Hamel saw where Andres was looking.

"And there is loyalty too, don't forget that," Cid-Hamel said as he drew Dantu to his side. The boy here wanted to come, but Itel would not allow it, so he snuck away and hid in the ship. I found him there last night. He tells me that his father Tupas died eight days ago, and now he is the Dato of Cebu and he thought he should be here with his people."

"He should be where it is safe, safe from battle and from treachery. He'll see enough of that when he is grown."

"He said he wanted to be with his people, and to be with you. He says he owes you his life."

"Perhaps," said Andres, "but he doesn't owe me his death."

"It's the same thing, isn't it." Cid-Hamel placed his hand on Andres' arm. The arm was sore from burns and Andres winced. But he felt the companionship that Cid-Hamel was offering, and he accepted the comfort. When you are in a fight, Andres thought to himself, all you have is your own courage and the loyalty of friends. Trust, he concluded, is worth an entire battalion. Without it, any enterprise is doomed. They had been betrayed by someone they trusted, and they were in danger of losing the battle. They could even lose all of the islands if their defeat were complete. "All right. For now. He's here and he's not any worse off then the rest of us, which isn't saying very much."

Andres surveyed their situation. Three men in a charred boat drifting in a sea of smoke and flames. Smoldering debris from the other boats floated about them. Legaspi had pulled far away by now and they were alone in the middle of the bay.

"Let's make for shore," Cid-Hamel suggested. "Grab some of those planks. We can use them to paddle in." Andres and Dantu followed the Muslim's orders and in less than an hour they were within a hundred yards of the shore when their little blackened skiff began falling apart. They eased themselves into the water and swam to a point of land near where Andres and Cid-Hamel had come ashore two weeks ago.

Andres now began to take charge. "De Goiti is attacking from the other side of the city so there shouldn't be too much resistance on this side. Let's see what we can do to take this city ourselves."

Andres started out up a muddy embankment to the base of the high wall encircling the city. Cid-Hamel and Dantu followed. "Give me a hand here," Andres barked, as he pried at the base of the wall, trying to unhinge one of the poles. Cid-Hamel bent over Andres' shoulder to lend a hand. Together they pulled. And surprisingly the pole came loose with little resistance. And the one next to it. And another. Then another. It was all too easy, Andres thought.

On the other side of the wall he discovered why. The wall was a facade. It was a deception. It was not intended as a real wall to stop real soldiers storming the barricades. It was an illusion of a stiff defense intended to keep an attacker at bay. From a distance it appeared to be an impregnable fortification to discourage attack. If someone were foolhardy enough to attack, he would expend his munitions on a mirage. Then, thinking he was about to triumph, the attacker would come ashore, breach the pretend wall and find himself in the gun sights of a palace guard firing from atop an interior wall some fifty yards away. The pretend wall behind them would serve well enough to keep them from retreating, and they would be trapped like rats, easy targets for just a small troop of men with guns and cannon.

They covered the distance to the base of the interior wall swiftly, crouching in the shadow cast by the north rampart. The sun was high overhead. It was now midday. Andres stood on Cid-Hamel shoulders and pulled Dantu up to him and then shoved him onto the parapet just above his head. Cid-Hamel climbed over Andres to reach the top and then pulled Andres up.

They found themselves on a paved veranda lined with cannon pointing not out to the bay but down at the pretend wall of bamboo. Behind the cannon were stacks of muskets and cannon balls. In a building to the left were tables and chairs. The mess hall, thought Andres. The men had left their midday meal to watch the sea battle in the bay. They were standing along the low wall that hid the cannon from view, at the far end of the veranda, pointing, laughing, enjoying the show and waiting. One, nearest to them, had his arm around a woman and was eating a chicken leg. His white teeth glistened in the sun as he picked gingerly at the roasted meat, cleaning the bone.

Andres looked in the direction the men were pointing. He saw Salcedo's ship listing slightly amid billows of smoke. It was badly damaged. Legaspi had arrived in time to drive Saluddin off before he utterly destroyed the young Spaniard's ship. Legaspi gave chase for a short distance, and then he turned to renew his assault on the citadel.

"Damn." Andres spat out the word. "We've got to warn Legaspi what he is up against. If he comes ashore before we have dismantled these guns, he will be slaughtered. Any idea?"

"We could make off with all their flints," Cid-Hamel offered. A smile cracked on his thick lips, and there was a glint of mischief in his eyes. The muslim was in the mood for a fight but he knew they were seriously outnumbered. The two of them and a boy, crouching in the shadows of the enemy's mess hall on a parapet lined with cannon. It was time for something devious.

"Or we could pack mud into the firing chambers. Or better yet, we could blow them up with their own powder. Look there." He was pointing at a trail of gun powder that ran between them and the low wall on the north side of the veranda. About ten yards farther on it arched toward the building and stopped. Cid-Hamel crawled on all fours along the messhall wall, like a blood-hound on the scent, following the powder trail. He stopped for a moment and then scuttled back.

"There's a door there. Probably a munitions store. If we could get in there...." He did not finish the thought. Dantu, who was huddled against a cannon at the corner of the building, shifted his position to relieve the strain on his knees. A portion of his bare shoulder that had been burned earlier touched the cannon which was hot in the blazing sun, and he squealed as the pain, like a needle, shot into the raw flesh. He pulled instinctively away from the source of the pain and with the abrupt motion his knife fell on the pavement.

The sound of metal on stone caught the attention of the guard with the woman. He disengaged himself from her and began walking suspiciously toward the north end of the veranda. He held the chicken leg in his teeth as he pulled a curved blade from his belt. Cid-Hamel stood up and pressed himself hard against the wall at its corner. He clutched his knife tightly, ready to spring as soon as the intruder's shadow appeared on the pavement beside him.

When the shadow appeared, Dantu sprang up as if on cue, then squatted down just as quickly. The Moro guard turned toward him and froze. It was the split second that Cid-Hamel needed. He reached out and pulled the man into the shadow of the wall, away from the view of his fellows who were still distracted by the events in the bay. With his right arm around the man's chest Cid-Hamel pinned him against his stomach. With his free hand he reached over the man's left shoulder and shoved the chicken bone down his throat. There was a wet crunching sound as the bone cracked and splintered and lodged itself in the soft tissue of the throat at the base of the tongue. "Try to call to your friends now," Cid-Hamel hissed in his ear as he dragged him further into the shadow, his fingers now clamping the man's nostrils shut.

The man flayed wildly, gasping for air. He tried gamely to get his feet under him, emitting spasmodic wheezing sounds as the air sought passage to his lungs through his mouth. With a desperate effort he managed to free his left hand which held his knife. He stabbed wildly backwards under his right armpit. Cid-Hamel let out a muffled groan. The knife penetrated his abdomen about three inches. But his assailant could not drive it in further or slice outward with it because of his awkward position in the struggle.

Cid-Hamel instinctively reached for the knife to draw it out. When he did he had to release the man who now turned toward him, his arms outstretched. Before he could move, Cid-Hamel lunged forward and drove his knife up to the hilt just below the man's sternum. The Moro made a preposterous sight, standing there, his eyes bugging out, his face flushed, a knife protruding from his chest which he held with both his hands like it was a life rope, and sticking out of his mouth, the lips turning blue, was a chicken leg, with a little piece of flesh dangling from its end.

In an instant, before the man could muster a dying scream or hurl himself backward into the sunlight and the view of his comrades, Andres reached around his frame and brought his knife swiftly and surely across his throat severing his neck muscles, the aorta, and the windpipe. There was a rush of air as if the lungs were pulling it directly through the man's neck. Blood spurted out and struck Cid-Hamel in the chest. Andres cupped his hand over the gaping wound, forcing the warm red fluid back inside. There was a long, low gurgling sound. And the man died, drowned in his own blood.

"Nice work," Cid-Hamel congratulated Andres as he slumped against the wall in a crouching position. "And they didn't hear a thing. Good for us." Andres dragged the dead guard further down the wall toward the door to the storeroom. He came back to Cid-Hamel who was holding his right side.

"Are you all right?"

"It's just a scratch," he lied. "I'll be fine." Dantu had left his position behind the cannon during the struggle. He moved down the parapet and was picking over the dead man as Cid-Hamel and Andres considered what to do next. He hurried back to them, running crouched over, his bare feet slapping the stone pavement.

"Look what our friend has found," Cid-Hamel said as he reached out to receive the set of keys that Dantu proffered toward him.

"Let's hope they're for that storeroom and not his whore's bedroom," Andres whispered. A glimmer of hope was beginning to appear in his eyes. "But we still need to get word to Legaspi."

"That won't be so easy now." There was a tone of resignation in Cid-Hamel's voice. "Look there." Andres followed the line of his companion's outstretched arm. A white flag was rising up a pole. It was now about half-way up. Soon it would be clearly visible above the bamboo wall.

"That's the sign," Andres said. "The sign that de Goiti's troops have taken the city. But where are they. The city is intact. There's no sign of de Goiti."

"It's part of the trap," Cid-Hamel said flatly. They are luring Legaspi in for the kill."

Andres crept to the low wall and peered cautiously over it. Below on what looked like a parade ground or a piazza of some sort was a central flag pole and a lone figure working the ropes to raise the flag that would bring Legaspi ashore. Right into a trap, thought Andres. "We've got to do something," he hissed through clenched teeth as he returned to his companions.

"You do what you can to keep that flag down. I'll arrange a surprise for our friends down the line there." Cid-Hamel rolled over on his left side and gestured toward the veranda with the keys. His right side was covered with blood.

"Dantu." Andres turned to the boy and put his hands on his shoulders. He was all business now and he spoke with authority. "You must get to Legaspi. Do whatever you have to. Find a boat, swim, whatever it takes. Get to him and tell him what's happened. Something is wrong with de Goiti. Or he would be here by now. Tell Legaspi to delay a shore landing until... until." He stopped to think. Until what?

"Until he sees a great explosion," Cid-Hamel broke in. "When this building blows up, then he can come. But not until. Have you got it?"

"Yes." The boy looked up at Andres, and then over to Cid-Hamel. "I've got it."

"Good," said Andres. "We're counting on you. Be careful, but get the job done. Now off with you." Andres patted him on the back and lifted him to the parapet wall and watched him slide over silently to the ground below. "And you, old friend, you must be careful too," he said to Cid-Hamel.

"Don't worry about me. You just bring that flag down."

Andres crept over to the wall and lay down flat upon it. He looked up toward the bay and could see Legaspi's ship. The admiral had begun to deploy boats for the landing of his troops. "I've got to hurry," Andres said muttered his breath as he jackknifed over the wall and eased himself down to the ground below.

He worked his way along the wall in the shadow, keeping low to avoid the sight of anyone looking out of the building across the piazza. Above him, Cid-Hamel was opening the door to the storeroom. When he reached the east corner of the building, he paused. There were fifty yards of open ground between him and the figure raising the false signal to Legaspi. Andres had to trust that everyone else was occupied with the show on the other side of the building, watching the naval battle or preparing to spring the trap when Legaspi's men came ashore. If he could bring the flag down, maybe Legaspi would hold off, at least until Cid-Hamel could disable the guns on the parapet.

Andres covered the distance swiftly. As he approached the flagpole, the man working the ropes turned. The ropes fell from his dark hands, and a shawl slid from his head as he stood erect, facing Andres.

"You!" Andres shouted. "What are you doing here?" It was Humabon. In a flash it was all clear to Andres. Saluddin had been one step ahead of them all the way. The Moro in Manila were ready for them, Saluddin lay in wait in the bay, the trap was set, all because Humabon got word of the attack to Saluddin.

"But why?" Andres demanded. "Why throw in with them? It is not the wish of Tupas."

"Tupas is dead," Humabon spoke for the first time. "We can do business with the Moro, with Soliman, the raja here in Manila. And with Saluddin if we have to. You do not do business, you just take."

"But we have given you much in return, you ungrateful heathen." Andres shifted his knife to his right hand and bound part of his torn shirt around his left arm to act as a shield as he began circling to the left. He was thinking of the night he saw Humabon in the jungle, the ritual of the harvest, the slain carabao.

"Yes, your soft religion. It is not a faith for warriors. You will drive out Laon. And then where will I be?"

"And our culture and language. We will give that to you, too."

"Your language." Humabon spat out the words. "I learned it only so I might curse you."

"But the Moro. Are they really any better? They are murderers, pirates." Andres was not in the mood for a debate. He was simply maneuvering for position. Humabon was a much larger man, and he needed to find an advantage. But time was getting short.

"Perhaps. But you Spanish dogs are more dangerous. We have to stop you here or you will take everything." Humabon lunged forward and stabbed at Andres' chest. Andres stepped nimbly aside and tripped the larger man who fell onto the pavement, rolled over and, before Andres could gain an advantage, he scooped up some loose gravel and threw it into the Spaniard's face. Humabon pulled himself to his feet and rushed the distracted Andres, burrowing into his midsection with his right shoulder and driving him to the ground at the base of the flagpole, his left arm pinned beneath his body. Andres' knife fell free and clattered across the pavement. Desperately he reached up and found one of the ropes dangling loose. He deftly circled Humabon's neck with it and then pulled violently downward on the other rope jerking the Bisayan's head upward. Humabon growled with pain and reached behind his head with his free hand to cut the rope.

The rope cut, Humabon sensed victory. He edged forward pinning Andres' shoulders to the ground. Andres looked up and could only make out the outlines of his enemy's head. The sun was directly behind and a fiery halo seemed to encircle his head like a solar eclipse.

Humabon dropped his knife and leaned over to gather up a large slab of the pavement which had been dislodged in their struggle. Anger flashed in his eyes and he spit out a curse as he lifted the stone over his head before bringing it down on Andres' face. The slab appeared like a huge black disc in the white hot sky. It is the last thing I will see, thought Andres.

But it wasn't. As he stared up, Humabon hesitated, then froze, motionless. His eyes registered surprise. The curse trailed off into a gurgling sound. Andres looked more closely. A pinpoint of steel, then a wedge of silver shining in the sun appeared at the base of Humabon's neck. Blood dripped, then spurted onto Andres' chest. The Bisayan's eyes glazed over and rolled back. He slumped sideways, the slab fell harmlessly onto the pavement, and Humabon crumbled in a pool of his own blood. Andres was still looking up. Where Humabon had been, now there was the silhouette of a young boy. Andres wriggled out from under Humabon's corpse and then he saw the hilt of Dantu's knife sticking out from the base of the priest's skull.

"Dantu! I thought I told you to get the word to Legaspi."

"This seemed more important," the boy replied. Andres was busily bringing the flag down, pulling on the ropes, one hand over the other.

"Well, I guess I'm fortunate you made that choice." He looked down at Humabon. "That wasn't an easy thing to do."

"No. It was not. But I had to decide." Andres knew what he meant. In that one action, Dantu had chosen Andres and the Spanish over his own people.

"It was a wise choice," said Andres. "I hope Legaspi sees this flag coming down and makes a wise choice, too. If this doesn't stop him, at least he will approach with caution."

"Come with me," said Dantu as he pulled on Andres' hand and started to lead him out of the courtyard, "I know where the raja of this place is. And he is not well guarded." After leaving the parapet, Dantu had made his way around the other side of the mess hall, looking for a way to leave the compound without attracting attention. It was then, just a few minutes before he was diverted to the struggle between Andres and Humabon, that he discovered Soliman's palace in a cluster of buildings at the rear of the piazza.

Andres hurried after the boy whose young legs carried him swiftly along the pavement. Andres was beginning to feel the fatigue of his day's adventures. The sea battle, the burning skiffs, the man on the parapet, and then Humabon. They were running toward the mess hall when the force of the blast hit Andres' chest like a gale force wind, driving him backward onto the pavement. A cloud of dust followed and the sound of the explosion echoed in his ears.

Before him the mess hall had been elevated thirty or forty yards in the air. It seemed to hover, collapse, and then fall to earth in wreckage. A series of explosions followed as the powder kegs of the munitions store ignited. Cid-Hamel had done his job well. The parapet had collapsed; the room under the veranda was aflame and the floor on which the cannons set had sunk. Those cannons that had not fallen into the room below were pointing awkwardly and uselessly to the sky. "That will make things easier for Legaspi," said Andres as he and Dantu ducked around a corner and into the great hall of Soliman's palace.

There was much confusion. Where before the attack had seemed an entertainment for the palace guard, now there was chaos. Usually in such a turn of events there is first a plan of action, a strategy to address the new situation. But on this occasion, the Moro went directly from confidence to despair and resignation.

Andres found Soliman sitting at a table amid his papers. He was surrounded by men who looked more like accountants than military guards. Several of them were Chinese. He was dressed in silks like an eastern potentate. He did not seem alarmed.

"Well, young man," he said in a calm voice to Andres, a voice belonging more to a man about to introduce a dinner guest than to someone who had just lost a battle, his livelihood, and perhaps his life. "You seem to have seen through our little masquerade."

"It does seem that way, if that is what you wish to call it." Andres had authority in his voice, the confidence of someone who had just beat his opponent in the last game of a long match. Andres moved toward Soliman with his knife drawn as he spoke. Soliman did not move or give any sign of resistance. The men around the table, stepped back, as if in surrender.

"What do you suggest we do now?" Soliman asked. My men, the few that are faithful to me, are in disarray. The rest along with the townspeople are fleeing for the mountains in the interior. They will return when they know things have settled down. Saluddin's men, foolishly, are trying to get back to him now. He will probably cut off their heads for their failure here. So what do you wish from me."

"Nothing, I suppose." Andres was a bit confused. Up to this point he had been uncertain of the outcome, and had worked against great odds. Now it all seemed so simple. Were there any further deceptions? "No wait. Some of my people are approaching the citadel from the north. What do you know about that?"

"They were ambushed. They are probably all dead." Soliman was matter-of-fact in his pronouncement.

"Send somebody to tell your men that the fighting is over," Andres ordered. "Tell your men to surrender."

Soliman summoned a guard, spoke briefly with him, and he left hurriedly. "As you wish. I always comply with the man who has the heaviest cargo. Anything else? Would you like some food." Andres was starving. He had not eaten since dawn. He knew Dantu was hungry too. Andres did not even have to respond. Soliman had snapped his fingers and a bowl of fruit was placed on the table before them, and a jug of sweet-smelling wine.

Andres wondered if de Goiti had been killed in the ambush. Humabon's treachery! And what of Cid-Hamel. Had he survived the blast in the mess hall? Both questions were soon answered. Within an hour, de Goiti and his surviving troops marched into the palace leading Manila's other raja Alcandoro in triumph. Two of his men were carrying Cid-Hamel, who was badly injured, but not mortally.

"What's this? de Goiti asked surprised when he saw Andres and Dantu sitting at table with Soliman. He had thought the victory was his when Alcandoro lifted his attack and surrendered to him. "How did you get here?"

"It's a long story, de Goiti," Andres replied. "If you don't mind I'll save it for Legaspi when he arrives."

Legaspi landed below the bamboo wall and met with no resistance. He made his way to Soliman's palace an hour after de Goiti's arrival. Andres presented Soliman to him, but there was no time for his story. Legaspi thanked him for his service and then turned to the business of taking over control of the city.

That night there was a great banquet in Soliman's hall. It quickly became a ceremony for the transference of power.

Legaspi began with a speech. "By the grace of God and in the name of Philip, King of Spain and the Islas del Poniente known as the Philippines, I claim this island, its possessions, and its people as subjects of King Philip."

Soliman raised a glass and answered, "I declare my allegiance to King Philip and promise to be his vassal from this time forth."

Legaspi then turned to Alcandoro. "Do you swear allegiance to our King and swear on pain of death to renounce hostilities toward the rightful possessors of this island, of all these islands?" Alcandoro agreed as Soliman had, but he added, "We may give up to you now. But there will never be peace in these islands as long as Saluddin is left free to prey on them. He is an evil you must destroy."

"Let him go for now," Legaspi said. "Our victory is sweet. Tonight we celebrate." He raised his glass and faced the men gathered around him. "Gentlemen, a toast. To King Philip."

"And to our General," the men shouted.

Legaspi then continued in a more somber tone. "Our mission is nearing completion, gentlemen. We have secured most of the islands. And with Manila as our base we can control shipping and trade throughout the archipelago, from China to the Moluccas. For your service there are rewards. You each will have estates and an allotment of natives to work your land. Andres, you are to take possession of a large portion of Cebu, and the land just north of Manila, for yourself and your heirs. De Goiti, this land on Cebu is yours, and a portion of Panay. Find suitable lands on Leyte, Samar, and Masbate for yourself and your men, since you discovered these islands. Salcedo, Mindoro is yours to divide among your men. After you have settled with Saluddin. But first I want you to explore up the coast of Luzon and take possession of the northern territories for King Philip. I plan to return to my camp at Panay. I will return to set up headquarters here next year. Manila will be my capital. In the meantime I want you, Andres, and Father Martin to remain here and establish the settlement. The natives will return soon and we will need your skills in language and leadership to keep things under control.

Andres was taken by surprise. After all he had done that day to bring Legaspi a victory. To be rewarded with exile from Itel and his home on Cebu. He could only stutter, "But, sir.... I..."

Legaspi continued. "These are your orders, Sergeant. This is where you are needed. Your affairs on Cebu will have to wait. And now, gentlemen, here is to a restful night after a tiring day. To Philip. And Manila of the Philippines."

* * * *

That night when Legaspi gave Andres his orders and stationed him in Manila he thought he might never see Itel again. That was two years ago. He would never have guessed then that now he would be dressed in Chinese silks sitting at a mahogany writing table from Seville, waiting for Father Martin to arrive for their annual celebration of their victory over Saluddin and Soliman twenty-four months ago. Martin had begun immediately to build his church. And after some of Andres' men fished two Chinese merchants out of the bay when their junk sank, the Chinese rewarded the "humane" Spaniards with trading rights to the mainland, and Andres was on his way to becoming a very rich man. Then, true to his word, after a year, Legaspi had returned from Panay. It was a rainy spring night. Andres and Martin were having a little supper in Martin's half-finished rectory. The door swung open and there was Legaspi standing in the doorway, beaming with pride and confidence.

They spoke for a few moments. Legaspi noted Andres' prosperity and Martin's added weight. Then he asked to see Andres the next morning for a full briefing. He stood at the doorway once more, turned to Andres before exiting and said, "Oh, by the way, Andres, I have a little surprise for you." He ducked under the sill and disappeared into the darkness, leaving a vacant frame for a second. Then it was filled. "Itel!" Andres shouted. "Is it you?" Itel appeared in the doorway, hesitated, then stepped down into the room. Martin cleaned off the dishes they had been using and retired into the next room.

"Is it you?" Andres was still incredulous. Then he noticed the bundle that Itel carried carefully under her arm. She held it forward and unwrapped the blanket. It was a child of less than a year.

"What is his name," Andres asked. "What is our son's name?"

"Carlos," she answered. "After the little priest in the village." She stepped forward again. Andres reached out and threw his arms around her. He held her tightly, but softly. Little Carlos wriggled between them and let out a tiny cry.

And now Carlos, at a year and a half, was crawling and stumbling towards him, falling at the base of the chair Andres sat in before his mahogany table. "We are a family," Andres thought as he pushed the chair back carefully so as not to pinch Carlos' fingers or toes. "But what kind of family?" Andres had done well in the trading business. He had ships bringing merchandise from China and galleons carrying it to New Spain in return for silver and gold. But he could not strike a bargain with his family. He could not negotiate a deal with Itel. As he became more prosperous, she became more wild. The jungle would return in her as it had in their child. Little Carlos would not wear the clothes Andres bought for him. Or Itel would undress him as soon as Andres left the room. He would nestle against Itel's breast but he would not sit still in Andres' lap. He was surely Itel's child, but was he Andres' too?

A knock at the door brought a serving woman into the room to collect little Carlos who continued to scurry across the floor, naked. Itel followed her into the room and she handed the child to his mother. Andres opened the door and Father Martin strode into the room. He was carrying a bottle of Madeira.

"Good evening to you all," he bellowed cheerfully. "Evening, Andres. And how is little Carlos this fine night? And his mother? Beautiful as ever. Good evening, Lady Urdaneta."

Itel offered her free hand which Martin shook. He perhaps would have preferred to kiss it in courtly manner, but Itel gave him reason to suspect this would not be to her liking.

"Say goodnight, Carlos," Itel said holding the boy up like a small animal. "We must let the men talk." Itel then turned on her heels and shut the door behind her.

Andres sat at the table in the center of the room and began to uncork Martin's bottle of wine. "You see how it is, Martin. I dress him in the finest silk blouse. And she takes it off. I give her this fine house and servants. And she consorts with the market women. And she takes Carlos with her, and he plays with the native children.... in the mud. What is the point of it all? I tell her he is the son of a rich Spaniard and the grandson of a Dato. And she says, "a Dato, yes, a raja, no." I tell you, things are getting out of control.

Martin collected two glasses from the side table and moved over to the table where Andres sat. He placed the glasses down for Andres to fill with the dark red liquid. "She is not a carabao, Andres. You cannot domesticate her."

Andres raised his glass and examined the color of the wine in the light from the oil lamp overhead. "I just want to love her, Martin." There was desperation in his voice.

Martin knew Andres had a problem. But he did not have a solution. So he decided it was better, among friends, to change the subject. "And how is business?" he asked. "Your business men seem to work only one month out of the year."

"Actually it's more like three. Trade takes time, Martin. The merchandise must get here and then be consigned, and then shipped to Acapulco. And then there is more time before the silver returns."

"And what do you do?" Martin sipped from his glass. There was mischief in his voice.

Andres laughed, "I wait, and take my profit. It is nice being the middle man. Manila is in the middle, and I am the man in the middle. Like you."

"Like me? How so?"

"Like you are the middle man between God and the lost souls here on earth. And what is your profit?"

"Heaven, Andres. Heaven."

"Yes, but you have to work twelve months out of the year for it. Speaking of business, I have some on the dock right now. A junk has come in with a cargo of silk, porcelain and ivory. There is musk, borax, and camphor too, I believe. Want to come along?"

It was late evening and Andres was leaving his comfortable home to conduct business. Maybe this is what is causing trouble at home, Martin thought. On the way to the dock Andres continued to talk business. Martin came to the conclusion that he was trying to convince himself more than Martin.

"I tell you, Martin, there is more money to be made here than anyone has yet imagined."

"If there is something for the church, I want to know," said Martin, trying to pretend that he was interested in the subject that so engaged Andres.

"You have lands, don't you? On Luzon. On Cebu. All over the islands. And you grow things on this land? Rice. Corn. Well, Right now we all grow just what we consume. We sell what comes from China. But what if we could sell what we grow. What if the galleons could take something of ours in addition to the consignments? The only thing of any worth that I have sent to Spain is Dantu. If we could sell directly to Spain, we would no longer be middle men. We could make all the profits for ourselves.

"What are you thinking of?"

"I am thinking of sugar." It was a bold idea. One that would make Andres and men like him a fortune. But the Spanish government was not ready to listen to such a proposition, and Andres knew it.

When they reached the docks they found a Chinese junk bobbing next to the pier. Bundles of merchandise were stacked on the dock. From behind one of the stacks a tall dark figure appeared. A figure out of Andres' past, not from his conscious memory but out of his nightmares. It was Saluddin!

"You!" Andres mingled fear and rage in his voice. "What are you doing here? Have you so little regard for your life?" Andres drew his sword and stepped forward. Saluddin did not flinch. Martin stepped between them, his huge bulk obscuring Saluddin from Andres' sight. Saluddin quietly, with the aid of this distraction, cocked the hammer on his pistol.

"I have much more regard for my life than for yours," Saluddin threatened.

"Now gentlemen," Martin interjected, trying to forestall any violence and bring the tempers down.

"He's no gentleman," Martin. "He's a lying, murdering, treacherous, bastard."

"Now hold on, son." Saluddin's voice was calm, businesslike. No need to get off on the wrong foot. I believe you are here to talk business with these gentlemen. Well, that means you're going to do business with me. You see, they already have come to terms. I let them sail in here with their goods. For a price. I'll let your ships sail out. Also for a price. I could attack them and take what I want. But this seems so much easier. And I am getting old."

"That's blackmail!" Andres was incensed. He also saw some of his profits disappearing into the pirate's pocket.

"I call it business. I'm just taking my percentage of the commerce that goes in and out of here. Isn't that what you do? I told you once before, we are much more alike, you and I, than you would care to admit. Think it over. I'll be in touch. You can take this cargo as a gesture of my good will. On account, so to speak. Let me know your decision before that galleon sets sail. Just think. For a few pesetas, you'll be able to sleep soundly at night."

That night Andres did not sleep soundly. But it wasn't because of Saluddin. He would play the pirate's game for awhile. Let him protect the shipping from China and to Mexico. At least this way Andres had only one pirate to deal with. Later when the trading was even more profitable he could afford to go after Saluddin. Or maybe the government would find it necessary. Until then he would do business with the pirate.

No. That was not why he did not sleep well. It was Itel. And the boy. They had argued again. When he had returned from the docks, Itel was waiting for him in the kitchen. She was wearing her sarong and doing the menial chores of the house with the serving women. Andres, as always, complained. She should be more mindful of his... their... position in the new society that was forming in the city. There were Spaniards there in great numbers now, from fine families. They dressed nicely, were building fine houses, and had fine dinner parties.

"I am yours," Itel said. "I will always be yours. But I will not be theirs. I must still be myself. And you must still be yourself. You are trying to be something you are not. And you are trying to make me something I am not."

"But we cannot stay the way we were," Andres pleaded earnestly. "The world is changing, this city is changing, and we must change with it. We are the ones changing it. Can't you understand that?"

"I don't want to change that much. You have already taken my brother away from me. Sent him off to a foreign land."

"That is to educate him," Andres interrupted. In Spain he will learn what he needs to know to be a fine gentleman. To run my business. To be a leader in our society."

"All I know is that I have lost him. And I will not lose my son. You won't take him away from me, too." Itel was angry, angrier than Andres had ever seen her. She ripped at her sarong and pulled it from her body. She stood there before him, gloriously naked, like she had stood before him in their hut on Cebu. She was defiant. Her eyes shown in the night. She pulled at the necklace with the crucifix hanging from it. Andres had given it to her on the anniversary of her appearance in that doorway the night she arrived from Cebu. She broke the chain from her neck and threw it at Andres as she ran from the room.

That night when Andres awoke, it was not Saluddin that disturbed his slumber. It was a feeling he had that he was alone. He thought of those nights on Cebu when Itel would disappear in the dark. He rolled over and felt the bed beside him. It was empty. Panicking, he ran into the next room. The crib was empty too. He ran downstairs and out onto the veranda and stared into the darkness under a full moon that left a trail of silver shimmering on the water in the direction of Cebu. The rage built up inside him, starting in his stomach and rising to his chest. It turned to pain and then to sorrow before it escaped from his tortured lips in a howl of agony and regret.

My dearest Dantu,

By the grace of God and the Captain of the San Lucas, I am in possession of your letter of December 4. It is now May on the fifth anniversary of our victory and conquest of Manila. And almost to the day, that day I will always remember, when you and Itel appeared in the door of Father Martin's little church. You had come all the way from Cebu to be with me. And now you are in Spain, and Itel is gone with our son. Back to Cebu and to I know not what.

I take pen in hand to tell you of this year's trading season and the great fortune we have had. I trust your studies are proceeding with all of the success that your industry and God's will can provide. I am delighted to hear of your visit to Seville in the summer and of your interview with Bishop Jofre. He is a great friend of Father Martin who sends his love to you and says he remembers you in his prayers. Martin has become a very important man here and will, we are hopeful, become the first Bishop of Manila. Never one to take the blessings of good fortune as free from taint, he believes of course that a bishop quite unfamiliar with these islands but more familiar with the courts in Madrid will be offered the benefice instead. The conquerors he has told me more than once are only good for conquest. It is the puppets who take over in the end.

Fifteen junks found their way into Manila harbor last spring and I dispatched two galleons with 712 pieces of Chinese silk of every imaginable weave and pattern and 22,000 pieces of gilt china and porcelain ware. This spring there arrived 20 more junks, heavy with silk, stockings, skirts, velvet bodices, cloaks and robes. And there were fans, and women's combs, and bibelots of ivory, jade and jasper, and bronze thimbles, and finely carved boxes, and spices, and tea, and perfume. They are as hungry for our silver as Acapulco and Madrid are for their fineries. We are the gateway between east and west, Dantu. Our city has the finest location in the world. There is a harvest of riches here.

The city has grown with God's blessing. Martin says it has become a copy of that Tyre so praised by Ezekiel. There are two new churches in the

Intramuros and the governor's palace with its many windows opening onto the sea and the Plaza is nearing completion. It is very beautiful and sightly with its two courts and its upper and lower galleries raised on stout pillars. There is a new hospital and the physicians and apothecaries perform miracles treating the natives for their diseases. The better Tagalogs now live beyond the walls of the city in the quarter of Malate which fronts the beach; others have settled in the lowlands beyond the walls. There are many Chinese among us now. They live together across the Pasig river and have many shops for goods that we need in our houses.

But you must see Intramuros. It is a splendid city with a gay social life for the Spaniards who have ventured here for their fortunes. Those who have survived shipwreck and fever crowd into the streets of Intramuros showing off their ornaments and fine clothes which are so readily available to them. The men and women go on promenades in the courtyard of the Cabildo. The city is a paradise for them providing as it does an abundance of food and the pleasures of life that humans are wont to enjoy. It is more than I could have ever dreamed it could be. And it is yours, my son, when you return. All I have will be yours, and I need you to help me with it.

And now to the story of your sister and your little nephew. Carlos has grown steadily since you left. He became like the jungle, growing out of control. Itel allowed him to run about unclothed. She let him play with the children in the worst parts of the town. And she herself mingled with the washerwomen, the maids, the field hands. I told her this was not the proper behavior for the wife of an important merchant. She would not listen. Martin told me she was not a carabao to be trained. The boy, he said, must be given his head.

He was right. I put the bit in their mouths. And they have left me. For several months, Itel had been disappearing at night as she did occasionally in Cebu years ago. You know of this, Dantu, do you not? You went with her to the clearing in the jungle where you worshipped your god in the carabao and your ancestors in the blue bird. For several days she did not return. I was frantic. The boy is so young. I followed them to Cebu. I went back into a dream I thought I had awakened from. The settlement was overgrown. Many of your people had returned to the woods. The grass was encroaching on the streets with nobody there to cut it back. I stopped by the chapel to see Brother Carlos. He was still there with several nuns. The church was finished half in stone, the rest in wood. There had not been enough help to finish the construction as it was planned. Carlos was tired as he cut away at the weeds growing up around the pavement of the little patio with the figure of the Virgin in the niche on the wall.

That night I went into the jungle. I was not sure where I was going, but I seemed pulled by a force. I have known for some time there is a power in the jungle, a power of life and a power of death. But I have not understood it. I found myself at the clearing. Itel in her robes with the figure of Laon. And little Carlos, young, innocent, sitting atop a giant carabao. I had seen this before. The people were there, chanting. Not so many as I had seen years before, but more than there had been last year, or last month, I imagine. When one version of the power recedes, another takes its place. Itel and Martin. And Saluddin. I realized that the power was one with Itel and she with it. It is not a power that I can understand. Perhaps one merely recognizes it. One uses it, for good. Or for evil.

You will finish your studies soon, Dantu. And then you will come home, home to Manila. You are my son now. You must come home.

Your loving father,

Don Andres Urdaneta

* * *

Carlos Martinez fingered the aging parchment lovingly, running his thumb over the signature as if to feel the presence of Andres Urdaneta lingering there. He stubbed his cigar out in a jade ashtray and muttered, "There was more pirate in him than he knew."

It was an ancient letter, full of strange names. Itel and Dantu, and Saluddin, and Laon the god of ancestors all mixed up with accounting figures and cargos from the early galleon trade in the islands. He liked to imagine what these people were, these ancient ancestors of his. The letter had been in Carlos' family forever. He often took it out and read it over. Especially in these days of trouble, this time of revolution when the future of his nation was at stake. There was a spirit in the letter that helped him to know who he was, who they all were, that gave him strength. A Power he needed to understand. To use.

"They are waiting for you, sir." A servant, small and brown in his loose-fitting barong, had entered the room behind Carlos. His words broke the old man's reverie. "Fine, fine, I will be right there."

Carlos delicately folded the parchment and returned it to its velvet pouch which he deposited in a small drawer of the mahogany writing desk at which he sat. The desk, a very ancient piece from Seville, or so some antique dealer once told him, faced a window that looked out over a sea of green that stretched to the horizon. The sugar cane swayed in the late April breeze. The heat was already beginning to rise and was visible in the air above the canes.

"And you might bring us something cool to drink," Carlos requested after the retreating house boy. "Angry men have dry throats."

The tall double doors creaked as Carlos opened them to enter his dining room. Around the long oval table sat men like himself, men of power and wealth who had turned the soil of their islands to useful produce and into riches for themselves. But they had suffered Spanish arrogance long enough. They had been patient long enough and had thrown their support behind the rebels. Now they were men faced with a decision.

"Have you heard the news, Don Martinez?" cried Enrico Hernandez enthusiastically. Enrico was the son of Jean Hernandez, a plantation owner who had recently died. The son, as is usual, took his father's place on the board. "We have won. The Spanish are in retreat. They have taken refuge in Intramuros where they sulk like wounded dogs."

"Wounded dogs can still bite," Manuel Lopez advised in his most dignified tone as he took a glass of lemonade offered him by a servant, spooned in several portions of sugar and gave the contents a quick stir to punctuate his observation.

"But we have still won. You can't deny that." Enrico was becoming insistent. He wanted someone to agree with him.

"It's not as simple as all that." Jean Luis Velasquez leaned forward, his elbows on the table, as if he were conquering territory. The more space one occupied, it seemed, the more right one had to speak. Velasquez based his right on his great bulk and his great wealth. He owned the largest sugar plantation in Negros and was the leader of the conservative faction of growers.

"We will have to root them out, of course," he said to Enrico. "And that will take time. And we don't want to destroy the city in the process. We must be cautious."

"Being cautious has gotten us nowhere," snapped Raul Dominguez. "Has Aguinaldo been cautious to get us this far? Was Rizal cautious?"

"Rizal was betrayed!"

"He was a fool!"

The voices raised all around as accusations shot back and forth across the table. "Gentlemen, gentlemen," Carlos soothed them down. "We are here to decide about the future, not debate about the past. We are about to become pawns in a chess game played by nations who do not have our interests in mind. I for one do not wish to continue as a puppet with someone else pulling the strings."

"Yes. We all fully agree," Lopez acknowledged. " We have won the battle in the countryside, thanks to General Aquinaldo and his brave men.

Now what are we to do about the Spanish garrison in Intramuros? How should we proceed?"

"We can starve them out," Hernandez offered. "They won't get any help from Spain. Spain has enough trouble in Cuba. And she is at war with the States."

"Yes. And what about the Americans?" Velasquez asked. "Where do they fit in? We will need them, you know."

Enrico did not know. "Need them? Why? We have taken the battle to the walls of the city of Manila. The Americans have their war with Spain in Cuba. This is our war."

"But after the war, my boy. What about after the war? Spain has provided us with our markets. Where do you think the sugar and rice from your father's fields were sold? Did it find its way to a plate in Quezon or in Madrid? When there are no more Spanish you will hope that your sugar will be sweetening the coffee of some businessmen in San Francisco. Yes, my friends, we will need the Americans."

"And they will need us!" It was Aguinaldo. He had come through the doors just in time to hear Velasquez' last words. I have just come from the Americans aboard Admiral Dewey's ship. They have asked us to storm the wall of the city while they engage the Spanish warships in the harbor. Tomorrow at dawn! It promises to be a grand day for our people. Victory on land and at sea and the islands will be ours."

He raised a glass of lemonade over the table. "Carlos, come, something more potent than this for such an auspicious occasion." Carlos gave the orders and two house boys went scurrying for the port which they brought in on carved silver trays, the delicate crystal glasses ringing a sweet harmony as they jostled on the tray.

"To the Philippines," Aguinaldo toasted, raising his glass in a broad gesture which the others followed.

"To tomorrow morning and victory," extolled young Enrico.

"To our markets in America," said Valasquez and Lopez in unison.

"And to the work that is yet to be done," Carlos said. He knew fully well that a battlefield victory was only a prologue to the truly hard work of forming a government, writing a constitution, and wrestling with the dangers of freedom. But tomorrow, it seems, they would be free. Carlos sipped at the port and thought, "The wine of victory is sweet."

* * *

Douglas Waters pulled at the last foamy ounce of tepid beer and dropped his cigarette into the green bottle. "God, where'd they get this stuff," he thought as he gently placed the bottle on its side, gave it a brief nudge with his forefinger and watched it roll overboard into the sea beneath Admiral Dewey's flagship. Waters had been on board since the admiral had steamed east ten days ago from Hong Kong with orders to contain the Spanish fleet at Manila. America had declared war on Spain April 20. If there was a war to be covered in Cuba, Douglas Waters would be the *Post's* man in Manila.

He had been waiting all morning for an interview with the admiral. The hallway outside the admiral's cabin served as a waiting room. Waters had inspected the pictures on the wall several times over. They told a history of naval battles going back to Odysseus and Poseidon. The famed battle of the Monitor and the Merrimack was his personal favorite, and someone else's too, since it occupied the favored position of the small panel just above Admiral Dewey's cabin door. "Now this is a sea battle," thought Waters. "How in the world did they keep afloat, made out of metal and all?"

The door to the admiral's cabin sprang open and Captain Buckley, the admiral's aide, stepped briskly into the hall.

"Any chance he'll see me soon, captain? I'm going to have these pictures memorized pretty soon."

"Just hold your horses, son. There's a big confab going on in there right now. You'll get to know all you need to know when the time's come." Waters eyed Buckley up and down and squinted at him as if to see if his shape would change. Buckley was a decent enough sort, Waters decided. Not real military, but friendly. He was from the southwest where the people are as open as the country. "That's a good line," Waters thought, "I'll have to work it in somewhere." Buckley was rolling a cigarette. "That's why he came out here, Waters concluded, to have a smoke, not to check on me."

"Yeah, well I'm a reporter and what I do is report the news. Get it. N-E-W-S," he spelled it out. "If my paper wanted an historian they would have hired Herodotus." This was a game Waters often played, dropping an esoteric name to see what kind of person he was dealing with.

"I prefer Thucydides myself," Buckley shot back. "He's more imaginative; he doesn't so much report the way things actually were, but the way they should have been."

Waters was surprised, but pleased. "Yeah, right, but you see I'm not an historian, I'm a reporter and my job is to report things the way they are."

Suddenly the cabin door swung into the hall and an official-looking man in a smart uniform with medals glistening from his chest filled the opening. Beyond him, Waters could see several men bending over a table cluttered with maps and navigational charts. The uniformed man turned sharply and saluted the men in the room. Then he turned crisply on his heels like a man folding his napkin after a meal he did not like, and with short, quick steps mounted the metal stairs leading out onto the deck. Two very junior officers followed dutifully in his wake as if to collect the sound of his sabre which clanged against the railings.

"What was that?" asked Waters, registering his surprise. "That was a Spanish officer, wasn't it?"

"Emissary from the city," Buckley offered matter-of-factly.

"What's he doing here? I thought we were at war with them."

"That's what they are working on." He motioned to the men behind the cabin door.

"What do you mean?"

"They're making arrangements for the battle tomorrow."

"With the enemy?" Waters was incredulous.

"That fellow you just saw here. He came to tell us that his men in the city are diseased and tired. They're hungry and they don't want to fight anymore."

"So the Filipinos have won."

"Right. But everybody concerned agrees that it's better if the Americans win."

"What do you mean? How can we win anything?" Waters sat down and pulled the makings of a cigarette out of his shirt pocket. His shirt was wet with sweat and the papers were all soggy. Buckley tossed some paper over to him and continued his explanation.

"You see, they don't want to surrender to a bunch of savages, the way they put it. I was in there. I heard it. They say they've ruled these people for four hundred years and they'll be damned if they'll give up to them. It's like giving your clothes to a servant and then standing naked there in front of him. It's too embarrassing."

"They'll surrender to us, though," he went on. Waters licked the paper of his makings and lit a match to it. The hot smoke burned his throat. He exhaled a cloud that rose to the ceiling and mingled with the smoke from the Merrimack's guns. Buckley was getting more animated. His interest in the tale was obvious. His eyes brightened. He spread his arms wide in a gesture of openness that says, "This is unbelievable, but I'm telling you the truth."

"So how are they going to surrender to us? We're out here, and they're barricaded in there."

"That's what they've just been arranging. We're going to stage a naval battle. We'll load our guns with powder and no balls, and so will they, and then tomorrow morning we light up the bay with harmless fireworks. Then after awhile, they run up a white flag, and later when the time comes, we can say they lost to us, not to the Filipinos."

"I'll be damned. But what am I going to report? I came here to cover a war, not a stage play. What if I tell my readers this is all a sham?"

"Do your readers want a war or a scandal? What are they reading about back in New York right now? About Cuba, I bet. And this is a sure thing. The winner is already decided."

Waters leaned back against the cabin door. He raised his leg to expose the bottom of his right shoe and crushed out his cigarette. All he could think about was a prizefight, one he had lost money on because the fighter he bet on went in the tank.

"You stick with us, son. We'll give you a war you can be proud of."

* * *

It was a pair of younger hands that reverently pulled the velvet packet out of the mahogany drawer and spread it out on the ancient writing table. Carlos' son, Pedro, pushed aside the other papers that cluttered the desk top to make way for the treasured document. A copy of the Malolos Constitution his father had labored so hard on fell to the floor. It was the long drawn out negotiations between Spain and America that had weakened him. The Americans claimed victory over Spain in the Battle of Manila and the spoils were theirs. And then in November the day after his son, Raul was born, the Spaniards had ceded the islands to the Americans who paid twenty million dollars for the public works and improvements they had made. Improvements! In four hundred years the Spanish took our lands, our livelihoods, they drained our marshes and our spirits. Pedro was repeating to himself things his father had told him, over and over. And he would tell them over and over to Raul. And now it was February. The rains were still standing in pools in the ruts in the roads and in the furrows of the fields which were untended. The men had gone off. The fighting had started again. A Filipino soldier did not answer an American sentry and he was killed. The next day an American was found. His body mutilated. His head cut off. All this just before the U.S. Senate voted to annex the Philippines. The American Vice-President cast the deciding vote. What went through his mind when he made his decision? Was it revenge for the mutilation of the soldier? Did he believe, as many thought, that the savages of the Philippines needed to be civilized? Was a war the most convenient way? Was he longing to provide a market for Philippine sugar? Had the islands driven out the Spanish only to let the Americans come in?

Pedro's eyes fell upon the parchment. He read his far-away ancestors' words: "When one version of the power recedes, another takes its place." There was a power loose in the islands again. A power for good. A controlled rage. A power for evil. Deceit and oppression, hunger and disease, the starvation of a people, the land laid waste, mutilated bodies, stomachs split open, heads on a pike. O Dangerous Grace.

Part Two: GHOSTS

TEN

"Senator Martinez! Senator Martinez!"

The young man leapt to his feet, nearly knocking over the sweating Coke can on his paper-littered desk. He shoved his chair backward into a huge pile of yellowed folders, which swayed and bulged at the middle. With one hand he tried to steady them, twisting his head toward the small old man in the doorway.

It really was Senator Raul Martinez, Sr.! In his doorway! Anyone would recognize the senator, his gray swept-back, thinning hair, his thin, brown, scarred face, anyone in the Philippines would recognize that face.

The face in the doorway smiled. "May I come in?"

"Why, Senator, why, yes, please," the little clerk bleated. He abandoned the swaying stack of folders behind him, which crashed in a dusty heap, snaked his way past other stacks, and gestured to a homely wooden chair in the middle of the office.

"Yes, Senator, right here, please sit down, I'm honored," the clerk tried to say as he pushed another pile of papers from the chair onto the floor.

"Please, Senator, here, just a moment ..."

The Senator stood in the doorway, smiling, then deftly worked his way around and through the stacks of books, folders, charts, maps, cardboard boxes, bulging three-ring binders, and tattered envelopes.

"Senator, sir, can I get you anything, a cool drink perhaps?"
"No, thank you," the Senator replied, sitting, at last on the office's lone chair. The mounds of papers around him looked like stalagmites, the books and papers hanging over the edges of the bookshelves along the walls looked like stalactites, the little clerk looked like some small, sun-shunning, cave dweller, suddenly stirred by unwelcome light.

"Am I disturbing you?" the Senator asked.

"Oh, no, not at all, Senator, I was just working on a few things," the clerk said, pointing vaguely nowhere in particular. He was standing next to the Senator, but even standing next to the seated man, he still looked small.

"Why don't you sit down, then, perhaps we can talk," the Senator said.

"Oh yes, by all means, of course," the clerk said. He bustled back behind his desk, feeling a little safer there, on the way, though, tumbling over two more stacks of papers. A cloud of dust drifted upward from each fallen stack. The light in the office from the overhead Flourescent light twinkled with dust.

"Senator, I'm really honored, no one told me, I would have ..." said the little clerk.

But the Senator seemed to ignore him.

"How is your sister's brother-in-law, is he working hard?" the Senator asked.

The little clerk thought and thought. He had begun to sweat like his abandoned Coke can. His sister. Her brother-in-law. Then he remembered. That good-for-nothing! Yes! His father had gone to the Senator for help, his father and the Senator were both in the war together, his father had asked the Senator to find a job for his sister's husband's brother, and the Senator had found something, in the post-office wasn't it? Yes, that was it, but I haven't seen him in years, the clerk thought. How do I know what he's doing, the good-for-nothing.

"Oh yes, Senator, he's working very hard, you'd be proud of him."

"And your father, his pension problems are all straightened out now, I hope?"

Pension problems? Yes, of course, the Senator had helped there too. And this job, for that matter, I got this because of the Senator. He wants something. Oh, no.

"Yes, Senator, we're all in your debt for all you've done for us over the years, and I really want to thank you too ..."

The Senator smiled, and waved away the thanks with a gentle gesture of his crooked, arthritic fingers. He had, of course, looked all this up in his vast collection of index-cards. People he knew, contacts here and there and everywhere, people for whom he had found jobs, old friends, debts he owed, debts owed him, all jotted down over the years. The collection was vast. And it had never failed him. "Well, Juan, I've come to ask your help." The

Senator had looked up Juan's name before he came. It was Juan. If necessary, the senator could name Juan's parents' names, his sister's name, her husband's name, even the name of the useless brother-in-law.

Juan was taken aback. The Senator knew his name! And now he wanted a favor. Oh no.

"Senator, what can I do? I will do anything, of course, but I'm only a humble clerk. As you see. I just catalog things for the national archives, I'm just a catalog clerk ..."

"Oh, no, Juan, I'm sure you can help me. It's a small thing, but, you see, a private thing. Between you and me. That's why I've come to you for help."

"Yes, Senator, of course, anything." But Juan was afraid. The Senator was a very powerful man. And Juan was in his debt. He could never turn him down. But Juan was simply a clerk, just a very small clerk, in the National Archives, and he could be fired in a moment. What if the Senator wanted something, well, bad, what if Juan lost his job? But then, if he turned the Senator down, then he would surely lose his job too. Oh, no.

"You see, Juan, I'm looking for something, and what better place to look than the National Archives? Where my good friend Juan works?"

"Yes, Senator."

"What I'm looking for is this. At the end of the war, when I was still a young man," the Senator smiled his crooked smile, there were gaps between his teeth, one tooth was silver, Juan noticed, "before you were even born, an American came here, to the Philippines, to make a film. A documentary. About the war. About the guerrilla war against the Japanese. His name was Pitfield. Ralph Waldo Emerson Pitfield. A very American name, don't you think?"

Juan had no idea why that odd-sounding name was particularly American, but he said, "Oh yes, Senator, very American."

"Anyway," the Senator continued, "this Pitfield came to make a film. He interviewed me, and many of the men who fought with me, and many others. He collected papers and diaries and things like that. All for this film of his.

"But you see, Juan, the film was never made. All those materials were collected together, those bits of film, and letters, and papers, and put in a large box. There was a big debate about what to do with that box. Some wanted it destroyed. Others wanted everything made public. I remember it because I was in politics then, it was one of my very first debates. The solution was a compromise. The box was neither opened to the public nor destroyed. It was sealed, and placed in the National Archives, sealed in perpetuity. Isn't that foolish, Juan, to keep something and then say 'sealed in perpetuity'?"

"Yes, Senator. Of course."

"Well, everyone, I suppose, has forgotten about that box. But, you know, Juan, I'm an old man now, and I think more about the past than about the future. About my adventures during the war. In fact, I'm thinking about writing my memoirs, and I happened to remember that box. And I wondered whether I could go through it. It would help with my memoirs, you see."

Even as he said this, the Senator thought: no, this is a lie. This box has to do with death. With terror. With bodies fished out of trash heaps. With evil that has come back. With evil I must find and kill. Finally. But the Senator did not say this. He did not cease to smile gently at Juan.

"So, I thought, who can help me find this old box? Who would know where it might be? And then I remembered my dear friend Juan."

Juan was thinking now. So this is it. It is not such a big thing after all.

"I'm sure the Director would be glad to help, Senator ..."

"No, Juan, you see, that would take time. The box is sealed, you see, and it would take a long time to get at it. And I'm an old man, why, I'd be enjoying my heavenly reward by the time I got to the box. You know how the bureaucracy works!"

"Yes, Senator," Juan smiled. But only on the outside. He was worried now. If this thing was sealed, who knew what was in it. And if he told the Director that he had given anyone access to it, even a Senator, he could get in serious trouble. Juan started to sweat again.

"And of course, there's no harm in it," the Senator said, looking and smiling at Juan. "Why, it has been almost fifty years since the end of the war. Fifty years. There's surely no harm in opening a fifty-year-old box!" No harm, the Senator thought.

No harm. Perhaps not. Perhaps this is a wild goose chase. But there could be harm. There could be death in it. For the box held memories. Ghosts. Maybe the ghost which had come back to Manila. The ghost which slaughtered people, flayed them, beheaded them. At least a sign of the ghost. In that box.

Juan was a young man, not quite twenty-four. For him, anything older than his own lifetime held little interest. A box twice his age was meaningless to him. Of course, he was an archivist, but he wasn't really an archivist. More a grave-digger. He buried old and useless things in the tombs of the archives, things which had exhausted their meaning long ago, things which certainly had no meaning for him. This was simply his job, like grave-digging was a grave-digger's job. A fifty-year-old box could be no danger. And to please a Senator, one as powerful as Senator Martinez, to find it could be beneficial.

"If you could help me find it, I would be in your debt, Juan," the Senator said. "And, of course, I'm sure I can rely on your discretion. This is a private thing."

Juan would, of course, not be discreet, if he had anything to gain, the Senator was sure, but he would be discreet for a while. If he told anyone, he would get in trouble, if he remained discreet, he could expect a reward, and as long as the reward was greater than the trouble, Juan would be discreet.

"Of course, Senator." Juan had never been known as bright, but this calculation was easy. If he could find the thing, the Senator might arrange a promotion for him. Get him out of this dank cellar. He would actually have something on the Senator, if anyone asked, he could go to the Senator and say, 'Senator, they're asking, and now I'd like a little something ...' And if they really asked, the Director or anyone, why, he could say the Senator made him do it. There was no way to lose.

"It will take a few minutes, sir, I'd have to hunt a little, it will just take a few moments ..."

"Please, I'll be happy to wait."

Juan bustled up from his seat. The Senator sat quietly. It took no more than thirty minutes for Juan to come panting back, carrying what looked like a footlocker, a dust-covered black trunk.

Juan was beaming.

"Here it is Senator, it took some work to find it, but no one knows this cellar the way I do! If you'd just come this way, there is a little office down here where you won't be disturbed, I can set everything up for you."

"Thank you," the Senator said, and followed Juan off into the basement corridor.

Juan left the Senator in the little office. It was much safer like that. If there was anything dangerous in the old trunk, it was better if Juan knew nothing of it. It felt very strange, Juan thought, as if there were a body in the trunk, as if the trunk were a casket, exhumed after all these years, and Juan didn't really want to know what was in it. There might be films in it, old films, so Juan had set up a rickety old projector and propped up a screen (the screen wouldn't stay up, it had fallen over twice, then there wasn't an electrical cord for the projector, and Juan had had to scurry off to find one, and then it turned out that the trunk was locked, and Juan had to find a screwdriver to pry it open (he had sweated even more then, not from the effort, but from the fear, and not just the fear that he would get in trouble with someone, but the fear that there was something inside which would leap out at him, grasp him with fifty-year-old dead hands, but the Senator had said it was his responsibility, the Senator's responsibility, and Juan had said okay, sweating) and finally everything had been set up and then Juan said that he really had to get back to his office, and the Senator had said fine.

When Juan left, Senator Martinez opened the trunk. The hinges groaned softly.

It was dusty inside, but dry. There were several stacks of manila folders, several notebooks, the kind children use in school, and small, round, metal film cases. Taped on each metal case were strips of paper. On the strips were names of the persons interviewed on the film.

The Senator worked methodically. One by one, he took the metal cases out of the trunk and stacked them next to the projector. One by one, he took the files out of the trunk, and stacked them next to the film. One by one, he took the notebooks out of the trunk and stacked them next to the files.

He had seen this all years before. At the beginning of his political career, just after the war, when he had been young. He had been on the committee which had voted to bury the trunk in the archives, though he had argued that all the contents should be made public immediately. That had been dangerous, and he had never been free from the danger he conjured that day. That had been long ago. He had changed in those fifty years. He was smaller, browner, more scarred, his fingers had gotten stiffer, his hair, what there was left of it, had gone grey. But the files, the notebooks, the film containers had not changed. It was as if they had all been frozen in time, as if time itself had been encased in the battered old trunk, as if opening it had plunged Senator Martinez through a hole in time, backwards, downwards, into what had been once, into what was still there, still here, only buried.

He knew Pitfield's method. The films were "takes" for the documentary that had never been made, interviews mostly, but background footage too. In the files were transcripts of the interviews, written like scripts. But it had been a reverse drama, the drama was real, and the scripts were not the cause but the product, the sediment, of what had really happened, what had really been said. And it was all preserved, frozen, suspended, in the amber of film.

The notebooks were Pitfield's notebooks. Miscellaneous thoughts, observations, lists of things to do.

Senator Martinez opened the film case for the first interview, and wove the old film in the projector. His fingers did not obey him well anymore, but when he snapped the "on" button, the projector clicked the film through the machine. The Senator turned off the lights in the office. By the light of the projector, he was able to follow the typed transcript.

The projector rattled and hummed. Dust particles danced in the projector's light.

Numbers flashed on the screen, in backward order, five, four, three, two, one.

Then the ghosts appeared.

"INTERVIEW WITH GUERRILLA FIGHTER RAUL MARTINEZ. Spring, 1946." A tall figure appeared on the screen, in fatigue uniform and pith helmet, holding a clipboard. Behind him were blasted trees and shell craters. The figure spoke.

Pitfield. I am Ralph Pitfield, and this is "You See It Now!" This is the Philippines. A tropical paradise. Blasted by war. (Pitfield gestured dramatically to his left and right.) All Americans know about the war in the Pacific, about Marines on the beach, and carriers on the high seas. But this war in the Philippines was a different war. A secret war. For four years, the Japanese occupied these islands, what were once our islands, America's islands. And our little friends, our little brown brothers, fought them in secret, in a war unknown to the rest of the world. For four long years the war raged, in the jungles, in the mountains, as brave Filipinos and a handful of Americans, struggled to preserve this nation from the Nipponese conquerers. It was a secret war, a jungle war, a deadly war of ambush, and treachery, and astonishing bravery. We Americans knew little of that war, but now, in the aftermath of victory, the secret can be told. And you can see it now.

The ghost vanished, the film blurred, then figures reappeared. Senator Martinez gasped. For the ghost which appeared was his ghost, the figure on the screen was himself, his younger self. He didn't remember that he was so small, not much taller than the enormous rifle he was holding, he did not remember that he was so thin, that his hair was so black and thick, that his voice was so high, that he spoke so quickly. But the ghost was his ghost, and, squinting in the darkness, he stared at his youth.

Pitfield. This is Raul Martinez, one of the heroes of the secret war. Raul, what was the war like here in the Philippines?

Raul Martinez. (Clears his throat). It was, I don't know, it was bad. I am only thankful that we won. I am thankful that it is over.

Pitfield. How long were you fighting?

Martinez. Since the beginning, since December 1941. I was in the Army at first. I was on the Bataan Death March. I escaped into the hills and with my friends, I fought the Japanese. For four years.

Pitfield. In the mountains.

Martinez. Yes. In the jungle. In Manila. There were many operations.

Pitfield. How old were you in 1941? When you went into the guerrilla army?

Martinez. Twenty-one.

Pitfield. How many fights were you in?

Martinez. I don't know. I didn't count. A hundred. Five hundred. I don't know. We didn't count.

Pitfield. You were the leader of a guerrilla band. How many men served with you?

Martinez. It varied greatly. At first, I was alone. Then, others joined me. At first, there were no more than a dozen of us. Then a score or more. At the end, I commanded a battalion, over five hundred men.

(The conversation went on and on, and as it did, the Senator's lips moved with his lips on the screen, as if some part in him were alive again. But he was not looking for all this, he was looking for something else. He skimmed through the transcript, found the fast-forward switch on the projector, and finally found what he was looking for.)

Pitfield ... that was the worst part?

Martinez. Yes. That was the worst part.

Pitfield. Tell me about it.

Martinez. Well. The Japanese secret service, their "gestapo," they could not defeat us in battle. This is our country, not theirs. They did not know our hiding places, they never could find us. So they had to rely on betrayal, on agents, on spies. They tried to penetrate our bands with spies. Not Japanese, of course, but Filipinos. Traitors. Pirates. Filipinos in Japanese pay. And in 1943, they penetrated my band. We were on an operation. An ambush. And, well, it failed. We were the ones ambushed. My men were slaughtered. Over twenty were killed and captured. Only a handful of us escaped. At first, I thought it just the fortune of war. But other operations failed too, and they failed only because the Japanese had advance information, they had to have advance information, someone in my band, someone close to me, was a traitor.

But even that was not the worst. They wanted us to know that we were betrayed. Not just to halt our operations. No. They wanted us to know we were betrayed so that we would not trust each other, so that we would fight each other, so that we would be afraid to be with each other. They did not just want to kill us. They wanted to kill our trust. That was even worse.

But not the worst. The worst was that the traitor had to be a Filipino. Someone close. A friend. That was the worst of all. Not the invader, but the traitor. Not death, but treachery. That was the worst. I was wounded many times, but that was okay. I was a soldier, I was prepared to die. The worst was treason.

Pitfield. How did they let you know that you had been penetrated?

Martinez. They didn't at first. At first, they just used the information to fight us, to disrupt our attacks, to arrest our people, our friends. But then, when we knew that we were penetrated, they toyed with us. Then sent messages, telling us that they knew where we were, where our families were.

Pitfield. Messages? In words?

Martinez. Yes. Notes and things. They would capture someone. Torture him or her, kill him or her, dump the body, and pin to the body a note. A laughing note. They, well, they, it is hard to say now, they dishonored the bodies. Beat them. Abused them. Some were flayed. Beheaded. Like animals. And notes were attached, warning us that they knew us, knew all about us, where we were, that we would be next.

But it wasn't really "them;" it was "he." One person. Of that I am sure. For the tortures, the notes, the threats, behind them was a single signature, a single voice, one hand. Someone.

Pitfield. Who? Who would do this?

Martinez. We never found him. We are still hunting. But we do know some things. We know he is one of us, of our generation. We know that he was close to us, knew our secrets. I say "he;" it could be a woman, but I think it is a man. My age. And you ask why? I do not know. Filipinos are honorable people. For us, honor is everything. We honor our parents, our friends. This man has violated honor. I think the only thing that could bring a man to this is power. The desire, the need, the lust, to manipulate, to dominate, to kill. He is not a soldier. Not a warrior. There is something wrong here, something more than just the killing in war.

Pitfield. A criminal? A psychopath?

Martinez. Yes. But more than that. He is an evil man. He is evil. I don't know, but, that is what I think, what I feel in my heart. He killed my brother. In, I cannot say it, in a brutal way. With torture. With flaying.

He killed my brother. And the note pinned to what was left of my brother, the note expresses pleasure at the cruelty. He is bestial. One day I will find him. I will kill him.

Pitfield. This is a personal thing?

Martinez. This is a personal thing.

The ghost disappeared. The Senator sat very still as the film flickered from its track and slapped mechanically at the projector. The Senator felt his heart beat, felt a rage of long ago well up in him, in his chest, in his hands, a heat, a fire, that made his hands shake. This man killed my brother. That was long ago. And now, fifty years later, this man, this thing, has returned. His sign is in the killings of the poor. The murders in Manila. He has returned. And now, I will remember. And with my memory I will find him.

ELEVEN

The Senator fed a second film in the projector. Snapped off the lights, gently opened the folder containing the transcript. The ghosts reappeared.

"INTERVIEW WITH PEDRO MARTINEZ, GRANDFATHER OF GUERRILLA FIGHTER RAUL MARTINEZ. Spring, 1946."

Pitfield. (Seated on the porch of a small peasant home. Next to him, a very old Filipino, dressed all in white, white trousers, white barong shirt, his face leathery, very thin. The old man sits stiffly, with great dignity). Thank you for seeing me, sir.

Grandfather. (Smiles, waves his hand as if dismissing the need for thanks).

(My God, the Senator thought, watching. It is as if he were alive again, as if I could stand up and speak to him again. That is his voice I hear, time scratching it, making it rustle, but it is still his voice. "Hello, grandfather," the Senator said softly.)

Pitfield. Your grandson, Raul, thought that I should speak with you. He said you could teach me about the Philippines.

Grandfather. I am an old man, still trying to learn. I do not know that I can teach.

Pitfield. Perhaps then you can tell. Tell me about the Philippines.

Grandfather. It is beautiful. It is green and blue and warm. There are grand mountains here, and waterfalls. The sky is vast here, and the air is bright. It is another Eden. I hope to be in heaven soon, and I hope heaven is as beautiful as the Philippines.

Pitfield. And Filipinos? Tell me about Filipinos?

Grandfather. Filipinos? They are the new human beings. Filipinos are Malays. And Chinese. And Spanish. And American. They are black, they are white. They are Asian. They are Western. In these islands, in this sea, all humans have come together. To make a new human being. Filipinos? They are very brave. They have much courage. They want to be free.

Pitfield. Raul says that you were a guerrilla fighter, too.

Grandfather. Yes. In my youth. I fought the Spanish. And later the Americans. With Aguinaldo. I was in the bush, fighting, yes. All Filipinos have had to fight. These islands, they are a prize. Many people have tried to have them for themselves. Filipinos have had to suffer and struggle to save them. You see, the Philippines is a door. A magic door. For Asians, for the Chinese, the Philippines is a door to the west, a place to rest on the long road to the west. For the west, the Philippines is the door to Asia, to China. So you see, everyone wants this door, this magic door, the Spanish, the Americans, the Japanese.

Pitfield. Tell me about your family.

Grandfather. Ah. To tell you of my family, that would take many days. I would have to tell you about Itel. In the old days. In my grandfather's grandfather's time. Before that. She was a priestess. Of the old gods. She was very beautiful, of that I am sure. She was a priestess and knew about the secrets of these islands, about the jungle and the mountains. Look at this. (Grandfather fished from his pocket a small object, a small bird. He held it gently in his hand).

Look at this. This is called Laon. Only a small thing. But he reminds us of bigger things. He reminds us that the past is everywhere, still alive, still acting, still aching. He reminds us that we and the forest and the harvest are somehow still connected. Itel knew about Laon, this small bird.

Now Itel, once she fell in love. With an invader, a Spaniard. His name was Andres. Andres Urdaneta was his name. He was brave, a conquistador, very handsome. They say that he saved Itel's little brother from death. His name was Dantu. This Andres had many adventures. Once, he was captured by pirates. Well, Andres and Itel, they fell in love. And they had children. And their children had children. And you see, these children were the new human beings. Were they Malay? Yes, of course. Itel was Malay. Were they Spanish? Yes, because of Andres. Were they Asian? Yes. Were they Western? Yes. They were the new people on the earth. Much like our cousins in Latin America. We Filipinos, we are the new people.

Pitfield. But like Latin America, the Philippines has suffered much.

Grandfather. Yes. Some people are blessed with riches. Others with suffering.

Pitfield. Blessed with suffering?

Grandfather. A strange blessing. Yes. But you see, it is our task to change suffering to good. To refine, to redeem suffering. Like Jesus. Who turned crucifixion into resurrection. It is our chance to be brave and good. I do not like suffering, I do not want to suffer. Suffering, alone, is an evil.

But to face this evil of suffering, to fight against those who make you suffer, to fight against that within you that makes you and your countrymen suffer, that then is a moment when we can be brave and good. To be blest with riches, that is fine, but that can only make people stupid and fat. But to face the sufferings we have had to face, to face them and not be deformed by them, to transform them, that is something worthy of a human being. We Filipinos have had to suffer. More than most peoples. More, I think, than many Americans. Sometimes, I wish we were rich, like you. But sometimes, I think that I would not trade our sufferings for your riches. To be rich is alone neither good nor bad. But to struggle, if necessary to suffer, that permits one to learn honor and dignity. We go to your country to learn about riches. But your people, they should come here. I think that here, in our islands, they could learn about dignity. And honor.

Pitfield. The pain of these islands, it is brought here by foreigners?

Grandfather. Yes. Because of foreigners, of course. Colonialists. Spaniards, Americans, Japanese.

Pitfield. Americans, too?

Grandfather. You are surprised?

Pitfield. But, Americans rescued you from Spanish tyranny. Brought you religion. Civilization.

Grandfather. When the Americans came here, they said they wanted to Christianize us. Spread the Gospel. They forgot that we had been Christians three centuries or more before they came, and that our ancestors had worshiped God in their own ways before that. Civilization? We had our civilization, our language, our customs. Who were the savages in those days? They called us "niggers." That is what they called us. But who were the savages?

I do not say all Americans were bad. I do not say all Spanish were bad. Some were good. Some were bad. The Spanish brought us convents. The Americans brought us Hollywood. And other things, of course. English is now, for many, our language. We have learned much, borrowed much. But freedom is the issue. Freedom. That they took from us. We will be free, we will make our own world, here, in our islands.

Pitfield. You were here when the Americans came. Did you see the great battle in Manila Bay? With Admiral Dewey?

Grandfather. Ah, the great battle! It was a battle. But mostly it was Hollywood. I knew Aguinaldo. He told me. It was all arranged. It was a play. The Spanish gave us to the Americans, they wanted to surrender to the Americans and not the Filipinos, so they staged everything. So the Americans simply replaced the Spaniards.

Pitfield. And you fought against the Americans.

Grandfather. I fought against the Americans. Just as my grandfathers fought the Spaniards. Just as my grandson fought the Japanese.

Pitfield. Your pain, then, is from the outside?

Grandfather. Yes. But not only that. Our islands are strong and powerful, more powerful than human beings. There are thousands of them, and to make a nation of them is hard. Volcanoes strike at us. Jungle wars with us for land. The sea roars at us. And too, I think sometimes that there is too much passion here. Sometimes, all the blood in our veins, Malay and Chinese and European, black and white and Asian, sometimes it is too much. Sometimes it explodes too.

Pitfield. Raul says that during the war, the worst thing was treachery. He says that he could fight the Japanese, but the worst thing was when his own people, other Filipinos, betrayed him.

Grandfather. Yes. I think that is the worst ... It happened during the war against the Americans, too, Filipino fought Filipino. Let me tell you a story. A true story.

Once, a village was plagued by locusts. Clouds of locusts. They too lived on our islands, and they attacked the harvest, and without the harvest, the people starved. So, the people and the priests, arranged a trial of the locusts. Some villagers dressed as holy saints. They were the witnesses for the prosecution. The priest, an important and powerful man named Martin, he played the great Saint Sebastian. A friar, he was the prosecutor, he played Saint Gregory. The judge was played by a woman in the village, she played the Holy Virgin. And there was a trial. And the locusts were found guilty and threatened with excommunication if they did not leave. And you know, the next year, there were no locusts.

The villagers were not foolish. This is not a foolish story. They knew they had to face the locusts, confront them. And they knew that the confrontation was not just a fight between humans and insects, it was a fight that involved good and evil and all the powers of heaven. That is where the fight must occur against the locusts, in the heart, in the soul ...

Suddenly, the old film snapped. It flapped madly against the projector. Broken; time had finally broken it. Senator Martinez slowly rose from his chair and snapped off the projector. "Goodbye, Grandfather," he said softly. "Goodbye."

"INTERVIEW WITH GENERAL DOUGLAS MACARTHUR AND AIDE CAPTAIN LIVINGSTON. Spring,1946."

The ghosts reappeared, flickering from long ago, almost as if they were reluctant to be conjured back. The Senator shifted in his hard chair, and opened the transcript of the interview with General Douglas MacArthur and a young captain on his staff. What was the Captain's name? In intelligence. A dangerous young man. Yes, there it was-Livingston. The Senator remembered. Perhaps here would be something. A clue. Something from the past with which to exorcise the evils of the present.

The projector clicked the film along. Dust particles danced in the projector's light.

And suddenly there he was, as splendid as he was then, General Douglas MacArthur, the American Caesar, and even now something tingled in the Senator's spine.

Pitfield. (Not on screen). General MacArthur, sir, this is truly a great honor, sir. I want to thank you for taking the time ...

MacArthur. (Smiles, waves his hand). My pleasure, sir.

Pitfield. General MacArthur, sir, few people know the Philippines the way you do. As you know, we are doing a film regarding the Filipino resistance to the Japanese during the war, and I was wondering, sir, whether you could give us your impressions of that resistance.

MacArthur. (Slowly, meditatively, solemnly). Yes, indeed. My father, you know, served in these islands in the early part of this century. And as you know, of course, my career has brought me back to these magical islands many times. I have spent my military life, it seems to me, in the Pacific. I am a man of the Pacific, and here, the Philippines is my home. And you know, I have always looked on these warm and gracious people as, if I may say so, my children. And they have always treated me with the honor and respect they would show a father.

(Puffing on his corncob pipe). Now, you have asked me about Filipino resistance to the Japanese tyranny. It was a brave resistance. A heroic resistance. From the moment the Japanese invaded, the Filipinos stood shoulder to shoulder with their American friends and allies. In Bataan, in Corregidor, the brave Filipinos fought like tigers. And during the long night of Japanese conquest, the Filipinos fought back again and again.

You know, young man, the Filipino has always been a warrior. Yes, even in the Spanish days, the Filipino served as a warrior for the Spanish crown. On many an island, on many an Asian field, Filipino warriors have struggled and prevailed ...

Pitfield. Yes, General, and the resistance ...?

MacArthur. You know, when the fortunes of war drove us from these islands, I promised the Filipino people, "I shall return." And that promise was a solemn vow. It was not theatrics as my critics have charged, no, it was a solemn vow. It was my vow as a soldier, to my comrade, the Filipino soldier. Americans who have never been here have no idea of the beauty, the power, of a vow made to a Filipino, or the vow a Filipino makes. It is a matter of the deepest honor. It is a matter of conscience, of dignity. And only the sombre mantle of death could interfere with it.

Many people know of my vow. But let me tell you of another. As I left the bloody island of Corregidor, pursuant to my orders from the Commander-in-Chief, I saw a tired, weary, bruised young Filipino soldier. He was no more than a lad, but already he bore the scars from a dozen battles. As I was leaving, with tears in my eyes, I grasped that young soldier's hand and said, "I shall return." That was when I made my promise. And that young soldier looked at me with manly eyes, and said, "General MacArthur, sir, we will never give up, we will wait for you." I do not know whatever happened to that brave young man, but for me, he will always be the Philippines, and his words will always echo in my heart.

Pitfield. And they waited, and fought, waiting for you?

MacArthur. Not simply for me, no, for the cause I represented. I have loved the Filipino people, and yes, I will say it, and they me. Not for MacArthur the person, but for what MacArthur represents. I think of the Filipinos as my children. And what I represent to them is, I think, freedom. Freedom from tyranny, from oppression. That is what they want, what they yearn for, what their history has been. Other nations have accumulated riches; other nations have tamed nature, or sailed wide around the globe. But the Filipino nation has lived for one thing — freedom. Unarmed, ill-armed, outnumbered, burdened with misguided leaders, the Filipino has always fought on, for freedom. Yes, I think I represented freedom for them, from the Japanese, of course, but freedom itself as well. Yes, I think of the Filipinos as my children. And someday, my heirs.

(A bustle off camera. A voice says something to the General. The film stops.)

Senator Martinez scanned Pitfield's notes, peppered with exclamation points, scribbled at the bottom of the transcript: "Another blast of MacArthur hot air! ... pompous! ... incredibly condescending! ... the arrogance of calling the Filipino people 'his children!' My God!!! ..."

Yes, the Senator thought. Yes, you're right, Mr. Pitfield. All what you say is true. Yet ... yet ... For me, for my generation, there is still something grand about that pompous colonialist. I cannot deny that tingle in my spine. And I think, despite everything, that he did know us. Perhaps he was the only one of you who did ...

Another film. The Senator pulled a legal pad to him, and began jotting, doodling. The images appeared.

Pitfield. (Sitting on a couch, next to a young American officer. The young officer is no more than thirty years of age; his light blond hair, faint mustache, and ruddy cheeks make him look much younger). Captain Theodore Livingston, thank you for giving us your time.

Livingston. (In clipped tones). My pleasure.

Pitfield. I understand, sir, that you have had extensive experience in working with the Filipino resistance during the war.

Livingston. Yes. I am with Army Intelligence ...

The Senator scanned the transcript, then fast-forwarded the film until he found what he was looking for.

Livingston. ... yes, the real hero was Hector Montoya. He is your man. Montoya single-handedly won this war, why ...

Pitfield. Ah, Captain, might I ask a delicate question? I have heard rumors that Mr. Montoya has a rather inflated war record, that he may even have been a collaborator, that the U.S. is promoting him now because he is, so to speak, our man in Manilla.

Livingston. (Heated). Lies! Communist lies! I know who told you this. Martinez and his crowd. Well, let me tell, you, Martinez simply has political ambitions and he is simply trying to smear a genuine war-hero. I've worked with Mr. Montoya for years, I've been his chief contact ... The Senator snapped his pencil point on his pad. He stopped the film, rewound it, played it again.

"INTERVIEW WITH GUERRILLA FIGHTER HECTOR MONTOYA. Spring, 1946."

Juan rapped softly on the office door, opened it just enough to poke his head through and asked: "Everything all right, Senator?" His voice sounded cheery enough, but Juan was still worried. The Senator had been in the office for a very long time. There was something strange going on, and Juan wanted no part of it.

"Everything all right, Senator?"

"Fine, Juan. Everything is fine."

"Can I get you anything, a drink or something?"

"That's very kind of you, Juan, but no, I'm fine."

"Okay, Senator. I'll just leave you then."

"Fine."

Juan softly closed the door and padded away. Back in his office, he began to write a memorandum-for-record. Just in case. He wrote that he hadn't wanted to do anything wrong. But the Senator had asked. And a Senator was a Senator. And Juan was just a very junior official. And how it all seemed all right ... Juan read his writing and sighed. He did not like this business. Old films in sealed boxes and powerful people like the Senator poking about in Juan's basement. He didn't like it at all.

A wobbly pile of books fell with a crash. Juan jumped. It was nothing. I hope it is not an omen, he said to himself.

The ghosts reappeared on the screen. Montoya. The dictator. The Hero. The Infallible Leader. He was gone now, the people had driven him out, Senator Martinez had helped drive him out. But there he was again, in the grey light of the old film, young and handsome, smiling at the earnest young Pitfield.

Pitfield. I'm speaking with Hector Montoya. According to Captain Livingston of General MacArthur's staff, Hector Montoya is the greatest hero of the Filipino resistance. Hector Montoya has won every medal for bravery that both the United States and the Philippines offer. If I may say so, Mr. Montoya, it is an honor to speak with you.

Montoya. (Smiling). My pleasure.

Pitfield. Hector Montoya, tell me about your exploits. Captain Livingston says that you, single-handedly, created the Filipino resistance.

Montoya. (Laughing). Well, Captain Livingston is my friend. But I won't pretend any false modesty. Yes, I did create the resistance. With help, of course. But I did it for the love I have of the Filipino people ...

Senator Martinez grimaced. Such lies. Even then. It was hard to listen to them. But didn't Pitfield ask some other questions? The Senator rummaged through the transcript of the interview. The pages were yellowed and stained. Yes. Here. He fast-forwarded the film. Montoya, the Greatest Hero, looked comic when fast-forwarded, gesturing frantically, sqeaking and squinting.

Yes. Here it is ...

Pitfield. ... traitors. Mr. Martinez says that the greatest enemy he had to face were traitors. Someone, in fact, infiltrated his own resistance group and betrayed his men ...

Montoya. (Interrupting) ... no! No! There were no traitors at all.

Pitfield. (Continuing) ... and he said that there were collaborators too, and that, well, this is a hard thing, I know, but he said that he thought you might have collaborated too, "trimmed your sails to the winds" was his remark ...

Montoya. Lies! It's jealousy, that's all it is! Sheer lies!

Pitfield. He did not say that you were the one who betrayed his group. No, he didn't say that. But he suspects that you may have part of the circle of informers the Japanese recruited ...

Montoya. Let him prove it if he can! He can't! He can't prove anything! Let him talk to Livingston, he is my friend, let him talk to the Americans, we have been friends for years, Livingston and me, talk to Livingston ...

Pitfield. Mr. Martinez says that someone betrayed his group, and arranged for horrible assassinations of his men, and that some of the collaborators might now decide that it was time to collaborate with the Americans. In fact, he says that the Americans have recruited the former collaborators. He told me that some collaborators were blackmailed by the Americans, that others were recruited because they were anti-Communist ...

Montoya. He's crazy! Does he really think that the Americans would recruit Japanese agents! It's preposterous!

Pitfield. Maybe not. Not so crazy. Here's what he said. He said: Filipino fighters fought the Spanish. The Americans helped them. The Americans were all for the freedom movement when it was against the Spanish. But, when the Spanish left and the Americans came to power, the Americans then wanted to suppress the freedom movement. And to suppress it, they actually recruited Filipinos who had fought for the Spanish against the movement. He says that the same thing is happening now. He says that the Americans want to disarm the resistance and suppress the resistance movement. And who knows more about suppressing it than Filipino collaborators who worked for the Japanese. And an added bonus: the Americans can blackmail these collaborators and threaten to expose them if they don't cooperate. And those who do cooperate will be handsomely rewarded.

Montoya. He's crazy. I want to stop this right now, this talk ...

Pitfield. Mr. Montoya, let me get to the point. Mr. Martinez says you're a fraud. A puppet of the American intelligence. He says you were not a guerrilla hero at all, but in fact a collaborator ...

Montoya. No more. The interview is over. Talk to Livingston. He will tell you everything. Talk to Livingston!

The film ended abruptly.

Talk to Livingston.

Senator Martinez rummaged through the file. Echoing still in his ear, though, was "Talk to Livingston." Pitfield had scribbled a note to himself. It was hard to read. It was written in pencil, and time had faded some of the words. The Senator stared at the note. He puzzled out:

"Lying. Follow this up. Either Martinez or Montoya is lying. Is Montoya a fraud? A front-man? Was he a collaborator? Did he have anything to do with the betrayal of Martinez's men? Talk to Livingston again."

The Senator gently placed the note in the folder again. Yes. He had not thought about all this. But could there be a link between the betrayer and the Americans? Livingston was dead, wasn't he? But had there been a link? And if there had been, why would the betrayer come back after all these years? Could Montoya have been the betrayer? No. Not personally. But he could have known the betrayer.

Talk to Livingston.

The CIA was blamed for everything. Crazy things. And usually, it was innocent. The Senator himself had had dealings with the CIA over the years. Sometimes their policy was bad, but they didn't make the policy. And for all their bad reputation, they were not thugs. Not murderers.

Talk to Livingston.

But the CIA did deal with bad people. They had to. And once in a while, there would be a rogue. An agent would go off on his own. The betrayer would know intelligence people. Not Livingston anymore. But people connected somehow to Livingston. Or if not to him, then to his heirs.

The Senator jotted a message to himself on his legal pad. The betrayer might still have links. To Americans, maybe. Yes. That might be a path to follow. Talk to Livingston.

TWELVE

"INTERVIEW WITH RAUL MARTINEZ AND RESISTANCE FIGHTERS. Spring, 1946."

This was the film the Senator had been looking for. The film they were all in. They had joked about it, joked with Pitfield. He had said that he would make them all movie stars, send them all to Hollywood.

They had all laughed.

It would be good to see them all again. The Senator felt strange as he fed the old film into the projector. It felt almost as if he were going to a reunion. As if he were meeting again with the people who had shared his youth.

All so long ago.

He was in this one. And his three lieutenants from those days, Carlos, Santo, and Emilio. And John Cleary, the American. And Corazon Chung Lee.

John and Corazon had had children, hadn't they? Yes. Cleary's son had joined the army. During Vietnam. And Corazon's daughter, hadn't she been close to Cleary's son? Yes. But they had broken up or something. And she had taken vows, become a nun. She worked in the villages north of Manila. Helena was her name. I wonder whatever happened to Cleary's son, the Senator asked himself.

Killed, I think. In Vietnam. He would be, what, about 15, maybe 20 years older than my son, Raul.

My son, Raul.

I must tell Raul all this. I must bring him home. He belongs here. But how can I bring him back to Manila from Harvard? To all this, from what he has now.

The Senator shook his head. He could not think about all that now.

Odd, in the Philippines, how everyone seemed to know everyone else, how everyone seemed related to everyone, or seemed at least related to someone who was related to everyone else. John had been killed during the Huk troubles, back in the 1950s. And Corazon had died some time ago. As for the others, they were still old friends. Emilio had been his aide now for a lifetime. Santo is my business partner. And old Carlos, irascible and cantankerous, still runs his big farm down south.

It will be good to see them all again, the Senator thought. The film clicked through the projector. Images danced on the screen.

(Seven people, sitting on rattan chairs, on a veranda in the bright sunshine. Pitfield in the center. Pitfield stares pleasantly at the camera).

Pitfield. Are we rolling?

Voice off screen. Yeah. Rolling.

Pitfield. Today, I have the pleasure of meeting with the leaders of one of the most successful guerrilla fighter bands in all of the Philippines. The gentleman to my left, Raul Martinez, was the guerrilla chief. And these were Raul's lieutenants. And today, we will talk about the war. But first, Raul, will you introduce the others for our friends back in America?

Raul. (Nervously). Well, at the far right is Emilio, next to him, Santo, and next to him, is Carlos. And here, on my left, is Corazon, and on the end, is John. John Wesley Cleary. (Laughter). We joke about John's name. Not too Filipino.

Pitfield. It seems like we have the whole Philippines represented!

Raul. Yes. I guess so. We're from all over the islands. Corazon and I are from here, north of Manila. Santo and Emilio are from Luzon too. Carlos is from the far south. He's the most Spanish of us all, I guess, but part of his family is Muslim.

Carlos. (Interrupting). Yes. Let's remember that the southern islands are part of the Philippines too! And so are my Muslim cousins!

Raul. And John here is officially an American. But he's really a Filipino too. And Corazon is from a Filipino-Chinese family. So we have lots of different colors in our flag, I guess.

Pitfield. I thank you all for being with us today. I have really a simple question for you all. Why did you fight? When the Japanese occupied the Philippines, why didn't you just lay low, and get along? Many people did when their countries were invaded, both here in Asia and in Europe. Why did you decide to take on all the dangers of resistance? Miss Lee? Maybe we can begin with you.

Lee. Well ...

Pitfield. (Interrupting). Maybe you could begin by first just telling our audience something about yourself.

Lee. My name is Corazon Chung Lee. My family came to the Philippines from China many generations ago. We are now all Filipinos, of course, though our ethnic roots go back to China. My parents, and their parents, were all merchants, They traded with China. I'm a teacher. So was my husband.

Pitfield. Your husband was killed during the war?

Lee. Yes. In 1942. During the Bataan Death March.

Pitfield. And you have a daughter?

Lee. Yes. She's four now. Helena is her name.

Pitfield. And you were in the resistance?

Lee. Yes. I did what I could.

Pitfield. I know you fought to get rid of the Japanese. That's clear. That's what you fought against. The Japanese occupation. But what did you fight for? What motivated you to take the risks you took? I guess I mean, what made you so brave?

Lee. (Laughing). I don't think I was very brave. None of us were. But what we fought for. (Pauses). I will tell you a story. I was at the market in our village, just after the occupation. Food had to be rationed, and the people were lined up to get food. There was an old man in line. He didn't quite understand what was going on, and when he got to the head of the line, he didn't have the right papers, or something, anyway, one soldier got frustrated with him and pushed him. Pushed him down. Another kicked him. The old man, he was very clumsy, and as he tried to escape the blows, he fumbled around on the ground. The soldiers laughed at him. And the other people in the line, they were frightened or confused, I don't know. Anyway, they just stood there and watched, while the old man was beaten up. I stood there, too. Finally, the soldiers dragged the old man away, and his people helped him up, and took him away. I had just stood there. Like everyone. But when I got home, I cried and cried. Not just for the old man. But for me. For us all. I cried and cried because at a time when I should have been brave, I wasn't. I had stood by and let injustice be done. I had looked the other way.

The next day, I tried to find the old man. I wanted to apologize to him. But I never could find him. And I thought: if I am ever to call myself a human being, I cannot just stand by again. I thought: I have sinned here, worse, in a way than the Japanese soldiers. I was a coward. And I decided that I could never live as a coward. That's all.

Pitfield. Did you have a program? Democracy? The American way?

Lee. No. No program. It wasn't that. It was just that I wanted not to be ashamed. I did not want to be ashamed of myself again. (Pauses). You know, I think that everyone has a chance, maybe once, maybe twice in a life, to be a coward, or to be brave. I had failed my first chance. And I thought, can I tell my daughter that I was a coward? Could I tell my husband that I was a coward? Could I live to be old, knowing that I was a coward? No. I couldn't live with that. That's all. I wanted to be human, to be able to call myself human again. I wanted my husband, my daughter, to be able to be proud of me, not ashamed of me. We had programs and things, but more important, for me at least, was dignity and courage.

And that has to do with being a Filipino. We do not have much, many of us. But we have courage and dignity and they are the most important things of all. You have to struggle to preserve them, to care for them above all other things. That's very Filipino.

Pitfield. But you said you weren't brave.

Lee. Oh no, I'm not! I was afraid throughout the whole war! I hated it! But, you try to let courage control your fear. You try to let dignity control your urge to run and hide. It's very hard. But that's what I tried to do. I think that's what we all tried to do.

Pitfield. Mr. Cleary, you were in the resistance, too?

Cleary. Yes.

Pitfield. But you're not a Filipino?

Cleary. (Laughs). Well, yes and no. You see, I came here as a missionary. I wanted to spread the Good News. But I learned that, in a way, the Good News was already here. I came to teach Filipinos the Good News and they taught it to me. My passport still says "U.S.", but my American friends think I've "gone native."

Pitfield. What attracts you about the Filipino people?

Cleary. Where can I begin? The land, the friendships. I can't say any one thing. But you know, if I can pick up what Corazon was talking about, I think that these people here, on these islands, have a dignity and an honor that I had never found at home. Don't get me wrong. Americans are fine people, I'm one of them for heaven's sake! and then, too, I don't know all Americans everywhere. But, what I mean is, here, Filipinos somehow know something about honor and dignity and courage that I think many Americans don't know. But it's not "know" exactly. It's more like "live." There are many problems here. To live amidst these problems and not be crushed by them demands a kind of daily heroism that you don't find at home. To care for your family, to aid your friends, sometimes that demands the kind of courage Corazon was talking about, demands it every day. Life is hard, and this hard life makes heroes. Again and again I've seen this daily courage in my villages. And I have admired that deeply.

Pitfield. Did you have trouble fighting for the resistance, as an ordained minister? Didn't that violate your calling?

Cleary. Yes, it was hard. I took no pleasure in killing. Killing brutalizes, deception brutalizes. The young Japanese soldiers here, they were boys, pawns of their government. It was evil to have to kill them. But it would have been even more evil not to stop them. I could not stand by in safety, I could not hide behind my collar and robes, I could not boast of my clean hands, when people were oppressed and abused. Clean hands are not always a mark of virtue.

Pitfield. I have heard that treason was a problem for the resistance. A major problem.

Lee. Yes, of course. Where was it not? Of course, there was poison here, some of our own people were poisoned. That was the most painful thing of all.

Cleary. Yes. And to root out that poison, it will be hard. And we have not even begun to do that ...

Pitfield. Carlos? Santo? Emilio? You were the actual leaders, with Raul, of the guerrilla band. Why did you fight?

Carlos. To get rid of the Japanese! For God's sake, it's not that complicated! We didn't want them here. We didn't want the Americans here before them, and we didn't want the Spanish here before them! We want to live our lives on our islands, to create our own lives, without being told what to do and how to do it ...

Raul. Now Carlos. The Americans are our Allies!

Carlos. All right, all right! Yes. Fine. And I like the Americans. I'm glad they're our friends. But they don't understand us. Never have ...

Santo. And who does understand us? I don't think we understand ourselves!

Carlos. Oh, come on, Santo! Look, Mr. Pitfield. It's this. You Americans fought in your revolution for freedom. Freedom from oppression. Freedom to take your own fate in your own two hands. Freedom. That's what the struggle was all about. And look, you have to see that this struggle against the Japanese, it was part of the same struggle against the Americans thirty years ago, and against the Spanish before that.

Emilio. (Softly). Yes. Carlos is right. We have programs and plans and all that. But it was more than that, more than programs and plans.

Generations have struggled before us. Generations will struggle after us. To build our own nation with our own hands. If others wish to help us, to wish us well, we welcome that. But the work must be our own, the successes and failures must be our own.

Santo. I don't know. This is too high flown for me. The Japanese were cruel to us. So we defended ourselves. That's all. Violence is just part of life, part of life especially on these islands. If you're not violent, if you don't understand violence, then you're a fool. And fools die.

Carlos. No. Wait. Look, Mr. Pitfield, do you know Rizal's poetry? He was one of our great heroes, killed by the Spanish. On the night before he died, he wrote one of the most moving poems anyone ever wrote, and you have to understand it to understand us.

Santo. Oh, Carlos, no poetry! Rizal wasn't a typical Filipino. He was educated, a world traveller, he was a middle-class intellectual, who represented nobody but his own middle-class ...

Carlos. No! You're wrong, Santo ...

Raul. No fights! Please. I think Carlos is right. We all know the poem so well that we think everyone does. But maybe you don't know it. Carlos is right. The poem does tell why Rizal fought, why we fought.

Carlos. I won't recite it all. But listen to it. Rizal was to be shot in the morning. In the night before he died he wrote this. He wrote it in Spanish, but I'll try to put it in English. Just listen to it. It goes like this:

Land that I love, goodbye, O you land of the southern sun! Pearl of the Orient! Garden of Eden we yearn for. Gladly I give up my life for you ... Far away, in the din and roar of battle, Others have given their lives, neither wavering or pausing in the giving ... O my country ... It is beautiful to fall, that my vision of you may rise, To give my life for you, to breathe your air as I die, Beautiful it is to sleep forever in you ... Pray for me, my fatherland, and Pray too for those who die in torment, for those who suffer in prison, Pray for the grieving mothers, for the widows, and orphans, And Pray for yourself, my fatherland, on your way to your redemption ... I will be the air in your streets, I will be the breeze in your meadows, I will be the vibrant speech in your ear ... O Philippines, goodbye ... Where I go, there are no tyrants ...

I don't think I got it all translated right. But look, this Philippines, we love this place! These islands, these skys, these hills, these people. We love this place. So many have tried to hurt this place, even some of us have tried to hurt our islands, but don't you see, we love these islands, and we will defend them, protect them, don't you see ...

The old film suddenly snapped and flapped frantically. The Senator tried to re-feed the old film in the projector, but it wouldn't work, the rest of the film wouldn't feed. He gave up.

There were tears in his eyes. He knew Rizal's poem by heart, too. Everyone did. But to hear it again, to hear Carlos recite it with such love.

It is late, the Senator thought. For now, I have seen enough.

A knock on the door.

Juan poked his head in. "Sir, it's been a long time. I think I have to go now, but if you'd like ..."

"No, Juan. Thank you. I have had enough for today. Thank you, Juan. I'll go now."

Later that night a spectacular moon illuminated the gently swaying palms, the sleeping jeepneys parked along the steet-sides, the sombre statues in Luneta Park. The night sky, as deeply blue as the ocean, flashed with patient stars. Boats in Manila Bay softly rose and fell.

In the Senate Office Building, Senator Raul Martinez, Sr., was still at work. His eyes were tired from his day of movies and transcripts. He sat at his desk, scribbling random notes on a legal pad before him. Now, he thought. Now. What is it that I know?

I know this:

A wave of murders has swept Manila. Terrorist murders, not just criminal murders. Very brutal murders. Torture and murder. I have been threatened.

And all the marks of these murders remind me of the old days, the war, when my friends and I were betrayed. When my brother was killed.

I think the betrayer is back.

I think the betrayer is behind all this.

I think he is very dangerous, very ambitious, very clever.

I think it is someone somehow connected to the past, to the war, to the old days.

But who from the old days is still alive?

The Senator began jotting on his pad.

Me. Emilio, my aid. Old Carlos, on his plantation down south. Santo, my business partner. It could somehow be one of us.

Montoya, the dictator, is dead. But what about his contacts with the Americans? What about Livingston, his old contact? Livingston was a young captain during the war, as young as we were. And if not him, could there be some American connection somehow?

Corazon Chung Lee is dead. Her daughter, Helena, is a nun. John Wesley Cleary is dead. And his son, Eddie, was it? I think he is dead too, in Vietnam.

It could be someone else, someone entirely different, but even if it is someone else, whoever it is, has some kind of connection with the old days. With the war. With the betrayer from the war. The past has come alive. The past has come back to haunt us. I must exorcise the past.

And Pitfield? Two months after finishing the interviews, he was found murdered in his hotel room. The official report said suicide, but no one believed it. And Montoya and his people demanded that Pitfield's notes be suppressed. No one has seen them since the '40s. Except for me. Today.

Or, yesterday, now. The Senator looked at his watch. It was just past midnight.

He switched on the small radio on his desk to catch the hourly news. The announcer droned on about wars here, disasters there. The Senator listened with only half an ear as he sketched on his legal pad.

Did the films contain something? Something I did not catch? At least they were a beginning. These killings today, they are somehow connected with the war, of that I am sure. And at least now I have begun to remember, remember clearly. And memory contains the clue. Somewhere. Memory contains the clue. I must talk to my son. I must talk to Raul. But I cannot get him involved in all this. I cannot set the ghosts after him. He has a good life now, in the States, at Harvard. He's even talking of marrying an American girl. That's good. That's his life now. He's cured of his student radicalism. But I was a radical too in my youth. My enemies say I still am. But it's good that Raul is settling down. He was never a communist, of course. But he was a patriot. A passionate patriot. Like his old man, they said, and I was proud of that. Headstrong too, they said, like his old man.

He's settled down now, to his studies. But he's still a patriot. But I cannot demand that he return to all this. But I have to. He is my son. He is still a Filipino. This is part of him, too.

I have to talk to my son. I have to ask Raul to return.

He rubbed his eyes. The glare from the overhead flourescent lights hurt his eyes.

The building was silent. Through his window, the Senator could see the brilliant tropical moon over Manila, that old witness to a thousand crimes, a thousand acts of bravery.

What have you seen, old moon? The Spaniards wading ashore in their armor? My ancestors from the olden times, chieftains and priestesses? Pirates and traders? Generation upon generation of my people toiling in this beloved land. Admiral Dewey and the great American Fleet? Japanese invaders? Me and my friends when we were young? The young today, full of love and hope? Traitors and heroes in this wounded Eden? What have you seen, old moon? Will you tell me? Do you capture time and hold it? Unblinking you look down on us all, on our islands, on our struggles, you have seen everything, and generation after generation have looked up to you on nights like this, and wondered, what do you see, old moon?

What?

The Senator was suddenly alert. What was the newsreader saying? He raised the volume of the radio.

"... latest brutal killing in Manila. Police report that the latest victim was tortured in a particularly violent way before being killed. The body was dumped on the steps of the National Archives Building in Metro Manila. The killing seems to be yet another part of the wave of killings that has terrorized Metro Manila over the past several months, though police say it is much to early to reach any conclusions. The latest victim has been identified as Juan Atacan, 23 years old, of Manila. He was employed as an archives clerk in the National Archives, and police have no idea why this young man was targeted for death.

The weather tomorrow is expected to be sultry, with thunderstorms expected ..."

The Senator gently turned off the radio. He closed his eyes.

I will call Raul. He must help. Not me, not just me, he must help us all, he must help rescue the Philippines.

I must call Raul.

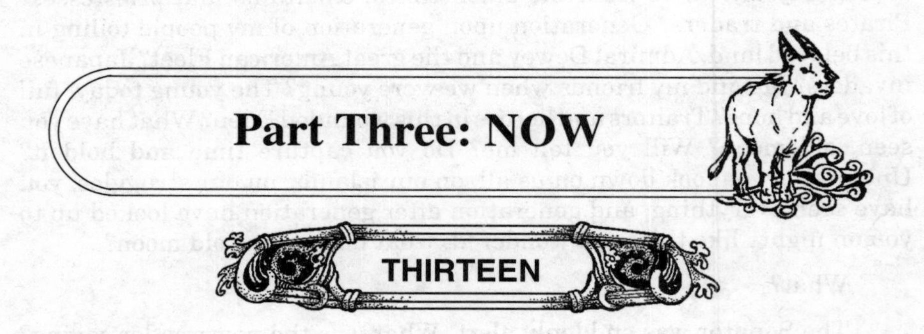

Part Three: NOW

THIRTEEN

It was a very nice day. Early summer in Northern Virginia. Flowers blooming. The air mysteriously fresh.

He parked at the opposite end of the parking lot, farthest from the office, and sat very still for a moment, looking around slowly, carefully. The offices in the complex were all pink and white stucco, all the parked cars glistening richly in the southern sun. He was thinking as he was watching, remembering, the thoughts more like a distant old half-forgotten refrain than a clearly formulated idea: park away from your destination; arrive early always; it is safest on foot; move slowly, deliberately ... Old habits die hard.

He had to smile at himself. This was America, after all, Magnolia spring in America, everything clean and bright and glowing, everyone moving in and out of the offices as trim and cheery as athletes and cheerleaders. But the summer sun had fired old juices, triggered old reflexes, stirred up old habits and memories.

He left his car and walked to the sidewalk, down the sidewalk, slowly, toward the office. The office complex was like a shopping mall, only with offices, not stores, but everything was as clean and tidily packaged as in a shopping mall. They all had small, tasteful signs which said things like "Management Associates," or "Financial Consultants," or "Corporate Attorneys." People who had done well were here. People well networked, who fit in, who knew just the right people, wore just the right clothes (elegant, but tasteful; confident but restrained). People with bright white teeth, and wavy hair, and trim waists.

His reflection, distorted, passed him by. He stopped, stepped backwards, to catch himself in the bronze sign. I'm old, he thought. My teeth are yellow. My hair is cropped, not waved, and falling out anyway. I look gaunt. Tired. He took off his sunglasses and looked at his eyes. They were black and there were dark circles around them.

He stopped at the office called “International Corporate Security.”

The door chimed softly when he opened it. The cool, air-conditioned air made him shiver.

“Yes? May I help you?” said a fresh-looking young woman. She was so very clean and tidy. She smelled very good.

“I have an appointment with Mr. D’Angelo. My name is Cleary.”

The young lady looked at the appointment calendar in front of her. A rubber band kept the pages on one side together. Little yellow reminders were attached to the pages.

“Yes, Mr. Cleary. Could you wait just a few minutes?”

That is what the young woman said, but what she thought was: I wonder who in the world this is! He looks, well, like nobody, really. A kind of tired nobody. She smiled to herself when she thought that. A tired kind of nobody. Maybe he sells floor wax or something.

The telephone on her desk buzzed softly. She spoke into it briefly, then looked at Mr. Cleary.

“Mr. D’Angelo will see you now.”

“Where’s Angstrom?” Cleary demanded.

The young woman had left, closing the door behind her. Cleary stood in the middle of the office. There were books on the walls, bright paintings, photographs, diplomas. To his left was a plush couch and a coffee table.

The man he was looking at belonged in this office. He was clean and tidy like the young woman, plush like the sofa. His cheeks were pink and white. His hair was blond and thin, pulled in wisps over his head. He wore glasses. They had wire frames and looked like aviator glasses.

“He is not on this operation.”

D’Angelo walked from behind his desk, and sat down on the sofa. He lay a thick folder on the coffee table. “I work for Angstrom.”

“Listen. I do not like this either. I did not ask for this or for you. We both work for the company. Why don’t we just get this over with?”

When he talked, Cleary could see his teeth. They were perfect. Cleary’s were yellowed. Like a dog’s.

Cleary sat down.

“I have been instructed to brief you on this operation. You must know that we are playing Washington rules. It is as distasteful to me as it is to you. But that is what our betters want. Washington rules. And I am your contact.”

"I never worked Washington rules with Angstrom. I am an independent. I have to have the freedom to work alone. I can't ask your permission for everything; I can't leave decisions up to Washington. To you."

"What you can do or cannot do is not the issue. Angstrom is not the issue. If you refuse this operation, say so. I will be more than happy to relay your refusal to the company."

Cleary said nothing. He was jumpy, that was it. He was supposed to be retired, they had retired him, set him up with the identity he had now, and a business, and a bank account. Set him up like one of their defectors; or a Mafioso. He was supposed to be retired. They said they would leave him alone. Angstrom had said so. Five years ago. And now they wanted him again. And they wanted Washington rules, they wanted to control the operation, they wanted reports, they wanted him to ask permission. They probably didn't trust him any more, didn't trust his judgment. They were probably right.

"You are to read this file, and return it to me. You may read it at your leisure next door. The room is secure. There is coffee in it; you may smoke in it. Sign the documents you need to sign. When you're finished, return the file to me. I will give you your operational materials." He paused, flattened his tie against his round stomach. Light glinted from a small ring on his baby finger. "In case you're wondering, I have no idea what is in the file. I am simply a messenger. I will pass along to you what they want. I will tell them what you say. That's all I have to do with it."

Cleary said nothing. He took the folder and walked into the adjoining room. D'Angelo closed and locked the door behind him. He was not an operations man. You could tell. Not just from his appearance; the best operatives made it a point not to look like operatives. Rather from his tone, his hands, his eyes. He had never gone on an operation alone. He did not know what it meant. He would go far in the company.

Cleary poured himself a cup of coffee from the white carafe on the table next to the room's only chair. He sat in the chair, lit a Lucky, inhaled deeply, and opened the file. That was when he first learned about Raul. This is what he told Leo later:

"You know, I had the strangest sensation. Or lack of sensation maybe. The room was clean and well-lighted and the chair was very comfortable, and it might have been in a bank or a library or something — no, not a library, they're too beaten looking, more like a bank — and I might have been reading a stock report or an investment plan or something. It was just pages, neatly typed on bright, white paper. I read them, page after page."

"I knew what sort of thing it was, of course, why else would they want me if it wasn't? And when I read through that neatly typed manuscript, I suppose I should have felt or thought something, not remorse or regret necessarily, but I didn't feel anything, or think anything. I wasn't excited or even interested. I simply read each page, memorized what I had to as I had always done, lay each page carefully face down on the coffee table, next to the white carafe. They made a rustling noise as I lay them down."

"I skimmed the preface. I knew that it would say that this document was top secret, that any divulging of it to anyone was a felony, that I was in no sense to consider myself an agent of the government, that I would, however, be compensated according to Internal Document Number 2741 (odd that I should remember the number). And that I was to kill a man."

"I memorized much of the rest. Names, dates, places. But when I had memorized everything, when it had become, then, part of me, that is when I felt very strange. That is when I began to shiver, shiver so badly that I spilled my coffee onto the cold white surface of the coffee table. It stained the white pages. I shivered because they were sending me to the Philippines. To my home. To kill a man."

FOURTEEN

As the Mercedes crept through the choking exhaust of Manila's chaotic traffic, past rows of shanties and mounds of garbage, he rehearsed again, silently, what he would say, but he was distracted again and again. The tinted glass concealed him from them, from the children and the cripples, who ran to his car at every stoplight. The tinted glass did not conceal them from him, though, and in their brown faces, in their dark eyes, reflected in the blue glass he saw himself. His face and their faces, merged together in the smoky glass.

He was not afraid of them. They did not disgust him. Even the toothless old man with stumps for hands did not frighten him. But there was something about them that was dangerous. Threatening. He hadn't noticed any of this in the men who had picked him up. His father's people. The older one, short and stout and jovial, embraced him when he stepped through Customs and playfully slapped his cheek. "Look at this!" the stout man laughed. "Look at this! The American boy! Welcome home, Raul!" He grasped Raul by both shoulders and shook him. "Juan, get Raul's bags! Your dad will be glad to see you, they all will!"

"Thanks, Philly." Raul had never known a time when he did not know Philly. Philly and his wife and his children either lived with Raul, or next door to Raul, or, rarely, down the street from Raul, and now that they lived in the compound, Philly and his family lived just across the street from Raul. He did things for Raul's father. His face was very broad, his teeth were widely spaced. He had very strong hands.

Raul sat in the back seat, alone. Philly drove. The other man sat in the passenger seat, in front. Philly did not introduce him. He was young, not more than Raul's age. He wore jeans and tennis shoes and a sport shirt and a windbreaker, despite Manila's heat. He was carrying something under his windbreaker, on his left side. He was an athletic young man. He did not smile.

"We've all been waiting, just waiting!" Philly was speaking Tagalog, now, spicing it with an occasional American word. "Your dad will be glad to see you. There's lots going on, Raul, lots, and it's not very good, I don't think, but your dad will manage it, and now that you're home, things will be great!"

Raul did not really listen. He was looking out the window at Manila flowing by. He had not remembered traffic as bad as this. There were hundreds of cars, thousands of cars, all herring-boned in the choked street, all coughing clouds of blue-grey smoke. Manila was made of cinderblock and asphalt and torn plastic garbage bags and exhaust fumes.

A jeepney crept past. The Philippines, Raul thought. A bastard thing, half jeep, half pickup, filled with coughing, choking people holding handkerchiefs to their noses. But a magical thing so gloriously and outrageously painted, in reds and whites and greens, so polished and chromed, so decked out in Jesuses who looked like Elvis, that Raul had to smile. On the windshield, at the top, bold letters proclaimed "Jesus Died For Your Sins." The jeepney rattled past, its passengers, jammed in the benches in the back, swaying.

At their first stoplight, the first crowd of beggars rushed around them. They were very quiet. They simply stood and stared. There were children, and old women with mouths filled with black stumps of teeth. They stood and stared in the smoky blue glass of the Mercedes windows.

The young man on the passenger side, in front of Raul, had had his window down slightly. When the beggars approached, he touched a button, and silently the window closed in the beggars' faces. Philly touched a button, and all the door locks snapped locked.

"There are lots of them now, Raul," Philly said, over his shoulder. The young man on the passenger side said nothing.

Alone in the back seat, Raul stared out the blue tinted window at the beggars. Behind them were palm trees. The fronds were moving gently against the turquoise sky.

"And can you believe this traffic!" Philly pounded the top of the steering wheel. "Just look at them!"

Traffic was stalled. Jeepneys and motor bikes, trucks and Mazdas, battered buses, and here and there a Mercedes and Volvo, all entangled with each other, in each other's way, all immersed in each other's choking exhaust. There seemed to be no rules, no plan. Cars crept into any lane, drivers shook their fists angrily at each other, there were no rules, there was no order, signs and lights were ignored, the mass of traffic, befouled and poisonous, lurched forward, hurly-burly, violently, spasmodically.

A river of debris, Raul thought. A fractured, broken city, pouring itself out in these foul rivers. A shattered world set in a tropic paradise. A jeepney crept by, gaudily painted in silver and red, half-truck, half-jeep, the outside American castoff, inside, weary Filipinos, the entire thing a frantic explosion of color and wild fantasy. A survival wagon, a mobile church with holy cards on the windows and plastic Jesuses on the dashboard, an explosion of junk and Baroque lunacy, creeping along in a river of dying technology.

This jeepney is my country, Raul thought. What has happened to my country? My country is a border town, a Juarez of the mind, Asia and America, both and neither, bruised and broken and extravagantly hopeful.

They entered Quezon City.

Quezon is different. Quezon is not Manila, though it is near Manila on the map. Quezon, with its skyscrapers and smart boutiques, its tasteful McDonalds and manicured gardens, is Miami, is Singapore, is Honolulu, but it is not Manila. Magically, the beggars disappeared, the trash and jeepneys disappeared, the traffic magically cleared, and, Philly at the wheel, the Mercedes coasted into another world.

He turned off the main street, and snaked through several side streets. They were like mazes, with high brick walls on either side. The high brick walls (some had broken glass and barbed wire on top) were the walls of the enclaves where the wealthy lived. Urban forts. Where Raul and his family lived.

Once he had explained to an American friend that these walls were just a Spanish custom, and maybe they were, but the mood was more Venetian than Spanish, or maybe Florentine, the mood was one of the Italian Renaissance, when powerful families built forts in the city, and plotted and conspired against each other. Forts in which families plotted a strange and cruel kind of intrigue, plots within plots in which assassins hunted assassins and poisoners were poisoned by smiling attendants whom someone else would kill in the heat and the warmth, beneath the blue tropical sky and the palms.

"Here we are," Philly said, as he turned into a compound. A man in a blue uniform, carrying an automatic weapon, waved them through the gate. The gate closed behind them. "Here we are," Philly said. "Home."

There were seven separate homes in the compound. Raul knew them all, had grown up in them all. Attractive, discreet, Spanish colonial homes. Airy. Most were built like Roman homes—squares, around an open courtyard in the center.

Philly pulled slowly into a driveway. As he did, three young men came out of the house. They wore barongs and jeans and tennis shoes. They were around Raul's age, in their early or mid-twenties. Raul did not recognize them. But he knew they were his father's people.

Philly turned the car off. He stepped out of the car and so did the young man in front; someone opened Raul's door for him. The young men nodded to Raul, but said nothing. He nodded in reply. One of them opened the trunk and pulled out Raul's bags.

Philly and Raul stepped into the house, walked through the vestibule into the living room. It was as he remembered it, dark but not sombre, filled with books and newspapers. Here and there, there were other young men.

"Johnny, here, come out into the garden, I'll let your dad know you're here." Philly stepped closer to Raul, and spoke softly. "Your dad's doing business. It's serious. You've seen how things look. Well, you know, something's got to change, somebody's got to take charge. Well ..."

Philly left. Raul stepped out into the garden.

He missed this garden. The house was built around it, the sky was open above it. A sliding glass door opened to it. His bedroom windows opened on to it. There was a huge palm tree in the garden, and mounds of fiercely green tropical bushes.

"It's like a Roman house," he had tried to explain to his American friends. "It's a square doughnut, with a garden in the very center."

They had laughed. "Filipino Romans! We thought Filipinos were all gentle and happy-go-lucky Polynesians."

"No," Raul had replied. "No, more like the Romans. Not world conquerers, but still Romans. We're stoics, and we respect our families and our parents. And we kill each other. The Sicilians of the Pacific."

"Raul." His father appeared in the doorway. There were young men in the background; they turned away. Raul stepped to his father. Silently, they embraced. Raul looked for a moment behind his father. Emilio was standing there.

"I am glad you are here," Raul's father said, after they had stepped apart. He had held Raul's shoulders when he said that: "I am glad you are here."

Raul's father was a small man. He was dressed in a simple but elegant barong and dark slacks. His brown face was battered and scarred, by the Japanese, by the secret police, by decades of political wars. His hair was still black, but there were hints of grey in it now, more grey than Raul remembered. His father looked thinner now. His movements were stiff.

Emilio was still in the background. "Good to see you, Raul," he said.

Raul nodded. He did not like Emilio. Emilio Dontar was his father's age; they even looked a little alike, two small, brown, scarred and battered old men. But Emilio was cold, distant. He did many things for his father, secret things. Among his father's friends, Emilio was perhaps the most important, the most powerful.

Emilio had always been there, in the background, like some sort of shadow. He and his father had met just after the war. Ever since then, one way or another, they had been together.

"Father," Raul had said once. "Father, I do not like Emilio."

"But he works for me, for us," his father had said. "I trust him."

"I don't," Raul had replied. He had not thought of him while he had been away, had almost forgotten about him. But now, seeing him again, he remembered.

Sometimes, people who were opponents of his father's had bad things happen to them. One was swept away by a scandal involving someone else's wife; another's business suddenly went bankrupt. Several died unexpectedly. Once, when one opponent was found floating face-down in Manila Bay, the police had arrested men who had worked for men who worked for Emilio. But they were released, and Emilio was never even questioned.

Raul had come outraged to his father.

"But he is a killer! Even I know that! How can you continue to be associated with him!"

"Listen to me," his father had said to him then, with a coldness and fury that had terrified Raul. "Listen to me. You are never to speak of these things again. Never. Not to me, not to anyone. You do not know what you are saying, you have no right to say anything, and I will not tolerate adolescent arrogance. Your mother, bless her memory, might have, but I will not. Listen to me." He was calmer now, but there was a seriousness about him that still frightened Raul. "One day, and it will not be soon, I hope, I will tell you all of my affairs, our affairs, and then I will retire and you can dispose of them as you wish. One day, I will say to you that it is time for us to discuss our affairs, and then, when you learn something, then you can judge."

That was long ago. But looking at Emilio now in the shadows, framed by the light shining through the glass sliding doors, he remembered it now. He did not like Emilio.

"Sit down with your old father."

His father motioned to the Spanish-style iron chairs off to the side of the garden. There was a table between the chairs. A young girl stepped into the garden and placed drinks on the table.

"Thanks, Emilio. Raul and I will talk."

Emilio nodded and disappeared into the house. He closed the glass doors behind him.

"We need to get you a barong! You look like an American. We need to turn you into a Filipino!"

His father sighed as he sat down. It was dark in this corner of the garden. The great, tumultuous green bushes were black now. The sky above them was black too, but speckled with dots of light. Men moved silently to and fro in the house, their shadows moving behind them along the garden doors. They sat the way they used to sit, the arms of their white rattan chairs touching. It was very dark but the darkness seemed very rich and velvet, more a presence than an absence. A soft breeze stirred the bushes. They spoke softly. Sometimes their voices mingled with the rustle of the palms.

The older man lay his hand gently on the younger man's arm.

"Father," Raul said. "Father," he asked, "what has happened to our beautiful country? It should be paradise. When I was young, we, and Singapore, and South Korea and Taiwan, we were all brothers and sisters. Now they've all grown up, now they're all strong. And we seem to be going nowhere. Or even worse, backwards. Every day, poorer, duller, more trivial, more violent. Our people are clean but our capital is submerged in filth. Our people work and work, and yet we're poor. We are peaceful, we are a family people, we are deeply religious, but every year there is more killing. Father, there is something bad here. It is almost as if something cruel and bad has selected our beautiful country as its lair. I read once that the opposite of the human is not the bestial, it is the demonic. It is not that we are becoming animals — would that we were. It's that .... I don't know. I think 'cancer' or 'poison'... I don't know. Father, what is happening to our beautiful country?"

Raul's father sipped his drink. The tinkle of the ice cubes seemed remarkably loud.

"You can read my speeches," he said. "There are many things. Many problems. We are seven thousand islands, we are an archipelagical culture, with scores of languages and customs. We have been wounded by stronger nations. Our elite have never developed a social conscience, a sense of noblesse oblige. Our poor do not have a sufficient work ethic, we have no sense of the commonwealth, everyone is out to enrich himself at the expense of the commonwealth. We are too tribal and clannish.... "

"But, Raul, there is something else, too. Yes, all of these are real problems. But there is something else, too."

"Think of this: time, we think, is horizontal. We move in the present away from the past, toward some ill-defined future. And as we move along this track, we leave the past further and further behind. Fine. The past is irrelevant, at best a curiosity. To think about the past is morbid, a waste of time, think about tomorrow, don't live in the past."

"You know, Raul, our people don't know our history the way they should. Our historical sites fall to wrack and ruin. We do not teach our children our history. Our politicians do not think about our history. OK. The past is behind us. Over and done with. Gone. Who cares?"

"But, Raul, think of this. Suppose time is not behind us. Not behind us at all. Just think. Turn our horizontal time by 90 degrees, and think for a moment, think for just a moment that time is vertical, that the future is above and the past is below. Think that what each generation does is gnaw its way into the future and transform it into the past, and build up layer upon layer of the past on which every generation lives. The present is just the most superficial layer of the past. And if this is true, and I think it is, then the past is not gone at all. It is still here, buried, yes, but still here, still active, still alive."

Raul's father's grip on the young man's arm tightened. This wasn't just an exercise, not just a momentary insight. It was important. Raul strained to listen, to understand.

The soft breeze stirred the flowers in the bushes. Shadows moved inside the house.

"No, Raul, the past is not gone at all. It is here, below us. It gives the contours to the present. And it threatens to erupt, to explode. For there are many things deeply buried, treasures, and riches, yes, but poisons, and fires. Courage is there, and hatred too. Still there, still active, still alive."

"Raul, think. Our language is laden with the past. We did not invent it, we could not invent it, the past invented it. Our faith is a great gift of the past. Our cities, our villages, our economy, they all grow out of the soil of the past. It's alive, Raul, even if we don't know it. And memory is not just the curious recollection of things dead and gone. Memory embraces our whole life, not just the superficial present, or the illusory future, but the past too, memory, when mingled with hope, is our only way to find out who we are."

"And, Raul, if you ignore the past, it will have its revenge. Something wicked from the past never dies, never disappears, it cannot simply be repressed, it must be faced, confronted, examined, and vanquished. Or else you go mad. The past, the present, the future, they are one thing. The past is always present. It shapes everything, it colors everything. And either you acknowledge it, try to understand it, try to control it, try to shape it, or you go mad. We do not know our past. Therefore we go mad."

Raul's father stopped. He seemed to need to catch his breath.

"I'm afraid I've turned into a philosopher," he said, and even in the darkness Raul could see him smile. "It comes with age," he said with a small laugh.

"But, Raul," he said, and his grip tightened again on Raul's arm, "it's true about the past. It has returned." He said it again. "It has returned."

"These are dangerous times," he said even more softly. "Ghosts walk. People die. I have called you home to help me in these times."

"Yes, father. And I have come home to be with you."

Raul's father folded his hands as if in prayer, his fingertips touching, the way he did when he was thinking. About something important.

"There are things I must tell you, Raul. Dangerous things. And things I must ask you to do."

"Yes, father."

Raul's father leaned toward his son, until his lips almost touched Raul's ear. Raul leaned toward his father. "Listen, son," his father whispered. And in the velvet darkness they sat, whispering together much of the night, their whispers blending with the rustling of the palms stirred by the warm and gentle night breeze.

FIFTEEN

His back, his legs, his neck were already stiff. All the comforts of business class, all the ministrations of the pretty stewardesses with the permanent smiles, and still stiff. He thought: I am getting old.

It wasn't this bad in the old days. The seats then were half this size and the flights twice as long. Like the flight to Bangkok from Tokyo in, when was it, '71? Odd that he could not remember. Life and death then. Forgotten.

His mind was drifting. Normally, in the old days, on an operation, he would jerk it back into focus, but now, he let it drift. It was dangerous to let your mind drift. It could get you killed. He did not care, really. He let his mind drift.

He sipped his scotch and let his mind roam. He lazily sniffed the cold airliner air, waved off dinner but ordered another drink, and plugged in his earphones. The classical station was playing something from Mahler. Something mournful and Viennese. He had never been to Vienna. He had been to Hanoi, Seoul, Tokyo, Rangoon, Bangkok, Beijing, Manila ...

He did not like this. Not one bit. (His mind began to focus again). The liquidation. The double game. Going to Manila.

He would liquidate the target. That wasn't it. Although why this one had to die he could not understand. True, he was into drugs. But what person of power in Asia was not somehow or other into drugs? And it was only some people, people who said, of course, that they were our people, who said he was into drugs.

It was the double game which bothered him. It made no sense. It violated everything he knew about this sort of thing. This target was a very public target. Very high profile. This profile worked like a shield. Therefore, the simplest means would be best. In country, execute the mission, exit.

But this charade, it was dangerous. Foolish. Not only would it most likely get him killed, but it would foul the operation.

It read like bad fiction. He was to disguise himself as a drug dealer. Establish contact with the target. Discredit the target via this association.

Agents in country would provide photographs and anonymous tips at the appropriate times to the opposition press. Then, once the dirtying was complete, then liquidate.

Destroy a person's reputation first. Then the person, too.

And how exactly was he to dress for this costume ball? Drug-dealers were young, macho. Not tired and old. They had thick and wavy hair, not close-cropped, steel grey hair (what there was of it). He could never do it. It was preposterous.

And dangerous. This stupid requirement would get him killed.

Because it wasn't a cover. D'Angelo couldn't understand that. Agents in operations, especially agents operating alone in a foreign country, needed hiding places, hiding places within hiding places. They needed covers, false names, blinds, false trails. But he was to call attention to himself. He was to be the big drug dealer come to the Orient. What if some police agency, what if some thug, what if some other secret agency spotted him and decided that he really was a drug runner? Where would he be then? No, this was the most ridiculous thing he had ever heard of. A high profile target. Liquidation. Inserting and extracting an agent. And instead of letting the agent prowl where he was safest, in the back streets, at night, in the drizzle and fog, no, they wanted to attach a spotlight to him.

Angstrom would never have stood for this. He would have laughed it out of court. He was the best handler he had ever had. He had been an operative himself. He understood this sort of thing.

Where was Angstrom?

This was wrong.

The day after the summons had come, disguised, the summons indicating that they wanted him again, the summons to see D'Angelo, he got the envelope. A simple envelope, postmarked "Chicago" and inside was a raggedly torn piaster, currency from the Republic of South Vietnam, from a country that had ceased to exist. When he opened it, it was as if a corpse had reached out and touched him.

In the old days, when he was young, in the jungle, during operation "Phoenix," this had been a sign. Phoenix had been the dirtiest side of the dirty war in Vietnam. Phoenix's agents were to infiltrate Viet Cong areas and assassinate Viet Cong leaders. It was dangerous and bloody. And a torn piaster was a sign. A warning. Nothing specific, no direct message, but a sign from a friend. A sign that said to hide. To go to ground. To find a hole, a cave, to lie very low and very still. Only the handful of people he had worked with knew about this private code. He had forgotten it. But from the past, this omen, this whisper had come to him. Leo, in Manila, knew what it meant. And Angstrom.

Where was Angstrom?

The lights dimmed in the cabin. The Mahler in his ear seduced him into a world of memory and melancholy. This interminable flight would have its termination. This flight through the dark, through memory, toward murder, would have its end.

He was going home. To the Philippines.

"No, you are not one of them," his dad had said, and he had cried. He was small then, and he cried easily. His dad put his arm around him, and dried his bitter tears. "I'm sorry. We are different. We can never really be one of them. We are Americans, not Filipinos." "No. We are not like them. I know you wish you were."

"But I talk like them. I play with them. I like them, my friends, I mean, and they like me. I was born here, just like they were. I don't understand what makes me so different."

"I don't know either, son".

His father embraced him, smoothed his hair from his forehead.

"When I came, before you were born, I came to preach the Gospel of Christ. To the heathen. Then being American and being Christian were all bound up together. The Gospel I preached was a mixture of Christ's message and Herbert Hoover's. Lots of people mixed up Christ and Hoover. At least before '29."

"I don't understand."

"That's all right. Anyway, to me, then, Filipino meant small and brown and savage. They are still browner than I. But I wonder who the savage was. I came to convert them. Then I married your mother. And I was the one who was converted."

"But we're still Methodist. We're not Catholic."

"That's true." His father smiled. He had a thin, long face, and his smile was very wide. His hair was light brown. His eyes were bright blue.

"I mean that they taught me as much about Christ, more, than I could ever teach them. You know what 'utang na loob' means?"

"Yes. It means that you owe someone a very large debt. That you would die for the person if you had to. It is a sacred thing."

"Well, that has something to do with being Filipino. It means honor and loyalty. It means that honor and loyalty are the most important things in life, far more important than things and money. Honor and loyalty and bravery. And that you must work very hard to attain them, but you know you never can because they are gifts. I'm not sure that Americans understand this any more."

"I still don't understand. Why can't I be a Filipino? I'll be honorable and brave."

His father squeezed his shoulder, and smiled his angular smile. "No. You will understand this someday, and much more. And as you learn more about honor and bravery and loyalty, about 'utang na loob,' then maybe you will become a Filipino. Because I don't think you are ever born a Filipino. You become a Filipino."

"Even the others?"

"Even them. They must become Filipinos. They must become who they are."

He could see himself. Not as he was now, lean, sallow, balding, his day-old beard black and grey. Not as he was then, either, in the first memory. But as he became.

And he learned something. He learned that people have eyes but do not see. He learned that you could hide in plain sight.

Because he did become one of them. A Filipino. At least superficially. With his brown skin, and his dark hair, dressed in a barong Tagalog and slacks, he of course looked like a Filipino. And when he spoke, he spoke not only perfect Tagalog, but Filipino Tagalog, spiced, connotative, nuanced. All the cues he knew, all the gestures and body language, all the winks and nods. Anyone who bothered to take a second look would see that he was just a little different, but few people bothered to take a second look. People lived on the surface, they looked but did not see, and on the surface, he was Filipino. Once, at the university, he was sitting with his Filipino friends in the cafeteria. There were a handful of Americans and Europeans there, too. He joined them and they wanted to know what in the world he had in common with those Asians. And afterwards, his Filipino friends wanted to know what in the world he had in common with those Caucasians.

He knew he belonged to the tropics. To the lush greens and rich blacks, to the rolling Pacific surf, to the enormous blue sky with its mountains of clouds, billowing like monuments. Palm trees and ocean breezes, the sudden storm hurled from the immense sky, the abrupt summer sunsets, they were all part of him.

But what about the other things? The things his father had talked about? Once, his father had tried to explain why he was sympathetic to the

Huks. Why, during the war, he had fought with the Huks against the Japanese. It had to do with suffering. Suffering was an evil. But in God's plan, suffering could never simply be abolished. It had to be redeemed. Which meant that one had to endure it, transform it, share the suffering of others. It was there that one learned about loyalty, and honor, and courage, and self-sacrifice, and "utang na loob." It was there, in redemptive suffering, that one learned to be a Filipino. His father had learned that. Learned that at the end. He had talked about that just before the soldiers took him. And killed him. And hid him deep in the Filipino soil.

He didn't think he had ever learned that. And that kept him from being a Filipino.

Maybe she had sensed that, young as she was. As he was.

He was a kind of a monster. An un-thing. That's what her family said. He sounded and smelled and moved and looked like a Filipino, but his father was an Anglo; and something about him was Anglo, even if he sounded and smelled and moved and looked like a Filipino. Often, one side or the other wouldn't notice his monstrousness at first. He had seen it a hundred times, a thousand times. He would be with Filipino friends, laughing and talking, and all of a sudden, one would ask him about his family. He would say that his mother was Filipino, but that his father was an Anglo. Then they would look at him as if he were a special kind of freak. It was as if you were chatting away with someone and only suddenly discovered that the someone was part horse, or part dog. Caucasians did the same thing. He would say something in Tagalog and their eyebrows would arch up. It was crazy. Everybody in the Philippines was a child of the whole world. Filipinos were all Asians and Caucasians, Polynesians and Chinese. Maybe, Cleary thought, it was him not the others. Maybe it was how he saw himself. Maybe he couldn't decide whether he was Asian or western, Filipino or North American. Anyway, he had learned to hide. To disappear into the background, into the bush. He had learned to be a chameleon. Among Asians, he was an Asian; among westerners, a westerner. It didn't always work, but mostly it did.

So that was who he was. A monster. In disguise. A monster of a thousand faces.

And an assassin.

"I want you to read about him," his father said.

He gave him a paperback book. On the cover was something that looked like people fighting. The Night They Burned The Mountain. On the back was a photograph of the author. Tom Dooley. A young man. Thin, but handsome. A doctor.

"He was a great man. He was a doctor, who dedicated himself to the Asian poor. A Christian. A revolutionary too. But not a Communist. A real revolutionary."

It was a warm night, they sat on the veranda of the little parsonage. The air was blue and black, slow-moving, heavy. The sky was electrified by a million stars.

He loved these times. Alone with his father. Just the two of them. He did not remember his mother very well, but his father said that she had liked nights like this too, nights very warm and heavy, with only muffled sounds in the distance, wrapped in the warmth and darkness.

Often his father would talk about America, about where he had grown up, about why he had become a missionary. About what it had been like when he had come out to the islands. About how he had met his wife, what she had been like. About important things, like how you ought to live, about why you ought to be brave.

"You were a revolutionary, too, father. When you were with the Huks. Against the Japanese."

"Yes. Maybe a little like Tom Dooley."

They were side by side, in the white rattan chairs, their feet propped up on the white veranda rail.

"The strong must use their strength to help the weak. That is the only thing which separates criminals from law officers, bandits from genuine soldiers. I have tried to use whatever strength I had to help the weak."

"Isn't that what the communists do too?"

"Some. Some are good people. But Communism itself is bad. Read Dooley's book; read what the Communists did to Laos. No, the Communists are just politicians like any others. They want to throw the ins out, they want the outs to be in. So they can exploit the old ins who are out. They want power, they are all for domination, they just want to be the ones doing the dominating. They are not heroes. They do not use their strength to help the weak, their conscience does not restrain their strength, and they do not guard their souls."

Often, when his father was talking about important things, he spoke in his preacher voice, deep and resonant, not loud, but rich, rolling. But he did not use his preacher voice this night. It was a voice the boy did not recognize. It was earnest, precise. It was as if his father were giving him very exact instructions about something precious and delicate.

"Guard your soul. Always. Use your strength to help the weak."

He was frightened. This sounded like his father's good-bye voice.

"Yes, father."

"Good. We'd better go to bed."

He remembered all this, every detail, the very tones of their voices, the small wrinkles around his father's eyes, he remembered it as if it were engraved on his memory, because it was the next day that the soldiers came and took his father away. And his father never came back to see him again.

"We will be landing in Manila very shortly," a chirpy voice said and rattled on pleasantly. He opened his eyes wide, stretched, and looked out of the airplane's window. There were clouds, great billows of white, cotton-candy clouds, which passed slowly, and below him, spectacularly green and blue, was the place where his memories had been born.

The business class was stirring around him. Everyone bleary-eyed from the eternity on the aircraft, but for all that clean and synthetic and polished. And safe. A world of muted desire, muted passion, minor danger.

He was glad to leave it, to return to the streets and the jungle. It had taken a very long time, but finally, the operation had begun.

SIXTEEN

“Raul! Welcome home. Welcome to the business!” He wasn’t really his uncle. But he was his godfather, which was much more important. He looked rather like his father; maybe it was just that all the men in that generation looked alike. All small and brown and battered. With broken and badly reset noses, or scarred faces, or crooked hands and fingers.

Godfather Santo—Uncle Santo—and his father had been in the war together. Raul didn’t really know much about that time, only that they had known each other. Santo had then been in Hong Kong for years. Then he and Raul’s father had started their business.

Raul always liked Santo’s name. His full name was San Thomas Aguiar. For some reason his parents had insisted on calling him San Thomas, and not just Thomas, maybe to convince doubting St. Thomas that this really was his namesake. Everyone called him Santo. When he was a boy, Raul had called him Santa, not Santo. It was a nice name.

“I’m glad to see you, Uncle Santo.”

“Your dad tells me you’re joining the business. That’s good, Raul.”

“I’m afraid I won’t be much help.”

“Oh, we’ll teach you.” Uncle Santo had a nice smile. He took Raul by the arm—his hand was firm, though his fingers were crooked—and led Raul into his office.

It was a fine office. Wood everywhere. Polished, reflecting, the books on the walls, the jet-black telephone on the desk, the framed photographs on the wall. Santo waved Raul to a sofa, and sat beside him. A young man slipped into the office with a tray. Cups with hot water were on the tray, and small dishes with instant coffee, sugar, and cream. He set the tray on the table in front of them and silently disappeared.

“Well, Raul, I’m glad to see you. Really. Though I’m just a little surprised. Your politics, I mean. I thought you were a revolutionary or something.” Santo smiled again.

"I'm just here to help Dad. I've nothing against business. I know you and Dad built this from nothing, I know it's honest. It's corruption I was against. I still am."

"Fine." Santo sipped his coffee. He had fine, delicate features. His fingers, though badly bent, were long, and seemed to move slowly. They seemed not to grasp the coffee cup, but to curl around it.

"A young rival! I admire that, Raul, I really do. But let's don't talk politics. I'm a simple businessman, trying to make a living. I'll leave politics up to you and your dad."

Raul smiled. "Fine. Will you teach me the business?"

"Of course. It's very simple, in a way. We are an import/export consulting firm. Foreign businesses want to work with a Filipino business, but don't know who to get in touch with. So they contact us, and we set them up with a local firm. Or a Filipino business wants to sell its wares in the U.S. or Australia or Europe, but they don't quite know how. So they contact us, and we help them get set up. We give advice on taxes, on banking, on real estate, on economic trends. We handle products too, although that's more of a sideline. We bring things in, ship them out." He sipped his coffee, delicately. "And make friends around the world. But concepts are easy. It's the implementation that's complex. Getting the accounts, keeping the records, doing the actual brokerage. But we make a living."

"I would like to start like any new employee."

"Fine. Although your dad wants you to be his representative, too. So we'll give you a crash course in business, introduce you to everybody, work you like a peon, then make you a top manager." Santo laughed. His teeth were yellow and silver.

"OK," Raul said. "I will be a success story. From campus radical to top manager." He laughed, but his laugh was a little ironic, a little sad. As if he had lost his virtue.

He hardly recognized himself when he dressed in the mornings. No jeans, no pullovers, no jogging shoes. The Harvard graduate student had disappeared. Sometimes a barong Tagalog, but not often. The Filipino, what there was of him, had disappeared, too. Now he appeared in Italian suits and silk shirts and ties. His skin had changed. Now he was sleek; now he glistened.

"This is the uniform, that's all," Uncle Santo had said. "We do business with people who dress like this. It means we share their values. It means we're dependable and successful."

"In the States, I was afraid of losing my Filipino soul. Then, I was even more afraid of standing out as a Filipino. I wanted to fit in, to be American. Inside, I was American. I knew more about America than the native-born. Inside, American, but outside, Filipino. And now here, now at heart, I want to be Filipino, but outside, I'm the All-American corporate manager. I feel like I'm in disguise."

"You are," Santo replied. "So am I. So are we all."

Raul and Santo talked for hours about Raul's job in the firm. They talked in Santo's mahogany office, sometimes in Santo's home. Santo lived in Makati, that glistening glass and steel, air-conditioned echo of Miami in the heart of steamy Manila.

"We are fixers. Brokers. Deal-makers. Business coming in, we organize; business going out, we organize. We advise, consult, guide. That's where your dad and I think you can fit in best. You know Americans well, you practically are one. You know Europeans. What do you speak, beside Tagalog? Three European languages? Anyway, your dad and I want you to be our contact with the West. We've got plenty of experts to handle technical stuff, technicians. But we need you to do the preliminary things."

"The wooing?" Raul asked.

"Wooing. But also negotiating. Arranging things. Drumming up business. It's important."

They were in Santo's home. It was much like Raul's father's. Lots of open space, dark wood. There were plants everywhere. It seemed almost to be a jungle. Servants silently brought them tea, emerging and disappearing from the web of plants. Santo had his young men, too. In tropical suits and windbreakers, some with barongs. Always, they seemed to be in the background. Silent. Ominous.

Santo seemed to be in an expansive mood. That was rare. He seldom talked about himself or his past. Raul suddenly thought that he really knew very little about Uncle Santo. He didn't even know whether he had ever been married, whether he had any children, any family.

All Raul knew was that Santo and Raul's father were contemporaries. That Santo and his father had somehow been together during the war, although not exactly in the same unit. That Santo had gone to Hong Kong after the war, and had managed his own business there and had become rich. That when Raul was a little boy, Santo had approached Raul' s father about a joint venture. So they had created the business, Aguiar and Martinez, Import-Export Consultants, "AGMAR."

Santo Aguiar, Raul thought, I wonder who you are.

"By the way, " Santo said, interrupting his stories about the business. "How's your dad?"

"Fine. Busy."

"I know. I seldom see him. He seems preoccupied with something. Worried about something."

"The situation. Something is wrong with the nation. It's like it's lost its way. Dad is afraid something bad is going to happen . He's taking measures."

"Of course." Santo sipped his tea.

So Raul Martinez entered business. And part of him enjoyed it . His ideas about business, he discovered, had been arrogant and narrow. Arrogantly, he had assumed that business people were less noble than intellectuals, which was preposterous. He actually came to admire the way business people were able to get things done, meet payrolls, make things and sell them.

Narrowly, he had assumed that no one could really enjoy business. But he discovered he did. He enjoyed the competition, the practicality of it. The sense of accomplishment, and the rewards.

Above all, he enjoyed the sheer pragmatism of it. People needed food, they wanted toys. So someone needs to make food and toys and clothing and transportation. Some systems need to match desires with products, dreams with realities. Ideologies couldn't do that; Marxist deconstructionism couldn't do that. The people of ideas could not feed the world. He grew more and more impatient with labels, ideologies, slogans. He wanted to know who, and when, and what it will cost.

So Raul entered business. He married sugar growers in Cebu to chocolate makers in Austria; Belgian electronic firms to small towns in Leyte that needed jobs. He flew to Tokyo to meet with bankers on behalf of Hong Kong merchants who wanted to set up shop in Manila.

But something bothered him. Worried him.

The situation, of course. That's what everyone called it. The swarms of beggars on the streets. The utter confusion in government. The bandit gangs in the southern islands. The inflation, and meanness that seemed to be taking hold of people.

But it wasn't just that.

It was his father. He seemed driven. Obsessed. He disappeared for days at a time, with only Emilio or one or two of his people.

Raul had asked Emilio what was going on. But Emilio only looked at him coldly, and said that Raul ought to speak with his father. Emilio was like Santo and Raul's father, the same generation, but colder, leaner, not really Filipino at all, machine-like.

And what are you doing while father is doing what he is doing, Raul thought.

Because Raul had seen things, heard things, downtown, in the restaurants in Quezon, he had heard that Emilio had friends in town, among important people, that important people spoke of Emilio as a successor to Raul's father.

I do not trust you, Emilio, Raul thought.

One evening, after dinner, Raul asked to speak with his father. Alone.

"Of course," Raul's father said. He gestured with his right hand, waved as if gently sweeping a fly away, and the young men went off. Emilio hesitated, but Raul's father nodded to him, and he left, a portfolio of papers under his arm.

"So, my son the businessman, what shall we talk about?"

"I want to help you with what you are doing."

"Close the door."

Raul stepped from the table, and slid the wooden door closed. He returned to the table and sat next to his father.

Raul spoke first.

"I know I should not interfere in your business. But since I have come back, your business is my business. You are preoccupied with something. I want to help."

Raul spoke in the same low tones he and his father had used in the garden when he first came home. Soft, low tones. The music of conspiracy.

His father did not reply at once. He toyed with the water glass in front of him, with the spoon. His brown fingers, crooked with age, with torture, were never still. Raul had inherited the trait.

"There will be a coup," his father said, matter-of-factly, without drama, without emotion. "Within six months, maybe eight." He tapped lightly on the table with the spoon. "Many people are preparing for what will happen. There will be blood. It is a time to be together with your friends. But that is not it." Raul's father sat back in his chair. His fingers tapped softly on the arm.

"During the war, when I was a guerrilla, sometimes we had successes, sometimes we failed. That was expected. But in the middle of the war, something very bad happened. Our missions began to fail, our men were murdered in their homes. In their beds."

"It was clear that we had a spy within. A Judas. Someone was watching. Listening. Someone very close."

"It was my job to find him out. He was very clever. He knew everything I did. He knew my moves before I even took them. He killed my friends."

"But I killed some of his. He had people around us, people who worked for him. I ferreted them out and destroyed them. But him I could never find."

"It became very personal with us. I thought of him not only as an enemy, but as the enemy. Because it wasn't just that he fought against us. It was that he was one of us, a Filipino, he must have been, but he betrayed us, sold us, he lived in lies and deception, he seemed to be everywhere, always ready to deceive, to betray, to trap, to murder. That I think was the worst part of the war. For me at least."

It had gotten dark, suddenly. In the rest of the house there were whispers, muffled movements. But Raul and his father sat quietly in the darkness, next to each other, so close they almost whispered in each other's ear.

"Everyone in that sort of affair develops habits. Calling cards. He had many. After a while, I recognized them immediately. They were a kind of language. He had certain ways of killing. He was remarkably brutal. He tortured people. Some he flayed or decapitated. In the forehead of his victims he carved a sign, three slashes, as if a tiger had clawed them. Certain kinds of people he recruited. The strangest of all was that he warned his victims before he struck. They would get notes. Messages. Things tacked to their doors in the middle of the night. Once, a farmer who had befriended us found a cat hanging from its neck on a tree. The farmer was murdered within the week. Rocks were thrown through windows. Children shouted things in the dark and ran away."

"It was bravado on his part, but it was also very calculated. It was designed to terrorize people, and it worked. It created confusion and great fear."

"He killed friends of mine. He tried to kill me. He sent me notes, threats, scoffing, mocking notes. When the war ended, he disappeared. I hoped he somehow or other had been killed. But I suspected that he had simply returned to whatever evil place he had come from. And was waiting."

Raul's father wiped his mouth with a napkin. He softly cleared his voice. It was very dark in the room.

"There will be a coup. Many have known that. We are all preparing. As I prepared, I began to notice something. I began to notice that in our politics, in Manila especially, there was, I don't know how to say it, a kind of growth, a kind of tissue. Something different from the usual factions, something different from even the usual criminals."

"Remember the winter we spent in the States, you were about ten?"

"Yes. I was nine. We stayed in New York. You were a guest professor. It was a very cold winter."

"You remember the flies?"

"My God, yes. I hadn't thought of that in years. I can still feel it. Not just disgust, but, I don't know, somehow dirty, putrid."

"At first, there was just the one little fly in the house. But strange. It would buzz in wild circles, hurl itself against lights, against your face even. Fall on its back and madly spin. At first we thought it was just one. We even laughed about the last fly of summer, trapped in the winter. But then there was another and another, then three and four at a time, on the floor, in the kitchen. They made your mother ill."

"Because they seemed sick. Diseased somehow. Insects are a nuisance, but you get used to them here. But those things. I was frightened of them. I was afraid to walk at night, afraid that I would step on them."

"We finally hunted them down, you and I. We tracked them into the attic. Into a dark corner amid the rafters. There were thousands of them. All diseased. All mad. Crawling on the rafters and falling off, crawling all over each other, devouring each other."

"What I have found is like that. Only I have found only the bunches of flies so far. I have not yet gotten to the attic. It is drugs, and bribery, and prostitution, but all strange, organized in a way I had not believed possible. And it has infected politics. If and when there is a coup, whoever is behind these flies, these vermin, he could be very powerful."

"Is it American gangsters, father? Chinese?"

It was as if Raul's father did not hear him.

"Seven months ago, just before I asked you to come home, I had driven into the city alone. It was in the evening. It was a routine meeting.

It lasted all night. When I returned to the car, it looked odd, as if it were squatting on the pavement. All four tires had been slashed. Every window had been broken. Red paint had been poured all over the inside. And in red paint, a finger had written on the driver's side door: "This is the beginning."

"A week later, one of our people disappeared. We still have not found him. The police found his head. On a post. With three slashes on his forehead."

"And then, a month ago, I got this."

Raul's father took out his wallet, and from it extracted a piece of paper, folded into a neat square. He handed it to Raul. Letters were pasted on it, cut out of magazines. The letters said: "I have returned."

"It could be anything, father."

"Of course. Anything. But the twisting of MacArthur's words in this way, the car, my man's disappearance. I feel him. He has come back."

"I asked you to come home before I was sure of all this. I hoped you would do what you have done, watch over the business with Santo, while I was in politics. But if this really is him, if he is somehow the organizer of this corruption, if he is alive and here, in Manila, then something is going on even more dangerous and deadly than merely a military coup."

Here his father fell silent. The shadows thickened around them.

"Who could believe that he is back after all these years?" Raul said. "It couldn't be."

"I hope it is not. I hope so with all my soul," his father said.

They were silent then for a long time. Then they began to whisper again, the young man and the old, sitting in the heavy tropical darkness, and they whispered long into the night.

SEVENTEEN

Chaos, as usual. A swarm of Filipinos coming home from Dubai and Bahrain and Kuwait and who knew where, each dragging a battered cardboard box filled with the wonders of the richer world. The Philippines had nothing to export but her children, and these she sent all over the world. They work as maids and scrub others' floors, they nurse others' ills, they dig ditches in others' soil, they spill their sweat and often their blood in others' lands, and then they come home. Like he did.

Already he felt at home, amid the chaos, the air filled with Tagalog cries and laughter, filled with brown eyes and jet-black hair, children underfoot everywhere. Magically, indestructible Filipino families coalesced all around him, like clouds in the tropic sky. He, of course, was alone.

Past customs. Off to the sides, in corners, hard-eyed young men in camouflage-striped uniforms, Uzis suspended lazily at their sides. He stepped into the terminal, into the heat of the tropic night. A young man, all in white, hurried up toward him.

"Transportation, sir?"

"Yes. Manila Hotel."

"Yes, sir. Let me take your bag, sir. This way, sir."

Behind the obsequiousness, cunning black eyes. The game between the colonial and the colonized. He often wondered who had colonized whom. We have colonized them. We have forced on them our language, our systems. But they, weaker than us, are stronger. For they have taken a language not theirs and made it theirs, a religion alien, and transformed it. They are the servants, we the masters, but this is their world and we are lost in it.

But who are we? Who are they?

I am not one of them. I am one of them. I am one of them pretending to be not one of them.

Outside, in the heat. The heat, a blanket, a weight, a cloak. His dark glasses fogged, and he removed them. One element of disguise removed, making his disguise, his foreignness, even stronger. Odors in the heat, of rich soil polluted by trash and engine exhaust, but rich and strong nevertheless. Each step was further into their world, which was his world, each step deeper into memory.

He sat in the back of the Mercedes. The driver was in white. He wore white gloves.

"First time in Manila, sir?"

"Yes," he lied.

"It is a beautiful city. The earthquakes were terrible, but, thanks to the Virgin, my family escaped. We're from north of here ..."

How we love to talk, how they love to talk. Gossip and stories and legends. Nowhere in Asia do people love words more.

"... but Manila at least has work, which is why we came here. You must go north, though, to the little towns. Of course, I'm sure you're here on business ..."

He stared out the window, the driver's voice humming pleasantly in his ear. They cruised through the darkness, into the choking traffic. Row on row of neon flashed past, snake shops and tumbledown bordellos, and he thought of Saigon. Western debris flowed past him, safe from it in the air-conditioned Mercedes.

They were on Rizal Boulevard now, the vast expanse of the bay to their left. Vast ships, dreamlike in the darkness, seemingly within touch. Glass and steel replaced concrete block; they were in yet another of the Philippines. It was right that the nation's name was plural. For there were many Philippines.

Palm trees illuminated by streetlight. On either side, now, Luneta Park, its monuments sepulchral in the night. A slow left, past an endless column of battered taxis, to the Manila Hotel.

The Manila Hotel. Incongruous, beautiful, all luxury now, but still with an ambiance of languid ceiling fans and white wicker chairs. More people in white, opening the Mercedes door, toting his suitcase, everyone smiling.

"If you please sir, would you step through our scanner? Only security."

He stepped through the scanner. Another young man in white ran a metal detector around him.

"Thank you very much, sir. Uncertain times. We cannot be too careful."

The lobby was as magnificent as ever. Vast, panelled in Asian wood, plush sofas in the center for weary Westerners and Japanese. Rock and roll from the bar on the left. Young Asians singing about Detroit. Reception to the left.

"Everything is ready, sir. We'd like to welcome you to our new luxury suite. Just sign here, please."

He signed: Philip Andrews. It was not his name.

He followed the bellman toward the elevators. That was when the memory came.

He had come to Manila with his father. His father had church business. He came along. He was small then. When they walked into the hotel, he had held his father's hand.

"This is a very famous and important place, John. When the war started, and the Japanese invaded, this is where General MacArthur was. And President Quezon. In this very hotel. Then, when the Japanese came closer, they went to Corregidor. Remember Corregidor?"

He did remember, because he had gone there with his father too. It was very green. There were cannons. He had climbed on one. There was a long tunnel too. "This is where General MacArthur was, too. There were soldiers here then, and fighting." They had walked into the tunnel, and he had been afraid. He had held his father's hand tightly.

His father had lived in the mountains when the Japanese had come. His father had been a soldier. A guerrilla. That was when his mother had died. Shot by the Japanese soldiers.

His mother had been shot by the soldiers.

He shook the memory away. They came on him too often now. And this place was webbed with memories; he could not walk ten steps without strands of memory gently enveloping him.

But he must not remember. He must think clearly.

In the lounge, on the business-class floor, a portrait of MacArthur suddenly stared at him as the elevator door opened. A final memory echoed.

The face was stern, but not frightening. It looked a little like his father, a little like the picture of God in his children's Bible.

"He looks like a daddy," he had said to his father.

His father had smiled. "Yes. He does. I suppose the Philippines are his children."

Dressed in his best Miami drug-smuggler costume—linen suit, Panama hat, dark glasses, tennis shoes without socks, alligator briefcase, Rolex—he strolled conspicuously through the Manila Hotel's luxurious lobby, and out into the Manila heat. Cab drivers languidly asked whether he wanted a ride, but he ignored them, crossed into Luneta Park, and walked south toward Taft Avenue. He spoke to no one, but made sure he was seen by everyone.

"People do not see people. They see types, caricatures. If you wish to disappear, dress and act more or less like everyone else, and you will disappear. People who bump into you will not really see you. When on a mission, if you need concealment, immediately dress nondescriptly like everyone else. And even if you would otherwise stand out, even if you are a black in Norway, a white in Zambia, you will all but fade away. But if you wish to stand out, dress and act again in a stereotypical way, but as a counter-stereotype. Wear a suit at the beach; a sweatsuit to dinner. Again, people will not see you exactly, but they will see your image. By changing these images, you can fade in or fade out at will."

He had given a talk about this once, at an Agency training center, and his words, long forgotten, echoed in his brain once more.

As he walked through the park, fragments of his mission came back to him, too.

Misinformation will be disseminated before your arrival. The lies in which you can hide. Our friends in the police, in the military, in the press, will learn that an important dealer is coming to town. They will follow you, but you will lose them, then let them find you again.

You must be seen several times with the target. You must discredit your target. Then you must liquidate your target.

And then I will change skins and disappear.

But what did that torn piaster mean?

Of course he knew what it meant. Danger. Caution. Go underground until the storm passes. Go to ground. But who had sent it? Why?

He walked slowly through Luneta. Memory came on him again. It bothered him now, this remembering. He could not control his memories; they came from nowhere and surged over him, voices and pictures. There were too many, that was the problem, he had done too much and seen too much and there was no place left in his mind; his memory had exploded, and they all came tumbling out, and he could staunch them briefly, but only briefly.

He began to sweat in the blazing sun, his white linen staining dark grey.

The martyr's monument was to his right; he turned left, past the statues of the carabao, across Roxas Avenue, between the hectic jeepneys, all painted in their turbulent, frantic colors, toward the Rizal Monument, pursued by his memories.

They would get him killed.

"On a mission, you are alone. Undercover, in disguise, surrounded by enemies, alone. On a mission, a thousand variables intersect each moment—weather, traffic, bystanders, police—and a small variation in one will transform all the others. Half of what happens, half of what happens, is sheer chance. Luck. And one day your luck will run out. That is inevitable. But the other half depends on caution. Caution on an operation is everything. You must be alert to everything, all the time, to sounds, smells, shadows. You are a lone wolf in a strange and dangerous forest. You must listen and sniff and tread silently and at the least strange stirring, you must go to ground. If you do not do this, you will die."

His words. From long ago. They were true, he knew they were true, he knew he had to discipline his mind, but he could not. To be honest, he no longer even tried.

There he was, younger, firmer, standing at the foot of the Rizal Monument in the flashing sunlight, the open horizon of the bay behind him, the flag of the Philippines snapping above him, standing perennially at attention as he did then, in his crisp tan uniform, the very picture of the New Frontiersman, a younger John Kennedy in khaki, his eyes masked by the aviator sunglasses which had become the lone-ranger mask of a new generation of cowboy heroes.

She was much smaller than he was; like many Filipino women she looked much younger than she really was, though they were both young then.

"I'm to be an advisor. I'm not to go into battle at all. An advisor. Just like my dad was here. I'm going there to help build a free society. The Viet Cong are worse than the Nazis ever were; sure, they promise to make a revolution, to help the poor, but they're tyrants. We're the revolutionaries, we're the ones who will save the poor."

"With your guns."

"Of course we need guns. They are killers, the VC. We have to defend the poor, and that means guns. But, there's good and bad, and you have to fight the bad. We're the good guys." They sat at the base of the monument, looking out at the bay. Great billows of white clouds set in the azure sky looked back at them. They sat on the warm base of the monument, their arms, their knees, their thighs, gently touching.

"Think of Rizal, think of the priest martyrs, think of all the people who gave their lives right here, for the Philippines. Think of Aguinaldo, Del Pilar, all the heroes. They fought, they gave their lives. When they had to. We are like them."

"Yes, you are. I understand that. And I understand that you are naive, too. Violence maybe is necessary sometime, but it is never good. Never. You say you are a radical, a real revolutionary. Fine. Just where do you overthrow the cycle of killing and death? Fight for the poor. I will fight for the poor, too. But killing breeds killing. And that is no revolution."

Helena gestured vigorously when she talked. She swept a lock of jet-black hair from her forehead.

"And who is naive now! Do you think that love without strength will transform the world? When a bandit attacks, will you stop him with kind words alone? When the murderer tries to murder, you must stop him. Is it more moral to stand aside just so you can keep your own hands clean?"

"And who then will break the cycle? Where is the real alternative, the radical challenge, the real revolution? I am sure the young VC talk just like you. And so you will kill each other and the poor will stay poor, if they're not killed in the process!"

They were getting angry now, and neither of them wanted it to be like this. They watched the clouds drift overhead, watched the small boats, beetle-like, scuttle over the waves to the tankers in the bay.

"We must go our own ways," she said then, softly. They had wept over this once, twice, wept over a future they had desperately wanted, a future they both could touch and taste and see, a future they had begun to conjure, but which they knew would never, could never, be. So they spoke softly now in respect to it, more fellow mourners than lovers, though they were that too.

"When do you leave?"

"Tomorrow. To Hawaii again. Then to Saigon."

He took off his sunglasses. They looked into each other's eyes, and saw the reflection of themselves in each other's eyes. They embraced, and cried for what had once been, for what never would be. He never saw her again. They wrote, but when he was recruited for Phoenix, when he was trained as a deep cover assassin, he was officially declared dead. It was a simple matter; he had no family and few friends. He was KIA. There was even a small obituary in the Manila papers. Son of American missionary killed in action in Vietnam.

He had heard that she had gotten involved in radical politics, had entered a religious order, had become a nurse, and gone to live and work in the villages north of Manila.

He had hoped that after the war, he could come alive again, resume his old identity, find her. But he did not. His life took on a different contour, a different trajectory. He continued to do what he had been trained to do. And the years went by more swiftly than he had ever imagined possible. And so he had stayed dead.

He walked through Luneta, watching over his shoulder. They were behind him. Stalking him already. Manila police do doubt. Sent to tail the dealer.

He walked more briskly now, toward Intramuros, the old Spanish settlement that was the baroque heart of Manila, past the green lawn which had been turned into a golf course outside the walls, past old women selling souvenirs, through the old gate into the maze of Intramuros.

And now he was Br'er Rabbit in the Briar Patch. Westerners were frightened of Intramuros, and Filipinos were, too. It could be beautiful one day, an old Spanish town here in the tropics, a maze of alleys and narrow lanes, but it had long since fallen in disrepair, the old stone houses were tumbledown, the alleys were littered with trash, squatter warrens blocked the streets.

It had become an urban jungle, a stone jungle with hidden paths and subterranean passages, but he was safe here. He had played here when his dad had come to Manila for church business, he had hunted through here when he had studied history at the university, he had dreamed of what it must have been like centuries ago when the Spanish were here.

Down one alley, briskly, into a doorway, through a hidden courtyard, always in the shadows which never left the narrow streets even at high noon, walking quickly, not running, glancing over his shoulder, pausing here and there, doubling back, cutting his own trail. His trackers were good, they stayed with him for nearly an hour, almost inconspicuous, but finally he lost them. From inside a courtyard, he watched them hurry past, cursing in Tagalog, whispering into their radios.

In his hiding place, he quickly climbed out of his drug dealer's costume, packing his clothes into a canvas tourist bag, sliding the attache case in the bag as well. He exchanged tennis shoes for his alligator shoes, jeans and a T-shirt for his white suit, a Timex for his Rolex, a battered baseball cap for his panama hat, a black-rimmed pair of sunglasses for the silver-rimmed glasses.

He stepped out of his hiding place, cut through side alleys, doubling over his own trail once, twice, just to make sure, and left Intramuros, heading across Luneta again, toward Del Pilar.

Sunset came quickly, as he knew it would. In the darkness, he felt safer.

Del Pilar Street came alive in the darkness. The row on row of bars and brothels stirred awake, the neon lights flickered and flashed on, the child prostitutes emerged from their lairs and began to prowl. The street throbbed with rap music and lust and fear.

He stepped into a battered bar, scanned the room swiftly, and quietly walked toward the back.

"Hello, Leo," he said softly.

Leo looked up over his newspaper, over his half-glasses, he laid his paper down, and slowly removed his glasses.

"Well, well, well," Leo said. He was a big man, not fat, but broad, his face red and wide. His white T-shirt exposed muscular arms. There was a tattoo on his left forearm, a blue-green anchor, hidden by black and grey hair. His hair, what there was of it, was cropped short. He needed a shave. His teeth were yellow and black and silver.

"Come into my office, you who are raised from the dead!"

He sat at the table across from Leo. The room was dark. A woman stood behind the bar. A dozen people, more or less, sat at small tables in the shadows. The darkness muffled the sounds of the street, the car horns and blaring music, and crude seductions.

"You look prosperous, Leo."

Leo laughed again. "Oh, getting by, getting by. Let me buy you a drink. San Miguel dark, correct?"

Cleary nodded, and Leo barked an order at the barmaid. She silently drifted to the table, placed the bottle and a fly-specked glass on the table, and disappeared back into the shadows.

"You look like hell. I guess that's where you've been." He flashed his yellow and black and silver teeth at Cleary, and lit a filterless cigarette. The smoke made him cough. It was a pulpy, heavy cough. The lazy fan above them caught the smoke and whirled it around and around.

Cleary poured his beer.

"I'll tell you something funny. My friends, business associates you might say, just told me that there was a new player in town, a big druggy. I wondered who it could ever be. Not that I would ever know such people, you understand. But I wondered who this newcomer might be. And now, my old friend from days gone by, who had been reported dead a half-dozen times, comes to see old Leo. Isn't that a funny coincidence?"

Cleary smiled. Leo smiled, too.

"Well," Leo said quietly. "I suppose you are on business of some sort. You know, sometimes I think of the old times. And I wonder what happened to us all. I mean, there we were in the old days, skulking around the swamps together. For how long?"

"Too long."

"I suppose so. But those were the days. But now, everyone's gone. Almost. Not the old networks, but most of the old team." He lowered his voice even further. "I heard that you were the only one who stayed with the Company. Always the idealist."

Cleary said nothing.

They sipped their beer in the darkness. They mentioned names to each other, strange-sounding names in faraway places, places they had known together when they had been young. They drank to friends who had been killed, or who had simply disappeared into the jungle and never returned.

"Well, well, well," Leo said. "Maybe we should talk business."

"I need some tools."

"Ah."

They spoke very softly now. About rifles and ammunition, and hiding places and money.

"No problem," Leo said.

They sipped their beer again.

"I got a torn piaster in the mail, Leo, just before I came here. Something's wrong. I don't know what it is. Be careful."

"Ah," said Leo. "I am always careful. But you be careful, too. The thing was sent to you."

He had urged his father not to go. Emilio had insisted that he go. Raul did not like Emilio, he did not trust Emilio, he did not know why exactly. There was something saturnine about him, something secretive. He had said as much to his father, but his father had replied that he needed Emilio, that the very things about him which Raul disliked were Emilio's strengths.

But maybe Emilio had been right.

Raul sat in the front row, just below the stage. Luneta was crowded with people, most strollers to be sure, but here, at the open-air stage, there was a good crowd for the rally. In fact, from the stage almost to the carabao and tamarau statues, there were people tightly packed together. A good crowd.

From the stage, speaker after speaker exhorted the crowd, urged them to vote, to vote a straight Liberal Party line, and the crowd cheered and sang. And when Raul's father was introduced they roared and cheered and leapt to their feet.

From behind the podium, Raul's father cheered back at the crowd. He had done this his life long, it seemed, and never tired of it. He joked about the opposition, and the crowd laughed. He told them sentimental stories, and they wept. Behind the podium, Raul's father was a small man, a wizened, battered old man, but he was a magician, a maestro; he conducted the crowd the way a conductor directed a symphony, arms cutting and jabbing, facing now here, now there.

Raul watched him with awe, and with love.

Maybe Emilio had been right. How could his father miss this rally?

"Listen to this," his father roared. "Listen to this," he whispered, and the crowd fell silent.

"They say there are no liberals left, they say I am the last liberal!" (No! shouted the crowd).

"I believe in the dignity of the individual person. Before class, before region, before nationalist cant, I believe in the dignity of the person. The left says, no, believe in class first. Pit class against class. The right says, no, believe in nation first, be a patriot, do what you're told. Of course, class is important, and I will struggle for the poor. Look at these scars; I have struggled for the poor. Of course, patriotism is important, and I have shed my blood for this nation!"

"Yes!" the crowd roared.

"And I believe in duty. Because when the person really grows in a free and open society, what grows is maturity, and responsibility, and a sense of duty to family and community and nation."

"And this is not foreign to us, this is at the very heart of being Filipino. We have suffered much in this land, suffered from foreigners, suffered from traitors, suffered from our own exploiting our own. We are a martyr nation; this park is a monument to our martyr nation, but our martyrdom has never been in vain, because always we have fought for dignity, for freedom, for duty."

"If I am the last liberal, that means I am the last Filipino! But that is not true! That is not true! For there are many of us, all of you, all of my brothers and sisters, my ancestors, my comrades, my heirs!"

The crowd roared, roared like a single organism, like a single vast animal, everyone on his feet, on her feet, cheering, Raul cheering, the cheers filling the brilliant sunlit sky, echoing from the Manila Hotel to the old Army-Navy Club, echoing and re-echoing through Luneta, out into the vast and beautiful bay.

Behind the podium, arms raised above his head in a grand V, Raul's father cheered back at the crowd.

And in that moment, in that ear-splitting thunder, Raul's father's head snapped up to the sky and he seemed almost to rise as if lifted up, lifted up in a burst of scarlet, lifted up and thrown back, and the cheers suddenly turned to screams—screams and chaos as the men and women on the stage scrambled madly around Raul's father, and Raul, frozen at first, cried out and cried out and pushed and shoved and tore his way over people to the stage, the screaming filling his ears, bursting his skull, rending the bright blue sky and the billowing cloud wrack.

Raul spent the weeks after his father's murder working through the tedium of death. There was the funeral itself to arrange, an enormous political event which brought Manila to a standstill. There were interviews to give, politicians to meet, scores of police to talk to. Fortunately, Uncle Santo handled most of the business. And old Emilio quickly emerged as the new power within his father's organization. Emilio was ever courteous; he insisted that he would run things only so long as Raul wanted him to, that Raul was the real heir. But Santo said, "Raul, do not trust Emilio." And Raul did not.

It was not that Emilio did anything suspicious. It was simply, that, well, there had been private meetings between Emilio and people Raul had never seen before, meetings Raul overheard, or heard about, meetings which Emilio had been reluctant to discuss. Emilio knew everybody, knew everything, and every day Raul felt himself more and more defenseless.

Above all, he was haunted by an obvious, terrible suspicion: was Emilio the one his father was searching for? Could Emilio be the enemy? If so, how could his father not know? But the enemy had known his father. During the war, the enemy had been part of his father's own organization. Raul spoke of this with Santo. Santo had been noncommittal. He had only said: "Be careful. Watch Emilio."

The police investigation accomplished nothing. Either the assassin had disappeared, or he had himself been assassinated. There were no clues. No trails. Nothing.

But Raul did not give up. He knew what his father had told him. He knew that his father had been killed because he had gotten too close. And so Raul searched through all his father's notes, all his private records, his journals and photographs. Day after weary day, alone, he scribbled words onto an untidy legal pad, sipped coffee far into the night. And found nothing.

Until the telephone call.

It was from Carlos Alvarez. Old Carlos. Raul's father's old friend from the war. Another old guerrilla. Could Raul fly down to Carlos' hacienda in Cebu? Yes, Raul could.

"I'm sorry I was so late in getting to you, Raul. We're a little out of touch down here. And I wanted to wait and listen and sniff the air a bit. Old habit from the war."

Carlos was thin and small and old and looked as fragile as a dried leaf. In his white trousers and white barong he looked like a wizard, a priest of an obscure and frightening cult. His gestures were all gentle, his words soft, but his skull-like face seemed hard and even cruel. His father admired old Carlos, and so did Raul. But Raul would not like to have Carlos as an enemy.

They sat side by side on Carlos' veranda, in white rattan chairs. Before them, stretching away from the house, a fine, green lawn dotted with luxuriant bushes and palm trees. The sugarcane fields, off in the distance, were alive with workers.

His father had laughed about old Carlos. A conservative radical, he had called him. Carlos was a landowner, a plantation owner, who believed in authority, discipline, tradition. He was also a firm Christian who believed that he was only a steward of his land, that his land was not really his land, and who, therefore, had turned his grand plantation into a cooperative. His workers were all co-owners who shared in the profits. Carlos was the manager, with an income fixed by the vote of the cooperative. Other landlords despised him, but stayed away from him, not only because Carlos' people would fight to the death for him, but because Carlos himself was an implacable foe. A man of great contradictions, Raul's father had said.

They sat on Carlos' veranda, in the shade, in the heat of the day, and talked quietly of Raul's father.

"So," Carlos said at last. "Let us talk business."

"Six months ago or so, your father came to see me. We sat here, in these very chairs. We often saw each other, though I make it a practice to stay away from Manila. We talked about the old days, about politics. And about this thing that obsessed your father."

"Your father was hunting. I assume you know that. And because he was hunting, he was hunted. It was the hunter who killed him, of that I am sure."

"He thought it was the same person, the traitor, from the war. He called him the enemy."

"The killings in Manila evoked the old memories, the sheer brutality of them. Then he received the notes, the threats that he had gotten during the war. Your father told you all this?"

"Yes. But I can hardly believe it. The war was a lifetime ago."

"I said as much. I said no, it could not be. But then came Jose's ring. He told you?"

"Yes, but I do not think all."

"Jose Concepcion was our leader during the war. A patriot, a very brave man. He was kidnapped and murdered because he was betrayed by this enemy."

"Yes, father told me."

"He had an unusual ring. Snakes coiled around each other. He was wearing it when he disappeared. It was not on the body. Your father received the ring in a package a month ago. There was a note. It said: "Here is Jose's ring. Yours as a souvenir. Be sure to wear it when I kill you."

"Father did not tell me that."

"I'm not surprised. He was sure you would try to make him flee. He would never flee."

"He gave me the ring. If anything happens to me, he said, give this to Raul. Whoever recognizes this is almost surely the enemy." Carlos reached in his pocket, extracted the ring, tarnished now, but an eerie thing, and handed it to Raul.

"There were a dozen of us during the war. But only your father and I and maybe one or two others worked closely with Jose. We were grouped into secret groups of threes and fours then, so no more than two or three people in the world would recognize this ring. So—you are looking for an old man, an old veteran, a cruel old man, whose eyes would glow when he sees this." Carlos smiled strangely. "You are looking for someone like me."

Raul slipped the ring into his pocket. They were silent for another few moments.

"A final thing. Your father asked me to help you in this. I will. There are limits to what I can do. I have little strength in Manila. But here, I have much strength. Should you ever need a refuge, come here."

"I don't want to endanger you or your family."

Carlos reached toward Raul, and lay his skeleton fingers on Raul's arm. "Listen to me, Raul, this is a matter of honor, of duty, of *'utang na loob.'* You would dishonor me if you made me break my word to your father."

"I will accept your help."

The sun had gone down, suddenly. There were lights in distant huts, but that was all. The stars above glowed in antic profusion, but the ground, the palms and bush were utterly black. But still the two men sat on the veranda, and talked of this and that long into the night.

* * * *

"Raul, thank you for coming to me. Come in, come in."

All around Raul, in the offices of AGMAR Import/Export consultants, everything was bustle. Men and women hurried to and fro, telephones jangled, a score of conversations ebbed and flowed. But when he walked into Santo's office, everything became still and calm.

Santo was old, as old as Raul's father, and Emilio, and old Carlos, but his movements were graceful, cat-like almost, and only the lines around his eyes — not his body, not his voice or hair — only the lines around his eyes betrayed his age.

They sat in the plush chairs in Santo's office. A secretary brought them coffee.

No, Raul said, no, he had not really learned anything. He was not lying, really. But Carlos had told him to say nothing to anyone, especially to the people around him, so reluctantly, Raul said nothing.

Santo nodded. Then, quietly, softly, he whispered: "Raul, I have found something."

"I need your help. It will be very dangerous. But I think I am on the trail of the murderer."

They leaned together. Santo sipped from his cup and set it gently on the table in front of them.

"Your dad was sure that the enemy had infiltrated our business in some way. We do many things. We are worldwide. He thought that the enemy had returned because of some sort of criminal business. Drugs. That is why he came back after your father."

"Yes. Father was not sure, but he thought that more than vengeance was involved. The killings in the city, they seemed to show that the enemy was building a network. A web, father called it. And he thought it all might affect the business. But it was guesswork."

"Listen, Raul. I think this is a big thing. Maybe this had nothing to do with your dad. Maybe it does."

"There is a businessman in Manila. An American. He has been here some months. He is in the drug business. He is a big man in the drug business. I do not know him, but he knows us. He wants to work out a deal."

"He says he needs contacts, an improved distribution network. He says he knows that our international links are among the best in the world. He wants to use our links, our transportation, our contacts, for his product. I think he may have thought this before, I think he may have come to Manila with us in mind. I think that maybe he decided to do away with your dad because your dad would never stand for any such deal."

"I have not met him. But I am told that he is in his late forties or early fifties. So he could not be the enemy from the war. Maybe that enemy no longer exists. Or maybe this man is an agent of the enemy. You see, all this I do not know."

"He does not want to be seen with me, he does not want me to meet with him. I must not have anything to do with operations, he said, or at least his courier said."

"Who was this courier?"

"I did not know him. He made a business appointment with me. He was an American, also in his late forties, balding, very bad teeth."

"Anyway, this man, he wants someone I name to be a contact. Someone he can talk business with. I told him I had to think about it. He said, or the courier said, that there were millions of dollars in this business of his, and little risk. I told him I would let him know."

"I shall be the contact?"

"It is very dangerous. I will not ask you to be. If you say no, I shall simply call the police."

"I do not trust the police."

"Nor do I."

"It is dangerous. I say it again to you, it is very dangerous. The man is a criminal. And if he is connected with your father's ancient enemy. . ."

"Then good. We know nothing. We have no clues. This is at least something. I will learn what I can. Then, later, we can go to the police."

"All right. I will set up a meeting. Be careful."

TWENTY

"Mr. Andrews?"

He stood before a man dressed in a light summer suit, wearing sunglasses and a white tropical hat. The man was in his late forties or early fifties, thin, haggard, but somehow dangerous looking. He was sitting in the bright sun on a bench in Luneta Park. The bright afternoon sun twinkled in the man's dark glasses.

"And you are Mr. Martinez?"

"Yes." The man rose, shook Raul's hand. "Shall we walk a bit?"

They strolled slowly through Luneta, past the Rizal Monument, past the monuments to the other Filipino martyrs, past the giant banyan tree, past the mothers and children, like friends, in the bright sunshine.

The older man, Andrews, spoke first.

"I heard about your father. My condolences."

Raul did not respond.

They walked slowly, casually, looking not at each other, but at their feet. A gentle breeze wafted in from the bay behind them.

"Perhaps we should talk business," Raul suggested.

"Fine. We shall talk business. You are in the import/export business. So am I. I have a great deal of money, and with my money, I would like to purchase part of your network, your transportation, I would like entree to your friends and clients. If we strike a deal, I will get a good way to move my products, and you will become very rich."

"And just what product do you sell?"

"Many products. It would be better, I think, if we discuss that in detail later. My products, I can say, are easily transportable. I would rather talk about transportation, storage, financial arrangements. For instance, I am very interested in investing some of my money here, but I would like to do it privately. I am a very private man."

"Do you speak for yourself, or do you represent others?"

"I speak for myself. I have friends, though. Many friends. Many rich and powerful friends. They would be very pleased if we could work out an arrangement."

They slowly walked round the park, not only talking but listening, feeling, sniffing. They walked down one side, toward Taft Avenue, and back up the other side, back toward the Rizal Monument, the reviewing stand, the bay. The sun was very bright and very hot.

They talked more about investments. Raul mentioned many possibilities. Andrews mentioned breathtakingly large sums. Raul mentioned possible returns on the sums. Andrews nodded. Andrews mentioned the weights he needed transported, hundreds of kilos, monthly, even weekly. Transportation, storage, they could be arranged, Raul replied. They agreed that this first contact had gone satisfactorily. They agreed to meet again, for dinner, in Quezon City.

The sun was very hot. The breeze from the bay had died down. They stopped at the foot of the Rizal Monument. The flag of the Philippines hung limply overhead.

They looked at each other now, each seeing himself reflected in the other's glasses.

"Who was this, this Rizal?" Andrews asked.

"A patriot. He was one of the leaders in our struggle for independence from Spain. Luneta used to be the Spanish Army's parade ground. The Spanish brought him out here and shot him. He's buried beneath the monument. He was a patriot. A hero."

"A fool," Andrews replied. "Fools die."

* * * *

They met several more times over the next few weeks. Sometimes, Andrews picked the spot, sometimes Raul. They met again in Luneta, they met in the exclusive restaurants in Quezon City. They talked in much more detail about Andrews' investments, about facilities Raul could put at Andrews' disposal, about payments and percentages. And each time they met, Andrews knew, and Raul did not, that people around them were listening, whispering, snapping pictures, watching. Among the tourists in the park there were watchers. They were good, Andrews thought, only once or twice did he spot one of them.

The mission was going well. When the liquidation occurred, the story would break that the son of the martyred political leader was involved with drug smuggling. There would be pictures, tapes, all the proof. Raul would be dead. His reputation would be dead.

The mission would soon be over. Accomplished.

But alone, in the middle of the night, in his armchair, sipping his scotch, staring out at the tankers in the bay, staring out, at dawn, at the smudge of Corregidor on the horizon, Cleary knew that it was wrong. All wrong.

He would sit very still, a cigarette smoldering in his hand, the blue smoke stinging his eyes, and he would think: No, this is all wrong.

He would think: When you are on a mission, you are alone and completely vulnerable. You have no friends. You must assume that everyone—everyone—is your enemy. You must use every sense—smell, taste, sight, feel. You must rely on intuition. Intuition is not occult, it is not magic. Your brain records more data than you could ever think possible, it sorts through more things than you are ever aware of, and you might not be conscious of all this, but the feelings you have, the odd sensations you get, they are often signs, messages, that you must pay attention to. Test them, of course. But these sensations, this intuition, is as important as taste and touch and sight, as important as reason.

It had been another lecture. At a safe house far up in the Georgia mountains. To a group of new operatives. He had felt sorry for them. They were young, men and women, blacks and Asians and whites, none ever out before, going to school. At least half, he guessed, would be destroyed on their first mission. A handful would survive as he had, until finally their nerves would fray as his had, finally, after hundreds of missions, and someone sharper, more cunning, more cruel, would hunt you down and destroy you too. He felt sorry for them. Sorry for all the people he had known in this twilight war, sorry even for himself.

When you think, he had said, don't just use your reason. Don't simply calculate. Even on a mission, rest somewhere, clear your mind. Pay attention to whatever pops in. You are a lone wolf in a dangerous country. Look and sniff and listen. Listen to everything, including your own intuition.

So he listened, alone, at night, when sleep would not come.

And he knew it was wrong.

The torn piaster. The murder of Raul's father. A local hit, bloody Filipino politics? No. There was a connection somewhere which they hadn't told him. And the cock-and-bull story he had been given as a mission. Raul was very dangerous. Both a dangerous radical and a dangerous drug smuggler. That was why he had to be liquidated.

Lies.

Even when he first read it, it sounded fishy. This boy knew nothing about drugs. That was obvious. And his politics? He was a reformer, all right, maybe a radical. Like I was, Cleary thought. He is like me. He could be my younger self. He could be me before my life went. Went the way it did. My younger self. Before the scars, and lies, and betrayals, and death. My self when I was alive.

This is wrong.

And where was Angstrom? Had he sent the torn piaster?

He spoke with Leo. They were in Leo's office, his bar, deep in the night. "Tell me about old man Martinez, the one who was hit," Cleary said.

"A good man. An idealist. Like you. Like you were. A hard man too, a hard enemy."

"Dirty?"

"No. He did what needed to be done. This is a hard world; he did what he had to. But never dirty. If I believed in heroes, I would say he was a hero. But then, I'm not a believer."

"And the boy. His son?"

"Never had anything to do with him. If you mean, is he involved in rackets, in anything dirty, spying and whatnot," Leo grinned, sipped his beer, "no. He is fresh and clean."

They sipped their beers quietly.

"Why all the questions, son? You're the Filipino. I'm just a humble expatriot businessman."

"I've been away a long time."

"I do have a bit of news for you, my son."

"Yes."

"They found Angstrom. Your old handler. Floating face down off Miami Beach."

"What happened?"

"Well, my information is all secondhand, you know. From friends of friends. Cubans I once knew, when we all were young, you and me and Angstrom, people involved now in other lines of work. Anyway, the word is that he was hit."

Cleary showed no emotion. He had been through this too often; death was too much a part of him to come as a shock, or even as a surprise. He ran his finger along the neck of his San Miguel bottle, tracing a path on the cool moisture of the bottle's neck.

"Why? Who?"

"Ah, that's the surprise. There's a rumor among people who know that it was a set-up. Our people. Either Angstrom was dirty and he had to go, or he knew someone who was dirty and they got him first. Nasty business."

"My piaster, I'll bet, was from him. He was one of us. He knew the code."

"Son," Leo said, "if I were you, I'd go to ground."

So now Cleary sat in his chair, in the middle of the night, sipping his scotch, listening.

He could simply go to ground, abandon the mission, disappear. They would record him as missing. And presumed dead. But they would, of course, think that he had gone rogue, and they would try to track him down. He did not worry overly much about that. He could hide here where no one could ever find him, not even himself.

But what was going on? What had happened to Angstrom? Where had this mission come from in the first place? There was something foul at home, something foul here.

Every instinct said: Go to cover. Go to ground.

But, sipping his scotch, squinting from the acrid cigarette smoke, another possibility came to mind. He could go double. He could continue with the mission and subvert it.

It might be safer. To seem to continue, to seem to act in ignorance, that might even be his best cover at the moment. And look and listen and try to find out what was happening. Because it was more than just him. He was a torpedo, a weapon, simply a trigger. Something much bigger was going on. Something dirty.

He began to get angry. He had trained himself for years to feign and never to feel. But now he was angry. His hand began to shake, shake so much that he dropped the cigarette. Not angry at being duped, being used. That was part of the game. It had happened dozens of times. He had been used as a decoy, as bait, scores of times. But always there had been a reason. Maybe a foolish reason, a stupid reason. But not now. There was something dirty here. Maybe this kid really was dirty. Maybe D'Angelo, back home. He had regretted his life but had never been ashamed of it. His sort of people were necessary in a world of international cannibals. But now, Angstrom murdered, now, he was being absorbed not merely into something foolhardy or stupid, but into something unclean.

He would fight it. Somehow. He would not simply save himself, he would fight this thing. Because if he fled he would lose himself, or whatever of himself had not already been lost.

And now, deep in the night, he was suddenly frightened, not of the fight, but of his own anger,for it was turning into something very strong, something very large, something he could feel in his stomach, in his chest, and if it ever exploded, if it ever roared out of him ...

Washington rules. He sent his coded reports as ordered. The meetings with Raul continued. Then the wire came. "Mr. Andrews," the obsequious desk clerk had said to him (sung really, in a tinny, whiny voice), "Mr. Andrews, sir, we have a wire for you." He signed for it, opened it as he wandered to a sofa in the lobby. It said: "Conclude transaction." It meant: kill Raul.

The meeting was set for dawn, an hour north of Manila, a mile off the highway, along a side road just north of a little village they both knew. Cleary had played here. Fished here with his dad. He had heard that Helena was up here somewhere. He had heard that she had become a nun, that she was a nurse up here in these villages where they had both grown up, where they had played together, where they had courted when they both had been very young.

He had scouted the field where they would meet. The ground was solid, though it was surrounded by paddies. There was dense undergrowth to the east. He would hide there. Immediately behind him would be a narrow gully, deep, and partially filled with stagnant water. It led off into a maze of jungle and paddies. If anything went wrong, that would be his escape route.

He would hide in the undergrowth, the sun behind him, the sun in Raul's eyes. He would set up early, before dawn. Raul would never know what hit him.

Washington rules. D'Angelo had demanded in another coded telegram to know all the details. Angstrom had never demanded such a thing. You never told anyone such a thing. He had refused. D'Angelo had insisted. So he had told him.

That was a mistake. He felt it, he was sure of it. But what could D'Angelo do, a world away in Washington? He could do everything. If he were dirty, he could betray the operation. This whole thing might be a double game, a triple game.

And he still did not really know what he would do. His mission was to kill Raul. He should accomplish his mission. But he was a double agent now; he should subvert the mission. And Leo's voice still echoed: he should go to ground.

He arrived in the darkness. There was no moon. He parked far away, and walked, stealthily, silently, toward the rendezvous.

He moved very slowly. Very quietly. His rifle cradled in his arm. He moved through the darkness like a man silently swimming, gliding through murky waters, gliding, only eyes and nose visible, and not really visible.

There were sounds in the darkness, night sounds, other animals moving as quietly as he was moving, other animals preparing to kill. With each footstep he paused and stared and smelled. If he had been betrayed, there would be others here somewhere, others hunting him.

He kept to the shadows, a shadow among shadows, alone, beneath the star-filled sky, and when he reached his lair, his hiding place, he settled in it slowly, softly, squatting first, then kneeling, finally lying on his belly, eyes unnaturally wide in the dark, listening until his ears ached, listening and staring and smelling ("Smell," he had told them at the safehouse in the Georgia mountains, "yes, smell, like an animal. Smell for engine exhaust, for aftershave, for tobacco smoke, for feces, know what the natural scent is of the place, and smell for anything strange, anything foreign, and if anything, if anything, is strange, foreign, move away, hide, go into your hole.")

Something? To the front? A movement? A ripple in the dawn's grey?

An engine's roar and sudden stop. Raul's sports car.

But what was that other thing? To the right. In the bush.

He extended his rifle slowly through the undergrowth. He caught Raul, emerging from his car, in the crosshairs of the nightscope, Raul, eerily yellow in the nightscope, standing now, looking stupidly at Cleary and not seeing him, captured in the nightscope like a fly, like a beetle, and a single twitch of Cleary's finger would destroy him, his head would explode in the roar of the rifle, and a voice said: execute the mission, do what you set out to do, do it, and another voice said (because even now they were talking in his head in a single raucous chorus, he hadn't stilled them): no, do not do this, he is you, he is a younger you, and this is not war, this is dirty, Angstrom ("If I were you," Leo said, "I would go to ground"), but what was that over there, to the right, what was that that Raul could not see but could feel, ah, so ...

The two roars were almost simultaneous, but not quite, for Raul heard two, yes, later, he was sure of it, two roars, yes, like they always said, like car backfires, like firecracker bangs, but two, yes, two.

Cleary squeezed the trigger, but jerked the rifle away from Raul; the bullet crashed through the windshield, shattered it, exploded it, and when the rifle lurched backward against his shoulder, he rolled to his left, but not in time, for the second roar, from off to the right, the second roar hit him, lifted him (almost gently, lifted him at the waist, to his knees) and then, having lifted him, hurled him backwards, violently, back over the gully's lip, hurled him and dropped him, stupidly, into the black and stagnant water below.

TWENTY-ONE

He tumbled into the car, panting frantically, fumbling madly for the keys, dropping them on the floor, the floor now covered with shards of shattered glass, his heart pounding, his head pounding, not thinking, acting crazily, in what seemed an eternity. Finally (it had only been a second, less than a second, but it had seemed hours, or rather, it had seemed that time itself had slowed, that everything was in slow motion, everything heavy, torpid) the engine came alive, and hunched over the wheel, Raul jerked the wheel, and the little sports car, like a frightened animal, leapt away, spewing sand and mud and grass behind it.

He drove wildly back the way he had come, back down the serpentine mud road, swerving, lurching, bounding over ruts, still panting, his ribs aching from his pounding heart. Here and there a startled carabao looked up to watch the wounded little car hurl itself past.

He drove and he drove, at last a little more slowly, off the back roads, onto the national highway, more slowly still, and finally he pulled over onto the shoulder, turned the ignition off, and sat, staring through the wreckage of what had once been the windshield.

All right. Stop now. I am all right.

The image of his father flashed through his mind, his father on the stage, arms above his head, suddenly flying upwards and backwards in an explosion of blood. He closed his eyes to drive out the vision. No. Not now. Think.

A truck sped past him, but he ignored it. In the paddies in the distance, farmers prodded their reluctant carabaos, huge and grey and sleek. The day was bright and clear and already very warm, but he was shivering, trembling.

Stop now. Think.

It was a gun. Someone had tried to kill him. Someone had killed his father. Now someone had tried to kill him. Inches. He could be face down in the dirt now, dead, a dead thing, a carcass, but for inches, but for wild chance. It was so inconceivable that he could be dead, that here, on this day, an hour ago, that he could be dead, that someone would want him dead, would want not only to hurt him but to destroy him. No. Stop now. Think. Think of what to do.

Two shots. Yes. He had heard two shots. Close together. Bang. Then a pause. Then bang. Two shots. Two shots at him. No. One at him. But the second, it sounded nearer, the bang was nearer, as if fired near him. Think. What had he seen? What had he heard?

All right. He closed his eyes and sat very still. The trembling stopped.

I pulled over. I was where Andrews said to be. I checked the odometer to make sure. Yes. It was the right place. But there was no one there. I opened the door. I got out. I looked at the side of the road Andrews said he would be on. I walked toward the front of the car. My hand was on the hood. Then. Then. All right. Then a crack, a bang, and the glass exploded, glass all over, on the hood. On my hands, Yes. I remember it on my hand, and it looked like snow. Absurdly like flecks of snow on my hand.

I ducked. As if someone had thrown something at me. I ducked and looked over the hood toward where I thought the crack, the bang, had come from. The field was open. It was very green and open. But farther, there was a bush, it was about waist-high, thick.

I ducked, crouched, and looked over there. Then I heard a second bang. Louder than the first. It sounded as if the bang were near me. Then the bush, part of the bush, leaves and branches, only a few but some, flew into the air.

Someone shot at me. And someone shot at whoever shot at me.

No. Crazy. Someone shot at me. Yes. He must have shot twice at me. There were two distinct shots. At me.

No. The second did not come from the same place as the first. And I saw the bush hit, I saw the leaves fly. And something move in the bush. Yes, something move in the bush, fall, or jerk or something. I don't know, maybe I didn't, but I did.

Suddenly, his eyes snapped open. Snapped open in terror. He was sitting here, my God, he was sitting here, and they or he or someone was only minutes away, someone who tried to kill him.

He drove off, spraying mud behind him. Tearing down the highway, he tried to think. What now? Where?

It had to be Emilio. It had to be. Who else? Kill dad. Then kill me. And my father's organization would fall to Emilio. But could father have been so wrong about him? He was during the war. The traitor had been one of them. The traitor was one of them again. Emilio. It had to be.

I will go to Santo. Yes. I have to talk to him. He will know what to do.

No.

They will see me. They have already called ahead. Of course they have. They will kill me as I go to Santo. I must not go to Santo.

And I cannot go home. Emilio is there. Yes, I could go there, and kill him myself. He killed my father. Kill him with what?

I will go to the police. No. I will not go to the police. There are many good policemen. But there are bad policemen. And what evidence do I have? And what will I say? Will I say that I was going to a drug deal with an American drug smuggler?

I will go to Carlos. To Cebu. "Raul," the words came to him, "Raul, if you are in danger, come here. I will hide you and protect you. No one will find you down here."

I will go to Carlos. And then I will come back.

He pulled off the highway, calm now, his head clear now. He drove slowly into a little village, coasted into a little garage. He stopped the car, and stepped out.

A mechanic, a small man in T-shirt and shorts and sandals stepped out. "I've had an accident," Raul said in Tagalog. "I ran into a tree limb. Wrecked my windshield. Can you fix it?"

A woman joined the mechanic. Children began to appear from the small building around the garage.

"A tree? It did this?"

"Yes. Can you fix it?"

"Yes. I must get the glass from Manila. It will take two days. Maybe three." He looked at the shattered windshield. "A tree did this?"

"Yes. Fine. Here, take this." Raul scribbled Santo's telephone number on a slip of paper. "Call me when it's done."

"OK. Fine. It will be expensive. Two, three hundred dollars."

"OK. Just fix it and leave a message at this number. My name," Raul hesitated, and decided there was no time to lie, "my name is Martinez. Just leave a message for me."

"OK. Two, three days."

"Good. Can I get a bus to Manila here?"

"A jeepney. It will be here soon."

"Good."

The jeepney arrived in minutes, already filled with people off to work in Manila. It was red and silver, and coughed clouds of exhaust. Raul climbed in the back, squeezed next to an old woman with no teeth. Bouncing over ruts and potholes, the jeepney headed for Manila.

In the city, Raul changed jeepneys twice. Each time he looked over his shoulder, looked around him, more frightened now than he had been, expecting each minute to see someone with a gun, a rifle, a knife, next to him. Once, a young man bumped into him and Raul swung wildly at him, then apologized profusely.

Finally he made it to the airport. With his credit card he bought a one-way ticket to Cebu.

He was leaving a trail behind. The car. The credit card slip. But he had to get away, and he could think of no other way. Anyway, Carlos would hide him.

He called Carlos from the Cebu airport. He came personally to fetch him.

Raul tried to tell him what had happened. It had only been hours ago, but it seemed like days. Carlos listened silently as he drove out into the country, into the bush.

"Of course, it was Andrews. But I don't know why." Raul was musing now, as the jeep bumped along the trail. The trees seemed to grow thicker, the bush denser, the green of the bush and trees more and more brilliant. But Raul scarcely noticed it, scarcely noticed the jolts as they bounded over ruts, scarcely noted the calls of the birds in the thick growth beside them.

"And it must have been connected somehow to what happened to dad. But why there were two shots, I don't know. Maybe I didn't hear two shots, maybe there was only one ..."

They slowed, the bush receded and became planted fields, they rounded a long curve, and pulled up in front of Carlos' home. It was a low, single-story ranch house, small when it was first built, but added to over generations so that it had acquired a find of labyrinthian quality.

They got out, walked into the house, Raul still talking, as much to himself as to Carlos, Carlos still silent. It was only later, after Raul had eaten, when they were back on the veranda, overlooking the trail up which they had come, that Carlos began to speak.

"You were right to come here. I do not know what is going on, of course. But I do know that your dad was hunting, and what he was hunting was very dangerous. And this thing which has happened, it sounds like him.

Like the one your dad was hunting, the one from the war. This double assassination business. Assassinating you, assassinating the assassin. Certainly that was one of his old tricks. I do not know that he is the one. I can hardly believe it myself. He must be long dead by now. Still, even if it is not him, whoever it is, is very dangerous. It is good that you have come here. And now, I must hide you. For the time being at least."

"I do not wish to hide. Father said this thing is dangerous not just to us, but to everyone. This thing is involved in Manila. In drugs. In politics. There will be a coup, father knew that, and this thing will come to power. Not directly, but indirectly. Its people will come to power. How can I hide? This isn't boasting, Carlos, it isn't panache. But I cannot simply hide in the bushes, while this thing does whatever it wants."

"No, you cannot. I know that. But we must catch our breath. We must think things out. I must contact friends. We must make our preparations. Then we can strike."

It took less than an hour for Carlos' people to prepare to hide Raul. Esteban, Carlos' aide, secretary, valet, and advisor, who had almost as many wrinkles as Carlos, Esteban brought everything out on the veranda. A large rucksack. A canteen, and knife and belt. Clean clothes, and sturdy, too. And heavy boots. A sack with provisions. And a pistol. A revolver, heavy, black and silver.

"You may need this, too," Carlos said. "There are extra cartridges in the rucksack."

Raul changed into the bush clothes and boots. When he returned to the veranda, there was a young woman next to Carlos.

"Maria, this is Raul," Carlos said. "Raul, Maria. Maria lives in the place where you will hide. Her people will take care of you. I trust her with my life."

"Yes. Fine," Raul said. Maria looked young to him, but he guessed that she was no more than a few years younger than he. She was small and thin. Her eyes were as jet-black as her hair. She was very pretty.

"It is best if you walk. Maria will show you the way."

"Fine."

"I will be back in touch. Soon."

"Thank you, Carlos."

It was a long trek up into the hills, through the jungle. By the time they had reached Maria's village, Raul was exhausted, though Maria seemed not winded at all.

Over the next few days, over the next weeks, they didn't speak very much either. Maria made sure Raul was fed, she made sure that he was able to clean his clothes. But they rarely talked.

It was a very small village, no more than a score of small huts spaced along a single road. Dogs and chickens roamed along the road, chased by little children. There were sugarcane fields in the distance. Beyond the fields was the jungle, thick, hot, heavy with plants and animals Raul had never seen before, never even heard of before. And beyond the jungle, were the hills, up which Raul and Maria had struggled.

The people left him alone. They pointed their fingers at him at first and laughed. They did not speak Tagalog, or English, and Raul spoke little Cebuano. So they grinned at each other, and Raul could only imagine what they said about this gawky foreigner.

In the mornings, just after dawn, when the sun had burned the mist and dew away, he would wander down the road, watch the farmers drive their animals out into the fields, and think. Or, not really think so much as let thoughts wander through him as he wandered down the road.

Sometimes he thought about the killing of his father, and Andrews, and the attempt on his life.

Sometimes he thought about other things.

He thought about Boston.

It was the other side of the world, it was another planet. The flight seemed endless, interminable, it seemed to take days and weeks, it seemed that he stepped into a hole in time and space in Manila, and centuries later, stepped back out, in another time, another space.

Every Filipino, he knew, had a cousin in the States. Part of every Filipino was really American. We speak English, he had told himself, we think of ourselves not as Asians, but as distant Americans. Everything is better in America; if it comes from the States it must be good. If it comes from anywhere else, especially from the Philippines, it must be bad.

His dad had been like that. His whole generation had been like that. All children of MacArthur, all convinced that the States was heaven to the purgatory of the Philippines. American cars were best, American books and ideas were best, American clothes and names were best. Everyone in the Philippines had to have an American nickname, "Joey," or "Johnny," or "Suzy." American schools were best.

That is how he ended up in Boston. There had never been any doubt about it. Of course, he would go to school in the States. And since his dad had gone to Harvard, of course Raul would go to Harvard.

Raul thought of himself as an American-Asian; he knew more about America than native-born Americans. Which was why it was such a surprise.

Boston. America. Such a surprise.

"I am afraid," he had said to Theresa. They had met in class.

They had become great friends. She was Caucasian, quite blond, blue-eyed, the mirror-image of Raul. White to his dark. Blond to his black. Aggressive to his reticence. Flirtatious to his shyness. He wanted, of course, an American girlfriend, and "American" meant, to him, Caucasian. And she wanted someone exotic, someone to shock her family. (No, he thought, unfair. Those things attracted us at first, me to her and her to me. But that wasn't all of it. That was just the beginning, just the superficial part of it.)

So they dated, so they went to concerts, so, most of all, they talked.

"I am afraid," he said to her.

They were walking through Boston Common. It was winter, there was snow on the ground, snow in the air, they were well-bundled, just strolling, hand in gloved-hand, and he had said, "I'm afraid."

It was getting dark. It was only late afternoon, but the snow-filled air was already turning from white to grey. They had been Christmas shopping.

"Sometimes, I am afraid," he said.

"Of what?"

"This sounds silly, I know, romantic and all that ..."

"Of what, Raul?"

"I think I am losing my soul."

"My, that does sound romantic."

"I know." They both smiled, and squeezed their hands tighter.

"I am not an American," Raul continued. He spoke quietly, undramatically. "I do love America, or rather, I love the ideals that America was founded on, which Americans do not always live up to. But I am not an American. I do not fit in here. I belong at home."

"It seems to me that you fit in here very well."

"No. I don't think I do."

"I really don't know what you're talking about.

"We've been over this a dozen times." She was getting angry now. She got angry quickly, unlike Raul. She calmed quickly too, she didn't brood. Unlike Raul. "We've been through all this. And yes, I do think it's romantic and adolescent. You will have a Harvard degree. You are well-liked here. You are no more Asian than I am. Oh yes, your eyes, your skin, your hair. Fine. My eyes and skin and hair came from Germany or Scotland or somewhere. And does that make me German? Raul, this is ridiculous. And I'm not saying this for my benefit. Yes, I want you to stay. I want to marry you. I want us to live together, here, in Boston, or New York, or wherever. But it's not just that. It just outrages me." She stopped and stood still, the way she did when she wanted to make an important point. She stood very still, wiped a wisp of hair away from her eyes with her mittened hand, and stood still. "It just makes me furious that you would waste your life, that you would throw everything away, by going back there."

"Listen. It is nothing racial. Nothing biological at all. No, you're not German because of German genes. No, I am not Asian because of Asian genes. It is a question of duty, and culture, and home. My home is there. My family is back there. How can I stay here, comfortably, when everyone back there is suffering? How can I make my life, when my life does not include my family, my country?"

"But listen to yourself. Just listen. You've just said you're losing your soul. Well, you had none to lose in the first place! No, that isn't right. What I mean is that you are not Filipino. No, no more than I am. You were born in Manila. Fine. Great. You speak Tagalog. Okay. I speak French. I am not French. And you are not Filipino. You know no more about the Filipinos than I do. You've always been with Americans, the books you've read are all American. I just don't understand. First you say you're afraid, because you've lost your Asian soul. I agree. You've lost your Asian soul, if you ever even had one. So now, you want to go back to Asia?"

They were walking again, not really paying attention to where they were going, still hand in hand. They stopped in a McDonalds for coffee. They pulled their heavy coats off, pulled their gloves off, still talking.

Because they knew that this was finally the moment, the moment that had appeared on the horizon soon after they met, the moment which grew bigger and bigger, like a cloud, like a storm cloud, the moment which they both knew would come, would burst, sooner or later, and now it had, not because either wanted it to, but just because it had to.

"You know I cannot go back to live with you in the Philippines. That is impossible."

"Yes."

"We could travel there. We could start a business, we could become part of father's business, we could join your father's business. I don't really care which. We could live in Manila part of the time. But we cannot simply move there. I cannot live there."

"I know."

"Then why do you say all this!" She spoke softly, but her hand shook, and she spilled coffee on the table.

"Why do you say this?" she whispered.

"It is not racial. There is no Asian soul, no biological destiny. I guess what I mean is this—I belong there. My father is in politics, he is working for our country, for our family, our friends. And I have a duty to be with them. I am not an individualist. I am not a little world all unto myself. I am who I am because of the many people around me. I am part of them, just as they are part of me. When I am not part of them, then I am less of me, less of who I am." They were quiet for a few moments.

They sipped their coffee silently.

Theresa spoke first.

"There's no use arguing about it. We've argued about it before. You have to go back. I don't understand that at all, I don't understand it at all. I don't understand it because it means that we are over, that you and me, that we have no future at all. I don't understand why you are doing this. But I accept it. But listen to me—you think you are a Filipino, but you don't really know what a Filipino is. You are no more a Filipino than I am. You don't even know what a Filipino is."

"No. Maybe that's the problem."

They did not see each other after that day. They did not go out with each other, but they literally did not see each other. She graduated early, in January, and went to Paris to be with her father. Raul finished in May and returned to the Philippines. They did not write each other. After that cold day, after that McDonalds coffee, they never saw each other again .

But on those scorching mornings in the little village, as he wandered down the dirt trail, through the cane fields, with the sky white and blue and the sun streaming overhead, he often thought of that frozen day in another world, in a very different time. And he thought: maybe Theresa was right. I think Theresa was right. I do not know what a Filipino is. I do not know who I am.

These people. What have I in common with these people? I do not really look like them, not really. Of course we look Asian, but that is trivial. Superficial. I do not speak their language. I do not share their hopes. Their world is not my world. I cannot live in their world, nor do I wish to. They cannot live in my world, nor do they wish to.

So. I am not an American. And I am not a Filipino. I was not at home there. I am not at home here. I am a false birth. A freak.

One morning, Maria walked along with him. She had come into the village on some errand or other (she did not live in the village, but in a house with her family some miles away), and had seen Raul wandering back from one of his strolls. He looked so forlorn, so bored and tired and lonely, that she had to smile.

"You look unhappy," she said.

"I'm afraid I'm about to go crazy. It has been nearly a month. I have to do something, I have to go somewhere."

"Carlos said you were to stay until he sent for you."

"I know. I know. I will wait. Would you like to go for a walk with me?"

He hadn't intended to ask this, but once he had he was glad. She hadn't expected him to ask, but she smiled and said that yes, she would like to walk with him.

So they got in the habit of going for walks. Once each day, sometimes twice each day. Down the trail out of the village, into the cane fields, sometimes off into the jungle where Maria seemed to know every tree, where Raul felt a little frightened.

Often they were very quiet—Maria did not like to talk very much; she seemed to enjoy silence as much as conversation—but sometimes they talked.

She had grown up here. Had spent her entire life here. She had been to school, the sisters, they had a school nearby, she had learned to read there, and do her numbers. No, she had never been away from Cebu, never been off the island, never been to Manila. She was a farm girl, just a farm girl. She would like to go different places sometime, but this was her place. No better than other places, but no worse either, though she didn't really know, of course. Maybe there were better places. Maybe there were worse.

He told her about himself. About his life in Manila. About his travels. At first he was shy about talking about places he had been and she had not, but she seemed not at all embarrassed by it. It was as if he had discovered a new animal in the jungle, a new plant, and was simply telling her about it, not to boast of finding it, but to share it. At least that's how she seemed to react. With interest, and curiosity, and amusement.

He did not know what to make of her. At first, he thought of her as a kind of noble savage, innocent, unspoiled, and so on, but he quickly discovered that there was nothing naive, and certainly nothing savage about her. He thought at first that she might be some kind of distilled

Filipino essence, some mix of blood and flesh and tropical soil, which would finally prove to him what being Filipino was, but she wasn't that. She was neither better nor worse than he was, neither kinder nor crueler, neither more nor less experienced. She eluded every category he tried to place her in. She was neither country-girl nor forest nymph, not sign or symbol of anything other than herself.

"You do not need to tell me this, if you don't want to," she said once, as they were hiking along one of the trails that she knew so well, that Raul had never seen in his life. "But I wondered, why are you in trouble? Why are you here?" "Of course you may ask. Because you are endangering yourself by being with me. It is politics. A political thing. My father was a politician. In Manila. Someone killed him. Then someone tried to kill me. Carlos is protecting me."

"Why did they kill your father?"

"I don't know."

"Do you know why they tried to kill you?"

"No. Not really. There will be a coup in Manila soon. Everyone says so. People are struggling to be on top, struggling to have power over one another. In the struggle, people use violence. My father struggled, too. I believe that he wanted more than power, I believe that he genuinely had an image, a sense, of the commonwealth, the good of all the people. But he did struggle, and he had enemies. One in particular. One that went back to the war. I think my father was trying to fight this enemy, so this enemy had my father killed. And tried to kill me."

"But you do not know who it is?"

"No."

They hiked along for a time, Maria in the lead, Raul following. The trail was narrow, the jungle heavy, it was like entering a tent, a tunnel, it was very warm and close and dank, and Maria seemed to be quite at home, but this was something Raul had never done before in his entire life. It was as if he were entering yet another world, some other place, different from Boston certainly, but different from Manila too. It was a place with different sounds and voices, different whispers and scents. Maria was at home here. Raul was not.

They stopped at a clearing, a stream wandered through the clearing, they sat next to the little stream, and tossed stones into it.

"Everyone speaks for the people. The people this, the people that." Maria was speaking. "The people. We have NPA up here, you know. New People's Army. Guerrillas. The Manila Army comes up here to hunt them. Once in a while they clash, there is shooting up here, you can hear it sometimes though the jungle muffles it. In the village, in the place where I live, we can hear it. And we wonder about it. The NPA are for the people. The Manila soldiers are for the people. But me and my people, sometimes we think that no one really is for us, that they are all for themselves, that they want a government not for the people or of the people, but over the people. The Manila soldiers steal our pigs. The NPAers steal our pigs. One says one thing, the other says the other. Either way, the pigs are gone. And we eat bamboo instead of pork. My father says: "When people say they are for the people, you had best hide your pigs."

Raul smiled. He tossed a stone in the creek. Once he thought she was naive. She naive, he sophisticated. He did not think this any more. Her experiences were different from his, but no better, no worse. And she had learned more from her experiences, he sometimes thought, than he had of his.

"Your father was a wise man."

"But your father was a politician, too."

"Yes. But he did not steal pigs."

They were sitting side by side, tossing stones into the creek. It was bright where they were sitting, brighter than the jungle around them, bright and very warm.

"Yes. My father was a politician. But I think that he really believed that politicians could do more than steal pigs. This is what he told me once: he said, Raul, remember, you have a duty to the world around you. You must not just take and take. You must give. And you will find that giving is better, that you will be stronger, that the more you give, the more you will have. It is not easy to give, it is easier to take, most people take and do not give, Lord knows that in politics that is true, but they are the poorer for it, their souls are poorer for it. And he said: of course, everyone wants happiness. Of course. You do, I do. It is not a question of rejecting happiness. It is a question of discovering where real happiness is, what real happiness is. And Raul, I do not think that happiness is in things, in getting and possessing and controlling things. And I do not think that happiness is in taking things. In having. I think that if you want to have a life that means something, if you want a life that is worth a life, it must have something higher than things in it, it must have beauty and justice and nobility and adventure in it, it must have loyalty and duty in it, and most of all, it must have giving in it. Giving of time and money and self."

Raul was speaking now very quietly and slowly, as if he were not speaking so much as listening again to his father speak, as if he were a boy again, and his father were speaking to him, seriously, but not sternly.

"My father said that there was such a thing as a commonwealth, as the general good, and that there was no better life than one lived trying to create a good and noble and true commonwealth."

"And they killed him?"

"Yes."

"I believe he was a good man. Most people go into politics to steal. Our pigs. To push us around. Power is a kind of addiction, I think, like the drugs the sisters warned us about, like the beer the villagers drink. I have seen NPAs and Manila soldiers when they have power, and it is as if they are intoxicated. People in politics want power so they can take. I don't think I have ever heard of anyone like your father. I am sorry that they killed him."

"Yes."

"Do you miss him?"

"I miss him." Raul began to cry. Maria put her arm around him. After that day, they loved each other very much.

TWENTY-TWO

"You've almost recovered."

"Yes."

"You look like you've risen from the dead."

"Another Lazarus."

"How does that make you, O You who have called me back from the dead."

She smiled.

It was almost like the old days, when they had been young together. It is a very great thing to be young together. To be a young man and a young woman, together. This is what they had been like then fencing, sparring, biting and tumbling puppylike, he the cynic and secret romantic, she the believer and secret realist.

He thought: I have forgotten many people, many friends and lovers, I have forgotten even myself. But you I cannot forget, even after all this, all that has happened. I have forgotten loves and hates, fears and triumphs, betrayers and those I betrayed I had too, that is part of the profession. But you I cannot forget. If I have a soul, you are its spark. We should have spent our lives together.

But now look at us. The assassin and the nun. A bleak tropical comedy.

"Would you care to take a walk," she said. "I think we need to talk."

"Yes," he said.

They walked out of the hut together, he balancing himself against her arm. Her arm was thin but well-muscled and very brown. She wore a white blouse, grey skirt, and sandals. A simple leather cord held a small wooden cross over her heart.

"You do not look like a nun," he said. He could see himself in her sunglasses, distorted, comic, his nose enormous, his forehead tiny, his face contorted, very tiny. "Nuns are porcelain. China. Wrapped in layers of black. With winged headdresses."

"Had I known you were coming I'd have put on my winged headdress."

"But I mean, you look fine."

"Thank you. You look like the devil."

They walked out of the hut together, he on her arm, his white T-shirt and white trousers a dingy white to her blouse, but his skin as brown as hers, and his arm, he was shocked to notice, almost as thin. They walked out into the blue and green sunshine, down the rutted path, through the village. The air was warm and glowing and thick, but not heavy. Children smiled at them. They called hello to "Sister Helena."

"This is my friend," Helena said to the children. "He has come from far away. Can you say hello to him?"

The children giggled hello in Tagalog, and when he answered in Tagalog they giggled again and galloped off in a small cloud of dust.

"It's time we made some plans," she said.

"Shall we run off together?"

"No."

They were quiet for a time. A light breeze ruffled her blouse, his T-shirt, both oversized, billowy.

"I need to decide what to do about you," she said.

He said nothing.

He had gone back into hiding again. It was nothing conscious, nothing on purpose, he hadn't decided to, but simply had, instinctively. He had gone back into hiding, hiding here in plain sight, even with her. Hiding in silence, in monosyllables. Nothing visible, nothing exposed. Watching. Sniffing. Listening. Make no noise, some voice in him said, an old voice, a familiar voice. Make no noise, and be very still. Be ready to run. Be ready to hide.

From his hiding place, he listened. Watched.

"After all these years, you return here. This way. Gunshot. Lying in a ditch. So, my friends and I in this village, we take you in. I did not recognize you at first. I thought someone had dumped you here, the military, the police, the guerrillas, the terrorists, criminals, I don't know. Another corpse in our fields. Someone else 'salvaged.' So we drag you here. Wash your face. I didn't recognize you. And then I said: 'My God.' That's what I said. My God."

They were beyond the village now. There were fields all around them, flat fields, brilliantly green, flooded with black water. Small brown people in shorts and shirts drove sleek carabaos pulling plows. The carabaos were huge and sleek and slow, in slow motion, as if they had the infinite patience of inanimate objects.

Even with sunglasses on, the sunlight stung Cleary's eyes. But the thick, rich air felt good on his shoulder.

Helena motioned to a felled log just off the trail. She helped him sit, then sat beside him. The sunlight twinkled in her dark glasses. The green horizon stretched off forever, and there it met the immense blue sky. Great white clouds lumbered lazily in the distance.

"So," she said. "So. We learn in the meantime from the Manila news that a man was found near where we found you. Dead. Shot 'execution style,' in the back of the head, the media said. And mutilated."

"And then a third thing. The media said that Raul Martinez Jr. has disappeared. The very day you were shot. The media said that Raul was involved in drugs, that it was a drug deal. But I know Raul well. And his father. They helped us with our work here. Years ago, I went to Raul's father for help with some political problem. He was a powerful man and a dangerous man, but I believe a good man. He helped then. And adopted us, our school, our clinic. Raul helped too. Often. I know him. I do not believe the business about drugs.

"Now, since we found you, people have been hunting for you. Not just the police and the military. But other people. Not guerrillas. I know the guerrillas here. These are not guerrillas. These are thugs. Gunmen. From Manila. They don't know your name, but they say that you should be around here somewhere."

"We have told them nothing. My friends say, 'We are just simple peasants, we don't know anything about anything.' I say, 'Why, I'm just a simple woman, a nun. What do I know?' It flatters their arrogance to believe this. But they are still looking."

"If you are a drug-dealer, I will turn you in. Not to them. To the army. Some army officers are corrupt. Some are not. Some are patriots. I will turn you over to them. If you have in any way injured Raul, I will also turn you in. If you have nothing to do with these things, I will do what I can to help you. In respect. To the old days."

He listened to her from deep in his hiding place. Without fear, without anger. But also with a strange apathy, as if he no longer cared whether he was found, as if the hiding were only a reflex now, a habit, which no longer really mattered.

His shoulder began to ache. He was dizzy. The heat was making him dizzy.

Helena touched his arm. She seemed to move slowly, everything seemed to move slowly, ponderously, as if time had slowed, become thick, turgid, in the heat.

He listened to himself speak, from his hiding place, and was surprised. He should be lying, deceiving, weaving webs of falsehoods to hide in, he would be safe there, safe as he had always been, in a labyrinth of lies.

But when he heard himself, he was surprised. Bemused. As if the voice did not really belong to him, or rather, as if the voice belonged to another him.

"There are many things I cannot tell you. For your safety, for mine, for the village's, for Raul's, if he's still alive."

The day's heat was weighing on his chest. His breathing was hard, it was hard to breathe.

"We'll go back in a minute," she said. "I'm sorry, we shouldn't have come out."

"I'm all right," he said.

And then: "There are many things I cannot tell you. But what I can, I will. And I will not lie to you. If I cannot tell you something, I will not. But I will not lie to you. What I tell you will be the truth."

"I am not a drug-dealer. I was told that Raul is. I was told that he was involved in an immense operation that was poisoning the nation, that he spread drugs, bred drugs. He is involved somehow, but I do not believe that he is a drug-dealer either. I believe that I have been lied to. The people who lied to me tried to kill me. They thought I would try to kill Raul. I intended to, but I did not. I would not, because he is innocent and I have been lied to. But they may have tried to kill Raul on their own. He may be dead, or in hiding or in their hands. I do not know."

"Who sent you here? Why did you come back?"

"I cannot tell you all that. Not yet. Someday."

They talked a great deal over the next days and weeks. Once, they were in the hut, he better now, stronger, but still in bed, she on the simple cane chair beside him. It had been raining for days. Outside, it was bleak and surprisingly cold. The rain poured down, not heavily but insistently.

"It's dark," he said.

They had been talking about this place, this village, their nation, the lives they had had when they were young. She had tried to explain why she came up to this isolated place, why she had plunged into poverty and isolation and oppression. Why she had set her life on such a course, why she had stayed on this course.

There is certainly nothing romantic about it, she had said. It is very tiring. And the people are neither good nor bad, poverty is no guarantee of sainthood. They are not saints. Neither am I.

But, she had said, musing, looking not at Cleary, but through the window next to him, at the rain and darkness, but somehow, I think this is important. It is a kind of a fight, a war.

Because, she had said, there is evil in this country. A poison, a cancer. Something cruel and cunning. I do not know where it came from, why it selected this time, this place, but it is here all right. And, she had said, looking at the rain still, and, this is one of the places where evil does its deeds. And so I have come here to fight.

And so, when he said "It's dark," she thought that he was talking about her fight, and she said, "Yes, it is a dark time. I want to fight against darkness. But I must enter darkness to fight against darkness. And I am afraid sometimes that darkness will capture me, that I will forget the light." Another time, when he was better, they had gone for a walk again, in the bright tropical light, through corridors of palm and bamboo, warm breezes caressing their cheeks, their hair, and he had said:

"This is a beautiful country, you know. Sometimes it simply takes my breath away. Sometimes, it's as if the colors, the blue and green and red, sometimes it's as if they suddenly come alive and dance and whirl and snatch me up and spin me and it's as if my heart clutches just looking at this place. The soil is rich here. The people are handsome. Brown skin, black eyes. The air is warm and comforting. There is passion here, passion in the scents, in the voices ..."

She laughed at this, and he looked at her, angry at first and a little frightened, but then he smiled and laughed.

"Look at you," she laughed. "Look at you. Skin and bones. Hair all messed up. Dressed like a beachbum, a ragamuffin. And talking like a poet. I thought you were beyond passion."

"I thought I was."

"When you were younger, you were quite the crusader. A warrior for the poor. Kennedy of the Tropics. Remember that? Young Rizal, we called you. Young Kennedy.

When you joined the army and went off to war, that's how you were, filled with idealism and lyrics. MacArthur's child, Kennedy's child. Chivalry. Camelot."

"You know," she continued, "in school, no one ever knew what to make of you. No one knew whether you were really Filipino or American. I loved you, for heaven's sake, and I never knew what to make of you."

They were silent for a long time, walking slowly, their shoulders and arms rubbing against each other as shoulders and arms of strollers do.

"Do you believe in God?" he asked abruptly. "I mean really? I know you're a nun and all, but do you really believe in God?"

"What brought that on?" she asked.

"Oh, I don't know. Maybe because we're like Adam and Eve in the garden."

"And will we be expelled because of our sins?"

"Yes. But answer my question."

"Yes. I believe in God."

"Dad was a missionary, you know," he said after a long pause. "I was raised to believe. But God won't speak to me. I know the usual responses — He won't speak because I won't listen, because I'm a sinner, if I repent, then I'll hear Him, all that. But that there is some other being out there somewhere, who raids this place like an alien or something, I mean, I don't understand. Sometimes I think it's like believing in elves or UFOs. It's not 'why there is suffering and all that.' That's a whole different thing. I'm quite prepared to believe that humans bring suffering on their own heads. And evil isn't so hard to believe in. But this other entity or whatever, I don't know. I don't understand."

They were well outside the village now. Ahead of them loomed an enormous mountain. It seemed to burst up from the horizon, its peak wreathed in clouds. Once it had been a volcano and had spewed fire and ash in roaring anger all around. It was quiet now. It no longer spoke. It was silent now too. Brooding. Like God, Cleary thought.

"I think," Helena said, "I think it is a mistake to think of God as some sort of separate entity, some other life form, which might or might not exist. That's a mistake," she said.

She spoke quietly, not preaching, not witnessing, not trying to browbeat or convince or recruit or convict. She spoke quietly, out of her own thoughts, out of her heart, the way people speak of things infinitely dear, infinitely important, shyly, haltingly, as if each word were very important, speaking because he had asked, honestly, looking not for a fight with winners and losers, but looking for directions from another traveller, or more, looking for companionship from a fellow pilgrim on the same long and hard road.

"I think," she said, "that God is not so much another being as the depth, the source, the heart of all being. I think of God not as up there, but down here, as depth, not just height. I think of God as the really real dimension of reality, as that spark of importance that makes things which are important, really important. God is the source of meaning when something matters, matters ultimately. And for me, when I shake off junk, triviality, superficiality, everydayness, when I experience courage, and goodness and loyalty, and beauty, there is where God is. And those moments are rare, but, I don't know, precious to me."

"Here's what I do." Her voice was very quiet now, barely a whisper. "I know that God is found in forgiveness, not vengeance. In truth, not lies. Courage, not cowardice. So I say, 'Today, I will forgive. Today, I will be brave. Today, I will not lie.' And that is when I encounter God, that is when my life has depth, richness. And God speaks, not in separate words, but much more directly than in words. There is a kind of communication which precedes words, it's as if words flow from it, as if words crystallize it, but as if words aren't it entirely. God speaks in words, but He speaks more directly than words. And you know, it's really true, it's not that I search Him out, it's really true that He searches me out, that truth and courage beckon, call, intrude even, all the time. As if love invades, intrudes, all the time, everywhere, and if you'll just listen, listen for depth, for truth, for courage, they're there."

They sat under an enormous banyan tree and looked not at each other but at the silent, cloud-wreathed volcano jutting out of the azure horizon before them.

"You can read the testimony of people who have heard God. That's important. It's easy to get confused. And it's dangerous. I think spiritual things are the most dangerous of all. So it's important that your ideas be clear and not muddled. When I think of God, I think of the depths of life, of my life, of all life, of the things that really matter, and those things become a compass for me, and I try to orient my life by them, and when I do, then I see His signs everywhere, and sometimes, not because I am good but because He is generous, I can feel His breath on my cheek.

They were both silent for a long time. Looking at the vast and brooding volcano.

"When we were young," he said, "when I was a boy, the old people told me a story about the mountain. They said that people go there to die. They said that God comes down to this volcano and finds the dying there and carries them off to heaven with Him."

"Yes. And people still go there to die. In fact, there is a hospice up there now. People are taken there and cared for. Old men and women care for the person. Then, they bury the body in some secret place. Where only God can find it."

"It would be a good place to die," he said. "Where God's hand touches the Philippines. That would be a good place to die. To be hidden in this island home. Until God finds your hiding place and carries you away."

"Sir! Sir! Wake up! Hurry! Please sir!"

A small figure tugging on his arm startled him from uneasy dreams.

"What?" he said, groggily, stupidly.

"What?" "O please sir, hurry sir, Sister said that when they come for you we must hide you immediately, and we have been watching day and night but sister isn't here, and they're coming for you, so get up sir!"

"The small brown figure was nearly in tears. A little girl. In tattered T-shirt and shorts.

The sunlight hurt his eyes. But it wasn't the girl's tugging, or her cries that startled him so much as the silence. Outside. There should be voices, noises. But there was nothing.

"Do what they tell you," Helena had said. "I'll be away for a few days. Trying to find out what to do with you. They'll watch out for you. So do exactly what they tell you. And stay out of trouble."

"I will," he had promised. "I'll do what they tell me. I'll stay out of trouble."

And now a child was tugging frantically at his arm. And outside, the world was silent. Ominous.

"Please sir! They're coming. Coming to get you! You have to hide. They told me to take you to hide right now. Please!"

Suddenly, he snapped bolt upright. He stumbled out of the cot, tugging his jeans on, snatching his pistol from where Helena had hidden it, stumbling down the bamboo steps, the child pulling him like a donkey, pulling and tugging him into the silent, dusty plaza.

Something was very wrong. Something very bad was happening. The sun beat down on his uncovered head, on the child, on the plaza, the sun silently flashed through the palm fronds, specks of dust danced in the beams of light.

"Here," the girl said. "Here sir. This way." She pulled and tugged him across the plaza, into the ruin of a hut. It was broken down and piled high with planks and bamboo. The little girl wriggled inside. He followed.

It was dark in the pile of debris, but he saw the girl tug away some boards, pull away a mat and point to a black oval she had uncovered.

She tugged and pulled and whispered: "Here. There is a tunnel here. You can fit. A long tunnel. It goes out to the fields. You go down. I'll cover the hole back up and run away. That's what Sister said. Please. Please!" She tugged and pulled.

"Wait," he whispered. "No. You go down the tunnel. I'll wait for a moment."

The little girl didn't move. She clutched his leg, her eyes suddenly very wide, and stared through a crack in the timber.

Cleary stared too, the little girl clutching his leg. Stared into the sun-bleached plaza, the tiny arena bordered by the green and yellow huts.

He heard them before he saw them. Metal clanking on metal. Grunts. Coughs. A frantic chicken scurried through the dusty arena and disappeared under a hut.

Grunts and coughs and voices now and the clank of metal on metal.

Cleary stood, frozen, staring through the lumber, the child clinging to his leg. Three of them.

Three men. Not soldiers, not police, though dressed in some sort of tattered uniform. Young men. Gunmen. He could see their faces clearly. One, scarred. Another, pitted by acne. Guns. Machine guns. Hanging lazily at their sides. One had a machete in his belt. Talking loudly. Coarsely.

They were pushing two people before them. A young woman and an old man. From the village. They stopped in the plaza. The men's shirts were dirty and sweat stained.

They stopped in the plaza, and formed a kind of crescent around the man and woman. They moved very slowly. Their gestures seemed to slow, their voices seemed to slow, to deepen.

"Where is he?" one man said. "This stranger. Where?"

Neither the man nor the woman said anything. They stared at the ground.

The sun was behind them. It made them glow, radiate. Cleary's eyes began to sting.

One soldier grasped his machine gun. Slowly. With both hands. He grasped his weapon and swung it in a grand sweeping arc, and struck the old man in the face and his head, the old man's snapped backward, and it was as if he had leaped upward and backward, in slow motion still, and then fell, crashed, in a clumsy heap on the ground. He twitched. The dust became very red near his mouth. Two of the soldiers kicked him. Once, twice, in the head, in the stomach, in the groin. Then he lay very still.

Their faces were scarred and pockmarked. Their faces glowed from the sweat which glistened like a sheen of oil.

One man grabbed the woman, stood behind her, held her by her elbows. He pulled her arms tightly behind her and she groaned but did not struggle. Another man stepped in front of her and slapped her face. He cocked his arm back to strike her again, but suddenly froze, his arm extended, his head cocked to one side, birdlike, and stared at the pile of lumber only a few feet away.

The lumber stirred. Pieces jumped out of the pile, one piece, two pieces, jumped out, and a man walked out, calmly, a man walked out, pushing a child away from him, behind him, a man walked out of the pile of junk, pile of lumber, a man in T-shirt and jeans. He walked like a robot. Like a zombie. His legs were stiff, unbending, his face expressionless.

The man, the zombie, walking forward, saying "no." "No." His voice grew in volume, in register, the "No" became not a word but a cry, a howl, a deep, furious roar, and he raised his arm, stiffly, there was something in his hand, a weapon, a pistol.

"No," he roared, howled, staring at the soldier with his arm frozen in midair, and the soldier with his arm in midair stared back, stared back until his head exploded in blood and smoke.

The second soldier tried to jerk his weapon in front of him, but the man turned toward him, howling and roaring, and the pistol in his hand roared as he did and in smoke and blood the second soldier crashed backwards, as if jerked by some mighty cord.

The third soldier, holding the woman, watched the two soldiers burst into blood and smoke, and he pushed the woman from him and spun around so that the bullet struck him full in the forehead, and later villagers peeking from the bushes and huts said it wasn't as if the bullet struck him, it was as if his head suddenly burst, it was as if his body didn't know that his head had burst because his arms had flailed about and he had run five (no, some said later, not five but ten paces), all right, then ten, he, it had run ten paces, arms flailing, his head a bloody pulp, until he collapsed.

And the man, the man who had emerged from the wood, Cleary, stood there arms extended, smoke wafting from the pistol, roaring and roaring, in the sunlight, in the dust, roaring and roaring, until a little girl stepped up to him from behind, took his hand, and led him away.

"We've buried them," she said. Matter-of-factly. Quietly. "They were assassins. From some private army. Not police or soldiers."

He was silent.

"The people say you ran amok. It happens. That's where the word comes from. From here. It's a Malay thing. People run amok. People think that someone running amok is not crazy but spirit-filled and very dangerous."

It was very dark, but the sky overhead was brilliant with stars. There were voices muttering in the darkness around them.

"You know," he said. "I don't really remember what happened. It's very odd. I've been in combat many times. I've been in danger many times. But I always knew what was happening. This time, it was like something came over me, like, I don't know, like something enormous burst in me, burst, exploded in me, I can't say it, but, I just erupted, blew up. I don't remember it at all."

"Do you know the statues in Luneta?" she asked. "The carabao and tamarau?"

"Yes."

"That's how we all are. Here in the sun. We are infinitely patient. But then, sometimes, I don't know why, everything explodes. The world explodes. Our heart explodes. It's been like that. Our Malay ancestors centuries ago were like that. Psychology, of course. Repression. I suppose we're all manic depressives." Helena was quiet for a moment. "The people say, such moments are explosions of God. Like fiestas. Lives are ruptured, transformed by God's hand. Such times are epiphanies. Pentecosts. One who runs amok, they think, he's been touched by God."

Cleary looked at his hand. It was still shaking. It was as if he had been shocked, as if the electricity was still throbbing in his bones.

"I have killed before," he said, "many times. But not like this. Not enraged, not furious. But this time, the man and the woman, they seemed like all the poor people in the world, they seemed like all the people who get pushed around, whose faces get ground in the dirt, and I don't know, it was like something hit me, charged me, I, I don't know, I just lost control, I was frantic, outraged. I can't imagine that it was God's grace. I thought his grace was meek and mild."

"No," Helena said. She was very serious now. "No. God's grace is dangerous. Very dangerous."

The sun was warm. They were sitting on the bamboo steps of Cleary's hut. The village was alive again, though quiet. No one spoke to Cleary, though they looked and nodded in his direction. An old lady was sweeping the center of the dusty plaza. It was still a dusty red.

Helena said: "We have to get you away from here. Others will come. Soon. The village, I think, will be all right. They're after you, not us. I have friends in the south. We'll get you down there. The trip will be dangerous, but we'll hide you as well as we can. We'll get you south. Then we'll see what happens."

For Raul, the days passed with a kind of narcotic languor. He felt like one of the lotus-eaters from Homer — dreaming his time away on a sun-drenched island, bathed in warm light, and in the perfume of a thousand flowers. But after a time, he had asked Maria to teach him how to work. It was comic at first. He stumbled into ditches, cut his hand instead of the sugarcane, and was even chased by a carabao – a carabao of all things. Maria smiled, the villages howled in laughter, and though his ego was mightily wounded, even Raul laughed. Mr. Manila; Harvard-educated; Mr. Filipino elite; chased through the fields like a child.

But the work was good. Hard. Certainly not romantic, and Raul had no desire to do it for a lifetime. But as he worked in the sun, chanting with the peasants in the sugarcane fields, chanting ancient songs about love and death and courage, Raul felt, it was hard to say, he felt clean and strong.

One bright day, Raul and Maria were kneeling together washing rice. The air was clear and warm, palms rustled behind them, children and chickens scuttled in the dust. As they rubbed and sorted the rice, Maria said:

"Are you ashamed to be here? With us? To work with us?"

"What? Ashamed?" Raul stopped. He wiped his hands on his shorts, and looked at her in amazement.

"Ashamed?"

"I do not mean that we are shameful here," she said. "I mean that you, well, you are from Manila. You have been to the States. Your father was a great and important man; even we, down here, have heard of him. You work with your mind, not just your back. Isn't this hard for you? When you go back to Manila, won't you say to your friends: How awful it was there! With all those peasants. And that awful Maria." She looked away from him when she said this, smiling, just a bit embarrassed, fishing for a compliment, fearing not an insult but indifference.

Raul smiled at her, touched her hair lightly. Then he went back to work with the rice.

"When I came here," he said quietly, "I felt two things. Two things. At first, yes, I felt, well, superior. Not morally, of course. I am enough of a believer to know that we are all equal in God's eyes and I believe that. But, I thought of myself as more sophisticated, more worldly. I love books and music; here you work and work then sleep then work. I thought, how isolated this place is. I thought, I can never live here."

"I've thought much about this. And now I think: I cannot idealize this place. I am not a farmer, farming is not my gift. And farmers are not innocents, they are good, some of them, and bad, some of them too. Once, I thought that people in Manila, they're not really Filipino, I thought, only farmers, only the poor, somehow they're nobler, purer, they're the real Filipinos. But that's adolescent dreaming. We're all Filipinos, the good and bad, the city mouse and the country mouse."

"But then I think too, yes, here, in this hard and simple life, there is beauty. In its own way. In its simplicity. You know, with all the digging in the dirt, there is something very clean about this place."

"Now, as for this Maria, well I don't know." He smiled and she smiled. "But if she would let me learn more, I would like to learn more."

"Well," Maria said, "about this big city Raul, I don't know either. But if he wants to learn a few things, maybe I'll let him. I think maybe he's not so bad."

Often they walked together in the evening, after the day's work. She told him about the village, about the animals, about the vast forest around them, about the even vaster mountains above them, about the great sea that surrounded them. About the stars. In Manila, in Boston, he had never seen so many stars. They were Christmas lights in the black sky, flashing, twinkling. He could not believe that they were there all the time; it was as if they were part of another reality, another dimension, a dimension of calm and coolness and infinite if distant light.

She was amazed at his wonder.

"Don't you have stars in Manila?" she asked.

"They're very hard to see," he said.

They talked about their lives. Raul talked about the mother he scarcely remembered. About his father who became both father and mother to him. Once, when he talked about his father, he wept. "I miss him very much," he said. "I can hear him still, see him, even smell him, feel his touch on my arm, but he seems so far away. It's just that I could always see him, he was always there. And now, I'm not sure where he is, and I wish and wish he were here. I can almost hear him sometimes. It's that I need to talk to him. To sit in our home, in the evening, to talk about things with him...."

He had wept then. As he had before. And Maria had comforted him.

She had told him about growing up in the village. Everyone wanted to leave, to go to the city, maybe even to Manila, maybe even the States. She would like to go someday to visit, to see what Manila was like, to see America. But this was her place. Her family was here. Not just her parents and cousins and brothers and sisters, but all her people, including the people in the graveyard. Maybe them especially. Someone had to care for their graves, keep them clean. Someone had to work the land, to keep it fresh, the old people said that the earth would weep if it were not properly cared for. Everyone needed a place, she thought. A place where the soil and air and smells were part of your own soul. It could be any place. This was her place. Someday, she might live elsewhere, of course. Maybe she'd be rich and live in Manila. But even then, this would be her place, and she would come back often.

They walked hand in hand.

Maria asked him about the things that had happened. He tried to explain, not only to her, but to himself.

"I think," he said, "I think that something very wicked and very dangerous is loose. There are lies within lies, deceit, blood. This thing has touched me, has killed my father because he had tracked it to its lair and had tried to kill it. There is money in this, crime, drugs, but it goes beyond that. It is as if all the badness in this poor country of ours congealed, came to a point, a focus, became a pus-filled tumor, and has burst, and will poison us all. The thing has to be lanced, has to be cut, the wound has to be stanched. But I don t know how. I don t know how."

Sometimes, Carlos came to visit. He looked thinner and thinner, his long brown arms and fingers more and more willowy. His sunken cheeks made his nose more hawklike, his eyes more glowing.

He brought news from Manila.

The news was not good.

They talked in the village plaza, sitting in the cool of the early evening, Carlos, Raul, and Maria.

Carlos said: "There have been more killings. Many more. Mutilations, terrible killings. And not just criminals now. Priests. Social workers. There have been bombings. Threats against the media. And now there is lots of coup talk. People say that only the army can stop all this, that only a strong-man can protect people."

"I don't think these are two separate things. I think that whoever is behind the killing, is also behind the coup. It might be someone in the army. Or some gangster."

"Do you think it really is father's old enemy. The old man from the war?"

"Yes. I do. I see his sign everywhere. He is old now. But his sign is unmistakable. It's eerie. It's as if he had come back from the dead, where he belonged. But I see his sign in all this. I smell him. These are his bloody tracks."

Villagers came by as they spoke, nodding to Carlos. He asked them how their crops were coming. They asked for favors, for advice.

"You are their king," Raul said.

"Yes," Carlos said, and he said it a bit wearily. "Neither they nor I choose this way of life. We were born into it, and sometimes I fear we cannot change it. It is feudal and backward, and I am no reactionary, I do not defend it, I certainly do not idealize it. But it is a way of life. And in some ways it is good. Many landlords abuse their people. And that is why soon, we all must go, this way of life must end. But in the meantime, I will try to be a good landlord."

The scene fascinated Raul. There was no doubt that Carlos was the patron, and the peasants were his peasants. But it wasn't as simple as that. Carlos was unfailingly polite, deferential even, almost disclaiming his role, and the more he did so, the more the villagers gave him respect. They did not fawn, they did not bow and scrape, they held themselves as people of importance too. Yet they were not equals either, the patron and his people. Yes, Raul insisted to himself, this is a bad system, it has to change, but it is not a simple system, and on those rare occasions when it was good, when there was respect, it even had its virtues, and to change it would not be simple.

When the villagers had gone, when the last new baby had been shown him, when the last dispute between neighbors had been solved, when the last wedding invitation had been offered, Carlos took up his story again. He spoke in whispers, as if the night, despite the stars, had darked his voice.

"I see his sign. He wants power, he wants the ability to control, to manipulate people, that makes him feel alive. And he enjoys killing. Killing to him is the ultimate power, the final power, when he kills, when he tortures, then he knows he has real power, then he knows he is alive. He is a man of death, of lies and death. He believes in death, and violence. He is in love with death. During the war, and after, your Dad and I talked about this often. For us, the war was the key experience in our lives. And this enemy, who hurts us so badly, was part of all that. He hurt us very badly."

Carlos grasped Raul's arm with his bony fingers. His dark eyes seemed to glow.

"This man is dangerous. And now that he is old, I believe he is even more cunning."

"So what do we do?"

Carlos spoke very softly. Raul thought he glanced to his left and right, cautiously, surreptitiously.

"We trap him. Then we kill him. And you, Raul, you must be the bait."

TWENTY-FIVE

The trip was long and hard. They travelled by jeep, by mule, by steamer, by canoe. They travelled through grasping and choking jungle, up and down mountains so steep they snatched your breath away, they travelled along winding tracks that, it seemed, even God had never seen. His wound had healed, but he was still weak. His shoulder and chest still ached.

But all in all it had gone smoothly. He could only marvel at her network of friends. If only spy-networks could be as good! Her friends passed him along the chain of friends, from church to church, convent to convent, village to village. They travelled by night most often, and moving through the thick and velvet tropical darkness, he was more helpless, more vulnerable than he had ever been in his life. Darkness, of course was his old friend, he was safest at night, when honest folk were abed, in the stillness, among the anonymous cries and moans. But he had always picked the darkness, he had always been the one to decide when and where he would prowl. But now, he was in Helena's hands, and the hands of her friends. Helpless in their hands.

They travelled by night. They holed up by day.

Each time he was exchanged, the guides whispered softly to each other. They would smile, trade messages. The old guide, whom he knew only by a first name, would introduce the new guide, mentioning only her or his first name. Sometimes they were men. Most often they were women, or even girls. Somehow, they seemed stronger, more competent, than the men.

None knew who he was. Each only knew that someone back along the chain, a friend, asked that he be protected. And each one in the chain trusted the other, so he was handed along, ever southward.

More than anything, it was this trust that struck him. These nuns and peasant women and priests and farmers placed their lives in each other's hands. And there didn't seem to be any double blinds, no deceptions, no tricks. Of course, he might be wrong, but he, who had spent a lifetime weaving lies, normally could spot them, or rather, feel them, smell them.

But he couldn't see, or feel, or smell them among these people. Even stranger was his reaction to all this. It was dangerous, of course. He was sometimes afraid. But all his old fears, all his old disguises, they all seemed to fall away.

He had gotten in the habit of lying. Swaying along on muleback, he suddenly realized that lying had become a habit, a characteristic. Even when there was no need to, he lied. "Have a match?" "No," he would reply, even when he grasped them in his pocket. "Seen the game on TV?" "No," he would say, when of course he had. He lied by instinct, by habit, constantly, to everyone. Including himself. Disguised himself from everyone. Including himself. But here, high up on muleback, swaying along a jungle trail, with a tiny nun on a tiny mule in front of him, the disguises fell away. And he felt, not exactly that he could tell the truth, but, somehow, that the truth would let itself be told by him.

He was filthy, sweat-stained, bearded, his hair was matted. But, exhausted and aching, he felt clean.

"They'll take care of you," Helena had said.

"They'll sell me," he had replied. Matter-of-factly. With neither anger or fear. "They'll sell me. One will. And, you know, I don't blame whoever it is. Unsold, I'm dangerous. A problem. But on the market, I'll bring a nice profit. Whoever the hunter is will pay a good price. For my head."

"I trust them. They won't sell you. It will be dangerous. But I don't think you will be betrayed."

"You're naive. This is my world now, not yours. And my world is a funhouse world, a world of mirrors and illusions. And violence and deception and death."

"Your world, yes. Not mine. In mine, people know all about your world, they know your world, it stalks them, it steals their crops, it murders their sons, it rapes their daughters, oh yes, they know your world only too well, they know it better than you do. And they knowingly reject it. They knowingly and consciously say that trust is more important than lies, that love is stronger than death. And that is how they live their lives. They have all the vices everyone has. But they have also the courage to say that they can escape, and overcome, your world of lies. And they will win. Because this world is better than yours, braver, nobler. It is poor, but braver and nobler."

"I'm sorry," he said, "but I trust no one."

"Ah," she smiled, "but I trust you."

The tiny nun drove the landrover as if she were in a cross country roadrace. The two of them bounced crazily in their seats as if springs were attached to their bottoms. She was a kaleidoscope of motion behind the wheel, her enormous wooden cross swung wildly back and forth, her feet pumped frantically on the clutch and accelerator (and rarely on the brake), her brown child's hand shifted the huge gear in every conceivable direction. The sun flashed and glittered on the shiny hood, the rich green cane fields bounced and lurched past.

At first Cleary thought she was doing it on purpose, but her tiny face, masked behind her sunglasses, betrayed no mischief. Well, he thought in amazement, she must drive like a lunatic normally. So he clung to his door and the dash and stared stoically ahead at the leaping and jolting road.

She did not tell him where they were going. He did not ask.

He had been underway now for over three weeks. Oddly enough it seemed that the faces along the trail, the words he had heard, only took form after he had taken leave of the people they belonged too. It was as if he had to think, and brood, and ponder over the faces and words before he could really see them and hear them.

There was, for example, the face of the Irish priest who had spent his entire adulthood, almost his entire life, in the jungle, among the poorest of the poor. He had hidden Cleary for five days, and had laughed heartily at finding "another Irishman" deep in the jungle. The priest's face was leathery. His hair was very white, but his skin was as brown as any Filipino's. He spoke Tagalog with an Irish accent.

There were the washerwoman's words. She was a widow, not as big as a minute, her face webbed with a million tiny lines. She took him from the priest. She shared with him what she had, some fish and some rice. Surrounding her in her hut were little mounds of other people's laundry, some soiled in little piles, some clean neatly stacked.

One night, after her only son had gone to bed, she and Cleary had a long talk. They sipped tea in the darkness, both making slurping noises.

"I do not like being poor," she said. She spoke quietly, so as not to disturb the boy.

"I do not like being poor. The rich say we are poor because we are lazy. That is true sometimes. My brother-in-law was so lazy he wouldn't even wash himself for days.The stink was awful. Finally my sister couldn't stand it anymore. She started to beat him with a stick. Then he washed himself. But I do not think only the poor are lazy. Maybe the rich are lazy too. I do not know."

She held her hands before her face, and wiggled her fingers. Her fingers were knotty and callused and bent.

"I do not think these are lazy hands." The knuckles were large. They were well-used hands, very clean, but scarred and hardened.

"I was born on a farm," she continued. It was darker now. Cleary could barely see her. "I liked that. We had animals. We worked very hard. But one day, a man came and said that he had bought the farm. This is a joke, we thought. Because it was our farm, you see. But it was no joke. This man, he knew all about the law, and we didn't know anything about the law, hadn't time to learn anything about the law, we worked too hard, in the heat, but I liked it. Anyway, he said he was buying many farms. He said he was going to make one big farm. To grow sugar. Nothing but sugar. To sell to the Japanese and the Americans."

"But what about us? Where were we to go? This is our land, we said to him. But he had soldiers on his side, and we did not, so we had to go. Go anywhere, he said. This is a free country. Go to Manila, he said. Just get off my land. I want to grow sugar on my land."

"So my family was broken up. Some went to Manila. I have nieces and nephews who went to the States. I'm sure they're rich by now, but I don't know. I just stayed here. My husband, my parents, they're buried here, so I just stayed here. With my youngest. But he doesn't want to stay. And there is nothing for him here. He'll leave when he can. Maybe even leave the Philippines. I don't know."

Her voice blended with the night breeze. In the other room of the little hut, Cleary could hear the boy sigh in his sleep.

"I clean the clothes of the wealthy people. Some are good people, some are bad. Just like with us poor. It's not one person or another is good or bad. That's not it."

"This is it," she said, and her voice seemed to take on an edge of not anger exactly, but intensity, of certainty, as if she had puzzled and puzzled and had come to this clear and cutting idea. "Think of this: you're poor in a very poor family. Your food is not too good. Your house is not too good. For you there are no doctors, no schools, no books, no radio. So you have none of these things. Then how will you make your way? The others, the ones I clean their clothes for, they have all these things. And they have the police, and the army, and the politicians, and the lawyers to protect them. We do not, so how will we make our way?"

"It's not that they should be poor like me. May Our Lady preserve them from that!" She chuckled softly. So as not to disturb the boy. "And it's not that I want their money, though I wouldn't turn it down if it came to me! It's just that I want to make my way. I want my son to make his way. And the way it is now, I do not think it is fair. For us, it is too hard, the burdens they lay on us are too heavy, they set traps for us. We cannot make our way."

"I am only a little mouse," she said. "Only a little mouse, and I run and I run. I poke my nose here, I poke my nose there, I try to find a way up, but there is no way up, there is no way to climb up."

They sipped their tea. The darkness gathered around them, slowly wrapped its velvet arms around them.

"You are a guerrilla then," Cleary said.

"No. Some of them are good. Some are bad. I do not think killing each other will help. A poor servant lives in a rich man's house and wants to share the rich man's table — is it a good idea to burn down the rich man's house?"

"Then how will you ever share in his table?"

"You must convict him of his greed, bring him to repentance. For we are all God's children, even the rich. And I think we can show him how. Greed and resentment and a spirit of vengeance, they are wrong whether in the rich or the poor. But maybe God has given us our poverty to cleanse us, to burn us clean, so we can show the way to others. Sometimes, that is what I think." She paused. Sometimes, in the moonlight coming in the window, Cleary could just make out her features.

"Sometimes, that is what I think," she said. "I don't know. But you, young man you are not well, I think. You should sleep."

Cleary smiled. "I'm afraid I'm not exactly young."

"Younger than I am. But sleep. I will pray for you in my night prayers. That God will keep his hand over you on your journey. And heal you."

"Thanks," Cleary muttered. He wanted to say: I will remember you in my prayers too. But he couldn't say it. The words stuck in his throat. It suddenly struck him that he didn't say his night prayers. It echoed in his head. She says her night prayers. But I do not say my night prayers. He wanted to say them, he wanted to say God bless her and her son and my mother whom I scarcely knew, and my father and all the people I've killed, and he wanted to say God bless me too and the wife I never had and the children I will never see, and he wanted to say God bless me but the words caught like a bone in his throat.

"Here we are," the little nun said, and at first, Cleary thought it was the washerwoman speaking still. Her words jolted him from his revery. He looked over at her, and saw himself reflected in her glasses.

She pointed off to the right. Sugarcane fields, swaying gently in the breeze, as far as the eye could see, a green sea surging, undulating slowly, mimicking the deep blue sea. In the farther distance, buildings. White buildings. With bright red roofs.

They followed the road which wove through the cane, bumping on ruts, splashing water from puddles. It must have rained. That was why the air was so crisp, so transparent, so shimmering.

There were people in the fields. Some looked up from their work and waved. The little nun waved back.

They drove past outbuildings, drove up to a plain white building that seemed to be the residence. It was large, Spanish looking, but simple. A wide veranda wrapped around two sides of the house. There was white rattan furniture on the veranda. A child playing on the steps with a cat jumped up and rushed into the house calling "They're here, they're here!"

In the background, Cleary saw young men. They were not farmworkers. They moved slowly, watching, always in the background, keeping up with them, watching them. They wore T-shirts and shorts. All had guns.

They climbed out of the landrover, the nun quickly, Cleary awkwardly. Once, his mind would have been racing. So, he would have thought, so, now is the time of betrayal. These men, they were not simple peasants. They were somebody's gunmen. So, he would have thought, now is the time of betrayal. His mind would have been racing, once, he would have looked for cover, for places to hide, he would have counted the gunmen, looked over their weapons, he would have looked for a time to bolt. But that was then. And now, he did none of that. Then, he would have thought, this is a trap, I have fallen into a trap, I am caught, and now they will kill me. But now, he thought nothing. He was too tired. Too tired. The journey had been too long.

An old man stepped out of the house. He was very thin. His snow-white barong darkened his leathery face. His hands were thin, his fingers were long.

So, Cleary thought. This is the end. Partly, he was simply curious that it should happen this way. He had thought of it so often, been so close to it so often, that it seemed odd, that this finally was it. It seemed so mundane. So routine. A quiet day. On a farm. He would be alive one moment. Not the next. But the farm would stay, and these people, and the sun and the sky, only he would not. And all his life had led to this moment, to this place, all the contorted trails he had followed all led here. All time led to now.

The thin man in white walked down the steps toward him. Cleary felt strangely calm. Relieved almost that it was almost all over.

TWENTY-SIX

Midnight in Manila. The heat, so oppressive during the day, had become a blanket, had become thick and dark. The air along Del Pilar Street still smelled of sweat and brackish water and rotting food. Del Pilar normally came alive at night. When the immense sun set over Manila Bay, the lights in Del Pilar Street came on, giddy neon lights, flashing, writhing, accompanied by their own music, driving, pounding rock and roll. When the sun went down, and the neon lights and rock and roll began, Del Pilar began to dance, to boogie, tawdry, lewd, sweat covered, smelling of brackish water and rotting food. And when the sun went down, the prowling began. Girls as small as children, girls who were still children, began to prowl, wearing little more than the heavy blanket of the thick, dank, oppressive night air. Up Del Pilar and down they prowled, hunting, purring wanna have some fun? you got dollars? Pimps and hustlers and fat bellied white men (tourists, thinking themselves hunters, really the hunted), the blind drunk and the drugged, the desperate and the violent and the lost, all began their prowl when the sun went down, elbow to elbow, jostling each other, mingling their sweat, disappearing arm in arm into the flashing lights and throbbing music.

But not tonight.

Leo looked up and down the street from the doorway of his bar. He had never seen it like this. Everyone in Manila was afraid. Even the lowlife, even the frantic and crazy, even the teenage whores and especially the fat tourists. It was silent and eerie on Del Pilar. Rats scuttled in the mounds of garbage on the street corner. In the darkness, there was a moan somewhere.

Leo wiped the sweat from his face, from his eyes. He shifted the pistol from his right hand to his left, and closed and double locked the door to his bar.

Something was out there. Something else was prowling tonight.

The rich had left the city. They created hour-long traffic jams, the cars so close together, creeping so slowly, that they looked like a single creature, like some sort of immense snake, writhing and rippling its way out of the city.

Politicians and lawyers and bankers left the city. Makati, Manila's rich and beautiful neighborhood, was a ghost town. Women and children left the city. Only soldiers and police and the very poor seemed to be left. The poor hid in their hovels. The soldiers and police patrolled in threes and fours.

It was as if a plague had hit the city, as if cholera or bubonic plague had struck. That's what foreign journalists thought.

"Manila," the young woman said, "is a dead city". She was young and pretty with perfect hair and teeth and she was dressed the way her producer thought daring foreign correspondents should dress in the tropics, in a white, open-collared, short-sleeve blouse, tight jeans, and calf-high black boots. She stared at the camera before her and said: "The air seems foul, heavy, torpid, the night air stinks of rotting bodies, of death. Death squads are on the loose in Manila, killing, and mutilating, but no one seems to know who they are or what they represent. Each of their victims, is savagely disfigured. On the forehead of each victim a mysterious sign is carved. First reports indicated that this was war between rival criminal gangs. Then the government said that it was the work of terrorists. Now there are rumors that some sort of cult may be behind the killings."

Even as she spoke, bathed in the lights of her cameraman, the sinister city seemed to close in on the young reporter.

"Rumors swept the city today that a coup was coming, that the army would seize power in a last desperate bid to restore order to this terrified city."

The young woman handed the microphone to her soundman. "Let's get out of here. This place gives me the creeps."

All the night's sounds were different sounds now. New sounds, human sounds, had suddenly disappeared. Old sounds returned, emerged from the earth, atavistic sounds not heard in Manila in centuries, ancient sounds, always there, of course, but only now, in the dying city, re-emerging, reclaiming what belonged to them. Palms rustling softly in the humid night air. Animals scurrying from darkness to darkness. Garbage shifting liquidly as something stirred in it. The ocean wind, blowing in off the Bay, sighing, whispering, muttering, down the long, dark, empty streets.

The four soldiers were heavily armed. They wore helmets and flakvests and carried automatic weapons. With their helmets and vests and weapons and boots and thick belts, they looked like invaders who had just landed in a city of the dead.

They walked through Luneta Park. The monuments looked like tombstones in the velvet darkness.

They walked side by side and watched nervously all around them.

"What do you think it is?" whispered one soldier.

"I don't know," the soldier next to him whispered back "Criminals, maybe. Terrorists. But they make no political demands. My mother says that its evil. She said there are vampires in these islands. She thinks the vampires are loose." The soldier laughed nervously.

"It can't be that, can it?" the first soldier asked.

"That's crazy." He paused. "But why are they all so torn up?"

"I'll tell you what it is," a third soldier whispered. "It's a cult of some kind. Satanic. These are ritual murders. They're all tortured and marked. It's some kind of human sacrifice."

Their whispers were the only sound in the vast park, the only sound except for the signing of the breeze in the darkness, and the crunch of their boots.

"Oh no," the fourth soldier said. He stopped and pointed.

"Oh no."

The others squinted where he was pointing. Something seemed all heaped together, something black, piled up helter-skelter.

"All right," the fourth soldier said. "Cover me."

The three fumbled with their weapons, knelt down, their hearts racing, squinting toward the heap in the park. The fourth soldier crept forward.

He moved slowly, cautiously, crouching, feeling with his boots for booby traps, his machine gun in his right hand, a flashlight in the other. He flashed a beam of light at the heap, but he still couldn't make it out. He flashed his light around the heap. All around it was black, opaque. He crept forward.

Suddenly he stopped and shivered and knelt down. His own breathing had startled him. He swallowed hard. His mouth was very dry. He glanced behind him. His comrades were still there, shadows now. His light grabbed his attention and he thought, my God, I am a target, a walking target, something will hit me, hurt me. He snapped the flashlight off and scuttled to his left, his weapon pointed stupidly before him, reaching out all the while with the blind flashlight.

The heap did not move. The palms, the grass, sighed and moaned in the soft breeze.

He crept forward. He snapped the flashlight back on. He flashed his light on the heap.

It seemed to be wet. Shiny. It smelled bad, like human waste. He ran the light along it. Arms. They looked like arms. Brown skin, but opened, cut open, it was like in a butcher shop, in a butcher shop window, meat red, cut open, slabs of meat piled stupidly on each other. He ran his light along the pile. Something twinkled in the light. Eyes, cat eyes. No, human eyes. Staring, unblinking. Staring eyes in human heads, heads with some sort of mark carved in them, heads with lolling tongues, piled up on the meat, severed heads.

The soldier stood up, stock still. He motioned awkwardly to his comrades. "Radio someone," he said to the soldier with the walkie-talkie. "Call this in," he said again, and pointed to the heap.

Then he lay his weapon on the ground, stumbled into the bushes, and was ill.

TWENTY-SEVEN

"Hello. My name is Carlos. This is my home." The old man extended his hand, shook Cleary's, the old man's hand was cold, and very bony, but his grip was remarkably strong.

"You are welcome here."

"Thank you. My name is ... Cleary." His name sounded odd to him. It sounded odd to say his own name.

"Please come this way. There are people here to see you. We have a great deal to do."

"Hello."

Cleary started. Then he laughed.

"Helena. You certainly do get around."

"Hello," said another voice. Cleary looked to his left. The room was very light, sunlight streamed in the windows, he had to shade his eyes. He scarcely recognized Raul.

Carlos intervened. "I think we should all be seated. We need to talk." He waved to one of his young men, who disappeared and instantly, it seemed, reappeared, with a tray of cool drinks. "Shall we sit down please?"

It was a simple but elegant room. The walls were white, the furniture was light colored, the air seemed alive with sunlight. There were many plants in the room, on the table in the middle of the room, in the corners.

The old man sipped from his drink. He left fingerprints on vapor on the side of the glass.

"Let me begin," he said. He cleared his throat. "We have important business to discuss. And dangerous. May God help us."

There was a fan in the room, overhead, and it turned lazily. In the silence it was a good thing to look at, to avoid each other's eyes.

"Let me begin with this." The old man carefully unfolded a newspaper and rested it on his knees. He put on a pair of black reading glasses. They made his eyes look very large.

"Yesterday's paper," he said. "This is from the front page: 'Seven more bodies were discovered in Metro Manila over the weekend, bringing the number of unexplained assassinations over the last fourteen months to 116. Each of the bodies was brutally disfigured. Each had cut into its forehead the mark which has become the signature of the killers. The bodies have not yet been identified but there are fears that at least one priest and one prominent political leader may be among the massacred. ...' Let me see ... 'Rumors are flying through Metro Manila that police and army authorities are preparing for a military coup. There appears to be widespread support for such a move ...'"

The old man took off his glasses and gently lay them on a small table to his right. He folded the paper and set in on the table as well.

"There is much more, of course. In all the papers. Editorials calling for a coup. They say that no one dares go out at night in Manila unarmed. Can you believe that? Even the poor, they say, huddle in their hovels. Tourists, of course have all left. Businesses are rushing their money to Singapore and Hong Kong."

He was quiet for a moment. The others looked at him, or at the fan, turning lazily above them.

"Now," Carlos continued. "This is what I think. I think these two things are related. This madness in the city. And the talk of a coup. I think someone is provoking this violence in order to justify a coup. I think the person behind this is not a soldier or a politician. I think the person behind all this is a criminal, but a remarkable criminal. I doubt that he has more than a hundred or so people in his organization, but I think that he has powerful allies. And I think that behind him is vast wealth."

"He could never come to power himself. But he can make a deal with ambitious elements in the military. They will seize power. But he will be the real power. He will have the Philippines."

Carlos paused and sipped his drink. The ceiling fan hummed softly. Sunlight poured into the room, and flecks of dust danced merrily in it.

"All this is like an animal. And this man is the head. The head must be cut off. Then the animal will die."

He then told them what Raul's father had found, signs, signs from long ago that he couldn't believe at first. But then he found more and more. Until this thing found him. And killed him.

He told them about the war. About their betrayal.

Raul then spoke. About his father. About the betrayer. Then Raul turned to Cleary, and said: "Now. You. I want you to tell us what you have to do with this. I believe you tried to kill me. Helena says that you will tell us the truth. I'm not sure. I think you are an assassin and a liar and may even be involved in my father's murder. But I will listen."

It was very quiet again. They all looked at Cleary — Helena, Raul, Carlos. Every instinct in Cleary said: go to ground, tell them what they want to hear, lie, deceive, trust no one...

Never tell anyone your name. That is what he had said once to students. Get in the habit of using an alias. Always have a false identity, a false persona, and if that is penetrated, have another and another, have a mirror reflection of a mirror reflection for an identity. Forget who you are, deny it, lie about it, obscure it. That is the first step underground. Underground, you can hide in all these lies. They will keep you safe. For a time.

But this time, somehow, he did not lie.

"My name is Cleary. I am called Eddie. But my real name is Emilio Aguinaldo Cleary. A funny name. I am named both after our great national hero, and my father, a Methodist missionary.

"I am an American. My father was American, Caucasian. My mother was a Filipina. Hence I look like you. I have your skin, your eyes, your hair, your memories. But I am not like you. I am different."

"The Philippines is not my place. The Philippines is my place. I cannot explain. I do not even understand myself."

He listened to himself speak, surprised, not so much by what he said as by how he said it. Quietly, without fear, almost confidently.

"I have done many things in my life. I have been a soldier. Many different kinds of soldier. I have done many things. I do not regret the doing of them, they had to be done then, though now it is sometimes hard to know quite why. But no, I do not regret the doing of them, but I do regret that they had to be done. I regret the cost of them. The cost was very high."

But he was drifting here, he was not so confident here, his fingers tapped on his knees, his voice became much quieter. No, he could not go into all this, not now. Someday.

Cleary looked at Raul.

"I came here to kill you. And discredit you. It was a mission. Nothing more. I did not kill your father. And although I could have killed you, I did not."

"I did not, because I believe that the people who sent me here are traitors. Moles. They, I think, are linked to this person behind the terror. He is not only strong in Manila. He has, I think, strong friends in very influential places. I think he has plotted with them."

"I think I was to eliminate you, because you knew what your father knew, so they thought. And because you could be your father's heir. His political heir. So I was to eliminate you, and discredit your memory."

"But," Raul objected. "Why go to all the trouble of sending you? Why did they not simply kill me the way they have killed all the others."

"I don't know, but this is what I think. First, I was to be a blind. After your father was killed, people were very angry. People loved your father And they will love his heir. It was safer if a stranger took you out. Safer for them."

"I think that after I took you out, I think that I was then to be killed. And that would be another advantage to them. These people want American support, but they do not want American restrictions on their drug business. So, by killing me, and exposing me, they could claim to be nationalists, shift guilt on to the US, and for a time at least, restrict America's role here. Everyone believes that everything that happens in the Philippines is planned in America anyway, so this would be believable."

"And another thing. I think this person in Manila wanted to involve his American allies in a killing. Once involved, they would have a vested interest in protecting him. And they would gain too. By doing him, or them, this favor, they had a claim on his wealth, his power. If he could expose them, they could expose him."

"I know something of this sort of business," Cleary said. "It is often like this."

Cleary was quiet now. He looked at his hands. They rested on his knees.

"I am afraid I am rather tired. Whether you believe me or not is up to you. I have not lied."

Helena spoke first. "I believe you. I believe you have told the truth. And now," she said, "and now what can we do for this suffering land of ours?"

Night fell, suddenly, as it does in the tropics. They didn't even notice the darkness at first, so immersed they were in all their plans. Carlos' young men tiptoed into the room and lit the lamps and refreshed the drinks. Because of what they said that night, people would die. Perhaps themselves.

Because of what they planned to do, many would be saved, although the saved would never even know how great was the danger they were in. Or many would suffer, this poor suffering land would suffer, for decades, for generations, something foul and cruel would take their islands. And as they sat in that soft night, far in the Pacific, in the heart of the Philippines, it was as if all the turbulent currents of Philippine history, all the ghosts of all the martyrs who haunted Philippine history, it was as if all the currents and all the ghosts flooded into that room on starlight.

The next morning, before dawn, Cleary left, alone, for Manila.

TWENTY-EIGHT

"Wake up! Wake up, Cleary, you fearful Jesuit!"

"What?" Cleary stirred on his cot. He was dressed only in shorts and T-shirt and hadn't shaved for days. It was already warm and humid.

"An allusion, son! Ain't you educated at all? Joyce! Ulysses! You know!" Leo laughed heartily, banged the door closed behind him and heaved himself into a chair. His heavy belly made a round bulge at his waist, and his T-shirt ("Surf's Up!" it exclaimed in foaming blue letters) and shorts didn't quite meet. His tanned, bald head glistened with perspiration.

"Your message has gone out," Leo said much more quietly.

Cleary sat up on his cot, cross-legged.

"I expect," Leo continued, "that this ferret down his hole will spook him out pretty fast." Leo wiped his head with an enormous red and white check handkerchief. "Just like the old days," he chortled, "intrigue! conspiracy! adventure! sweat!"

Raul smiled and said: "Leo, be careful. I want you to be careful in this."

"Son, I'm always careful."

The ferret had spooked him. It was just two days later. Cleary was in the back room of Leo's bar where he had been staying since he had returned to Manila. The backroom was shadowy, and Cleary sat quietly, a shadow among shadows. Outside, in the bar, outside, on Del Pilar Street, the sounds and smells of sundown in the tropics, rock and roll and trash and sweat. Motorbikes backfired, old convertibles spewed exhaust, the neon lights throbbed to the driving rock and roll beat. The killings seemed to have died down and Del Pilar was back alive.

The lock on Cleary's door clicked open.

A man stumbled in. He was dressed in a rumpled pin-stripe suit. He looked as though some mean matter scrambler had snatched him from some Wall Street bank and dumped him in red-light Manila, beating him about the head and ears on the way. He wore a black sack over his head.

Leo stepped in behind him, pushed him into a chair, closed and locked the door, and roughly snatched the hood from his head.

D'Angelo squinted and blinked. Even in the shadows, he looked puffy and wrinkled. He was unshaven, his suit was sweat-stained. It had been a long flight. And an even longer drive from the airport.

Cleary sat Indian-style on his bunk. Leo stood behind D'Angelo. A small corner lamp provided not so much light as a greyer shade of darkness.

"Listen," Cleary said. He spoke softly and very coldly. "Listen: I have Raul. Stashed away. He's told me everything."

Cleary paused. He watched D'Angelo.

Then he continued: "I want no games. If I even think you're lying, I'll have you killed."

Leo placed a pistol to D'Angelo's head, the muzzle in his ear, and cocked the hammer back. D'Angelo closed his eyes. His face began to quiver.

"My friend here will kill you in a heartbeat, and we will dump you in a garbage heap, and the dogs will eat you. You are nothing here, nothing to me, nothing to anyone. Do you understand me?"

D'Angelo nodded. It looked like he was going to be sick.

Leo put the pistol away.

"I have Raul. I know that you set me up. I know that you wanted me to kill Raul and then planned to have me killed. I know that this is a rogue operation. I know that you are dirty."

D'Angelo coughed. "Look," he said. "Look. This is very big business. Very big. There is money here, you wouldn't believe the money. This is big. Very important people are in this. And, OK, you can be in this too."

"Fine," Cleary said. "I think we may be able to do business. I want to meet your boss. The big man over here. This is the thing I want from you. I want you to set this up."

D'Angelo looked very nervous. "That isn't easy, you've got to understand, this is a very important man, and he's very cautious ..."

"Shut up. Listen to me. You tell him this. Tell him, I have enough from Raul, and Raul's father, to blow him out of the water. If he wants that, fine. But what I want is a piece of the action. That's all. If we do business, he can have Raul, he can throw him, and his father's files, to the fishes. And tell him this, tell him I want to meet him. Alone. Him and me. No musclemen, no buttonmen. Alone. My friend will give you the details. And tell him to pray for my good health. Because if I sneeze, if someone looks at me funny and hurts my feelings, my friends will take Raul and the files to the Americans, to the media, to the government, and he's dead meat."

"Wait," D'Angelo said. He was panting, as if he had run a dozen laps, panting and sweating. "You don't know this man, this is an important man, I work for him, I don't order him around, no one does ..."

"Shut up. You have 48 hours. If it isn't set up in 48 hours, he's dead, and you're dead. And by the way, tell him that I'll know him. From Raul's father's files. So no ringers, no double-crosses, no crap."

D'Angelo attempted to say something, but Cleary waved toward the door and said to Leo: "Get him out of here."

Leo quickly slid the black sack over D'Angelo's head, and jerked him to his feet. As he pulled D'Angelo from the room he looked back at Cleary. They smiled and nodded to each other.

Within 48 hours, Leo reported: "It's all set up. Tomorrow. In Luneta. Dusk. You're to meet on the reviewing stand. Out in the open. He'll say, 'Look at the Tamarau and Carabao, that's us. That's the Philippines.' He knows who you are already."

"OK. Are we ready?"

"My people are ready." Cleary smiled. "What do you reckon the odds are?" It was an old game they played, they had played it in the jungle a hundred times before a hundred operations, Cleary always asked: "What do you reckon the odds are?" and Leo always said what he said now: "A million to two, and we're the two."

"By the way, old son," Leo added. "A friend of mine found D'Angelo. Part of him, at least. In a trash bag. And his head was pitted on a stake."

That night, Cleary tossed and turned. The night was sweltering; just past midnight there was a fierce downpour. His shoulder ached. He drifted in and out of sleep.

He was in his village again. Where he had been a child. It was dark and warm and there was no breeze. He was running, sweating, his lungs were bursting, he was a little boy, running everywhere, shouting, calling, "Father, Mother" but he could hardly say it, his lungs hurt so, and he could see no one. There was no one in the village. But there was groaning, chanting, throbbing, drumming, there were flashing lights, serpentine, undulating, swaying and there were people, hundreds of people, people from Vietnam and Bangkok and Del Pilar Street, flowing, out of the village. He followed, but they all seemed to be disappearing into the darkness, into the jungle. He still called "Mother, Father," but softly now."I want to go home," he said. "Take me home," he said, but there was no one to hear him.

They disappeared into the bush, but around its edges was a fence, no, not a fence exactly, but posts, like a post fence, and on top of each post was something, something dark and leaking, and he saw, saw that the things on top of the posts were heads, severed heads, Leo's head, his father's head, his mother's head, Helena's head, his own head ...

"Wake up! Wake up, son!"

He jerked upright, stared ahead, covered in sweat.

"It's me. Leo. You're all right."

Leo was holding him now, cradling him. Leo smelled of whiskey and tobacco.

"You're all right," Leo said, "you're all right."

And for a long time that night, the two of them sat on the foul cot, in the steaming Manila darkness, locked in a firm embrace.

In front of him Luneta sank slowly into twilight. The monuments blurred into shadows, then the shadows took on shadows. The raucous city became surprisingly still, in the twilight. Behind him, the vast Bay murmured.

People strolled through the grand park, lovers holding hands and whispering to each other, the lonely, the thoughtful, and the despairing. Parents warned their children not to run too far. He was tense. Not cramped, but tight. Like in the old days.

Steps behind him, to his left, coming up the concrete stairs.

Cleary looked to his left. An old man was approaching, alone. White trousers, white barong. He wore dark glasses, despite the twilight. His face, as it emerged from the,twilight, was leathery and wrinkled. He stopped a few steps away, and turned toward the park. He gently placed his hands on the rail. His fingers were long. And so were his nails.

"A pleasant view," the old man said softly.

"Yes."

"Look there," the old man pointed, "at the Tamarau and the Carabao. That's us. That's the Philippines."

Cleary mentioned names Raul had given him, names of men who had served in the war with Raul's father. He said the last names only, and asked whether the old man had ever heard of them. The old man had; he knew all their first names.

Cleary took a ring out of his pocket, held it in the palm of his hand, and showed it to the old man. The old man picked it up, delicately, and smiled. "Ah,

Jose's ring", he said. "Fine workmanship, don't you think?" He gently placed the ring back in Cleary's palm.

"Now," the old man smiled, "now that all our games are over, might we talk business?"

My imagination, thought Cleary. Only my imagination. But I am afraid of this man. He is twice my age, he is an old man, he looks fragile, he is thin and bony, but I am afraid of him. He has teeth, and nails, and because of his glasses I cannot see his eyes. This man is dangerous. Sinister. His skin is snakeskin.

"We do have much to discuss," the old man added.

"Fine, " Cleary replied. "In my car. I will drive."

"Fine, " the old man said.

They walked down from the reviewing stand, side by side, in the swelling darkness. Each knew that the other had allies hidden in the darkness, somewhere. Behind this monument? In this jeepney? Each knew that a score of eyes were watching them, predatory eyes, glowing and bloodshot, out there. But neither could do anything at the moment, except walk, silently, down from the stand, and over toward the Manila Hotel, where Cleary's car was parked.

Cleary glanced in his rear-view mirror as he pulled away from the curb. Two cars pulled out behind him; there were three, maybe four men in each car.

"My insurance," the old man smiled. He turned his head and stared at Cleary, though his eyes were invisible behind the dark glasses. "Let us hope we have a safe trip. Otherwise, my insurance will have to intervene."

Cleary did not reply. He pulled out on to Roxas Boulevard, and headed south, bisecting Luneta Park, the vast sweep of the palm-lined Bay on his right.

He drove normally, part of the normal flow. He drove calmly, glancing at his followers, letting them keep up.

A light turned red. He stopped. His followers stopped.

And suddenly he stamped on the accelerator, jerked the wheel to his left, the car screeched and tore across two lanes, brushed a half-dozen outraged cars, and roared down a side street.

The chase was on now, in earnest the chase was on, he flew down a blackened street, snaked through traffic, slammed on the brakes, fishtailed crazily, spun completely around, hurtled past his pursuers, careened off to the right, down another side-street, jammed on the brakes spun around again, backed into an alley, watched his pursuers fly by, tore out from his hiding place, the car screaming now, jerking, bounding, leaping, every bump now a bone-shattering jolt.

They were a rabbit now, alive, darting frantically from hole to hole, in the deep darkness. Palms, flying past them, had become ghosts now, buildings had become ghosts, people had become ghosts, even the ghosts had become darker ghosts. The running car had itself become a ghost flashing down the rivers of street light which slashed through the darkness.

They were in the southern suburbs now, sailing along a main avenue, Cleary's heart was throbbing in harmony with the engine.

Somehow, behind him, they were still there. Inexorable.

Cleary grasped the wheel with both hands, hit the brakes, the car, terrified, it seemed, screamed again, Cleary jerked the wheel left and right, spun around again and again tore past the pursuers.

And they were flying again now, tearing down the street now, the engine, the tires, screeching, they were flying, into a warren of alleys and litter-strewn lanes, jeepneys, garbage, shocked shadows waving them on.

Left, right, down here, back up, sit (quietly now, watch!) tear out again, sweating, panting, arms, eyes, legs aching with the strain. Cars, wagons, trucks, trees, flying past them, kaleidoscopic, wild, vertiginous.

Neither Cleary nor the old man saying anything.

Until something behind them exploded.

The first pursuer. Something had crashed into it. A truck. A garbage truck. Smoke poured from the pursuer.

Men tumbled out of the first pursuer. The second stopped. Men leaped from the garbage truck. Men leaped from jeepneys which appeared magically.

Cracks, flat and sudden, cracks like firecrackers, like backfires (Cleary and the old man watched, their car halted, the engine slowed, but still shaking), flashes in the night illuminated suddenly frantic men around the jumble of broken vehicles.

Gunfire. Sudden like tropic lightening. Begun suddenly, become frantic, stopped just as suddenly.

A man stepped into the street, from the wreckage. A big man, heavy. He waved his arm back and forth. Leo.

Cleary pulled away. Headed back north, toward the dark heart of Manila.

No one followed.

TWENTY-NINE

Cleary snaked into Intramuros, through a narrow gate, the black stones sweating in the humid night. He drove very slowly, through the maze of ancient alleys, bumping along over stone and sticks, nudging boxes and trash and debris out of the way. He snapped off the car's lights, and the yellow streak before them disappeared into the sweltering night.

It seemed now, that they were underground, in a mine, in a tunnel, under the water, everything only varying shades of darkness. It was as if they were going down and down, back and back, into the heavy stone world the Spaniards had made, back and back, down and down, slowly, slowly, into the heart of the islands.

After the frantic chase, Intramuros seemed to envelop them, engulf them with something heavy and cloying, something which slowed them, pulled at them, something thick and viscous and time slowed and space contracted.

The old man stared ahead, his skull-like head expressionless, staring back at him from the windshield.

This is death's time, Cleary suddenly thought, glancing at the old man who suddenly looked like a cadaver, a mummy. This is death's time, this is death's place, someone will die tonight.

Cleary stopped the car. He stepped out, stepped around the car, opened the door for the old man. Cleary unlocked a door. They stepped into a building. Walked down a set of groaning steps, the old man first, Cleary following.

The air was stale, it smelled as if it were decomposing in the liquid heat.

Up another set of stairs. Through another door.

Lights flashed on, blinding them, someone rushed toward them.

"Cleary, you all right?"

"Yes, I'm . . ."

"My God," the voice said. "My God . . ."

"Hello, Raul," the old man croaked.

"Santo . . ."

"May I sit down?" Santo asked. He glanced at the pistol Raul held and added, "I really don't think you'll be needing that. It appears you and your friend here have won."

They were in some sort of warehouse, long since gone derelict. There were boxes and crates here and there, paper and string and shards of glass were scattered on the greasy concrete floor. The windows were filthy; two panes of glass were missing. A single lightbulb glowed nakedly overhead.

There were several metal folding chairs in the center of the room, arranged around an upended crate which served as a rude table.

Santo sat down. He placed his hands on his knees. Raul sat across from him, the pistol resting on his thigh. Cleary sat to Santo's right.

Cleary felt ill. Dizzy. The light seemed to blind him. The shadows seemed to dance.

Helena had warned him. He still had some lingering infection from his wounds, for the past several days it had gotten worse, nausea, cramps, dizziness. Leo thought it was some old Vietnam disease come back to haunt him (Cleary had had a touch of malaria once, in Thailand) and had urged him to postpone all this, but of course they couldn't.

He clung to the side of the metal chair. It seemed to sway beneath him. He was drenched in sweat.

Santo looked at him quizzically, then looked away, at Raul.

"Shall we conclude this melodrama and get to business?" Santo asked. "I assume the point of all this is that you want to be included. Fine. You have impressed me. I can use you. We need only negotiate your price."

"I ..." Raul murmured. He shook his head, shrugged his shoulders.

"And my father?" Raul asked.

"He had to go. That's all. He had to go."

"Listen," Santo said. "Listen. I am in business. That's all. I am a simple businessman. And my business is satisfying people's pleasures. Look," he gestured to his right, the sleeve of his barong billowed around his thin arm, "look. Over here are peasants. In Burma, in Thailand. In Peru. They grow opium, they make cocaine. A thing, a product. That's all. And look here," he gestured to his left, "over here are customers. They want the opium, the cocaine. It makes them happy. Like nicotine. Like caffeine. They will pay a vast amount of money to get their opium, their cocaine. But how will the rich customers get in touch with the poor peasants? That is my business. Listen. These peasants, for a gram of rice, let's just say, for a gram of rice they can earn a penny, US, let's say. But, if they grow cocoa, or poppies for opium, they can make, let's say, a dollar a gram. So what should they do?"

"I give them the dollar. And I take their gram to the Americans, to the Europeans. And I sell their gram for $100, or $200."

His voice was suddenly quiet.

"There is money in this. There is a vast amount of money in this. I have built up a network of suppliers and distributors from Bangkok to Manhattan and Paris. I move hundreds of pounds of product every month. And now I am the wealthiest man in the Philippines. In Asia maybe. And I can make you rich."

"But it isn't money, Raul, it isn't just money. Power follows money. I have much money. And soon I will have much power. These events in Manila, of course they happened because I willed them to happen. I push a button and a man dies. That is my power. And now the people are clamoring for law and order. For protection. Fine. And when the military takes over, I will be behind the military. This will be my country."

"Join me, Raul, not for the money, but for the good things you can do. I will tell the generals, and they will make you Prime Minister, President. You want the poor to read, fine, give them books. Join me. You will be rich and powerful, and you can do good things for this nation. Join me, Raul. If you doubt, fine, join me for just a moment, just a time, then, fine, if it's wrong, expose me, leave me. But now, join me."

His voice seemed calm, enticing, honeyed. He slowly extended his hand.

"I know you think me a wicked man. A monster. But it isn't true . What I have done, I have had to do in secret, that's true. But you know me. I am still your uncle. Do you know me to be evil?"

"Wait," Raul said. "Wait."

But Santo did not wait. "OK, maybe my business is bad. I do not think it is, I think everyone gains, but fine, maybe it's bad . But listen, I am a patriot. I love this country. I want to help this country. Raul, we are falling apart, you can't deny that. We must have a strong and powerful government. You can't deny that. The military must take over, for the good of the nation. And wealthy men like me, we must use our wealth for the good of the nation. That has been my only thought."

"Wait," Raul said. "Wait." Santo did not wait. His voice was soft, but insistent. He sat upright in his chair, his back was straight, he sat on the edge of his seat, his outstretched hands closer and closer to Raul.

"Raul, you loved me once. I know you did. And you were right to. Because I loved you, I still do. And I trust you. I know you do not want to hurt me, your uncle. I know you don't want to hurt your nation. I have known you since you were a child, Raul. You know I would not hurt you."

"But father," Raul said. "Father . . . "

"Ah, your father was a good man, and a patriot. He would understand. We were in the war together, you know. Comrades. But something tragic happened. He did not understand what was happening. I did not want to tell him because he was too innocent, too gentle, too good. And that is the tragedy. He thought criminals were doing all this. He investigated, he threatened to overturn everything. And against my wishes, against my wishes, Raul, some military hotheads did, well, they did what they did. I wept, Raul. You know I wept. He was like my brother."

"But this is not right," Raul exclaimed. "Not this way. These killings."

Santo interrupted. He was sitting on the edge of his chair, his back was very straight, his fingers touched Raul's knee.

"Raul, is this righter? Is it right that a nephew should hold a gun to his uncle? That a nephew should ally himself with a drug-dealer," Santo nodded toward Cleary, "against his own uncle. Is that right? Do you feel good about that, Raul?"

"No, Santo, no, but ..."

"You know me Raul! Are you crazy? I bought you presents when you were small. I held you in my arms. And now you threaten me with guns?"

"Listen, Raul, we must get this sorted out. We must talk. We must have a long talk together. I will tell you all, and then, if you don't believe me, fine, that's it then. But for the love you had for me as your uncle, on your father's name, talk to me!"

"All right," Raul said uncertainly. "All right ..."

"Fine." Santo had half risen from his chair, Raul could smell, feel, Santo's breath on his face, "Hand me the gun, you don't know about guns, I'll get rid of it, hand it to me, and we'll leave and talk all this out, uncle and nephew, like when you were a boy, just hand it to me ..."

A scream, Cleary screamed "No ...!" and leapt from his seat, the seat crashed backwards, but too late, too late, Santo snatched the pistol, spun about and crashed it into Cleary's face, felling him like a steer, fired wildly, catching Cleary in the thigh, spun again, faced Raul (half-seated, half-standing, staring stunned), and fired pointblank at Raul's chest, the shot hurtling Raul backwards, filling the room with an acrid stench. With his free hand, Santo snatched up one of the metal folding chairs and hurled it through a window, destroying the glass and frame, and with a remarkable agility, he disappeared out the window.

The naked light overhead streaked the acrid smoke, coiling and writhing above Raul, above Cleary, coiling and writhing and snaking slowly toward the shattered window.

Pounding at the door. Pounding, blow after blow, pounding. Groaning, the door gave way.

Leo, his boys, and Helena rushed into the room.

Cleary heaved himself up on an elbow. His mouth was bloody. His thigh was gashed, as though by a knife.

"Raul," he said, "there, look to him, I'm all right, look to him."

Helena climbed over the boxes, shoved aside the overturned chairs. Raul's chest was covered with blood. She tore at his shirt, wiped at the blood with her hands, "Give me some cloth," she said, "a shirt, anything." One young man snatched off his shirt and handed it to her. "Find some water, and get an ambulance."

Leo knelt next to Cleary.

"He's bolted, Leo. A second ago."

"We'll get him, son, don't worry."

Leo barked something at the men in the room. Several disappeared.

Cleary struggled to his feet. Leo tied a rough band of cloth around his thigh, and helped him into a chair.

"Helena," Cleary said. "Helena, how's Raul?"

She was drenched in blood, she looked like a butcher.

Without looking away from Raul, she said: "I think I've found the wound. I think it's along his side, along his ribs. It's a bad tear, he's bleeding badly, but I don't think the wound itself is mortal. I don't know though ..."

"All right," Cleary said. "Let's go."

"What?" responded Leo. "What?"

"We've got to get him. If he gets out, we'll never find him.

"You're in no shape ..."

"I'm going out after him. Stay if you want. Come if you want."

Leo shook his head. He pointed to one of his young men and told him to stay with Helena. He pulled out a pistol and lay it at Helena's side. "Just in case," he said.

Cleary was already out the window. Helena looked up at them, watched them go, and turned back to Raul.

In the humid darkness, surrounded by decaying stone, in the hushed air, feeling his way like a blind man, Cleary hobbled along an alley. Leo and two men were with him.

Leo grasped his arm. "Listen. Eddie. You're in no shape for this. Let us get him," he whispered. "Be reasonable, Eddie, let us get him. You'll just slow us up."

Cleary was leaning against a wall. The sweating stone felt cool on his back. He didn't feel so dizzy anymore. Must be adrenaline, he thought. But he felt tired. He felt like he might fall, he felt his legs quiver and he thought, yes, I'm going to fall.

"All right," he said. "I'm all right. Just go after him."

Leo motioned to one of the men; the man handed Cleary an automatic.

"Be careful," Cleary whispered. But the darkness swallowed the whisper, just as it swallowed Leo and his men.

The night was his friend. The stone on his back felt cool. His legs still quivered, but he did not fall. He blinked away the sweat in his eyes, cocked his head backwards and stared overhead. A million stars, cool, indifferent, infinitely distant, stared back at him.

He smelled the smells of Asia, fetid, rich, intoxicating, he closed his eyes.

Think, he said. I think of other times, of Rangoon, Bangkok, Saigon, Djakarta.

I think of other hunts through blackened streets, I am hunting, I am hunted, I think of running, past stalls with dried squid, past toothless crones hawking mangoes and lychees, I think of stalking and listening and smelling, in the night, in Rangoon, Bangkok, Saigon, Djakarta.

No. Think of now.

Now. Where? Were it me, he thought, I know where. The best hiding place. I know where it is. With a tunnel through the walls. That is where I would lay low.

I know where, he thought.

He crept along the wall. Beneath his feet, liquid sounds, around him, hisses and squeaks, night sounds, and here and there, he thought he saw burning eyes dart his way and vanish.

Down one alley, up another, feeling his way along the wall.

I know where. Helena does too. We played there. It is the best place. I would go to ground there. Maybe he has too.

He found it easily, even though he felt like he was in a dream, even though he felt that this was no longer real, that this was fantasy, a hallucination. He no longer felt bad, he no longer felt anything. He felt his way along a wall, the pistol hanging in his free hand, swinging pendulum-like, stupidly.

He found it easily. And crept inside.

It had been a building with a cellar, and the cellar had a cellar, and from the second cellar a tunnel extended underneath the old city and out beyond the massive walls.

He crept inside, down the stairs, down into the first cellar, down the second set of stairs, creeping, smelling, listening.

It was as if he were going underwater, as if he were sinking deeper and deeper in dark, brackish, thick, turgid water. It was as if he had stepped into a cesspool and were sinking lower and lower, it was as if the water were foul with waste, with debris, it was as if the foul water had covered his feet and legs and waist and shoulders and now his head, pressing him, engulfing him, filling his mouth, his ears, his nose.

No, he couldn't continue down there. He was drowning. He was drowning, his mouth, his lungs filled with this liquid and turgid waste, he was drowning in this cesspool, in this grave, in this pit, in this quagmire. Down and down and down, his tongue lolling, his arms slowly flailing, swaying, his head rolling in slow circles, sinking, down and down and down.

Until the flash and the roar hit him in the chest and threw him down on the cool stone floor.

He was wet. His chest was wet. He could feel the wetness. It was sticky. His ears rang. He smelled the stinging smoke. He felt no pain, but he was out of breath, as if he had run his lungs to bursting. He gasped and gasped.

Foosteps approached.

They stopped. There was a face above him. The old man's.

The old man stood above him. He cocked the hammer on his pistol, aimed the pistol at Cleary's head.

Cleary stared upward at the pistol's mouth, at the long thin, hairless arm, at the phosphorescent eyes of the old man.

A roar, a flash, the old man leapt upward, arms outstretched, leapt backward, his face exploded, falling backward, his blood arching like a black rainbow.

Cleary turned his head to the side. A pistol in the distance, smoke streaming out of it. An arm, a hand behind the pistol, face behind the arm.

Cleary squinted, swallowed, the face was sideways to him, he tried to focus.

And it emerged from the darkness, from behind the pistol, the face emerged, materialized, and he could just make it out, the eyes, the forehead, the cheeks and chin, he knew this face. Yes. The face was the face of Helena.

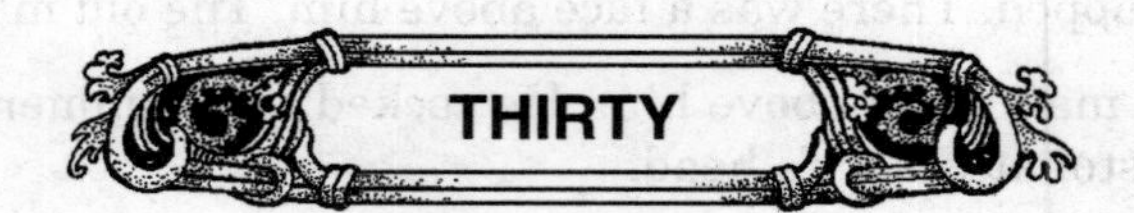

THIRTY

"Well, old son, you've gotten into a fine fix this time." It was Leo's voice. But it was hard to see him, the sun was behind him and Leo seemed to glow.

"Leo? "

"Yes."

Leo sat on the edge of the bed, careful not to disturb the web of tubes and wires which hid Cleary. Cleary reached upward (there were tubes in the hand) and patted Leo's cheek.

"By God, Leo, you've shaved!"

"Well, yes." Leo seemed embarrassed by this respectability. "For you, Eddie, I'd even shave."

They talked about old times for a minute. Then Leo explained what had happened.

"She picked up the pistol I'd left, and when the ambulance picked up Raul, she went out hunting. My boys and I stumbled all around the place, but she knew right where to go. Blew the top of his head clean off."

A doctor suddenly intervened. She whispered to Leo, nodded toward Cleary, and tiptoed out of the room.

"Got to leave you, Eddie," Leo said. He coughed. He took Cleary's hand in his. "Got to leave you now."

"You'll arrange it, Leo?"

"I'll arrange it."

"So long, Leo."

"So long, partner."

"Leo took care of it," Helena said. "It's all set. Raul arranged a helicopter."

"How is he?"

"Fine. Sore, but the wound was nowhere near as serious as it looked. It's only been two weeks, but he's up and about. In fact, he's going to make a speech today. About the time we fly out."

"Sorry I'll miss it. " Cleary closed his eyes. He felt very sleepy. He felt no pain. Just sleepy. Just very sleepy.

Helena took his hand.

"Tell me again about the mountain," he said.

"The people say," Helena began, "the people say that God visits the mountain to take home the souls of the dead. The people say that if you're on the mountain-top when God comes, He'll take you straight to heaven with Him. Old people are on the mountain, old men and women, and they'll take care of you. They'll hide you where only God can find you. And then you'll be safe."

"God comes to the Philippines?"

"Yes. Even to the Philippines. Because we are sinners and need Him, because we have suffered so much and need His comfort, because our islands are so beautiful that this is where He rests."

"This is the Gate of Heaven?" Cleary asked. He was drifting now, he was just so sleepy, so tired, he could scarcely keep his eyes open.

"The people say it is the Gate of Heaven. There is a hospice there now. My friends run it. It's called Gate of Heaven too."

"And this time, when I hide, I'll go home?"

"Yes. This time, Eddie, you'll go home."

It was not so much a crowd as a sea, a sea as vast as the sea behind him, with all the crests and undulations of the sea behind him, with all the echoing roars of the great ocean behind him. Every inch of Luneta was filled. People were perched on Rizal's Monument, people clung to all the martyrs' monuments, far off, people gawked from windows in the buildings that ringed the park.

The microphones sent his voice booming and ricocheting around the park, from the Manila Hotel on his left, to the white stucco Army-Navy Club on his right.

When he was a boy, he had been down there with them, staring at the small brown man in the dazzling white barong who was his father, staring up behind him at the vast white cloud wracks adrift in the brilliant blue sky over the Bay. He had felt like wax in the melting heat, he had jumped and giggled at the screeches of the sound system, he had felt his heart swell to bursting when the vast crowd cheered his dad.

And now here he was, up on the same reviewing stand, looking out at the sea of a million faces.

"My sisters," he began. "My brothers."

His voice boomed and echoed and drifted off over the city.

"I want to talk to you from my heart. You know what has happened in these days. You know of the evil which struck me, struck us. You know that I was away many years, but have now come home. This you know. So now, I want to talk to you from my heart."

"Here, in this place, we are one people. And as one people, we stand for our one people. We are young and old, men and women, but one. In our veins course many bloods — Malay and Chinese, and Spanish and American. We are very different from each other, and yet we are one. We are Catholics and Protestants, Buddhists and Muslims, and some of us profess no faith, but still we are one. We come from many homes, from all over our 7,100 islands, but still we are one."

"The rich are not the Philippines, but neither are the poor. The Malays alone are not the Philippines, and neither are the Chinese or Spanish or Americans. No class, no race, no region alone can claim to be the only Philippines. For this one nation is many, and this multitude is one."

"We are many. We are one. To affirm who we are means to affirm plurality and paradoxes."

"We are one not in blood, not in speech, not even in dreams."

"But we are one in suffering. We are one in the face of the typhoons and earthquakes which hurl themselves against our island home. We are one against the invaders who have tried to enslave us. We are one in suffering from poverty, from crime, from injustice, from oppression. For make no mistake, even the rich will suffer if poverty is not checked; the just will suffer if crime is not suppressed; the comfortable will suffer if injustice is permitted; and even the oppressor will be de-humanized by his oppression."

"We have suffered much in this our island home. This soil is soaked with our blood, with our tears."

"But we shall be one as well in our resurrection. For we shall be redeemed. If we suffer with nobility, with bravery, with gentleness and decency, if we suffer with each other's suffering, we shall be redeemed. If we embrace each other's right to be different, to be free, if we bear each other's burdens, share each other's sorrows, if we pledge ourselves to democracy, to freedom, to an unshakable respect for human rights, then we shall be redeemed."

"My mother rests in this soil. My father rests in this soil."

"When my father suffered a painful blow, he would say: 'I am wounded, but I am not slain. I will lay me down and bleed awhile, and then I will rise and fight again.' His lips speak no more. But he will not be slain forever, evil cannot slay him forever, he will rise in us, bleeding but not slain, and we will rise from all our suffering and redeem our island home."

"Long live the Philippines!"

For an instant, there was silence. Raul's words echoed over the vast crowd. And then the crowd began to cheer, to roar, to bellow, the crowd with its head high roared, not like a carabao, weary and patient, but like a tamarau, brave and furious and free.

Overhead, far up in the blue sky, a helicopter made its way over the crowd. On its belly was a bright red cross. Against the blue sky, it looked like a strange and exotic bird, fluttering over the vast human sea, then turning, delicately, off to the north, off to the bright green mountains.

The helicopter touched down on a little pad carved into the mountainside. The whirling blades flattened the grass, stirred the palms. Even before the blades stilled, young men hurried over to the helicopter, and unloaded the stretcher. They carried it away from the pad, down a trail, toward a small clutch of buildings. Cleary's head rolled gently to the right and left; Helena walked at his side, holding his hand. With a roar, the helicopter took off. The young men carried the litter up a path, higher onto the mountain, deeper into the bush. Trees, branches, flowers, grew in greater profusion, in more wild abandon, the farther up the path they walked. When they reached a small, garden-like clearing, they halted, and placed the litter on trestles. There were several small huts around the clearing, and from the huts came old men and women who gathered around the litter. They were very small people, with faces formed mostly of wrinkles and bright eyes. Some stood around the litter and touched Cleary's arms, his head, his legs. Others squatted on their haunches, in the ancient peasant style, and began to chant a strange, sing-song hymn, swaying back and forth as they chanted. The air was green and yellow and black and scented with camellias. On his litter, Cleary looked very small.

Helena stood next to him, held his hand, smoothed his hair.

He was drifting, his head lolled gently back and forth, when he opened his eyes, they were unfocused, and the pupils seemed very large. "Am I home?" he asked, very quietly.

"Yes, Eddie, you are home now," Helena said.

"They'll hide me here, and I'll be safe?"

"Yes."

"And God will find me where they hide me?"

"God will find you, Eddie."

He smiled. A tiny little woman, no bigger than a minute, touched Helena's elbow, and motioned to a donkey one of the young men had brought. Helena nodded, and squeezed Cleary's hand. She turned away, and without looking back, mounted the donkey. The young man handed her the reins. She shook the reins, poked the donkey in the ribs with her heels, and set off down the trail. As she trotted down the green and swaying mountain path, she heard the old people behind her keening an ancient song of the Philippines, a song full of pain and joy, of defeat and endless suffering and inextinguishable hope, of farewell, and grief and homecoming.

Manila, Vienna, Charlotte, 1990-91.